# PRAISE FOR W∆NT

### AN ANDRE NORTON AWARD FINALIST

"Vividly conjured . . . positively chilling." —*NEW YORK TIMES BOOK REVIEW*

"A spectacular, fast-paced, action-packed novel full of brilliant suspense and vivid characters." —*BUZZFEED*

"Pon's tale of a group of young people who want to make a difference in their difficult world is a rewarding, and ultimately uplifting, story." —*LOS ANGELES TIMES*

"Fresh, compelling—and timely." —**VERONICA ROTH**, #1 *New York Times* bestselling author of *Carve the Mark* and the Divergent series

"A story brimming with high-octane action. What a roller coaster!" —**MARIE LU**, *New York Times* bestselling author of *Warcross* and *Wildcard*

"An exciting, socially conscious futuristic thriller." —*KIRKUS REVIEWS*

"Pon excels as this society's architect, constructing sights, sounds, and smells that make this Taipei come alive." —*BOOKLIST*

"A strong sci-fi novel that will entice an array of readers." —*SCHOOL LIBRARY JOURNAL*

"A gripping, fast read." —*BCCB*

"Pon is a science fiction writer of the highest order." —*VOYA*

## ALSO BY CINDY PON

*Silver Phoenix*

*Fury of the Phoenix*

*Serpentine*

*Sacrifice*

*Ruse*

# WΔNT

## CINDY PON

**SIMON PULSE**

NEW YORK   LONDON   TORONTO   SYDNEY   NEW DELHI

〰〰〰

SIMON PULSE

An imprint of Simon & Schuster Children's Publishing Division

1230 Avenue of the Americas, New York, New York 10020

First Simon Pulse paperback edition March 2019

Text copyright © 2017 by Cindy Pon

Cover illustration copyright © 2017 by Jason Chan (front) and Thinkstock (back)

Also available in a Simon Pulse hardcover edition.

All rights reserved, including the right of reproduction in whole or in part in any form.

SIMON PULSE and colophon are registered trademarks of Simon & Schuster, Inc.

For information about special discounts for bulk purchases, please contact

Simon & Schuster Special Sales at 1-866-506-1949 or business@simonandschuster.com.

The Simon & Schuster Speakers Bureau can bring authors to your live event.

For more information or to book an event contact the Simon & Schuster

Speakers Bureau at 1-866-248-3049 or visit our website at www.simonspeakers.com.

Cover designed by Karina Granda and Regina Flath

Interior designed by Steve Scott

The text of this book was set in Adobe Garamond.

Manufactured in the United States of America

10 9 8 7 6 5 4 3 2 1

The Library of Congress has cataloged the hardcover edition as follows:

Names: Pon, Cindy, author.

Title: Want / Cindy Pon.

Description: First Simon Pulse hardcover edition. | New York : Simon Pulse, 2017. | Summary: Jason Zhou is trying to survive in Taipei, a city plagued by pollution and viruses, but when he discovers the elite are using their wealth to evade the deadly effects, he knows he must do whatever is necessary to fight the corruption and save his city.

Identifiers: LCCN 2016047522 |

ISBN 9781481489225 (hardcover) | ISBN 9781481489249 (eBook)

Subjects: | CYAC: Pollution—Fiction. | Virus diseases—Fiction. |

Survival—Fiction. | Taipei (Taiwan)—Fiction. |

Taiwan—Fiction. | Science fiction.

Classification: LCC PZ7.P77215 Wan 2017 |

DDC [Fic]—dc23

LC record available at https://lccn.loc.gov/2016047522

ISBN 9781481489232 (pbk)

*For Malinda Lo, who told me from the beginning that everyone loves a bad boy who plays with knives*

Taipei in an alternate near future.

*Mei*: without; pronounced "may."
*You*: to have; pronounced "yo."

# CHΔPTER ONE

## THE KIDNAPPING

I watched the two *you* girls from the corner of my eye as the crowds surged around me. Eleven o'clock on a balmy June evening and the Shilin Night Market in Taipei was spilling over with *mei* shoppers looking for a way to cool themselves. Stores lined both sides of the narrow street, and music blared in Mandarin, Taiwanese, and English. The road was closed to traffic, overtaken by vendors with carts selling noodles and oyster omelets, cold juices and shakes. Others spread their merchandise on the ground over blankets, hawking cheap toys and knickknacks.

I slouched lower on the plastic table, faded black boots planted on a stool beneath, taking in the stench of cigarette smoke, stale beer, and sweat. I flipped my butterfly knife rhythmically between my fingers, enjoying the feel of cold steel and the sound of blade and handles snapping in my hand.

Men glanced at me warily, touching the places where they hid their own weapons. Girls clustered closer as they edged past,

1

chattering. One *mei* girl, barely fifteen, raised her kohl-smudged eyes from her heap of chua bing smothered in red beans and smiled at me, electric blue bangs brushing against her lashes. Most teens were maskless tonight, wanting to have fun and pretend that they led lives from some other era, when going barefaced was normal. Pretend that they breathed good air.

The *mei* girl's friend elbowed her and loudly uttered something about delinquent *mei* boys hiding their faces behind face masks. She cast a pointed glare in my direction. They sashayed past, legs bare beneath short, ruffled skirts, the friend with her nose in the air. Smiling girl's pink mouth was now pursed in a pout.

"Hey," I called.

She half turned, careful not to spill her iced dessert. Her black brows were raised, widening her dark eyes. I winked at her, spinning my knife, then tossed it in the air before catching it in one swift motion. She blushed, and her giggle carried to me even as her friend tugged her away, disappearing into the throngs.

But I never lost sight of the two *you* girls bent over a round tub, trying to toss plastic balls into floating dishes. The prize was a koi—genetically engineered to never grow beyond two inches—in iridescent oranges, reds, and greens. Hell, they probably glowed in the dark. The girls were flanked by three bodyguards, beefy *mei* boys with muscular arms crossed against their bulging chests.

I had volunteered to do this, because if I were caught, I alone would be prosecuted. I would be the only one to be put to death. My friends would be safe. They all had family, or someone who loved them. *I* was the dispensable one, and I would give my life to protect them.

A *you* boy strutted toward the girls, his features obscured by his glass helmet from this distance. We called them "bowl heads" in derision, as their helmets looked like fishbowls. His sleek suit was black, with an indigo dragon breathing orange flames woven down one long sleeve. The suit ensured that he got the best oxygen available, that his temperature was regulated, that he was always plugged in to the *you* communication system. The taller girl in the white-and-silver suit ignored him, intent on winning a koi in a jar, but her petite friend nodded to the bodyguards, and the *you* boy swaggered through.

I snorted under my breath.

They chatted, probably pulling up info on their com sys, assessing weight, height, and genetic makeup even as they exchanged first names. This was what it meant to be *you*, to *have*. To be genetically cultivated as a perfect human specimen before birth—vaccinated and fortified, calibrated and optimized. To have an endless database of information instantly retrievable within a second of thinking the query and displayed in helmet. To have the best air, food, and water, ensuring the longest possible life spans as the world went to rot around them.

Me, I'm like the other 95 percent of the *mei*s in this country—*without*. We want and are left wanting. I'd be lucky if I lived to forty. I'm almost halfway there.

The *you* boy fiddled with his collar, then took his helmet off, handing it to one of the bodyguards with studied nonchalance. He coughed for a long time into his sleeve, attempting to adjust to the filth we breathed every day. What a rebel. Without his helmet, I got a better look at him. His blond hair was chin-length, streaked

3

in red, his features Asian. He looked about seventeen.

He pulled a cigarette from a sleeve pocket and lit it, inhaling deeply, tilting his head to blow the smoke out. He leaned toward the petite *you* girl, his expression flirtatious. I watched as the taller girl threw them a glance, then turned back toward the tub. She was broad-shouldered yet slender, her suit decorated in neon pink lines with a jeweled Hello Kitty sewn above her heart. Real gemstones, no doubt. The way she tensed her shoulders told me she wasn't pleased by the *you* boy's intrusion.

I'd been studying the suits for my task. Victor had gotten his hands on all the relevant info. "You don't want the more square helmets," he had said, showing me images on the screen. "That's an older model from two years ago. Any embellishment like jewels would be real. Nothing but the best for Jin's suits. So the shinier the suit, the richer the *you*."

Although the shorter girl's purple suit was more eye-catching, the taller girl had probably $100K worth of diamonds stitched to her chest.

I tucked the knife away and retrieved two small items from a pouch strapped to my side. I wore a sleeveless black tee and black jeans to match. Not only did I blend in, but it allowed me to move with ease. I jumped off the table and stretched my arms overhead, flexing my shoulders.

Now or never.

I cut a quick path through the crowds, moving diagonally, thumping into others as they scurried out of my way. Steam rose from the pot of the chou doufu vendor stirring her spicy broth, and my eyes watered from the scent. I was behind the bodyguards within a minute. Their massive backs blocked me from my target. I tapped the middle one on his shoulder. He twisted, fists clenched.

"Move," I said.

"What?"

I cocked my elbow and punched him hard in the nose, breaking it. The oaf roared, covering his face as blood spurted. I barreled past him and slammed into the *you* boy, who was gaping, bug-eyed. The other two bodyguards swiped at me with clumsy hands. I leaped out of the way, but not before one of them managed to grab my mask, pulling it off so it hung at my neck.

*No matter.* Grinning at him, I smashed the vial I held to the ground. Noxious smoke billowed around us. The bodyguards and boy dropped like sacks of rice within five seconds. Bet that *you* boy would regret taking off his helmet tomorrow morning. The petite girl screamed shrilly beside me as passersby shouted, but everyone steered clear of the fumes.

I lunged for the tall girl, pulling her tight to my chest, and plunged the syringe into her hand, the only exposed part of her body. The needle hissed as it dispensed the sleep-spell drug. She sank against me and I hefted her over my shoulder, dashing into the dark alley behind us, finally allowing myself to take a breath when I cleared the smoke. She wasn't heavy, but all cumbersome limbs.

"Eh, you!" a man shouted, his running footsteps echoing behind me.

I cursed and spun around the corner into a black alley. My pursuer followed immediately. I stuck out my foot, and he tripped over it, thumping hard onto the uneven pavement.

I ran without looking back, gripping the girl tightly by her legs, the streets' layout etched in my mind. The distant din of the night market reached me, accompanied by the shriek of police sirens as they inched their way through the crowds. No one followed. I burst onto the main street at the far end of the market, hailing a taxi. It screeched to a stop, spewing foul exhaust. I slipped my mask back on before yanking open the door. "Take me to the end of the bus line," I said.

The driver nodded, raising an eyebrow as I gently lay my hostage on the backseat. "She drank too much," I muttered. "I tried to warn her."

He flicked a cigarette butt out the window before merging back into traffic. "Those *you* girls have everything, but they always want more."

I stared out the open window as the driver zipped through the streets with expertise, honking at pedestrians and mopeds alike. "You her bodyguard?" he asked, catching my eye in the rearview mirror.

I shook my head.

"Ah, her boy toy, then." He grinned. "Whatever pays the bills, right?"

*Right.* My friends and I had decided the best way to gain info on Jin Corp was to get suited, infiltrating the *you*s by becoming one of them. Victor was perfect for the task—with his charm and good looks, he'd fit right in. But we needed funding. And who better to fund us than those who had a few hundred million to spare?

Neon signs flickered in a kaleidoscope of colors, washing my vision in reds and blues, oranges and greens. I kept a hand on the *you* girl's arm, so she wouldn't tumble over with the taxi driver's sudden braking. Her glass helmet reflected the lights around us, and I couldn't make out her features. I swallowed, suddenly afraid. There was no going back now. I jerked my face away, loosening my grip when I realized I was squeezing her arm.

She was unresponsive, her chest barely rising with each breath. She'd be out until tomorrow morning at least.

The taxi slammed to a stop, and I threw my arms around the girl to keep her from falling onto the floor.

"Here we are, end of the line," the driver said.

I handed him the cashcard tied to a fake identity and bank account Lingyi had set up. "Thanks," I said. "Add five for tip."

He smiled, the corners of his eyes creasing with deep lines, and saluted me. He couldn't have been more than twenty-five.

I got out and lifted the girl from the seat, kicking the door shut with my foot. The driver blared his horn twice before tearing off. It was almost midnight, and I needed to be within Yangmingshan as soon as possible. The end of the bus line was near the mountain's base. I shifted the girl so her head rested against my shoulder, her helmet smooth and cold against my cheek, and started my long climb home.

The half-moon was wan, obscured by clouds and pollution. The Vox on my wrist provided scant light, but I navigated the muddied roads without trouble, stopping twice to catch my breath. Each time I laid my captive down, setting her head on my thigh, not knowing how else to place her. She seemed inhuman encased in her glass

7

helmet. Alien. The neon pink lines of her suit glowed in the dark, and her exposed, soft hands lay limp at her sides.

How had we drifted so far from what it meant to be human? I could remove her helmet, but it seemed too much of a violation. I smiled sardonically at the irony.

I rose, throwing the girl over my shoulder. She no longer felt light—it was like hauling an elephant, and my arms were dead weights. Finally, I spotted the outcropping of jagged stones marking where I should turn off the path. Darkness enveloped me as I picked my way between thick brush and massive trees. Three years ago, mudslides after a bad typhoon season were followed immediately by a massive earthquake that swallowed teahouses, roads, and homes alike. Half of Yangmingshan went up in flames. Survivors fled, and due to the economic depression and rumors of the mountain being cursed, no investors ever bothered to rebuild.

Now the once-scenic getaway was deserted, lush, and wild, its only occupants the dead in overturned graves. And me. If anyone else lived on Yangmingshan, our paths never crossed.

I counted my steps, legs trembling with the effort. Near my four hundredth, I spotted the first garden light, glowing like a flower spirit. I had planted them for the last fifty steps leading home. Each light was solar-powered. Sweat stung my eyes, but I was too close to stop. The heavy wooden door to the laboratory clicked open by my voice command, and I stumbled inside, laying the girl on the cot in the small office that served as my bedroom.

I slumped to the floor, arms draped over raised knees, and sat there until I caught my breath.

Leaving her, I stripped and washed myself in the makeshift shower, wishing I had cold water instead of the lukewarm spray that pattered over me. Every muscle shook as I soaped myself, before drying off and pulling on some shorts. The front door could be activated by my voice alone, but I took no chances and rummaged through the green metal desk, finding the key that I needed. I locked us in, then slipped the key on a string and tied it around my neck.

I didn't even look in on the *you* girl again before crashing onto the worn sofa in the main room, falling immediately into an exhausted sleep.

Something prickled my consciousness awake; it wasn't the brightness of day. My eyes snapped open to find the *you* girl peering at me, her bowl head not an inch away from my nose. I glimpsed her face for the first time. She'd had little work done that I could see: eyes halfway between almond-shaped and slender, a rounded nose, and a full mouth. Her eyes were a light brown, like the watered-down coffee I'd buy with fake cream. Her fingers were extended tentatively above my throat. The back of her hand was bruised where I had jabbed her with the needle. She jumped back when she saw that I had woken. I looked down and remembered the key, then cursed myself for not putting on any clothes the previous night.

"It was only a precaution," I said, my voice cracking. I cleared my throat and sat up. "You wouldn't have been able to get out even if you'd gotten it."

She stood over me, appearing even leaner in the daylight, all long lines and sharp angles.

"The back door's blocked," she said in perfect, educated Mandarin.

Her voice surprised me. Rich, like dark chocolate—more womanly than she looked.

"Mudslide," I said.

She nodded and drew her other hand from behind her back, revealing a pair of dull scissors I kept in the desk. "I could have killed you in your sleep."

"You would have had to try hard." I rose, reaching for a clean shirt draped over the back of a wooden chair. It was black, like most of my clothes. "Those scissors are from another century." I pulled on the shirt, then some blue jeans, and scrubbed a hand through my dyed blond hair, suddenly self-conscious. I had taken off my mask the night before, assuming I would wake up before she did. Now it was pointless, but seeing each other face-to-face like this felt odd. We'd become a society that barely showed our faces to strangers anymore.

*Now what?*

We stared at each other for a long moment. If she were a feline, her tail would be thrashing.

"How much do you want?" she asked.

I reached for the scissors, and she let go without protest but said, "They were still sharp enough to stab you in the throat."

I paused, surprised by her boldness. Maybe if I hadn't woken when I did, I'd be bleeding out on the sofa right now. Game over.

"Are you hungry?" I asked.

Her eyes narrowed, and she shook her head.

10

"I know you must be thirsty. The sleep spell will do that to you." I crossed the spare chamber to the corner kitchen and pulled the refrigerator door open, grabbing a bottle of fancy *you* water, purified and enriched with gods knew what. A case of it cost more than most *mei* folks' weekly salary. "Here." I offered it to her.

She sat down in the wooden chair, turning the bottle in her hand, examining it.

"It's not tainted," I said. "The seal's unbroken."

She raised her eyes. "How do I drink it?"

*Ah.*

"Haven't you ever taken—"

"No. Never in unregulated space."

"The air isn't as polluted up here," I lied.

"I can't call anyone in helmet."

"No." I knew the first thing she'd try upon waking was to call for help. "I've jammed the signals."

She blinked several times, and her nostrils flared.

I glanced away, tamping down my sympathy.

The girl fidgeted with her suit collar, finally lifting her helmet. It came off with a low hiss. Her ponytail sprang free, black and uncolored. The scent of strawberries filled the air, and I took a step back, caught off guard. I had expected *you* girls to be scentless at best or to smell clinical at worst, like some specimen kept too long in a jar.

Not like fresh, sweet strawberries.

Her eyes truly watered now as she breathed our polluted air for the first time in her life. She doubled over, coughing. I grabbed the bottle from her hand and twisted it open. "Drink."

11

She did so, sucking down the water as if it would save her life. Finally, she wiped her mouth with a handkerchief that had been tucked in her sleeve, then pressed it against her eyes. "How do you live breathing this every day?" she asked in a weak voice.

"We don't have to live for very long," I replied.

She dropped her handkerchief and stared at me with red-rimmed eyes. "That's not funny," she said.

I smiled. "I wasn't trying to be." I sat back down on the old sofa, so there was some distance between us.

She was pretty in a way I wasn't used to. Not like most *you* girls bowing to the latest beauty trends, indulging in temporary body modifications from reshaping their noses to plumping their lips, or hips, or rears, depending on what was *in. You* boys kept pace with pec implants and by buying new, chiseled jawlines. But fads came and went, and the *you*s altered their looks as often as the seasons. The *mei*s, lacking the funds for such drastic changes, resorted to painting their faces in bright colors, using semipermanent tattoos, and dyeing their hair.

Taipei's youth had become chameleons. If we couldn't change the dirty smog that smothered our city, we could at least control how we appeared, each metamorphosis more colorful and extravagant than the last.

She finished her water and cast a wary glance my way. "What's your name?"

"Seriously?" I laughed.

She lifted her shoulders. "I'd guess you're one year older than I am. Eighteen. Born in the Year of the Horse." She nodded at the black clothes strewn on the few pieces of furniture in the room. "Dark Horse, I'll call you."

I almost smiled but instead pulled out my butterfly knife and began the familiar pattern of flipping it between my fingers and spinning it in my hand. It helped me to think. She tensed, clutching her thighs. She was afraid I might take advantage of her. I wouldn't, and I had to fight the urge to reassure her, to explain.

"Why so Ro?" Her throaty voice broke my reverie.

*Why so Romeo?*

She didn't mean Romeo as in romantic; she meant Romeo as tragic.

I took in my surroundings through her eyes. I lived in an abandoned laboratory that used to belong to Yangmingshan University, an experimental "home" run on sustainable energy. Back when some thought we could still salvage our planet by "going green." We might have, if enough people had cared. But they hadn't. The rich were too rich, the poor were too poor, and the middle class—let's be honest—were only poor people with bigger houses, driving better cars. Now that the majority of us didn't live past our forties, we cared even less.

My current home consisted of just three rooms: the office, a bathroom, and this main chamber, which included the small kitchen. It held a large, round dining table with a couple of mismatched stools, the ragged turquoise-and-yellow sofa that was at least four decades old, a metal desk, and the wooden chair she sat in. Large windows flanked the southern wall, revealing a thicket of jungle beyond.

I tossed my knife three times, savoring the *snick* and *snap* of the blade and handles, before shrugging. "It's easier to kidnap in black."

13

Bad joke. I think her eyes actually smoldered.

I jumped up and grabbed my ancient MacPlus from the desk, opening it. "Put your helmet back on," I said.

"Why?"

"You're calling your family."

She did as I asked, securing her helmet, then took such a deep, full breath, her breasts swelled against her suit. I pretended not to notice.

"You have one minute." I tapped the necessary commands into my laptop and nodded at her.

We waited in tense silence, but their was no response to the call request.

"My father's not picking up," she finally said.

How was that possible? His daughter had been kidnapped.

"Call your mom, then," I ordered.

Her mother accepted the call immediately. *Thank gods.*

"Ma!" Her voice changed, sounding younger, helpless.

Although her helmet had darkened slightly, I still glimpsed the tears brightening her eyes, seeing her mother's face in the glass.

I could follow the entire conversation from her one-sided replies.

"Mei you, Mei you. Wo mei shi." *No, he hasn't tortured or raped me.*

She clasped her hands in front of her face, fingers trembling as if she could keep her mother's image there.

"Tell her I want three hundred million," I said.

Her pupils dilated, then shrank, and she saw me again.

"Now!"

"Ta yao san yi," she whispered.

14

"Put it in this account." I gave her the cashcard number for the ghost account that had been set up, and she recited it. "You have two hours."

"You liang ge xiao shi," she repeated.

Her mom began asking frantic questions.

Who is he? "Wo bu zhi dao."

Where are you? "Bu zhi dao!"

I typed a command and severed her connection.

She leaned forward, disoriented, almost falling off of the chair, then tugged her helmet off, throwing it to the ground. It bounced on the bamboo rug and spun twice before I snatched it up.

"Shit!"

She had pulled her legs into her chest on the chair, burying her face between her knees. Her shoulders heaved. When she lifted her head, her pale face was mottled.

"What if you had broken it?" I carefully placed her helmet on the dining table.

"Three hundred million? Are you serious?"

She had some nerve. I'd admire her for it, if her entitlement didn't piss me off so much. "What? You probably have twice that waiting for you in your trust fund." The *you*s didn't lead the lives that they did without having a few billion to spare.

"What do you want with it?" she asked, crossing her arms, assessing me.

"What do *you* want with it?" I countered.

We stared at each another, both our breaths coming too quickly. Hers because she was unused to our foul air; mine because I was rattled. *Damn* this *you* girl.

"How does my family know to trust you?" she demanded. "That you won't kill me anyway?"

"You know how it works." There was an unspoken rule between kidnappers and their targets. The victims always paid in full, and the criminals never killed anyone. Not yet, anyway. But then, no one had ever asked for three hundred million before. That wasn't my problem. And if I were a betting man, the ransom would be in the ghost account within the hour.

"Can I use your bathroom?" she asked.

I nodded toward the door and she disappeared within, shutting it behind her. I took the moment of privacy to pace the room and analyze my situation. I'd give her family two hours to hustle up the funds. Once cleared, I could deliver the girl back to the night market.

The shower had been running for some time, and I went to the bathroom door, which didn't lock. "The window's too small to crawl through," I shouted. "And the drop to the other side will break your legs, if not your neck."

The water turned off after another minute. She came out, looking exactly the same and still smelling of strawberries.

"Do you need a towel?" I asked, hiding a smirk behind the last apple I had found in the refrigerator drawer.

"No, thank you," she said coolly, then proceeded to drink the vitapak I handed her with dainty sips. "Don't you have any solid foods to eat?"

"Does this look like a five-star *you* establishment to you?" I asked. "I've only got liquids." Because I couldn't afford anything more.

"Although . . ." Suddenly remembering, I opened a kitchen cabinet. "I do have two rousong bao from the bakery."

I gave her one of the buns. "Don't blame me if you get a stomach-ache," I said, taking a big bite out of mine.

She stared at it for a long time, finally trying a nibble and chewing slowly before swallowing. Then she sat very still, as if waiting to die. I finished mine and brushed off my hands. "Well?" I was still hungry.

She took a full bite the next time, challenging me with a lift of her chin. "It's good," she said. She glanced out the expansive windows. "Are we on Yangmingshan?" she asked.

"No," I lied. "Is that the only mountain you know in Taiwan?"

"I haven't traveled much out of Taipei." Her face took on an expression that looked like yearning as she gazed into the trees. "Can we go outside?"

I couldn't hide my surprise. "No."

"I've never been in the mountains before. I won't run away."

"You'd get lost. And die."

She walked to the giant window and pressed herself against it. I wondered what it was like, never having been in the mountains or seen the jungle so close—never to have gone outdoors without a glass bowl over your head.

"All right. Your helmet stays inside. If you're willing to breathe the air, we can step out for a while." It was a risk, but so was our entire plan. I was no kidnapper or thief—even if kidnapping and stealing were exactly what I was doing. I hadn't gotten this far worrying over risks.

She turned, silhouetted by the afternoon light, and actually smiled. The most natural thing was to smile back. I ducked my head and turned. There was nothing natural about this.

"Come on. Stay close." The heavy door clicked open with my voice command. "I've got cucumbers and tomatoes to harvest anyway."

"What?"

I grabbed her hand, feeling the softness of her skin in my own rough palm. She jerked her arm back, startled, but my grip didn't loosen. "Do you want to see or not?" I asked.

She nodded, jaw tense, two bright spots on her cheekbones.

I led her along the edge of the house, sweeping aside giant fronds and leaves, past a dozen massive cisterns that collected rainwater. The smell of wet earth filled my senses. We picked our way through the shaded dirt path and veered into a small clearing, where the view of the sky was unobstructed. The sun burned above us, a blistering orb tinged in orange.

The sky used to be blue. This was what my research on the undernet told me, some sites even displaying actual photographs from another time—a pale blue skyline punctuated by skyscrapers or in a deeper hue over a calm sea, so two shades of blue melded like some old painting by a landscape artist. My mind kept returning to this image, the crisp purity of it. Unapologetic and true.

But what could you believe from reading the undernet? Images were more easily manipulated than a *you* boy's face. I didn't know anyone who had ever seen a blue sky. It wasn't until I had read a novel—published over a century ago—where the author described something in *sky blue*, that I let myself believe it, feeling wonder and joy and grief all at once.

I never did finish that book.

I suddenly felt the pressure of the *you* girl's hand clutching mine. Her flushed face was turned up, eyes squinted against the dull sunlight. She coughed into her sleeve, and when she finally stopped, her breaths came quick and shallow. It was late afternoon, the summer day's humid heat oppressive.

"Are you all right?" I asked.

She turned to me, eyes gleaming, and said, "I've never seen the sky like this before."

"You mean without your helmet?"

"And so wide. It's always a dirty brown over Taipei," she said.

The skies above us were tinged gray with pollution, but not the opaque brown that's so often seen directly over the city. I led her into my small garden. Cucumbers dangled from a bamboo trellis I had made, nestled within their giant dark green leaves. We stepped between the tomato plants, their fruits small and marred. I stooped down, and she crouched with me as I selected a tomato, dusting it off, then taking a bite. More tangy than sweet. She stared as if I had plucked a rat off the ground and eaten that instead.

"The sky used to be blue," I said, after I finished the tomato.

"That's what my grandfather says."

*Grandfather.* I'd never met my grandparents, didn't even know their names. My paternal grandparents were long dead before I was born. As for my maternal grandparents, they lived in America, and I wanted nothing to do with them.

"He's seen it, then?" I tried to keep my voice from rising. "With his own eyes?"

"He thinks so. But he was very young." She ran her fingertips over the ridges and bumps of an orange tomato. "He says it feels like a dream when he remembers it."

Sweat beaded at her temples, and there was a sheen of perspiration above her upper lip. I swiped my arm across my forehead. "I can't believe how hot it gets," she said, licking her mouth.

I mirrored her without thinking, tasting the salt on my tongue. "This is what summers are like in Taiwan when you're not wearing an air-conditioned suit," I replied and grabbed the woven basket near my feet.

"I'll help you," she said.

We spent the next twenty minutes in silence, filling the basket with imperfect tomatoes and cucumbers. The mountain breeze rustled the leaves around us, and the birds sang deep within the jungle's thicket. When we were done, the *you* girl's lips were leached of color, and wisps of black hair that had escaped from her ponytail clung to her damp neck.

Her breaths still came too fast, like a frightened hare's. "I think we should go back inside," I said, lifting the basket.

She rose with me. "I want to try one."

I angled the basket, and her hand grazed over the tomatoes and cucumbers, touching them as if they were gems instead of meager crops. She finally selected an oblong tomato, redder than the others, and brushed a thumb over its skin before taking a bite. She immediately made a face and shuddered.

I laughed. "No good?"

"It's more sour than I've ever tasted."

I smirked. No doubt, she'd only ever had perfectly grown specimens. We walked back toward the house, and she appeared thoughtful as she finished the fruit.

"I like that it tastes . . . earthy," she finally said. I saw her eyes sweep our surroundings as we approached the front of the lab.

The door unlocked with my voice and we stepped back inside the relative coolness of the building. I set the basket on the dining table and nodded at her helmet beside it. "You should put it back on."

"Later," she murmured and walked back toward the windows, gazing outward.

I sat on a stool and tapped a few quick commands into my laptop. The funds had transferred in full. I let out a breath, releasing the tension I had held ever since stealing this *you* girl. Three hundred million had been a gamble, but a gamble worth taking. It was enough for Victor to suit up as a *you* boy and pretend to be one of them, to infiltrate their closed and elite society. We'd destroy them from within.

We wanted blue skies again.

"What are you going to do with the money?" She turned, her hands clasped in front of her.

I jumped at the sound of her voice and shut the MacPlus. "I don't know. Redecorate?"

She gave me a leveled look, and I broke away first, taking in the chamber I had called home for the past year. I'd have to leave immediately. I would miss this place.

21

"I'd suggest a new wardrobe first, Dark Horse."

I laughed despite myself. "What's your name, then?"

"Seriously?" She raised her eyebrows in mockery.

I shrugged. "What does it matter now?" I did like her. I wanted to know.

"Daiyu," she replied.

"From the novel?"

She smiled in surprise, and it made her truly beautiful. "You've read it?"

I read voraciously, most often from the undernet, but had found an actual copy of *Dream of the Red Chamber* stuffed and forgotten in the desk drawer of a junk shop. The owner had given it to me for free, waving me off without a glance. Books weren't worth the paper they were printed on.

"Flowers in my eyes and birdsong in my ears," she murmured to herself.

I'd read the book enough times to recognize the line, from a poem that the hero Baoyu used when thinking of the heroine, Daiyu's namesake.

"Augment my loss and mock my bitter tears," I replied.

She glanced toward me, eyes gleaming from the pollution—or fear, I didn't know. "You have read it."

It was a favorite of mine. But she didn't need to know that. Instead, I said, "You don't look the tragic heroine to me."

"Don't I?" She had been leaning against the glass and straightened now, squaring her shoulders. But not before I caught a glimpse of wistfulness in her eyes. Of longing. What more could a *you* girl possibly want when she already had everything?

"We better go," I said. "I need to return you to your family, and it'll be dark soon."

Daiyu lifted her helmet and adjusted her collar before fitting it over her head. And in an instant she was something *other* to me, something less human. It was hard to believe there was an almost-normal girl beneath the glass. A smart one with a sense of humor.

"I'll have to give you the sleep spell again," I said apologetically.

"No. Blindfold me if you have to."

"I can't risk it. I've added something so you'll forget." I could see her eyes widen in panic, even with her helmet on. "Not everything. Just the past twenty-four hours."

She shook her head. "Please don't."

But I took her hand, was already pulling her to the door. "It's safer for us both if you don't remember anything. Trust me." I felt stupid the moment I uttered the last words.

We were out in the muggy humidity of the late afternoon again. It would take a few hours at least to walk to the mountain's base, and by then, night would have fallen. Even if I were abandoning the lab, I still couldn't risk her remembering this place, remembering me.

The sunlight glinted off her helmet, and I was glad I couldn't see her features clearly as I tugged her to me. She resisted, but I was stronger. So she stepped forward instead, bunching the fabric of my shirt in one hand.

23

"But I *want* to remember," she said.

I grabbed her wrist. Stuck the syringe into her open palm. Its hiss seemed too loud to my ears.

"We all do," I whispered and caught her as she fell.

# CHΔPTER TWO
## TWO MONTHS EARLIER

A storm was going to hit, the first big one this spring, and I could sense the anticipation: in the tension from those around me, in the stillness of the dark clouds that swelled overhead. I slipped through the crowds in Ximending. Dusk, and the air in Taipei was cold and brisk. Three girls swept past, chattering, swathed in nervous energy, eyes bright above their face masks. One clutched a fuchsia umbrella and its tip tapped against my shin as I dodged out of their way.

I glanced over my shoulder a few times to be sure I wasn't being followed. After five years living mostly on the streets on my own, I was used to watching my back. But Arun had warned us that his mom, Dr. Nataraj, might be under surveillance. She didn't know by whom.

I tugged my worn blue cap lower, satisfied I wasn't being tailed. Workers were just beginning to trickle out from their office jobs, rushing to the metros to commute home to their families or to restaurants and eateries to meet friends. Still too bright to turn on their neon signs, the windows of the shops and boutiques appeared unassuming, not yet ready for the throngs of fashionable teens and twenty-somethings to trample through once night had fallen. Street vendors shuffled and rearranged their merchandise: jewelry, purses, and shoes; I saw two cast a wary eye to the skies above. One vendor set out a colorful array of umbrellas especially coated to last against our acid rains.

I knew it would be a rowdy night, as everyone tried to stay out for as long as they could before the winds and rain hit. If it weren't for meeting up with my friends, I'd be back at my makeshift home on Yangmingshan, reading, cruising the undernet, or working on something nefarious with Lingyi. Arun had called for an emergency meeting, and he wouldn't have unless it was serious.

A silver limousine inched through the narrow street, hulking and ludicrous. It didn't take a genius to know that some *you* teens had probably gotten their daddies' permission to make an excursion out among the masses, to one of the exclusive clubs or restaurants pumped with regulated air, open only to those who were rich enough to be members.

Tucking my chin into the collar of my black denim jacket, I sneered as I strode past the limo. The vehicle pulsed from the music within, a steady, strong bass beat. A commercial for the limo company played across its opaque windows, featuring a gorgeous Taiwanese woman dressed in black showing off the car's luxurious interior, lithe arms moving gracefully as she pushed buttons and was served champagne by a barbot. When I passed the back window, the flickering glass suddenly became transparent, revealing the actual interior with white seats bathed in bluish light. A *you* girl rapped on the windowpane, fingers curling, the other hand clutching a crystal flute filled with a liquid that glowed pink, the bubbles rising like bright stars.

The limousine had jerked to a stop, trying to navigate past the crush of people, and I stopped with it, staring at the *you* girl pressed against the window. She wore a silver dress beaded with crystal, the top revealing her full breasts. Though her features were Asian, her sleek hair was as deep red as her lipstick. Lifting her glass, she toasted me. Another girl leaped from the back of the car and wrapped an arm around the redhead's shoulders, giggling. Watching them was surreal, like I was viewing another commercial projected on the limo's window. The two dipped their heads together, animated, laughing. They looked no older than sixteen.

Pedestrians pointed, and I heard their complaints in the periphery: *rich, useless* you *girls drunk already*. There was no reason the limousine needed to be on the street—it could easily lift into the sky, avoiding congestion. Aircars were a luxury, even among the ultrarich—they could fly unpoliced above the masses and arrive at their party before they finished their drinks. The girls *wanted* to be in the crowds. They wanted the attention. "Get out of the fucking way!" some old man shouted and kicked at the limousine tire. The silver limo lurched forward, breaking through the foot traffic, and the girls within shrieked; I could tell by the set of their mouths, as their bodies swayed together from the momentum. The redhead then pushed her lips against the window, smearing the clear glass with the imprint of her mouth. She winked at me, and before I could react, the window was opaque once more, brightly lit with the moving image of the limo commercial.

I raised my fist, ready to pound on the glass, hard enough to scare the girl, to shock her from her comfortable stupor. But the limo had sped ahead, only to brake hard at a red light.

*Forget it. Not worth my time.*

"Eh!" The man who had cursed at the limo broke through my thoughts. "She wanted you for a boy toy."

He laughed, spittle flying, and I was glad he stood a short distance away. You never knew what you could catch these days. Gaunt, with shoulders hunched forward, he looked like a grandfather. But he was probably in his forties. Dressed in rags, he shuffled toward me, finger outstretched, before a fit of coughing seized him. He doubled over, pressing both hands to his thighs, his body literally shaking from the episode. After what seemed like a full minute, the coughing finally eased, but he remained stooped, rasping, trying to catch his breath.

People steered clear of him, so it seemed we had an invisible barrier around us. Concerned, I took two steps toward him, battling my own fear of becoming tainted by his illness. But he held up his palm and fixed his sharp black eyes on me. They were wet from his violent coughing.

"If I were still young and a good-looking kid like you, I'd do it," he said, voice grating. "Good money, good food, fun times."

I laughed. It was short and humorless. "And be at a *you* girl's beck and call? Be kept like some dog on a leash? No, thanks." I took another step forward, my arm outstretched. "Uncle, let me buy you a hot drink. You should sit down—"

28

"Don't come closer!" he shouted, his words thick with phlegm. "Are you stupid? I'm diseased. You want what I got?" He dragged a filthy sleeve across his mouth, muttering to himself before saying, "It's easy to be idealistic when you're young and pretty, boy."

I turned and walked away. He didn't want my help. And what could I do for him in the end anyway but buy him a hot tea? He needed the hospital and medicine, just like my mother had. I swallowed the sourness at the back of my throat, my grief suddenly as sharp as a fresh cut wound. There was nothing more I could offer—I didn't have anything myself.

Another limousine zoomed by, this one overhead, followed by three muscular *mei* boys on airpeds—bodyguards or boy toys, most likely both. At least they weren't adding to the rush-hour madness below.

"Truth is, reality *always* crushes your ideals," the guy shouted at my back. "Just you wait and see."

The clerk in the lobby of the run-down karaoke joint didn't look up when I strolled in. The place must have been built in the '90s, when the popularity of karaoke was at its peak, and appeared as old and tired as the outdated machines they still used. A dim chandelier barely lit the dark foyer; the old carpet reeked of grease and must.

"I'm meeting some friends," I said.

The clerk flicked his cigarette butt into an ashtray. "Tall Filipino guy?" he said, still not bothering to glance up. "Hot chick in a fluffy skirt?"

I nodded and wondered how he had guessed, then realized there probably weren't more than two rooms rented out in the entire pathetic place.

"Upstairs," the clerk said. "Suite two-oh-three." He lit another cigarette, breathing deep, then coughed as he blew the smoke out, eyes glued to an old box television placed on the counter in front of him. The TV was the kind where you had to twist a knob to change the channel—it'd be an antique if it weren't such crap. That's what most *mei*s were left with these days: crap.

Taking the creaky stairs two steps at a time, I found the dark brown door with faded 203 brass numbers tacked on and the muffled tones of a Jay Chou ballad coming from beyond it. Knocking once, I twisted the sticky knob and pushed the door open before I got a response. Four pairs of sharp eyes met mine; I was one of the last to show as usual.

Dr. Nataraj sat in the middle of a worn black sofa, its fake leather hiding decades' worth of stains. Arun was to her left, his usual bright orange spiked hair pulled conservatively back in a ponytail. Lingyi sat on Dr. Nataraj's right, wearing a bright green tee and full white miniskirt plastered with bright flowers—tulips. Victor was slumped in a red velvet armchair beside Lingyi, his long legs sprawled in front of him, lazy as a cat. And just as cool. "Nice of you to join us, Zhou," he drawled.

Seeing that Dr. Nataraj had turned away and was speaking to Arun in soft tones, I flicked a rude gesture at Victor, and he widened his eyes in pretend shock, laughing under his breath.

Lingyi arched one eyebrow, lips pursing, a not-so-subtle reprimand for me to behave; I grinned charmingly and shut the door behind me. Iris stood behind it, and I jumped. "Gods, Iris!" I said.

"Hey, Zhou." She was dressed in black, like always, and tucked the syringe she held casually between her fingertips back into some hidden pocket at her thigh. A quick stab in the arm with the sleep spell, and I would have dropped within seconds.

"Hey," I said back. She was already slinking away from me, falling carelessly into the other armchair, throwing her legs over its arm, and settling in.

"I'm sorry I'm late." I could see again the resemblance between Dr. Nataraj and Arun—both had dark brown eyes with high cheekbones and strong chins. But Dr. Nataraj's black wavy hair was threaded with gray.

She shifted over on the large sofa and smiled at me, patting the place beside her. "Only a few minutes, Zhou. We haven't started yet."

I slipped over to sit between her and Lingyi. Even Dr. Nataraj referred to me by my family name alone. I never shared my given name, and my friends never asked. After years on the streets on my own, it afforded me the anonymity I wanted. Zhou was a common enough surname.

Dr. Nataraj pushed a white plate toward me, stacked with perfectly triangular samosas, fried to a beautiful golden hue. "I made your favorite, Zhou. Take some." She flashed her warm smile.

"Thanks, Auntie." We all called Arun's mom "auntie" because she insisted upon it. None of us had a mother figure in our lives to speak of, and she'd made sure to welcome us into her home and heart from the start. For over three years she'd played the role of listener and advice giver, and was simply there to give hugs when any of us needed it. The dinners she invited us to in her and Arun's home were the only home-cooked meals we had. But it wasn't the delicious saag paneer or aloo gobi she made that drew us the most, it was the feeling of comfort and belonging she offered each of us.

My stomach was already growling as I heaped three still-warm samosas onto a paper plate, wolfing two large bites down before saying, "Your samosas are the best." They really were.

She angled her chin a fraction, her gold pendant earrings swaying, and replied in a conspiratorial tone, "I've wrapped up a few for you to take home."

I made the pretense of kissing her cheek, but stopped short as my mouth was full and that seemed rude. She laughed, shaking her head. Dr. Nataraj had a way of making you feel special, like she *saw* you, and that you *mattered*. We both knew she'd made takeaway packages for everyone there. Arun was so lucky.

The ancient karaoke set was playing its music on a large box television, just loud enough to drown out our conversation for anyone listening at the door. A young man and woman danced alone in a sunlit ballroom, gazing lovingly at each other as the lyrics scrolled across the bottom half of the screen. There were no windows, and the only light came from another cheap chandelier that hung over the seating area. Two plastic-covered menus were thrown haphazardly onto the low, black table in front of us beside the plate of samosas.

The room stank of stale cigarette smoke.

Dr. Nataraj didn't begin until she met each of our eyes, knowing she had our full attention. She was a prominent professor in ecology at National Taiwan University. Not only was she well respected in the field as an educator, she was also a vocal activist, tirelessly trying to get the government to pass more restrictive pollution laws in Taiwan to help clean our filthy air and dirty waters.

"I'm sure that Arun has told you there's been no progress. I have approached six officials who are part of the legislative yuan and have been stonewalled, met with silence, or had doors slammed in my face." She spoke perfect Mandarin, tinged with the lilt of her native Hindi. It didn't matter that she was dressed in jeans and a black sweater—her presence, her poise, commanded your attention. "I was even escorted out by security twice!" Dr. Nataraj let out a soft laugh. "Me, thrown out by burly guards because I'm such a threat."

She sank into the sofa and folded her hands in her lap. "It's clear that someone very powerful doesn't want the legislation to ever be presented. I appreciate all your help so far in being my eyes and ears. I didn't want to break any laws, but I have a feeling whoever we are going up against has no such qualms." She paused, then turned toward Lingyi and me. "I think my communication is being monitored."

Iris straightened and Arun's knee jittered with nervous tension.

"Written communication?" Victor asked.

"And voice," Dr. Nataraj said. "Anything going through my phones or computers."

"Have these people left any threatening messages?" I asked. "Any clues at all?"

"No," she said. "They're pros. And I have no evidence other than my intuition." She gripped her hands tighter, tight enough that the knuckles turned white. "I was almost run over twice this week."

I leaned forward, meeting Victor's eyes; he was still draped haphazardly in the armchair, but his jaw had tightened.

"What?" Arun exclaimed. "Why didn't you tell me, Mom?"

"I didn't want to worry you," she replied. "The first time I thought it was just an accident . . . but then it happened again."

Lingyi reached over for Dr. Nataraj's hand and squeezed it. "Tell us."

"I was returning home after shopping at the market," Dr. Nataraj said. "It was Saturday, and the streets and sidewalks were crowded. I was waiting at a corner to cross, when someone from behind bumped hard into me, so I stumbled in front of an oncoming bus."

Victor cursed under his breath.

"Thankfully," Dr. Nataraj said, "the bus was moving slowly, and the driver hit his brakes. A kind woman pulled me back by my coat. Two days later, I was leaving the university late in the evening, and a car almost ran over me coming out of one of the parking lots at full speed."

"Did you catch the license plate?" I asked. "Were you able to see the driver at all?"

Dr. Nataraj shook her head. "It was an expensive car, and the windows were tinted."

"Iris, why don't you start shadowing her?" I said.

Dr. Nataraj began to protest, but Arun grabbed her arm. "I think we should, Mom. For your safety."

"The sooner we find out who's behind this," I said, "the better."

"I can help, too," Lingyi said. "If you give me permission, I can secure your accounts. I can make them impenetrable." She gave the professor a bright smile. But Lingyi wasn't playing around; she was one of the best in cybersecurity, just like she was one of the best to hack through it.

The professor smiled back at Lingyi. "Thank you." Then her expression turned serious. "But I would ask more of you, if you're willing. I'd like you to hack into these six legislators' accounts and see if there are any clues—anything at all to tell us who we're up against."

"Of course," Lingyi said without hesitation.

"It might be dangerous," Dr. Nataraj said. "I wouldn't ask if I saw any other way. But I've tried for months going through the proper channels, meeting with officials who obviously don't want anything to do with me, and I have nothing to show for it but the unwanted attention of a possible stalker and attempts on my life." Even though she spoke in soft tones, she still spoke with vehemence.

"They're not playing by the rules—," Arun said.

"So why should we?" I finished.

"Don't worry, Auntie. We're happy to help," Lingyi said. "I'll start on it right away. And, Victor, keep all your channels and contacts open for any underground info that might help us."

"Anything for you, Auntie," Victor replied.

Dr. Nataraj extended her arm and Victor clasped her hand in a rare show of genuine affection. Usually, anything Vic ever said was in half jest, overexaggeration, or sarcasm. But not this time. He looked ready to hunt down those who were accountable and beat the shit out of them. I was prepared to join him.

"We'll get to the bottom of this, Mom," Arun said. "We'll have answers before you know it."

Gray haze lay thick over Taipei. I set a brisk pace, my hands thrust into the pockets of my black denim jacket. The sleeves were too short, the

35

cuffs hitting a few inches above my wrists, and the material so worn, it had faded to a muddy gray. But it was the only jacket I owned, and one of the last things my mom had given me. Back then, it had been too big; she had laughed when I tried it on, the cuffs almost hanging below my fingertips. My mom had bargained for a cheaper price. "You'll grow into it," she had said, then touched my cheek.

In the end, she never did get to see me wear this jacket. She caught a cold that turned into a virulent strain of pneumonia. We couldn't afford the medical care or medicines that might have saved her life. And at thirteen, I watched her die.

I shivered and drew the thin denim tighter around me.

Meet me at my mom's office, Arun had messaged me an hour ago. I'm worried about her

Arun came from a family of prominent scientists, and Dr. Nataraj had encouraged his inquisitive nature since he could pose a scientific question. At eighteen, he was getting his doctorate in virology at the university. Arun was a genius. And being as logical and pragmatic as he was, he'd never worry without reason.

I walked faster.

College students on bikes emerged like phantoms toward me through the polluted haze. I'd walked this promenade lined with palm trees many times before to meet Arun. We'd been friends ever since I met him at my favorite cybercafe four years ago; he had been getting some secret gaming in after school. The university's grand library was at the end of the wide path, but like the palm trees, I couldn't see it. I might as well have been marooned on some desert island—the only inhabitants, the ghostly images of students on bikes floating past me and disappearing again into the gray smog.

Like everyone else, I wore a mask over my face. But this didn't stop my eyes from burning, feeling as if they had been rubbed with sandpaper, and each choked breath still somehow tasted of ash and dust. My throat felt raw, irritated. The air was still as a held breath. This filth was going nowhere.

I jogged through the mist toward our meeting place, in front of Dr. Nataraj's building. Swerving at the last moment, I avoided a bike ridden by a girl wearing two long braids. She yelped in surprise, dark eyes wide above her hot pink mask, the sound sharp and out of place, then cycled on and disappeared from view. We were far enough within the large campus that the noise of Taipei's traffic was only a low hum in the distance.

My black boots sank into the wet grass before hitting concrete, and the grand arches of the science building manifested before me; some long, rectangular windows above them were lit up like blank eyes. Arun's bright orange spiked hair drew my gaze immediately, and I broke into a wide grin until I saw his panic-stricken face. He lunged at me and grabbed my wrist. Something was seriously wrong.

"I still haven't been able to get in touch with my mom," Arun said while dragging me as he ran into the building. "Since yesterday afternoon. I came home late last night from the lab and didn't see her this morning. She always returns my messages."

We skidded through the foyer filled with arches leading into other corridors. Our footsteps echoed through the grand space. Arun pressed his palm to the scanner at the glass barrier allowing access into the interior, then tugged me through when the door swung open.

We took the stone steps two at a time. The long hallways were empty this afternoon. Most people had already left for the Qingming Festival tomorrow, making long trips to their ancestors' gravesites for the annual tomb sweeping. The air was muggy in the stifling building, and coupled with the eerie quiet, the place felt abandoned. We stopped in front of Dr. Nataraj's office. The wooden door was shut. Arun pounded on it.

"Her office door is *never* shut, much less locked," Arun said. "And it sounds like the screen is on inside."

Our eyes met, and the hairs on my arms rose.

"Mom?" Arun shouted this time and threw his shoulder against the door. It thudded loudly, reverberating down the empty hallway. "Help me," he pleaded.

We counted to three and launched our bodies against the door. Arun was stocky and I was lean, but we both had some muscle. The door looked old, original to the building, and creaked in protest.

"Again!" I said.

We rammed ourselves against it once more, and this time, there was a loud snapping sound. We fell into the room.

Arun jumped up as I straightened.

"Mom!" He ran and crouched down beside Dr. Nataraj, who was sprawled on the floor near her desk. A purple scarf was unfurled beside her, like an afterthought. He was stroking her cheeks, smoothing the tangle of hair from her eyes. But just one look at the pallor of her face, and I knew. Her warm brown skin was tinged an ashen gray, the set of her limbs that of a corpse, not someone who was unconscious.

38

"No!" Arun wailed as he pulled her inert form to him, so that he was cradling her in his lap. "No, Mom!" He rocked her, grabbing her hand, rubbing her fingers, as if holding her could somehow bring her back.

His grief brought a knot to my throat. I kneeled beside him, clasping his shoulder. I went through the motions of searching for a pulse, and Arun raised a fist, as if to punch me, or hit my hand away. I shook my head, confirming what we both already knew. Sorrow and rage washed over me, and suddenly I was thirteen again, alone, helpless, holding my slack mother in my own arms. I didn't want comfort then either. I wanted to beat the world to a pulp.

Not Dr. Nataraj, too. Not our auntie.

"But how?" he roared, my gentle friend who never raised his voice. "Why?" He grabbed a cushion from a nearby chair and placed it under her head. Arun then lunged to his feet and cast his eyes wildly around the room.

Dr. Nataraj's neat desk was in disarray, with the top drawer pulled out. Two empty plastic tubes were discarded on the desk and another had fallen to the floor. Arun stumbled to the desk and picked one up. "Epinephrine. These were her injections in case she suffered an allergic reaction." He shook the empty syringe. "She's allergic to peanuts—but was vigilant."

"We should call an ambulance," I said.

On the wall behind us, the screen was on, but I wasn't paying attention to the murmur of voices on whatever program it was tuned in to.

"No," Arun replied. He picked up one of the empty syringes,

tapping it against his palm. He lifted the syringe and held it to the fluorescent light above us, shifting it this way and that, then repeated this with the other two. Arun brought his fist down hard on the desk, his pupils constricted to sharp points. "All three syringes' liquids are tinged brown. Epinephrine is clear."

What he said took a moment to sink in.

"Shit," I said.

"It means they've expired," Arun said, "but the dates on them are current. She was so careful. There's no way she would have let one syringe expire, much less all three. Her life depended on it."

I leaned down to pick up Dr. Nataraj's MacFold, which was smashed against the concrete floor. "And there's her Palm." It lay a short distance from Dr. Nataraj's body. The screen on the com device was smashed too—not as if it had been dropped, but like someone had stomped on it. Then I noticed Dr. Nataraj clutched something in her hand. Her arm was curled against her chest, as if protecting it.

The screen control.

I jerked my head toward the wall screen, and the voice finally registered over the rush of panic and confusion. Dr. Nataraj sat in a red leather chair, her hands clasped within the folds of her deep green-and-gold sari. She looked as regal as a queen. "We *must* do something to change the destructive course we've set upon. We must work together to decrease the pollutions we're pumping into the air we breathe, into the water we drink, into the very soil in which we grow our food. I urge the Taiwanese government to push through the necessary legislation to right the wrong we've inflicted upon ourselves. Upon our Mother Earth." She gazed directly into the camera, dark brown eyes gentle yet forthright. "We are poisoning ourselves. Our planet. Our home," Dr. Nataraj said emphatically.

The young hostess of the *Go, Go, Let's Chat* talk show nodded, then leaned in, crossing her perfect, long legs. "And what do you say to the *you*s of Taiwan, who manage to lead healthy and long lives in regulated spaces and in their suits? Who contend that no problem exists?"

Dr. Nataraj's smile was pointed. "That is a poor and temporary solution. I say to all the *you*s of Taiwan, to *all* the haves of this world, who believe that you can live in a literal bubble and survive: you cannot. We are all creatures of this earth, of this shared ecosystem." She raised her hands, which were still clasped, her fingers intertwined. "We are integrated. We're one. You cannot survive if the ecosystem is dying around you. You cannot hide from the effects of global warming. It's bad now. I urge that we don't continue to make it worse locally. It is not too late to change our ways, to alter our course."

"And how has progress been on introducing legislation to help our environment, Dr. Nataraj?"

Dr. Nataraj's kind face hardened, her mouth pulling into a tight line. "Harder than I expected. I've been trying to encourage the introduction of legislation in the legislative yuan for almost a year, with absolutely no progress. In fact, I have proof that someone has actively worked against implementing these laws."

The hostess widened her eyes in shock. "Who would do that?"

"I don't know." Dr. Nataraj looked straight into the camera. "But when I find out, I'll have no qualms about exposing them. This is no

41

longer about business, politics, or profit; it's no longer a matter of health; it is a matter of our very survival."

The image froze on-screen, with Dr. Nataraj's expression imploring yet intense, her elegant hands held before her, as if literally pleading with the audience.

"Why was this playing?" I twisted toward Arun, drawing a shaky breath.

"This interview aired yesterday afternoon." Arun stooped beside his mom again and touched her slack arm, the one clenching the control. "She never watched her interviews on-screen." Even as he spoke, the program rebooted again to start from the beginning of the show. He glanced up, the whites of his eyes standing out in his face. We were both thinking the same thing: Dr. Nataraj had been murdered.

Arun swiped a hand over his eyes. In that instant, he looked like he had aged ten years. He tugged his Palm from his vest pocket.

"Are you calling the police?" I asked.

"We can't," he said. "We can't go to the police. What proof do we have?"

I cursed. After meeting with Dr. Nataraj, Lingyi had managed to hack into a Taichung legislator's account, finding a message between him and a "Mr. Wu." Since then, she had extracted five more similar exchanges with other legislators Dr. Nataraj had tried to meet. All with the same veiled threats, all with the hint of large bribes if they obeyed. Still, we weren't any closer to discovering who was behind Mr. Wu's work. And now Arun's mom was dead.

"Hey, Arun." Lingyi's cheery voice carried through his Palm. "What's up?"

Arun opened his mouth, then clamped it shut. Tears streamed down his face; his throat worked.

I looked away, feeling a hot pressure behind my own eyes. "Lingyi, we have to meet," I said. "Something's happened."

A pause. Then she replied, "Tomorrow morning? My apartment?"

"Yes," I said.

It had all seemed harmless before, working with Dr. Nataraj. To help someone we loved and respected. To help the *mei*s, to save Taiwan. Playing the *good guys*. Now, with Dr. Nataraj's calculated murder, it was obvious we were screwed—up against professional criminals who were older, wiser, better funded. We could be the ones suffering an "accidental" death next.

"Done." Lingyi's voice floated to me. "See you tomorrow." A soft chime; she had clicked off.

Arun was holding his mom again in his arms, rocking her. I clenched my jaw.

"Let's get the assholes who did this," I said.

He raised his head and jerked his chin in agreement.

No. We wouldn't let the bastards get away with this.

Rain drizzled all morning on Qingming Festival day. Taipei seemed empty, subdued. Most shops were closed, and only a few pedestrians wandered on the sidewalks, some holding colorful umbrellas. I wore a cap but chose to go barefaced this morning. The rain was warm where it hit my exposed skin, on the backs of my hands, my neck and cheeks. Not heavy enough to sting. It wasn't often the *mei*s of Taipei could go barefaced in the day. Our rains carried enough pollutants to taint our waters, but they still had the ability to wash away our brown air, even if for a few hours.

We were meeting at Lingyi's apartment in central Wanhua, the oldest district in Taipei. I passed vacant storefronts and abandoned buildings, boarded up and scrawled with graffiti, but the mood changed when I neared the Longshan Temple, a few blocks from where Lingyi lived. Clusters of people who couldn't leave the city to pay respects to their ancestors and many foreigners were gathered around the temple, wandering in and out of its main courtyard. The tiles of the curved roof stood stark against the ominous sky, smears of red and green. Smoke curled into the air, and the scent of sandalwood carried to me, defying the weather. Hundreds of incense sticks would be lit today to pay tribute to the dead.

I glanced at the Vox strapped to my wrist. Jogging past the crowds, I found a monk selling incense at a table tucked into the corner of the large courtyard. No cashcards here. The monk, his face untouched by age except for two deep grooves marking either sides of his mouth, gestured to a wooden bowl on the table. I was poor. Not enough to be starving, but enough to be hungry all the time. My friends were good to me, especially Lingyi, but I didn't want to be their charity case. I did translations between Chinese and English and earned enough to survive. But a kid without a high school education could only get so far. My clients were referred out of kindness or used me for my cheap rates.

And there was Arun's mom, who had always made sure she passed me something delicious to take home whenever I saw her. Just last week, I had stopped over at Arun's to check out his latest game purchases, and Dr. Nataraj had sent me off with a stack of naan wrapped in aluminum foil and a container of bhindi bhaji. My vision blurred, remembering her warm brown eyes crinkling with a smile when she pulled away from our hug. It would be the last time I saw her alive.

Digging in my jeans pocket, I fished out two yuan coins and tossed them in the bowl. The monk handed me three incense sticks without a word. I took the incense and jostled my way to the closest brass urn in the courtyard. It rested on a pedestal, its domed top towering over me. A small fire shimmered like a mirage at its center, and I lit the incense sticks, breathing in the sandalwood smoke before closing my eyes. I clasped my hands together, bowing.

It took a moment before I could remember my mother's features. My mind then leaped to Arun, clutching Dr. Nataraj's slack body, his face twisted as if in physical pain. At thirteen, I had been too young to understand the injustice of my mother's death. I only knew that we didn't have money, which meant we couldn't get her the help that she needed. Now, after almost five years living on the streets on my own, I understood. I saw the city I loved teetering on the edge of ruin, on the verge of taking its people with her. Only the *you*s remained untouched in their wealth, impervious. Now Arun's mom was gone—murdered—and I felt again that anguish. I bowed once more, heart heavy, before opening my eyes and planting the three incense sticks in the urn. There would be no grave sweeping for my friends and me today.

I arrived fifteen minutes late to Lingyi's apartment, and everyone was already there, making the space look even smaller than usual.

45

Lingyi sat at her workstation, while Arun slouched on the white sofa, dark circles marking the curves beneath his eyes. Iris was swinging from one handgrip to the other on the target wall, not using her legs at all. She was dressed in cargo pants and a T-shirt, a knit cap pulled over her short hair—all in black.

Victor paced the room in long strides, both hands thrust deep into his trouser pockets, shirt cuffs folded crisply and secured with silver cufflinks. Not a hair out of place, but his eyes were red and swollen. This shocked me more than anything; it drove our loss home. Vic had no immediate family in Taiwan that we knew of, although he'd occasionally refer to cousins who lived here. Lingyi had told me she suspected Victor sent most of what he earned in his deals back to his family in the Philippines, but he never hinted as much to me. The facade of careless ease was what he projected best, but Dr. Nataraj had found ways to win even Vic over, always pulling him aside to speak to him in soft tones. Asking how he was doing. Making sure he was all right. She was the one person he talked to after Lingyi broke it off after a few months of dating. Once, when he had had one too many shots, he confessed that Dr. Nataraj reminded him of his own mother. It was the only time in the three years I had known him that he had ever mentioned his own mom.

Victor nodded at me, his tanned face drawn. He made a strong impression. No wonder he was faceless in all his transactions. You didn't often see a striking, young Filipino man wearing sleek suits and a silk tie wherever he went in Taipei. If you saw Victor once, you'd likely remember him. He wasn't born to blend in.

Today, he was dressed as sharp as ever but lacked the usual

swagger. I nodded back at him but went immediately to sit by Arun, who looked broken. I didn't know what to say and clasped his shoulder for a second.

"Sorry I'm late." I took a butterfly knife from my jacket pocket and began flipping it between my fingers. "I stopped by the Longshan Temple on the way."

No one had to ask why.

Iris jumped down from the wall onto the bamboo floor, stalking, noiseless as a cat, to sit on the rug near Lingyi's feet. She looked pissed. But I'd learned some time ago that this seemed to be a default emotion Iris displayed in place of sadness, fear, or disappointment. Lingyi's eyes were red-rimmed, but she thrust her chin forward, as if ready for war. "I've found something," she said.

The energy in the room coalesced. I swung my blade closed, feeling its cold weight against my palm.

"I've finally been able to break into Mr. Wu's Vox account." Lingyi met each of our eyes. We all knew the significance of this. It had been much easier for her to hack into the six legislators' accounts than it had been to crack Wu's. "I still don't know Wu's true identity," Lingyi said in a tight, tired voice. "All the billing info is bogus, leading to cash payments at various 7-Elevens across Taipei. He doesn't keep all of his message exchanges, but I found two more sent out to legislators—that makes eight total that we know of."

She twisted the thick cuff at her wrist, neon green and painted with bright circles. Her fingers shook a little. I straightened, my senses buzzing. If Lingyi was fazed, then we were even more screwed than I had thought.

47

She continued. "But I was able to find a deleted voice message. Usually these are wiped—he either knows his shit or has someone who knows how to clean up his cybertracks. Wu slipped, this once." She drew a breath. "Arun, it's about . . ." She swallowed. "It's about your mom."

Arun's brown face blanched like he'd seen a ghost. He nodded. Lingyi's fingers glided over her keyboard, and two men's voices filled her living room. Wu had the rough voice of a smoker, and the man he called "boss" sounded educated and suave. His voice was oddly familiar to me. A chill slithered down my spine, despite that warm baritone. The man asked how Wu was doing, if he had anything to report. Wu coughed, then said everything was going as planned. "I'm very convincing," Wu rasped, "when I give them all the info you provide, boss. You should see their faces when I show them on-screen with photographic evidence that I know where their mom lives, but also their niece and nephew down to their second cousin on their mother's side." Wu laughed. "Shit, we even know where their dog's groomed."

"It doesn't take much," Wu's boss replied.

"No," Wu agreed. "Never more than that and the blaster I've got to convince them."

"I have another task for you," Wu's boss said. "The info's sent. Make it look like an accident." The connection was crystal clear, and we heard a muffled knock on someone's door. "Yes?" Wu's boss said. "Mr. Huang is here for his appointment—," a woman's voice interjected, clear but faint.

"Give me a minute," Wu's boss replied, cutting her off.

48

My heart was pounding so hard that I heard it in my ears. She had almost said his name—almost given away his identity. There was a crackling, indistinguishable noise in the background, then silence. "As I was saying," Wu's boss continued, "get rid of her."

"Info received. Her again," Wu said. "When do you want me to do it?"

"Tomorrow. She's done enough damage."

"I'll take care of it," Wu replied.

A chime, indicating that his boss had clicked off.

The silence was heavy after the playback ended.

"This call was made two days ago, after Dr. Nataraj's interview had broadcasted," Lingyi said. "It's no coincidence."

Arun dropped his head into his hands, his knee jittering. His grief and fury were palpable. I sat beside him, feeling useless, impotent.

"We were so close to finding out that asshole's identity," Iris said. She sat casually on the ground with her arms propped over raised knees, but her shoulders were tensed into a straight line. "It's my fault. . . ."

Lingyi reached down and gripped Iris's shoulder. "No, it isn't. *I* had sent you on another task for a few days."

Iris had been shadowing Dr. Nataraj since our meeting at the karaoke joint a few weeks ago. But nothing suspicious had happened again . . . until yesterday.

"It's the killer's fault, Iris," I said. "And whoever is behind this."

She shot me a murderous look and jerked her arm so Lingyi dropped her hand.

Lingyi colored and cleared her throat. "There's more," she said, and her voice cracked. "When his secretary opened his office door, there was some background noise. . . ."

I nodded. We had all heard it.

"I analyzed it using Clarity—it's the best voice-analysis program out there." Her eyes flicked to Victor—he must have gotten it for her. "Listen."

There was a faint crackling, then a woman's voice spoke, almost in a hiss. But what she said was clear: "Ladies and gentlemen, we are honored for your visit today. The next official tour of Jin Corp will begin in five minutes at four p.m. in the lobby."

*Jin Corp.* I felt a cold sweat break at the back of my neck. The company that manufactured *you* suits for all the rich people who wanted to live life in a self-contained bubble while the world went to rot around them. These suits were sold worldwide, but only about 5 percent of the population could afford the twenty-million-yuan price tag.

"I knew I recognized that voice," I said.

We didn't look at each other. All of us were thinking the same thing.

Jin Feiming was the richest and most powerful man in Taiwan. He owned half of Taipei. And he had ordered Arun's mom killed like she was an annoying pest, a mosquito buzzing in his ear. He could kill each of us just as easily, making them look like accidental deaths. Nobody would care. Lingyi might garner some attention, being the daughter of the disgraced CEO of Fortune Securities, but even then, a week's worth of headlines, at best.

50

"What can we do?" Arun finally asked after a long silence. "Jin can get what little evidence we have dismissed. He'd buy his way out of this easily. We'd never get a conviction."

"Assuming he doesn't have all of us murdered," Victor said.

Arun flinched, and I glared at Vic. But he was right. Victor only said aloud what we were all thinking.

"So he's been systematically threatening and bribing politicians to stop any environmental legislation from being introduced for years—," Lingyi said.

"For the sake of profit," Iris interjected, jumping to her feet again, prowling the room like a caged panther. "He's unstoppable."

"Is he?" I flicked the blade out on my knife, then spun it. "There's no profit to make if there's no product to sell."

Victor cracked his knuckles. "What are you suggesting, Zhou?" As successful as Vic was at running his business and doing deals, he was cautious. He made decisions only after thoughtful consideration of all his options. Victor was careful and restrained—basically the opposite of me.

He'd be the hardest to convince.

"I've read up on Jin Corp, on Jin Feiming's success," I said. "He's currently got plants in Nevada, outside of London, and in Mexico City. But they're assembling factories. Jin's said in interviews that he's kept all the production and development in Taipei—he's proud of that fact."

"So, what—we blow up the building?" Arun asked.

Iris was swinging up the wall again, her toned arms flexing as she skipped from one handgrip to the next, using her upper body

51

strength only, with obvious ease. "He'll just rebuild."

"But that'd take time," Arun replied.

I nodded. "We leak the evidence we have *after* we destroy Jin Corp. The media will have a feeding frenzy. Jin will be under heavy scrutiny—and it'll give us time to work on pushing through legislation."

"To finish what my mom started." Arun rubbed his hands and stared at the floor.

"The suits won't work if Jin Corp blows—Jin's said as much. Suits power off if the servers at headquarters are down," I continued. "Two or three years without a suit might be what the *you*s need to pull their heads out of their asses and really take a look around. See how bad things are. Breathe the air we breathe."

"Or they can just stay shut in, flying from one extravagant regulated space to the next," Victor said.

"Like trapped dogs?" I smirked. "I think some of them would be pissed. The *you*s aren't used to being denied anything."

"It's impossible to pull off," Victor said. "We're outmatched in every way. Jin Corp uses the best security, the highest tech. No chance in hell you just walk in and blow the place up. Not all of us seek danger, Zhou, just for the thrill."

I cocked an eyebrow at Victor. "Jin *killed* Arun's mom, Vic."

Victor winced, as if I'd punched him in the gut. I knew he cared for Dr. Nataraj as much as I did. Pushing away my guilt for speaking so bluntly when we were all still grieving, I went on, "We have evidence that he's bribing members of the legislative yuan to keep Taipei polluted so he can continue to turn a profit with his suits. At the cost of *mei* lives. We can *do* something." I slammed a fist hard on coffee table in vehemence, and Lingyi jerked at the loud noise, while Arun clutched his hands tighter. "So what if the odds are against us? We can try to fix this. I'm so sick of doing nothing."

Iris, the only one who hadn't reacted to my fist pounding, had slipped over to sit by Lingyi once more, leaning against her chair like a cat. "I agree with Zhou," she said simply.

I tried to hide my surprise.

Iris was fearless, but not rash. Her love and devotion to Lingyi was probably only rivaled by her love for Taipei. She was an orphan with an obscure past, and her fiercest ties were to this city. That much I knew. She roamed it every day, laying claim on the only thing that had been a constant in her life.

"Jin's filth. A murderer," Lingyi said after a pause. "But we wouldn't be much better if we blew up Jin Corp and killed innocent people to stop him."

"No one has to be in the building." I spun the knife in my hand. "We can secure it somehow."

"We'd need millions just to pay for the equipment alone," Victor said. "Never mind the logistics of breaking into Jin Corp. It's impossible. And we'd be risking our lives. Is this worth dying for?"

My eyes swept the room. Iris was in. Arun's jaw was clenched; his knee hadn't stopped bouncing this whole time. As if he felt my gaze on him, Arun jutted his chin out. "I'm in. Smite the fucker."

I couldn't keep the grin off my face. Leaning over, Arun and I bumped fists.

Victor slouched lower in the armchair, folding his arms and

kicking his long legs out in front of him with an air of resignation. "You'll get us all killed," he muttered.

"Maybe it isn't impossible." Lingyi pushed up her black frames and regarded each of us. "I think we can do this. I know I can gain access to Jin Corp's security system. We just need some time, and a good plan of attack."

Time, a good plan, and for the gods to be on our side. For the stars to align and the wind to blow just right. We'd also need a shitload of money, like Vic said. All that and we might have a slim chance of succeeding. I felt my body tingle with a rush of excitement. "I can't see any other way to force Jin's hand." I ran my thumb over the cool handle of the knife, then met Victor's eyes in challenge. "The man isn't just underhanded or greedy—he's a murderer. He needs to be stopped."

I flicked my gaze toward Lingyi. If she was in, then everyone else would follow.

She gave a single nod of her head. "Let's start planning, then," Lingyi said.

# CH∆PTER THREE

## ONE MONTH
## AFTER THE KIDNAPPING

The July swelter didn't stop the Taipei youth from coming out in droves, seeking some sort of entertainment and escape on a Friday night. Pedestrians jostled against me, many sipping teas and juices kept at an icy temperature in slender takeaway bottles. The thick, stagnant air reeked of perfume, cigarettes, and exhaust. Everyone was barefaced, wanting to flaunt their features instead of hiding beneath blank masks. To be able to flirt with their lips, to be able to kiss. But I wasn't fooled by the dark—the air was still poisonous. Even if we couldn't see the brown haze, it smothered our city lit in neon.

I passed a corner 7-Eleven, its glass doors opening for a group of teens who could only afford to "party" in the convenience store. A column of cold air blasted toward me before the doors slid shut. The group—three girls and two boys, their hair dyed in bright fuchsias and purples, joined friends who were already inside, sipping on cheap beers and smoking even cheaper cigarettes beneath a large vent, which sucked the crap right back out into the night sky.

The truly poor huddled along the sidewalks, propped themselves against buildings, or lay like sick dogs. They murmured in hoarse tones, begging for food, coin, water, drugs, clothes—anything. They'd lick the grease off of your Snappy Chicken wrappers if you tossed them over.

A woman with matted hair and hollow eyes didn't have the energy to extend a hand, much less raise her arm; her open palms sunk like dead weights in her dirty dress. I'd been that hungry before, at my lowest. It's a gnawing emptiness that stays with you. But she was wasting away from more than hunger. I reached into my wallet, something I hadn't carried for years, not until after we all got a cut from the kidnapping, and dropped a wad of large bills into the sick woman's lap. She didn't notice, but a thin man beside her did, and he stared at me, his eyes too large in his gaunt face. I reached in again and thrust the rest of my bills at him. He took the cash, bowing his head over and over.

I was rich now, not rich enough to buy myself an twenty million *you* suit, but richer than I had ever imagined possible. Yet giving everything I might have to the sick *mei*s did nothing to lift my mood. Because I knew that it changed nothing. Simply throwing money at them was not enough. Their existence wasn't the heart of the sickness in Taiwan—it was a merely a symptom.

The smell of steamed buns and fried sausages from the food carts mingled with that of urine and vomit as I walked past dark, narrow side streets filled with more sick *mei*s. I didn't need to see them to know they were there. My stomach turned from the clash of odors. My throat felt dry, scratchy, and I wished I had an ice-cold beer to drink myself. To try and shake the futility of it all, the desperation.

*Soon.*

I was meeting Victor to discuss our group's plans—and everything we needed to do before he took on his rich-*you*-boy identity.

I quickened my pace, broke through the covered walkways, and crossed the crowded intersection with other pedestrians, swarming like cicadas, toward my destination. The cool neon blue of the Rockaroke Building did nothing to dissipate the oppressive heat of the summer evening. Known to provide the best simulated entertainment in all of Taipei, with opulent suites to cater to your every whim and pleasure, Rockaroke was a major *you* destination every evening. And if your vices ran deep and you really needed to check out, the suites were available for long-term rental, starting at $250K a week. Blue and red laser lights darted and crackled over the windows of the tall glass-and-steel building, and a rooftop projector swept a neon green *R* and *K* across Taipei's hazy skyline.

Victor had checked in to oversee a big transaction with a rich client, anonymous but present for those who worked for him, in case anything went wrong. He never dealt drugs, but could get you just about anything else. Lingyi had told me Vic once got hold of a dozen sought-after purses before they were even set out for display in the Paris flagship's storefront, causing an actual riot among the *you* girls and their moms.

Aircars and -peds glided overhead, disappearing into Rockaroke's private garage for *you*s twenty floors above us. They never needed to set foot on a filthy sidewalk if they didn't want to, could avoid the sickness and poverty that we *mei*s lived with every day. I entered from the ground floor, adjusting my face mask and pulling my cap lower. I had already memorized the entire lobby from scoping the place virtually on the undernet.

The opaque glass doors closed behind me, and it was like stepping into another world. The air cooled, and the loud noise and honking from the city streets were replaced with the soft notes of Mozart being played on a grand piano in the middle of the foyer. I breathed the clean, regulated air and walked across the plush carpet toward the elevators. Gigantic chandeliers hung from the magnificent arched ceiling, casting a soft, muted glow on everything below. There were more solicitous attendants—young women and men dressed in brocade jackets—than there were clients.

Rockaroke prided itself on its impeccable service. The establishment reeked of money and class. A pretty veneer for all the depraved indulgences that took place in the private suites above.

Even as I quickened my step, a young woman approached me, trailed by a silver barbot floating behind her shoulder. Her pale pink lips pulled back to reveal perfectly white teeth. None of the attendants were *you*, but Rockaroke hired only the most attractive *mei*s— attendants who were willing to use their pay to make themselves even more beautiful. Saving up for an ass injection here, pec implants there. Lingyi told us how she had met one beautiful woman who worked as a Rockaroke attendant, and said she was altering her face, one feature at a time, to look more like Mingmei, the hottest singer in Taiwan. It guaranteed higher tips, she had divulged to Lingyi with a bright smile.

"Can I help you, sir?" The attendant inclined her head.

"I'm meeting someone," I said in a brusque tone. "I've got the access codes."

"Can I offer you a complimentary beverage, sir?"

The barbot whirred behind her, its blue buttons flashing as if eager to serve.

"I'd kill for a cold beer," I said.

Her lips pursed for a moment. "I apologize, sir. My barbot only provides wines. But I could call my colleague over—"

"Never mind." The last thing I wanted was to be stuck in the foyer. Even with my face covered, I didn't want to be seen. "I'll grab one in the suite."

The attendant lowered her head graciously. "Enjoy your stay," she said in a melodious voice. "Rockaroke has everything you want and anything you need." She flashed another flawless smile at me before gliding away.

I made it to the golden elevators without further interruption and punched in from memory the access code Victor had messaged me earlier. The mirrored interior was as opulent as the rest of the building, its ceiling gilded with the Chinese symbol for prosperity. The bell gave a pleasant *ding* after a fast trip up to the twenty-third floor. I searched the numbers on the red doors, passing a drunk teen *you* boy with indigo hair tottering down the wide hallway. He waved enthusiastically at me and shouted, "Hey, party!"

I didn't bother to reply, but he didn't take the hint.

"Room twenty-three-sixteen! All paid for, man!"

*By your parents*, I thought as I turned the corner and jogged down the hallway, an exact replica of the one I had come from, finally stopping at 2338. The door pulled open before I could punch in the access code, and Vic dragged me in by the arm. I tripped into the room.

"Gods, Victor." I straightened. "I'm happy to see you too."

"Why didn't you reply to my messages?" Victor hissed. He twisted the silver cuff link on his perfectly ironed shirt and glared at me.

"My Vox ran out of juice." Good thing I had already memorized the access codes. I glanced around the large suite with a plush sofa and matching chairs. A smaller chandelier, similar to the ones that hung in the foyer, illuminated the rich, wood-paneled room. Two cylindrical enclosed pods were set on either side of the wall screen. I'd never tried it myself, but Vic said combined with the sim suits, gamers who were in pod had a completely immersive experience. Two sim suits were draped over the back of the sofa. It couldn't be more different than the spare, concrete studio I'd been renting for the past month. "Why?"

Victor grabbed me by my shirt collar and shook hard. I shoved him off, more surprised than angry. "What the hell?" I asked.

He smoothed his hair with a hand, but not one carefully styled lock was out of place. "There are four men wandering Rockaroke asking about you."

"What?"

"I was trying to warn you not to come tonight. To stay the hell away." He cracked his knuckles in frustration. "But you, nitwit, couldn't be bothered to recharge your Vox."

"Who are these guys? Did you talk to them?"

Victor studied the monitor showing an empty hallway outside our door, then turned on the wall screen with a control, revealing a life-size sim. She had long brown hair, pretty Asian features, and wore a sheer white tank top that revealed every inch of her perky breasts. Inexplicably, the lower half of her body was that of a golden-colored mare. Vic was going to play with *her* after zipping into his full sensory sim suit?

I didn't ask.

"No. My sources messaged me." He flipped his Palm from his trouser pocket in one smooth motion, showing me the screen. It was a rendered image of me, with shoulder-length blond hair like I had during the kidnapping. But it wasn't *quite* right; my eyes were off, as was the shape of my nose and face. It was like looking at myself in a distorted mirror. I'd since cut my hair short and dyed it back to its original black.

"How's this possible—"

"Maybe the bodyguard you punched gave a description," Vic said, tucking the device away.

"No. The smoke I used on them memory-wipes."

"The friend, then. The shorter girl you mentioned—"

I shook my head. "I was turned away from her when I attacked, then dropped the smoke bomb. If she saw me, it was only in profile, and not for more than a second."

Victor let out a frustrated breath. "Well, *somebody* saw you. Maybe snapped a blurry photo." I'd never seen him like this before—and suddenly realized he was really worried. That's why he was so pissed. "They were on the twenty-second floor an hour ago, making their way up." He punched his fist into an open palm. "Thank gods you didn't run into them in the hallway."

"Look, I'm sorry I was offline—"

He waved a hand, adopting his usual laid-back manner. "Forget it. You've been keeping a low profile, but you need to be even more alert now. These guys are killers—"

A loud knocking startled us, and we spun at the same time to look at the door monitor.

"We know this room's occupied," a man with a gruff voice said. "We've permission from Rockaroke to ask you a few questions." Four men dressed in black suits stood outside our door. The man who had knocked was short and thin, but there was one behind him built like a tank, and the two others were tall and lean. Dangerous. They reminded me of sharp blades.

I flipped my own butterfly knife out within a second and snapped it open, exposing the five-inch blade. Victor cursed under his breath and pressed another button on the screen control. His sim girl-pony reached down and pulled off her sheer tank top, revealing breasts even better than I had imagined. She pawed the ground with one hoof and tossed her thick hair.

"Let's play, big boy," she said in a sultry voice and swayed her pony ass at us.

I gaped, and Victor shoved me toward the wall of glass. "Get out."

"I can hide in the bathroom." Flicking the blade closed, I tucked the knife back into my jeans pocket.

"No," he replied. "They'll check the bathroom. I would." He punched more buttons on the screen control. "You'll have to go out on the ledge."

I stared at him. Victor, who was always so collected, had lost it. "There aren't any windows."

"One panel opens," he said. "I charmed it out of one of the attendants. You just need a specialized code. Safety measure." The glass panel on the very far side of the room slid aside, and the street noise from below reached us, even as the humid air rolled in. "Quick!"

"We're twenty-three floors up!" I protested.

"You're a climber." He pushed me again toward the gaping space. "Just stay put till I let you back in."

I almost laughed at the absurdity. "It's a *crap* image."

"*I* recognized you from it," Vic said. "We can't risk it."

Another knock. This time, even louder. "Open up!"

There was no fighting Victor. And there was no other option. I carefully stepped out onto the metal ledge, not more than a foot wide, and the glass immediately slid shut behind me. The windows went opaque, their surface crackling with blue and red laser lights. I stared straight ahead at the skyline, forcing my panic away. *Don't look down.* I shuffled my feet until I was flush against the metal divider separating us from the other suite, also extended twelve inches out. The humid air made my skin sticky, but I was grateful there was no strong wind tonight. Sweat rolled down my back, and I suppressed a coughing fit, my eyes tearing with the effort. Coughing, even a sneeze, could send me plummeting to my death. I pressed my hand against the side wall and found a round metal hook set there. *Gods.* I curled my fingers through it, gripping so hard my nails dug into my palm.

The rumble and hum of aircars and -peds entering the garage a few floors below swept hot air upward. I only hoped none of them would pass too near, spot me, and call Rockaroke security. My palm grasping the metal hook was slick with sweat, and I felt it gather at my hairline, then slide down my forehead.

I blinked, keeping still—fighting the tickle at the back of my throat, the sweat that stung my eyes. I focused on the ad playing on a board mounted on a rooftop across from me. Time dragged. Maybe only a few minutes had passed—I had no idea—it felt like hours.

A filthy pigeon flew by, and I felt the flap of its wings. My body seemed to vibrate, strung too tight. A maniacal chuckle escaped my mouth, irritating my dry, swollen throat, and in that instant, the glass panel opened behind me, releasing a whoosh of cool, clean air. Victor threw his arm around my waist and dragged me backward. I fell in a heap, boneless, to the carpeted floor. The panel closed, shutting the noise and heat out once more.

"You all right, kid?" Vic was kneeling beside me, a hand on my shoulder.

I laughed, my body shaking. He was six months older than me but used it to his advantage, asserting his seniority at every turn, like some pain-in-the-ass big bro. I loved that about him. As well put together as he was, Vic knew what it was like to be an underdog, an outsider. He was a self-made success, and he had clawed his way to the top. My laugh turned into a rasping cough. "A drink?" I asked between breaths. But it was like he didn't hear me. I rose unsteadily and grumbled at the barbot; it floated over, giving me an ice-cold bottle of beer. I drank half of it in two long

64

gulps, savoring the sensation of the liquid sliding down my throat. My scalp tingled.

Victor was still kneeling on one knee, his tanned face pale. "What happened?" I'd never seen him so obviously scared before, and it was weirding me out. "Did they rough you up?"

He glanced over after a long moment. "No." Vic straightened, so out of sorts he didn't smooth his hair, didn't adjust his expensive cuff links. "We had a lot of fun drinking and playing with the sim suits. I charmed them. They loved me."

I shrugged. It was what Victor did; he rolled high in charisma. "Great. The better to get info from them."

Victor's expression darkened. "They were out for blood—and Rockaroke actually gave them access to do this, go from suite to suite. It's unheard-of."

"What'd they say?" I leaned against the back of the sofa, still feeling unsteady on my feet.

"All they had was that bad image of you. Made up some story that you were a murderer—some sick sociopath."

I snorted.

Victor scrolled through his Palm. "The leader gave me his contact info. Said his boss wanted to bring you 'to justice.' That's thugspeak for 'dead.'"

I shook myself, trying to get rid of the queasy feeling in my stomach. "Great," I said and rolled over the back of the sofa to slide down onto its thick cushions. I stared at the wall screen. "What in all hells . . . ?"

Victor's sim girl-pony had morphed into a buxom, blue-eyed

blonde with three pairs of gigantic breasts lining her torso. The fact that she remained upright defied gravity. Two curved horns protruded from her forehead, and her lower body was that of a white goat's.

"Vic, I'm worried about you."

He didn't laugh, didn't even crack a smile. He sat down beside me, crossing his long legs in front of him. "It's Victor."

"'Victor' makes you sound like a grandpa."

"And 'Vic' makes me sound like a scrappy teenager." He flicked something off the sleeve of his expensive shirt, then nodded toward the wall screen. "It served as a distraction. One of those goons wanted to try his hand at character creation. Let's say the group lost its focus on the mission for a bit."

I smirked, then, suddenly realizing, said, "You planned it. Showing that naked sim pony."

"Of course."

We sat for some time in silence, each watching the sim's strange, goatish cavorting, her short tail wagging with enthusiasm. It was grotesque, yet hypnotic.

"They say money can't buy you happiness," Victor said, clicking the screen off. "But those *you* kids try hard. They spend and spend. Then when *things* aren't enough, they plug into the sim world so they can create and *be* whatever they want."

I flipped my butterfly knife out, turning the blade through its familiar rhythm. "As if being filthy rich weren't enough." My hand wasn't quite steady yet.

"You don't know how often a *you* kid has to be dragged off by ambulance because he's been plugged in for too long," Victor said. "A few have actually died. 'Sim sickness,' the medics call it."

I shrugged, unsympathetic to their tragic ennui as *mei*s died on the streets below their glittering high-rise worlds. Because what, they were *bored*? Because they couldn't find *meaning* in their lives?

"So now what?" I asked.

He shook his head, looking tired and weary. "We have to call it off." When he brought a tumbler of scotch to his lips, his hand shook hard enough for the ice to clink against the glass.

"What?" I stared at him, trying to process what he meant. Why he was suddenly so afraid.

"Me going in as a *you*," Vic said. "I'm out."

"We *have* to have someone on the inside. You're the only one in the group who can—"

"No."

"Why not?"

"Let's call Lingyi," he said. "She needs to know too."

"If you're pulling out, everyone needs to know." I prompted my Vox to call the group, then cursed. I'd forgotten it was out of juice.

Victor took out his Palm. "I'll call a group meeting—"

"*Now*," I said and glared at him.

Lingyi swept in forty minutes later, shadowed by a silent Iris, and the suite filled with Lingyi's vanilla scent.

"Can't I leave you boys alone for just one night?" Lingyi asked. Her hair was pulled back with a large orange daisy tucked into it.

"Apparently not," I said.

She sat down, adjusting the short summer dress she wore, splattered with bright geometric designs. "What happened?" she asked, removing her face mask.

Iris had wandered over to the sim suits, touching one with mild curiosity. She wore black fingerless gloves, as always.

Vic flipped out his Palm and leaned over, showing Lingyi the poorly rendered image. She looked from the image to me, then down at the screen again. "I see a little resemblance," she said. "How'd they get this?"

"We don't know," I replied.

Someone knocked, and both Victor and I jumped. Iris raised an eyebrow at us and stalked over to the door, glancing at the monitor. "It's Arun." She pulled the heavy door open and he entered, lifting his chin once in greeting.

"What's with the emergency meeting?" he asked as he plopped himself on the long sofa near Vic.

Lingyi handed Victor's Palm to Arun. "Zhou is on someone's radar."

Arun examined the rendering. "It could be worse. They have a likeness, not an actual image." He yawned. "I got out of bed for this? I'm working in the lab early tomorrow—"

"You're here," Victor said, "because we need to call the whole thing off."

Lingyi made a noise in the back of her throat, and Iris slipped over to drape herself on the wide arm of Lingyi's plush chair, staring unblinkingly at Victor like a cat contemplating her prey. Iris hadn't bothered to remove her face mask and looked like the ninja that she was.

"Why?" Lingyi said after a loaded pause.

Victor sighed and took his Palm back from Arun. "I recognized the leader of the group—he's Jin's right-hand man."

"*Jin?*" Lingyi and I said at the same time.

"Yes. Goes by Da Ge, but he's no big brother anyone would want to have," Vic said. "He heads Jin's security team but is not above kicking the shit out of someone, or having one of his goons knife and kill a guy in a dark alley. Hell, I've heard of him being responsible for assassinations in bright daylight in a crowd—but no one can actually pin it on him. Jin's power and wealth protect him."

"Is he our 'Mr. Wu,' then?" Arun asked in a quiet voice, but I didn't miss the steel beneath. The anonymous Wu, who murdered his mother.

Tension in the suite coalesced as sharply as if a gunshot had gone off.

Vic swiped a hand over his face. "It's impossible to know. Jin's got a lot of people working for him. I can see him going outside of his legitimately employed men to . . . to"—Victor cracked his knuckles—"I'm sorry, Arun. I don't know."

Arun nodded but didn't meet our eyes, instead staring at his black workman boots, hands clenched together in front of him.

"So Jin is onto us?" Lingyi said. "That's why you want to abort?"

"Da Ge *knows* me now. He's sharp and spends much of his time near Jin," Victor said. "There's no way I could go in as the *you*. He'd recognize me and dig deeper into my background than we want. I gave him the false name I used when I checked in remotely. I had no choice."

Rockaroke prided itself on the privacy of its clients. As long as you were able to gain access to the elevators with a code, you were a valued guest. Victor had checked in online without ever talking to a Rockaroke attendant in person, remaining anonymous. It didn't matter as long as you could afford the suite.

"But I didn't expect a face-to-face interrogation," Victor continued. "If I'm a rich *you*, Jin's people would have known about me already."

Arun cursed. "And no one else can take your place. I'm too well known at the university—"

"And you're Dr. Nataraj's son," Lingyi finished. "Everyone knows me as the daughter of the infamous hacker, never mind my dad's wide network when he headed Fortune Securities. And Iris—well, Iris would just as likely kill everyone first."

Iris stretched her arms languidly overhead. "It always does seem to be the easier option."

I thought she was joking—with Iris, you never knew—but none of us laughed. Vic was right: His cover was blown before it even started. And no one else could go in. . . .

"What about me?" I said.

Lingyi gave me a look so sharp it'd cut if she could will it. "No."

"Why not?" I looked her square in the eyes, challenging. We'd known each other since I was thirteen—Lingyi had befriended me in a used-book store soon after my mom had died. She was the oldest one in our group at nineteen. Lingyi was the boss. Didn't mean I never disagreed with her or always did what she told me, though.

"They were going around with an image of *you*, Zhou," she said.

"A very bad image—"

"*I* recognized you well enough."

"It's because you know me," I replied. "You love this face too much."

Iris and Victor snorted at the same time, then stared at each other suspiciously.

"Victor said that Da Ge is no fool," Lingyi said. "He'd make the connection—"

"So we're just going to give up?" I jumped up from my chair and paced in front of my friends. "After I risked my life kidnapping that *you* girl? What are we going to do with all that money? *Return* it?" I spat.

"Maybe we could donate it anonymously—"

I cut Lingyi off with a sharp laugh. *"Donate* it? Will that change how bad things are in Taiwan?" I turned to Arun. "Would a donation be enough for what your mom wanted to do—the changes she wanted to make?"

He reared back as if I'd slapped him. I didn't care, fueled by a frustration and anger that felt as if they could burn a hole through my chest.

"That's not fair, Zhou," Lingyi said.

"There is no 'fair' in this scenario." I fell back into my seat because Iris had begun flexing her fingers, danger lurking behind her dark eyes as she tracked me. I didn't think I could win against her in a fight. Actually, I knew I didn't have a chance. Any advantage in strength I might have she made up for in agility and speed. Iris always sided with Lingyi. "I refuse to be a bystander anymore. It's bullshit."

We simmered in silence for a long moment. The silver barbot floated between us, offering drinks, as if trying to placate a tough crowd.

Then Arun said, "No."

We stopped sipping our alcohol.

"A donation isn't enough," Arun said. "My mom tried legislation, and look where that got her—murdered." He drew a long, shaking breath, his fierce orange spikes did nothing to make him appear less vulnerable. "We should stick with the plan. Target Jin."

"All Da Ge needs to do is put Zhou's face through a recognition system, match it with the image he has, and it's endgame," Lingyi said.

We all knew that "endgame" wouldn't mean a botched operation—it would mean me, dead. The thought of death didn't scare me. I'd glimpsed it enough times in my life. In my mind, the reward of shutting Jin down was worth every risk.

"I've got the best face recognition program on the market," Vic said. "Let's see, then."

He stood and passed his Palm over my face, bathing me in green light for a few seconds, then proceeded to type some commands into it. We waited. The suite felt too hot all of a sudden, and my hands dampened with sweat.

"Nothing." Vic grinned after a minute. "The program couldn't confirm a match between the rendered image they had and the scan I took of Zhou's face."

"So I'm in," I said triumphantly.

"You do know what this means, though, right?" Arun asked. We

72

all stared at him expectantly. "Jin's the one who sent those thugs after you," he said. "Which means *he's* somehow involved in this. He's the one who wants you dead. Maybe he's connected you with"—he swallowed, looking pained—"my mom."

"Shit," Victor murmured. "It's like sending poor Zhou into the lion's den."

I had been so distracted by the men showing up, my escapade out on the ledge, and Dr. Nataraj's death—I had failed to make the most obvious connection.

"It's too huge a risk, Zhou." Lingyi appeared physically ill, curled forward as if her stomach ached. "If something happened to you . . ."

Iris squeezed Lingyi's shoulder, her narrowed eyes still focused on me.

Lingyi had been an older sister to me for almost five years now, making sure I had somewhere safe to sleep every night, that I wasn't starving. She did this with everyone in our group—looked after us— even Victor, who I suspected was still secretly in love with her. I know she had been with Arun every day after Dr. Nataraj's death, helping with the necessary paperwork, making certain he was eating, that his kitchen was stocked with food.

Since her own family escaped to China, she had made us her family. Her responsibility.

I went to Lingyi and extended an open palm; after a long hesitation, she slipped her hand into mine, and I clasped it. "I want to do this," I said. Because there was nobody else, and Jin needed to be stopped. "But I need you to have faith in me. I need you to back me."

Her gaze swept over the others in the suite. Arun's expression was grim, but he nodded once. Vic was assessing me, more serious than I'd ever seen him. "I think Zhou can pull it off."

Lingyi stared into her tumbler of rum and Coke, already empty. I knew then how stressed she was—she rarely drank. "All right," she said. "If you're sure, Zhou, of course I'll back you completely."

"I'll start a rumor that the guy they're looking for has gone abroad," Victor said. "Keep an even lower profile for the next few months, Zhou."

Lingyi nodded. "It'll give me time to lay the groundwork for your *you* identity. And it'll take that long to receive your custom suit."

A *you* identity and my own suit. It represented everything I despised: greed, excess, selfishness, and complacency—a culture embodied and enabled by Jin Corp. I was going to become what I wanted to destroy. "Sounds good," I said.

Iris slipped off the armrest and came to stand in front of me. Other than Lingyi, she rarely acknowledged anyone in the group so directly. Alarmed, I had no idea what to expect. "Eat," she said.

I laughed. She didn't have to tell me twice. Never in my life had I had enough money to buy whatever I wanted to eat, and however much I wanted, whenever I felt like it. "Okay . . . ," I replied.

She reached over and squeezed my bicep hard enough to make me wince. But I didn't.

"Pack on some muscle," she said. "It'll help."

I saw Victor chortling behind her back and resisted the urge to flip him off. "Got it," I said instead.

74

Iris nodded, satisfied, and stalked noiselessly to the wall-to-wall windows, gazing out at the Taipei skyline lit in hazy neons.

It wasn't supposed to go like this, but life had never gone the way I had planned. I flicked out my knife and spun it. "Let's do this, then."

# CHAPTER FOUR

The Ximending District came alive as I veered away from it. Neon signs flickered on, framing storefronts in golden yellows and bright reds, while advertisements were broadcasted on giant screens across all the tall buildings, like birds trying to attract attention with bright plumage. More aircars and -peds appeared, zipping to their party destinations, some lit as brightly as the buildings surrounding us. Within fifteen minutes, the entire district had amped up for the evening to come. The sweet aroma of egg cakes being cooked by a vendor trailed me as I dodged down a side street, avoiding the large crowd of commuters exiting the metro station.

After staying holed up in my dank studio, I wasn't used to jostling with the crowds again, elbowing others for personal space. My forays out in these last three months had always been after midnight, slinking through near-empty streets. The humid air smelled of sweat and smoke and held that inexplicable electrified heaviness that only came with typhoon season.

Concrete buildings pressed in, facades filmed in decades' worth of pollution and dirt, their windows and balconies covered by metal bars. A few more turns and I had left the noise behind, as well as all the lights. The damp, narrow street had no lamps—I could have easily gotten lost if I didn't know where I was going. But I did. Lingyi had finally called an official meeting at our new headquarters. My custom *you* suit had been delivered.

The thought of it sent a wave of anxiety and excitement through me.

I stopped at the front of one of the gray buildings with a side entrance on its corner, edged with red tiles. A rusty mailbox was bolted to the left of the open door frame. It was empty. I nearly tripped over the purple bicycle propped against the side wall, with a large white basket strapped to the front of the handlebars—a new addition. I smiled. Arun was already here, then. Flying up the narrow stairway, I reached a dead end on the third-floor landing, which was just as cramped in space, and knocked hard on the dilapidated wooden door with a closed fist. A dim bulb flickered above me.

"Yes?" a muffled feminine voice asked from within.

"It's me," I said.

Silence. I knew full well that she could see me with the hidden camera that was trained on this narrow landing. Then came the whirring of multiple dead bolts unlocking, and the door slowly swung open. Lingyi peered from behind it, then seemed to do a double take.

I couldn't help but smile. "What?"

"You're late," she said.

"Yeah. Well." I slipped past her into our headquarters.

The door closed with a *snick* behind me, then the dead bolts all mechanically slipped back into place. What had looked like an old wooden door on the outside was actually a steel one, thick enough to be bulletproof. Our entire headquarters was encased in steel and could probably survive a bombing.

"Hey, Zhou." Arun lifted his chin in greeting and rose from the deep cushion of his armchair, coming over to bump fists and throw an arm around me in a loose hug. "We've missed you."

I hadn't seen any of them for some time, keeping all communication via Vox.

Victor raised a hand from where he was slouched on a leather beanbag, long legs in dark gray trousers sprawled in front of him. Too cool to get up and greet me. "When I said make yourself scarce, I didn't think you'd take it quite so literally."

Lingyi caught me in a hug, squeezing me tight across my back. I had to remember to wrap my arms around her—it'd been so long since I'd been that close to anyone. "Everything's set." She pulled back, studying me. "It's good to see you."

She wandered back to her MacFold, her thick purple hair, cut in a blunt bob, swaying. She was dressed in a pale green tank top and white shorts, and I caught Victor admiring her as she perched back onto her stool. *Poor wretch.* What a hopeless crush.

This place had been bare except for the large glass table Lingyi sat at when I had visited once, two months ago, but had since been furnished in my friends' eclectic tastes. Lingyi had selected the glass table and plush armchairs, the leather beanbag and modern art magnetized against the steel walls were Victor's, and the Chinese antique tea tables and gold brocade sofa were all Arun. The only hint of Iris were the ropes and bars set into the wall and ceiling in the padded corner of our large headquarters for her to practice jumping, climbing, and acrobatics.

Victor stood, smoothing back his hair, and then adjusted the cuff links of his pale blue pin-striped shirt. "Ready when you are, boss."

"Where's Iris?" I asked. Iris was brought in after she had stumbled upon a fight in some dark alley between Victor and three thugs trying to mug him. Vic said he could have taken care of the situation without Iris's help. I didn't doubt him; he was a strong guy. But I'm not sure if he would have kept his handsome face. Little did Victor know that he'd lose Lingyi to this enigmatic girl who spoke so few words when we welcomed her into our group.

"She's out wandering," Lingyi replied, her pink-glossed lips lifting into a smile. Iris had been an orphan since birth—and even more of a loner than I was. I had a feeling her wandering wasn't as innocuous as Lingyi made it sound.

"Why don't you suit up, Zhou?" Arun said. "We need to make sure everything fits and works properly."

I stared at the *you* suit in its clear, oval pod set in the corner, like some headless astronaut. The helmet had its own square cubby within the oval pod. My suit was a light gray, lit with dark neon blue geometric designs along the collar and the length of both sleeve edges.

Lingyi went over and punched clear buttons on the pod and the glass slid open without a sound, like double doors. "Normally, you'd suit up at one of Jin Corp's boutiques. But I didn't want to give away the fact that this was your first suit. So I thought it was better to give you an orientation in private."

Victor unhooked the suit and removed it from the glass pod. He unzipped it from the collar, continuing under the arm, then along the length of the left side. I shrugged off my jacket and stared uncertainly at the suit. It symbolized everything *you* to me, all that I never wanted to be. And here I was, suiting up to pretend I was a rich *you* boy, just like the rest of them. Pushing these thoughts aside, I carefully stepped into it, fully clothed. Victor zipped me up. I thought I would feel claustrophobic and hot, but the material was light and seemed to mold itself to my body.

Lingyi lifted the helmet from the cubby, proffering it. "Just place it over your head and you'll hear the mechanism latch at your collar. The minute you're in helmet, you're connected to the *yous'* com sys. I've jammed your suit signal for now, while we're at headquarters. But other than that, the suit and helmet should still work like normal."

Taking the glass helmet from her, I brought it over my head and had to fight a sudden wave of panic. Victor noticed my hesitation. "I'd suggest you buy into the suit mentality fast for the role you're going to play," he said.

"It won't be so bad, bro," Arun said. "You're doing this for us. *Our* cause."

Arun was right. I'd do anything to destroy Jin Corp. And although he didn't say it aloud, the memory of his mom lingered there, within all of us. Dr. Nataraj had loved Taiwan as much as we all did—that's why she had pushed so hard for reform. It was up to us now to finish her work. I slipped the helmet over my head and into the suit's stiff collar. I heard a hiss as the helmet's glass darkened a fraction and WELCOME MR. ZHOU flashed across it in blue. I took three long, consecutive breaths until my eyes watered, and I felt light-headed. The air in our headquarters was filtered, but it was nothing compared to this pure stuff.

"You okay in there?" Arun asked. His voice sounded as clear as if I didn't have a helmet on.

I nodded at him.

"There are sensors in the helmet tuned to your brain waves. You can control the suit or query the com sys by thought or through voice," Victor said. "Just start each request with 'command.' Go ahead and try changing your suit's temperature."

"Command," I said, throat feeling dry. "What is the suit temperature?"

21°C/70°F appeared in blue on the lower right corner of my helmet.

*Command*, I thought in Mandarin, *change suit temperature to 68°F.*

COMMAND RECEIVED. LOWERING SUIT TEMPERATURE TO 68°F.

The blue words flashed in Chinese at eye level, then disappeared after three seconds.

"I've set the default language to Mandarin for you," Lingyi said. "But your suit can understand and translate a multitude of languages, more than you'll ever encounter in your lifetime. If you speak or think your commands in English, it'll respond in kind."

I raised my arms to look at my hands, the only exposed part of my body, then flexed at the elbows, testing my range of motion. I walked away from my friends, who had clustered around me, still breathing in the pure air. The suit was comfortable, and I moved with ease, my actions unhindered. The helmet was the most awkward aspect. It

81

wasn't heavy and didn't distort my vision or hearing, but I was very aware that I was enclosed. Separated.

"The temperature's adjusted," I said, incredulous. "It feels cooler."

"You look good, man." Arun nodded in approval.

I squatted to the floor in one swift motion, bouncing to the balls of my feet, before jumping up into the air. The suit moved with me like a second skin.

"Once it collects enough data from your voice and brain waves—both are individually unique—the suit will truly be personalized. It'll only work for you when you put the helmet on," Lingyi explained. "This ability to recognize its owner makes stealing suits pretty much pointless."

"Lingyi's added a safety enhance to the suit upon my recommendation," Victor said. "Mainly for when you're riding on your airped. If you fall, the suit will slow your descent as well as inflate with protective padding. It isn't fail-safe, but it's been known to save lives."

"I've got an airped?" I asked, removing my helmet. It unlatched with a hiss. The sound reminded me of the girl I had kidnapped, when she had removed hers for the first time. Suddenly, it felt too warm in the headquarters.

Victor grinned. "Custom. The budget didn't allow for an aircar, but you'll look more badass on this."

"Yeah, the airped was a necessity," Lingyi said. "But not some of the other enhances Victor suggested."

"What?" Vic replied. "Like the Superman?"

"Superman?" Arun and I said at the same time.

"Ask him later. We have more important things to discuss."

Lingyi gave Victor a warning look. "Arun, your mom had only hit upon the tip of the corruption. We know now that Jin's padded the pockets of everyone who's supposed to call out violations to turn their backs on the people, on top of stopping legislation from being presented. In fact, a handful of influential politicians who couldn't possibly afford *you* suits have them." She tucked a sweep of purple bangs behind one ear.

"More reason to shut Jin Corp down," I said. "Blow it to smithereens."

"Let's go over everything together in detail. You start, Arun." Lingyi glanced at me and nodded toward a red velvet armchair.

I sank down, facing the wall screen. The main part of the spacious loft where we were sitting felt cozy, lived-in, with thick cushions thrown on the seats and old books spread on the long teakwood table before us. Metal pendants in geometrical shapes strung at varying heights dangled from the tall ceiling, making our headquarters bright, despite the steel-shuttered windows.

Arun clicked on his Palm and the chamber dimmed. "Lingyi's been working on establishing your new identity online these past months, Zhou. You've been studying like we've asked you to?"

"I've been reading more novels in English—"

"Who's your favorite American author?" Victor interjected.

"Poe," I replied.

"Poe! He's strange," Victor said.

"I like strange."

"Chinese?"

"Cao Xueqin," I said.

"You're a romantic." Victor draped himself onto the sofa beside me and smirked.

I ignored him.

Arun tilted his chin at me. "Zhou, in your new identity, you went to university at fifteen and are a prodigy." He spoke the last word in English.

"So act prodigious," Victor added, also in English.

"Are you joking? I haven't been at the American School since thirteen," I replied in Mandarin. "I'm a dropout."

Arun turned from the wall screen and caught my gaze, his brown eyes serious. "You're the most well-read guy I know. You'd run circles around all those spoiled *you* kids with your smarts."

"Your new identity will be solid," Victor said. "Jin's men are looking for a gambler, a druggie, some rich, stupid criminal. Not an educated *you* boy from the United States. Besides, I barely recognized you when you walked in that door."

"What?" I said.

"It's true," Lingyi replied. "You look like you've gained fifteen pounds of muscle since I saw you a few months ago." She squeezed my bicep for emphasis, and I felt my face grow hot. "What have you been doing in that apartment of yours?"

Sleeping past noon. Staying indoors all day and night, reading novels and comics, and trawling the undernet. Following the net diaries of a few *you* boys and girls, caught between revulsion and fascination over their vapid lifestyles. Then, come two a.m., I left my studio and headed to the twenty-four-hour gym, lifting weights and doing indoor rock climbing to blow off steam. "I'm eating more," I said after a pause. "And I go to a hole-in-the-wall gym in the dead of night."

"Well, it shows," Victor said. "You're bigger. And pale as a white foreigner. No one will make the connection between the blond, thin street urchin in that photo and your new, rich-boy identity."

Iris had told me to put on some muscle, which seemed to work out in the end. But I had been going to the gym because I needed to—because I *had* to get out of my dark studio, but also to sweat out my frustrations in having to wait, and to curb my anger over, well, everything.

"Let's continue," Arun said. "Zhou, you've just graduated with a bachelor's degree in world literature from Berkeley in their accelerated program. Lingyi's laid the groundwork to back all this for anyone who might want to dig up info on you."

An image of me flashed onto the projection wall. My hair was clean-cut and black. Instead of a worn black T-shirt, I was wearing a white dress shirt and a gray vest. "I don't look like that," I said, blinking at the dapper young man on the screen—Victor's clone.

"Actually, you look like *this* now." Arun pointed his Palm at me, and I was momentarily bathed in green light as the device scanned my face, just like when Vic had done the same three months ago at the Rockaroke. His fingers raced over the Palm. My tanned face with the sharp cheekbones and chin morphed before our eyes on the wall screen. My coloring grew more pallid, rendering my brown eyes almost black, even as my face filled out, making what had appeared sharp before more defined. Mature.

They were right. I barely recognized myself.

"You look the part of the pale *you* boy to me," Arun said. "Unless you're the kind to go for the unnatural tanned look."

Vic snorted, retrieving a monogrammed handkerchief from some hidden pocket to dab at his forehead. Our headquarters' air was cool enough that there was no way he was sweating. He just wanted to show off his latest Victor accessory.

"I guess we all know where your share of the cut went, Victor?" Lingyi said in a teasing tone.

Victor winked with his usual cockiness, but I didn't miss the color that rose to his tanned face.

"We've decided to go with your English name as your alias," Arun continued. "And your surname is common enough that you're keeping it. We've changed your birthday to May first from the twenty-third. The best false identity, for our purposes, is one that is most closely tied to your true one." Arun swiped a fingertip across his Palm. "It'll make you more believable in your role."

JASON ZHOU flashed across the wall screen next to my image.

I jerked and bumped Lingyi in the shoulder.

Arun lifted an eyebrow at me. "We're correct in thinking that no one called you by this name except for your mom, right? None of your records indicated an English name anywhere."

"Yes." I swallowed, trying to clear the knot in my throat. "Only my mom ever called me that."

She had given the name to me after my father had died. And she never spoke English or called me Jason except in private, as if it were a secret language between us, reading me Roald Dahl and Beverly Cleary when I was younger. She had enrolled me at the American School in

Taipei when I turned six, an expensive private school that she was only able to afford due to the annual allowance she received from my grandparents in California. They had broken all contact with my mother after she became pregnant with me at twenty-three and married my father; their sole acknowledgement that she still existed was the deposit they made into her bank account each year. My mother never talked about her parents with me, but even at a young age, I heard snatches of conversation that made more sense after both my parents were gone.

*I'm eating cold rice porridge with bamboo shoots and fermented bean curd, because it is too hot to light the stove. But this is one of my favorite meals anyway. All three of us sit in the cramped kitchen at the round wooden table; my feet dangle above the ground, and I swing my legs.*

*"Write to them; go see them," my father says. All I can remember of my father was the solidity of him, how high he'd lift me in his arms, how his hugs enveloped me entirely. To be with my father meant I was safe. "They'll be glad to meet their grandson."*

*My mother sets down her chopsticks, then dabs her mouth with a napkin. "If they refuse to see you, then I refuse to see them," she says in a soft voice.*

*Ba reaches over to fold his large hand over my mother's slender fingers. Leans over to kiss the corner of her mouth.*

*I am five years old, and I am happy.*

We never moved from the small, humble apartment that my father's construction job could afford, but after he was killed on-site in a freak accident, she opted to spend all the allowance my grandparents gave on my education. I was privileged to be taught by some of the best Mandarin and English teachers in Taipei, the best in the arts and sciences. At least, until she died. It was only then my grand-parents in California tried to contact me.

I rejected their overtures. I knew nothing about them, but I suspected they were wealthy. The one thing I knew for certain was that they had cast my mom aside, and *I* was the only one by her bedside when she died.

Lingyi touched my arm and brought me back to the present. "Are you okay?"

My heartbeat thrummed. I cleared my throat, then lifted a corner of my mouth up in my trademark nonchalant smile. "My English name is perfect. I'm game."

Victor and Arun grinned at me.

I hadn't fooled Lingyi, however. We were close, but she never pried unless I was ready to tell, and I returned the favor. I unzipped from my new *you* suit, placing it back in the pod, busying myself as my friends chatted.

Somehow guessing I was more affected by the use of my English name than I'd let on, she clapped her hands together and said, "Let's take a break and eat."

It didn't take more than that to convince us. Lingyi was a fantastic cook, and we boys seemed to be perpetually hungry. Soon, our headquarters began to fill with the mouthwatering aroma of stewed bamboo and tofu. "It's the perfect weather for tofu rice bowls," Lingyi said while stirring the pot, then sipping from the ladle to test its flavor. Victor stood beside her, cooking an eggplant dish, his height dwarfing Lingyi's. "I've stocked up for the typhoon," she said. "We should probably all stay here until it blows through."

Arun and I were helping to set the table, and I clamped down on my protest. If I couldn't stand being locked in for a few days, it was better just to slip out rather than argue with Lingyi. Because from experience, that had never worked in my favor. Victor ladled large bowls of savory bamboo and tofu over rice for all of us, while Lingyi brought the eggplants in oyster sauce and sautéed water spinach with garlic to the table. Arun was vegetarian, so that's what we mostly cooked.

We sat down and ate in silence for a while, making appreciative noises because the food was that good. Lingyi was buying organic now that we had the funds, and it tasted vastly different from what we were eating on a *mei* person's budget. But to get untainted meat and produce cost a premium, one that the majority of *mei*s simply couldn't afford. These days, if a food product was recalled—if they even bothered—the *mei*s simply hoped that they got no worse than vomiting and diarrhea. If your immune system was compromised and you were unlucky, you might shit to death.

*What happened to Lao Yang?* someone might ask.

*He ate too many of those pork chops.*

"Have you started to look at Jin Corp's security system?" Arun asked, leaning back after he had finished eating.

"Not yet," Lingyi said. "I've been focused on establishing Zhou's identity online. But now I'm ready to tackle their building security."

Lingyi's father, founder of Fortune Securities, had fled to China three years ago when his past criminal activities as the infamous "xiaoshu" hacker came to light. "Little mouse" might seem an innocent enough moniker, but there was no building security system that Lingyi's father, as a teen living in Shanghai, couldn't break through once he targeted it. He was the one who cracked Apple's high-security warehouse in Shenzhen three decades ago in protest of the corporation's labor and wage disputes in China. The warehouse was swarmed and dozens made out with hundreds of brand-new Apple products before the building was secured.

But her life had changed as fast as mine did, the daughter of a prominent millionaire most sought after for his expertise in building and cybersecurity, who fled Taiwan in the dark of night with Lingyi's mom and younger brother. Lingyi remained and survived by freelancing her own skills picked up from her father. Or "researching" for the greater good, as she liked to say. Her hacking abilities would make her father proud. Or make him deny all culpability.

Although rich, they had never gotten suited. Lingyi had told me when we first met that her father detested Jin Corp and everything it represented. The tech sites were abuzz when he had refused to revamp or manage Jin Corp's security system despite a multimillion-dollar bid. Not a few months later, his past as the "xiaoshu" hacker was leaked. In retrospect, it seemed eerily coincidental, and I know that same thought must have crossed Lingyi's mind. What would her father think of our plans now? Lingyi had chosen to stay so she could finish high school with her friends, not knowing the decision would cut her off from her family. If she wanted to remain in Taiwan, she had to disassociate herself from her father's infamy and scrutiny. But each day she watched Taipei—her city—deteriorate and crumble, and its people along with it. Soon, she'd often say, those only left living would be the bowl heads and roaches.

A sudden knock caused everyone to jump. Both Victor and Arun's hands went to where their tasers were. I preferred knives but took my cue from Lingyi's relaxed posture. "It's only Iris." She went to one of the two large windows covered in steel shutters and unbolted it, then pulled it open. "She does this when she wants to show off," Lingyi said over her shoulder.

Sure enough, Iris pushed through and climbed into our headquarters, located three stories up. To scale that height was probably child's play to Iris. I'd been bouldering for two years on Yangmingshan and had recently started indoor rock climbing but could never scale our building without equipment. Iris straightened, and ran a hand through her cropped hair, shorter than mine and bleached a platinum blond. She was Taiwanese-born and Asian, although her exact background was unknown.

"I heard that," she said.

Dressed in black cargo pants and a tank top that showed the lean muscles of her arms, she looked like she had stepped off the set of an action film. Iris smiled, and Lingyi's face softened. Then Lingyi grinned back. "We just ate, but there's plenty left over."

"I'm *starving*." Iris settled beside Victor at the table and thanked Lingyi when she brought her a large bowl of rice, the tofu still steaming. "You're a goddess," she murmured and grabbed Lingyi's hand, pressing it reverently to her cheek. Lingyi laughed.

Iris's entrance had broken the serious discussion we had been having, and everyone reverted to casual conversation as she ate, talking about the impending typhoon, where everyone would sleep in the headquarters that night, and what we should make

91

for breakfast. That was mainly Lingyi and Victor, setting the next morning's menu.

I kept silent as I observed Iris. Although I'd known her for two years, she remained an enigma. Her movements were as spare and concise as her physique—there was never anything casual in her motion, anything unnecessary or extraneous. She was tough because she'd had to survive for so long on her own, Lingyi had told me. Among our group of five, she was the most reserved in her words as well.

Iris began clearing the table after she was done. Arun stood to help. "Well, if we had leftovers before, we certainly don't now," Victor quipped.

"I said I was hungry," Iris stated.

"You're always hungry," Victor replied.

"Look who's talking!" Lingyi said.

We laughed as only people with full stomachs in the security of a warm home could laugh as a threatening typhoon loomed. I pushed back from the table, bringing the last of the dishes while Arun loaded them into the domed washer. Arun and I chatted about cheats for Frenzy, ready for a night of gaming soon, while the washer cycled through. Three minutes later, we were stacking the dry dishes back onto the kitchen's open shelves in exactly the way Lingyi liked them.

Victor brewed jasmine tea for everyone, and we all soon settled back onto various plush seats, nursing teacups in our hands.

"We were just going over Zhou's new identity," Lingyi explained to Iris. Lingyi sat in the middle of the sofa, flanked by Victor, who was leaning in toward her so their thighs almost touched, and Iris, who perched again on the armrest.

"I've already befriended the best tailor in Taipei," Victor said. "You'll have a complete custom wardrobe made. The *yous* are less likely to question your pedigree the more expensively you're dressed. No more ripped shirts or jeans—unless they're designer. I'll be getting you the best gadgets and accessories on the market too. You'll be decked out better than Bond."

I tilted my face up and suppressed a groan. How convincing could I be as an entitled *you*? I needed to pull this off. No fear. No hesitancy.

Victor reached over and swatted the back of my head.

"Ow!" I yelped.

"Ungrateful wretch. This is all coming out of the main fund. I'd love to get everything you're getting and play the cool, rich guy. I'll be securing an apartment for you soon as well. How would you like it furnished?"

"I'd like a rock wall," I said.

"A rock wall?" Victor shook his head. It was obvious he thought I was hopeless in my rich-*you*-boy role. "Anything else?"

I shrugged. "A bed, two chairs, a table, and an espresso machine?"

"All this money and you live like a hermit?" Victor paused. "A wall-climbing hermit?"

I smiled, and everyone laughed.

"What am I supposed to be doing in my new identity, anyway?" I asked.

"Our mission is to get as much information on Jin Corp as we can—and you'll be our link to the inside," Lingyi said. "The *you*s are a small group in Taipei, and the ones near our age have even tighter cliques. You're fresh blood. They'll be intrigued by you."

Arun swiped his Palm and the projection wall lit up once more. "Jin has one child, a seventeen-year-old daughter named Daiyu. She's been shielded from media attention thanks to her father and keeps a really low profile. No wild parties or media blasts of bad behavior from her."

I tipped my cup and sloshed hot tea over my fingers. Wincing, I glanced up at the wall to see an image of Daiyu looking back at me, dressed formally in a red evening gown, her black hair swept up to expose the graceful column of her neck. I felt all the blood drain from my face.

"Befriend her," Lingyi said. "She's our best access to Jin Corp directly."

"I recognize her," Iris said. "I've seen her coming in and out of Jin Corp. She's chauffeured in a white limo."

"Jin is divorced from Daiyu's mother, Liwen, Cambridge graduate and model–turned–variety show hostess." Arun's deft fingers worked his Palm screen, and an image of Jin and his ex-wife appeared on the wall: beautiful and dazzling in their wealth.

I leaped out of the armchair. "I can't. That's *her*."

I felt all eyes turn to me.

"What?"

"What do you mean?"

I stumbled away from everyone to stand before the wall screen so I wouldn't have to see the images behind me. "Daiyu was the one I kidnapped."

94

The chamber erupted in exclamations.

"It was Jin's thugs who were looking for you," Victor said. "*Of course* you had to kidnap his daughter."

"But if it was Jin's daughter, wouldn't it have been all over the news?" Arun asked.

That's what I had assumed too. Foolish me. "I had . . . her call her father first." I couldn't bring myself to say her name. "He never even picked up."

I had never told the group the name of the girl I had taken for ransom. Although the kidnapping was core to our operation, it seemed a personal affair. I had volunteered to do it alone, and the less my friends knew, the better. There had been no need to divulge Daiyu's identity. The ransom had been deposited anonymously from Taipei Bank into the account Lingyi set up. Daiyu had been gone for less than twenty-four hours.

I didn't share her name because I didn't want her, in my mind, to suffer the indignity.

I didn't share it because I wanted the memory of our short time together to be my own. As twisted as that was.

I didn't share it because I didn't want to think about her anymore.

"It would have been bad press," Lingyi said after a long moment. "Imagine the headline: 'Daughter of Head of Jin Corp Kidnapped for a Large Ransom—Easy Target as a *You* Girl Wearing One of Jin's Own Suits.'"

"You mean to tell me you didn't do an undernet search *all* this time?" Arun asked, eyes wide. "Never once? You had no idea you actually kidnapped Jin's daughter?"

I paced the length of the wall, avoiding the gigantic screen beside me. "No. I didn't. I didn't want to know, all right?"

"Well, surprise," Victor drawled.

"It changes everything, don't you see?" I touched the minimalized image of Daiyu on the screen, and she leaped back to full size—larger than life. "What if she recognizes me? What if she *remembers*?"

"It's impossible," Victor said. "I paid for the best memory-wipe that was available from a legitimate dealer. No one has ever remembered. Trust me. I'd wager my cuff links collection on it. You don't have to worry."

Arun tapped quickly on his Palm and brought up his search screen onto the wall for all of us to see. "It's true. Multiple studies and volunteer testimonies over a three-decade time span. No subject has ever remembered the period that was wiped from their minds."

"They can't even dream about it," Victor said. "It's gone. It never happened. Believe me, to Daiyu, it's like you never existed."

"We could change his face. Put him under the knife," Iris said.

I shuddered at the thought of altering my face. But for the mission, I'd do it.

"No," Lingyi replied. She sounded angry. "We can't risk medical records of any kind on Zhou. And we've invested too much money and time into his identity. We proceed as we have planned." She grabbed my hand and squeezed. "I trust you. Jin would never think to look for the kidnapper among his *you*s. Right under his nose. Play the part, and you've got this."

Somehow, that didn't make me feel better; then the projection

96

wall went blank behind me, and for a moment, we were pitched into darkness.

I closed my eyes anyway, and the afterimage of Daiyu floated there, burned beneath my eyelids.

None of my friends said it aloud, but it didn't need to be said.

What I was attempting to do wasn't just dangerous.

It was suicide.

Late afternoon and the sky was tinged with gray haze so thick, you'd think if you swiped your palm through the air, you'd be able to grab a handful. Victor and Lingyi were still working on my rich-*you*-boy identity, fine-tuning my records online and securing a bachelor pad. I wanted to enjoy these last days of freedom, even if I never left my dank rented studio without a cap, face mask, and sunglasses on—covered and unrecognizable. I was meeting Arun at his lab on campus before we headed out for dinner. I hadn't been back to the National Taiwan University since we had found Arun's mom in her office. Remembering vividly brought back my friend's rage and grief, something that he still struggled with. He was quiet more often, his easygoing manner and conversations at times falling away midinteraction.

I never knew what to do in those moments, other than rushing on where he had left off, as if his grief could be carried away by my aimless prattle, as if my words could fill those huge, empty spaces.

I entered the massive concrete-and-glass building where the science and technology labs were situated and signed in with the security guard at the desk. Arun had arranged for my building access.

I messaged him on my Vox after I gained entry, because I wasn't as familiar with this building, which was riddled with many corridors and turns. But he didn't respond. Apprehension gripped me suddenly, a sense of déjà vu like ice down my spine.

My hands grazed the places where I hid my knives, their weight and solidity grounding me, my senses going into hyperfocus. The white lights overhead were too bright, washing the corridors in that disinfected glow that reminded me of hospitals and death. All the thick doors were closed, though I could hear muffled conversations behind some of them as I walked past. Finally, after pacing the circumference of the sixth floor twice, I found Arun's lab. The door was shut, and I knocked, anxious enough now that I couldn't stand still.

"Come in," Arun said, and I let out a breath of relief to hear his voice.

I pushed the heavy door open and found Arun slumped on a stool, his elbows resting on a large black lab bench. He wore a bright yellow lab coat over jeans, and his orange hair wasn't spiked, but tied back in a ponytail. The chamber was ringed on either side with computers and large pieces of equipment I didn't recognize. There were three more lab benches cluttered with bottles and tubes. A low hum filled the space, coming from the ventilators and machines, and was devoid of any noticeable scent.

"Am I early?" I asked, pulling a stool up next to Arun.

He gave a dejected shake of his head. "They died."

My pulse picked up immediately. "Who died?" My words sounded like a shout in the empty laboratory.

"My monkeys."

Arun tapped on his Palm and the far glass wall screen lit up with a recorded image. It was muted, showing Arun in his yellow biohazard suit, with his head completely covered. He was facing a wall of six clear cages, with a monkey in each one. The monkeys all lay inert on their cage floors. They had brown fur, the fuzz around their faces reminding me of baby animals. I thought they were dead until two of them were seized with uncontrollable shudders, their mouths forming black circles in a silent scream, large brown eyes staring up unseeing into the lurid light. My arms goosepimpled, and I smothered a shiver. I was glad there was no sound.

"These monkeys were genetically engineered to have as similar a respiratory system to us as possible. I had given them avian flu and injected them with my latest antidote a day after they began showing flu symptoms," Arun said. "H5N1 is a particularly virulent strain with a sixty percent fatality rate. But none of the monkeys survived. The nanobots went rogue, and my antidote killed them all."

"You're creating an antidote for the flu?" I asked in amazement. I knew Arun was smart; he came from a family of eminent research scientists, but this was groundbreaking.

"Not just for the flu," Arun replied, rubbing the spot between his black eyebrows. "I'm creating nanobots to specifically target viral replication. It stops it in its tracks, then the body's immune system takes over and wipes out any lingering viruses."

"That's incredible."

"Only if I can get it to work." Arun pounded on the lab table twice with his fists. "I thought I had it this time. And look what happened."

The wall screen showed the monkeys twitching in their cages, a few jumping as if they were getting electrocuted, before blood seeped from their mouths and noses, darkly saturating the fuzz around their tiny faces. Then their small bodies finally stilled.

"Two of them even bled from their eyes," Arun said, sounding hoarse.

I swallowed, feeling sick. "Gods, I'm so sorry."

"Before my mom died, I had told her I'd do this. That I wasn't an ecologist and I couldn't be an activist or spokesperson like she was for our environment, but I'd try and curb the illnesses at least. If I could get this to work, *mei*s could live longer, have healthier lives—"

"You can't give up." I bumped my fist against his, which was curled tight in frustration.

"Never." Arun gave a shake of his head, the familiar fire returning into his dark brown eyes. "I've just got to refine the nanobots to inhibit viral transcription. I'm so close."

We left the science tech building fifteen minutes later. Arun had taken off his lab coat and was wearing an orange shirt beneath that matched his hair. I had to blink if I looked at him for too long. The color was brighter than I had ever seen from our pale sun. We had picked a hole-in-the-wall cafe that served delicious steamed dumplings and buns.

Walking through the campus, students on bicycles zipped past us on their way home or to an evening class. Lingyi was waiting at the main university entrance and gave a wave when she spotted us. Looking ready for spring, she had pulled back her hair with a bright green headband, and her white pants had giant pink blooms on them. She hugged us both, smelling of vanilla, and said, "Victor can't make it. He's meeting a client."

I wondered what Victor was selling this time.

We made our way through the rush-hour crowds on the sidewalks. The sky was darkening, taking on the muted grays of impending night, but I still kept my sunglasses and cap on. It wasn't worth the risk of anyone recognizing me, not when I was so close to taking on the role of Jason Zhou. Fortunately, my getup didn't get a second glance from anyone on the streets—there were stranger things to see than a guy wearing his sunglasses and cap at night. Like the man in a giant squirrel suit that we just walked past trying to lure customers into the all-you-can-eat buffet.

Lingyi led us down a side street as a shortcut to the cafe, when Arun let out a surprised yelp. "Gods, woman! Can you not be such a ghost all the time?"

I turned to see that Iris had joined us, clad in black, and silent as a phantom. She sidestepped Arun in one agile stride to stand by Lingyi's side, as if for protection. That thought, in itself, was laughable. "Sorry," Iris mumbled.

The truth of the matter was, I didn't think Iris could make noise even if she tried.

Iris caught my gaze, her slender eyes sharp as we walked past a massage parlor wreathed in neon signs and pulled down her mouth just a fraction. *What's up with him?* she was asking. But Lingyi, being Lingyi, said it aloud: "Is something wrong, Arun?" She was sensitive to our moods, always looking to smooth things over. That's what made her such a great leader.

Arun shrugged, the set of his shoulders sagging. "Hard day. I don't really want to talk about it."

"Well, dinner's my treat." Lingyi nodded, letting her hand brush Arun's arm for a moment. "Especially since Zhou will be going in soon."

Arun frowned. He was so upset, he hadn't bothered to put on a face mask. "Oh," he said.

I tensed, then rolled my shoulders. Although I had continued studying my fake identity and trawling the undernet following popular *you* exploits (any info on Daiyu had been impossible to find), I had not dwelled on the actual fact of *going in*. The prospect of being immersed in a world totally unfamiliar and aberrant to me was daunting. But there was no turning back—I *had* to pull it off.

"It's all set, then?" My voice sounded muffled behind my mask.

Lingyi nodded once.

We all smelled the mouthwatering scent of buns steaming in bamboo baskets and handmade noodles being stir-fried in a wok at the same time. The square entrance of the cafe, with its dark blue awning and verdant bamboo stalks and leaves planted on either side, greeted us as we walked in.

"To a good meal with good friends, then," I said, flinging an arm over Lingyi and Arun's shoulders, sounding more at ease than I felt.

It would be my last one out in public with them for a very long time.

# CHΔPTER FIVE

Neon lights pulsed to the beat of the taitronica music the DJ was playing on his dais over the crowd. Large glass orbs hovered in midair above us, changing from neon green to blue to purple, then red, splintering the air with its colors. New Year's Eve, and Taipei was in the midst of an especially cold and wet winter. You wouldn't know it by looking at this crowd. The *you*s were dressed in their finest, from silver leather pants that glowed in the dark to gold and crimson dresses encrusted in jewels. Diamonds, rubies, and emeralds graced the earlobes and throats of many, while a few still chose to wear traditional gold and jade. The young women, mostly in their teens to early twenties, were in fine form this evening, baring shoulders and backs with plunging necklines strategically adhered to offer a glimpse of their perfectly shaped breasts. The dance floor was filled with flawless physiques and proportioned faces, because contrary to popular belief, money *could* buy you everything.

They also got you wings, black and leathery, spreading wide enough to knock people out of the way if the *you* wanted to, surgically embedded into their shoulder blades. There were variations, some choosing lighter colors—feathered wings, like swans, or transparent wings, gilded in silver and gold. The love for all things supernatural, fey, and demonic was the current rage among Taiwan's youth, and the *you*s took it to the next level, surgically altering their physique, adding horns and tails, scaling their skin, be it mermaid or dragon. They were same-day walk-in alterations at the physique surgeons, the changes cast off in a week or two, replaced by some other trend.

I stood at the edge of the dance floor, one hand hooked casually in my trouser pocket, my body responding to the beat of the music as I observed the crowds. This was my first *you* party thrown by Jin to ring in the new year in the most extravagant way possible.

"Big things are coming from Jin Corp," he had said with a triumphant smile when he welcomed all the party guests, before an antique gong was sounded and the black curtains dropped behind him and the massive wall erupted in red-and-gold flames. The audience gasped and clapped as an elaborate cutout of a Chinese ox blazed into existence dramatically before our eyes, in anticipation of the lunar new year soon.

Partygoers wandered from the stage after that, to hurry to the multitude of gold fountains that had began flowing with bubbling pink champagne or melted Belgian chocolate. I had lingered, hoping for a glimpse of Daiyu, but no one waited for Jin beneath the stage except for his small entourage. I spotted Da Ge, dressed in a black suit, and felt a surge of adrenaline. No one would recognize me tonight; I had to sell my new identity.

Watching the dance floor, I was enthralled and repelled at the same time. I'd heard stories of the *you* youth's excesses. But it was different to be surrounded by so many beautiful, thoughtless people at a party so extravagant most *mei*s wouldn't be able to wrap their heads around it. It was obscene. What did it matter when everything was going to rot around the *you*s if they themselves thrived? Why should they care? I didn't think they even noticed.

I might have my own *you* suit now and an expensive, air-regulated apartment, but I'd never forget my childhood, growing up as the poorest kid at my private school, being grateful for every meal that my mom put on the table.

Those knee-high black boots that indigo-haired girl wore probably cost enough to buy the meds my mom had needed; that pair of sapphire earrings, to get her a private room at the hospital, and pay for top-notch medical care.

Enough to have saved her life.

I clenched both hands into tight fists without realizing, then loosened my stance. *Focus. Befriend them. Charm them.* That was my task tonight.

A stunning girl clad in a silver dress with purple-feathered wings unfurled behind her winked at me. Her eyes glowed lavender in the darkness, another surgical manipulation. Nothing was permanent in the world of the rich, except for their wealth. I winked back, but the wild movement of the dancers quickly swallowed her from view.

The *you*s danced with fervor, arms thrust into the air, some thrashing their heads, brightly colored hair whipping. The majority gyrated their hips as if in an aggressive mating ritual. The young women danced in groups or with each other, but some were partnered with young men, who were more than willing to keep up, hands gripping the women's waists—or lower. They bared as much skin as the women, many with glowing semipermanent tattoo sleeves, and others with designs across lean, chiseled pecs.

The regulated air was cool, but not cool enough to dissipate the human sweat and heat that rose from the crush of bodies on the massive dance floor. Silver barbots whizzed along its periphery overhead. A wave of the hand brought them hovering over a guest, who could order or take their drinks and never miss a beat of dancing.

I was overdressed for my first official party as Jason Zhou. With Victor's guidance over Vox, I put on slim-fitting dark gray wool trousers, a periwinkle dress shirt (I had made the mistake of calling it "blue" and got corrected by Victor very quickly), and a light gray vest that gave a silver sheen. I was overdressed not for the style we chose, but because I simply wasn't showing enough skin. Victor had insisted I wear a thick, square palladium cuff on my wrist with a matching square ring on my opposite hand.

"You have to wear some kind of accessories as a *you* boy," Victor had said, instructing me to fold my sleeve edges back so I looked more casual. "Besides, it'll show off your manicure."

I had laughed.

I searched the crowds again for Daiyu. For a moment, I thought I glimpsed a girl on the far side of the room, across the large dance floor, with Daiyu's height and graceful movements. She was speaking to a redhead, leaning toward her friend, so I could only see a quarter profile. Pushing past the dancers and guests holding sparkling drinks in glowing glasses, I made my way toward the figure but was not halfway through the grand room before she disappeared, too. It was too crowded for me to follow her movements.

*Damn.*

After another fifteen minutes nursing a glass of pink champagne, I got tired of standing on the sidelines. I had received curious looks all evening, but no one had yet introduced themselves. Since moving into the 101, I had joined in on a few conversations over the com sys, but found the response polite and guarded. Most of the *you* kids had grown up together and had known each other all their lives, and I was an obvious outsider. I suddenly thought of Tom Ripley from one of my favorite novels, and how he wholeheartedly took possession of a lifestyle and wealth that were never meant to be his. He believed it as he lived it.

Squaring my shoulders, I plunged into the thick throng of sweating bodies and saw the redhead Daiyu had been speaking with. She was half-turned from me, and I caught her arm; she shifted, an annoyed look on her face, until she glanced up. Then she smiled. "Why, hello," she said, and caressed my cuff, trailing her fingers across my inner wrist.

I resisted the urge to jerk my hand away and gave her a lazy grin instead. Girls had always shown interest in me on the streets, but they had never touched me so casually, as if I were an object to be acquired. But I supposed I'd started it. Blood rushed to my head, pulsing in time to the music.

"What's your name?" she shouted above the beat, but I could still hear the husky note of her voice.

It was the redhead that I had seen in the silver limo months ago.

She wore a crimson silk halter dress, the neckline plunging to her navel. Deep purple lotuses were tattooed above her chest, nestled beneath the arches of her clavicles. I stared at the elaborate tattoos, and she touched a fingertip to one of the buds painted right above the swell of her breast, drawing my eyes there. I let myself take in the view, feeling uncomfortably hot, before my gaze returned to her face.

Her lips were as red as I remembered, and she pursed them before they curved in a knowing smile. "Wait. Do I know you?"

A spike of panic.

Then I smiled back. "I've never had the pleasure." I extended my hand. "I'm Jason."

She clasped my fingers, amused by my formality. "Angela." Her hand was warm, and she didn't let go of mine when she said, "What's your surname? How is it that I've never met you before?"

"Zhou," I said. "Jason Zhou. I just arrived from California." I said the state name in English. "I'm new to the city."

"Well," Angela said. "Welcome to Taipei, Jason Zhou. Let's dance!" She tugged at my hand, walking backward onto the dance floor. People cleared a path for her, as if she were some kind of siren, until we were near the middle, almost directly under the DJ's dais.

The music filled me from inside out, and Angela wrapped one hand behind my neck, swaying her other in the air, flinging her head back as she danced with abandon. I held her by the waist so she wouldn't fall backward in her enthusiasm. She laughed, her brightly silvered eyelids fluttering, thick lashes brushing above high cheekbones. It'd been a long time since I'd danced so close with a stranger. I took the lead and matched her move for move, our bodies gyrating in sync to the music. She thrust her hips into mine, and my body responded. My hands moved lower to her hips, but I resisted the urge to slide them farther down.

She threw her other arm behind my neck and pressed closer, her dark eyes glowing with pleasure, locked to mine. She ran the tip of her tongue across her upper lip, and the corner of her mouth tilted into a seductive smile. I'd never been big on casual flings, though that was an invitation for a kiss if I'd ever seen one. But I didn't want to kiss her—not a *you* girl—even if my body was revving to go. Leaning in, I unclasped her hands from my neck, then spun her out with the next hypnotic beats. Her eyes had been shut in anticipation, but she gasped now, surprised. Laughing. I pulled her close again and she gazed up at me, lips parted, trying to figure me out.

It wasn't that I didn't find her attractive. She seemed almost normal in this setting—just another beautiful girl enjoying the celebrations. But deep down, part of me still balked over our differences. Any lust I might have felt for her, any desire, was edged with anger and dampened by contempt. After another twenty minutes of dancing, Angela pulled me down by the shoulders, one hand sliding carelessly to my bicep, and said into my ear that she wanted to go somewhere quieter. I nodded, but not before she brushed her lips against my earlobe. She drew me back off the dance floor, hand clasped tightly with mine. I had a feeling that Angela always got what she wanted.

We left the crowded dance chamber to the one adjoining, this one with fewer people and much more subdued. A circular bar dominated the large rectangular room, the edge of its counter lit in electric blue. Bottles of liquor were nestled on mirrored shelves behind the bar, also tinged in bright blue. Classical music played from the air vents that pumped out our regulated air as well—Bach. The walls were soundproof, so not a note of taitronica emanated from the dance area. Barbots still hovered overhead, ready to take a drink order, but actual bartenders stood behind the bar, for those who preferred to deal with humans. Angela ordered a typhoon cocktail for herself and I asked for a Jin beer—brewed especially for Jin's soirees.

The party guests here were older, much more conservative in their elegance, although their jewels were displayed just as prominently, even more extravagant than what I'd seen on the younger crowd. Large diamond chokers, bracelets, and rubies glittered even in the soft ambient light. I led us to one of the many tables by the floor-to-ceiling windows. The 101 building was encased in glass, and the party was held on the eighty-eighth floor, owned by Jin himself. The Chinese considered eight to be an auspicious number, so it was unsurprising that Jin had bought this entire floor for his personal use. Taipei's lights blinked and flashed beneath our gods'-eye view, and it looked beautiful from up here.

An attendant dressed in a gold qipao embroidered with dark pink chrysanthemums offered us finger foods from a large silver tray. Angela took two meatballs and I chose a stuffed mushroom. It was filled with tender bamboo shoots and was the most delicious thing I'd ever eaten, its flavors exploding in my mouth. Angela nibbled from one meatball but left them both on her gilded plate. It took all my willpower not to chase after the attendant and snatch more food from her, given so freely and endlessly. Leftover food and drinks were discarded everywhere around us, even as attendants came and

110

swept the plates and glasses away. What could feed entire hungry *mei* families—food better than anything they had ever tasted—thrown into the trash.

The waste was unfathomable.

"You're a good dancer," Angela said, sipping from the glowing straw dipped into her tall glass, watching me from beneath lowered lashes.

I raised my beer to her and took a swallow. "I had a fantastic partner." Jin's beer was a golden hue, the flavor crisp and cool, reminding me of wax apples in the summer. Mom would always save so we could share a few when they were in season. "I haven't danced like that in a while."

She widened her kohl-lined eyes. "Why not?"

"Too busy studying, I guess." I grinned. "Besides, the clubs in Berkeley don't compare to what you have in Taipei."

"Studying, huh?" Angela wrinkled her nose as if she smelled something rotten. "You're too hot to be a nerd."

I laughed, even though my initial reaction was one of scorn. "Sorry to disappoint."

*Play the part.*

Her gaze settled on someone behind my shoulder; she straightened, as she had been leaning closer across the small table. She raised her hand and waved, and the subtle scent of her floral perfume drifted to me. "I wasn't sure if you'd stayed," Angela beckoned.

I felt a cool breeze as someone swept up from behind me to stand beside our table. Another *you* girl, dressed in a flowing white dress, like the one I had spotted earlier across the dance floor: *Daiyu*. I drew a small breath when Angela said, "Jason, this is Jin Daiyu, the unofficial hostess of this party. And she *hates* parties."

My heart leaped into my throat, but I managed to swallow before lifting my face and smiling up at her. Her silk dress was sleeveless with a wide square neck, and she wore a choker of blue stones set in silver. They emitted a faint light, casting her face in its soft glow. Her hair was swept up, and she looked like some wayward goddess. It felt as if my heart stopped for a long moment, my grin frozen on my face, before I managed to say, "But your father throws a great party, Miss Jin." I inclined my head. "It's a pleasure to meet you."

I met her eyes, waiting for that inevitable moment of recognition. Her lips curved into a faint smile. Then her straight eyebrows lifted slightly, not from alarm, but in question. She thought I was flirting.

Angela laughed. "Isn't he cute? I'm keeping him."

"Another one? You're well on your way to establishing a personal harem," Daiyu said, and her rich voice was exactly as I remembered it. She must have been wearing heels, as she appeared even taller in her white dress.

"Do join us," Angela said. "I haven't seen you in ages. You never come out to play."

I made to rise so I could offer her my chair before getting another one, but she shook her head. "I can't stay." She studied my face, dark eyes lit with curiosity. "You're Tianren's cousin, right?"

One corner of my mouth slanted up even as I gripped the beer bottle tighter in my fist. "No. I've no cousins left in Taipei. I just moved here from the Bay Area."

Angela giggled. "Doesn't he look familiar? But I think it's because he reminds me of that famous Cantonese star."

"Perhaps." Daiyu tilted her head. "But I think Jason's look is unique."

Probably because I was the only youth in the room whose looks hadn't been genetically or surgically manipulated. My free hand almost went to where I usually hid my knife, but I swept my fingers through my hair instead. There were no knives on me tonight. Security was tight.

I took another drink of beer. "Sit down. We're taking a break from dancing." I willed my pulse to stop racing. Victor and everyone else had promised that there was no way Daiyu could remember me. What if they were wrong? There was an anomaly for everything. Never mind the photo her father had been sending around. Surely, she'd seen it too. Would I blow this on our first meeting? "I'll get you a drink."

I tried to stand again and Daiyu laughed, a surprisingly full sound. "I really wish I could." She touched my shoulder this time, a light touch, and I remembered how that same hand had grabbed my shirt with such strength during our last exchange. When she had begged me not to use the memory-wipe on her. "My father's waiting for me." She rolled her eyes and Angela made sympathetic noises.

"We could come with you," Angela offered. "Would that make it better? You could introduce him to Jason."

I swallowed my beer too fast and pressed the back of my hand to my mouth, clearing my throat. How could I get out of this?

Daiyu brushed her fingertips against my arm this time before I could respond. "You're a darling, Ange. But you know how my father gets with boys." She let her hand drop. The familiar way she had touched me made my palms sweat. "Nothing personal, Jason. My father's just a bit of a hard-ass."

"I get it," I replied.

She gazed down at me; her eyelids were shadowed in a silvery blue, matching the glow of her necklace. "But I look forward to meeting you again."

"Don't forget he's mine." Angela grabbed my arm and hugged it to her chest, dragging me toward her. She gave an impressive pout.

Daiyu's dark eyebrows lifted. "Are you?" she asked me. "Hers?"

I almost dropped the beer in my other hand as I pulled my arm back. "I . . ." My eyes darted from Angela to Daiyu, and I felt as if I were the punch line of some private joke between them. I'd never had to deal with *you*-girl games before. "No. I'm not." I grinned apologetically when Angela stuck her tongue out at me. "I don't belong to anyone," I said.

"You don't belong to anyone," Daiyu repeated. "I like that. See you around, then." She paused after a few steps. "Where do you live, Jason?"

I tried to keep my expression smooth, shocked that she would ask so directly. "Twenty floors below this one. On the sixty-eighth floor."

She nodded, but not before I caught her brief surprise. The 101 was the most expensive and sought after real estate in all of Taipei, with a long wait list to buy. Residential rentals were prohibited and inventory was limited. The majority of the building was still used as commercial and retail space. But somehow, Victor had managed it with his charm and connections. The apartments started at seventy-five million for a studio.

"Sixty-eighth? What a fortuitous number," she murmured, then blew Angela a kiss and gave me a small smile before gliding off.

Hell, Jin probably owned the sixty-eighth floor too, just to monopolize all the good numbers and good fortune.

We both watched her go. The layers of white silk swirled around her, and Daiyu seemed lit by the dress itself. "I think she likes you," Angela said. There was no hint of jealousy in her voice. "How strange," she added as an afterthought, and I burst into laughter.

What had I gotten myself into?

# CHΔPTER SIX

I ignored the sweat seeping into my eyes as I searched the wall above me, trying to decide which handgrip to grab next. I had set the climbing wall in my apartment to medium difficulty and in a moment of spontaneity had decided not to use the harness, belaybot, and rope. I was free climbing for the first time—something that was illegal to do at my old indoor gym. It was too dangerous and a liability risk. Selecting a red grip that protruded from the engineered rock wall, I got a good hold with my fingers before shifting my right foot onto another grip.

I was nearing the top of the twenty-foot wall and reached for the angled overhang above my head. Although I had only asked for a simple rock wall, Victor, in his usual manner, had hired an expert and outdone himself. The synthetic wall could shape and reshape itself to whatever level of difficulty I chose within minutes, in an endless combination, and it spanned from one wall, across the actual ceiling, where it could slope down in various overhangs, to meet the second rock wall on the opposite side. Victor had purchased a belay-bot for each side to work the rope as I climbed in harness. He even had horizontal bars installed to hang from the ceiling so I could use them to exercise or to rest from climbing, if needed.

I had pounded his shoulder then hugged him in my excitement when he had first shown me my new apartment. He had actually looked embarrassed as he grinned at me. "I only buy the best," he said.

A small voice in the back of my head whispered warning as I reached upward, searching for the best path to climb across the ceiling. I'd done it dozens of times before, but never without a harness on. The danger sent a surge of adrenaline and forced me to hyper-focus even more. I selected a purple grip, shifting upward so I hung at a slant from the ceiling. I loved the tunnel vision I experienced when I was climbing. No other thoughts or doubts intruded except for the next best grip to choose for my hands and my feet. My breath quickened and my muscles strained. I consciously drew in a long breath then let out a longer one. I kept moving, shifting, gauging the landscape of grips scattered across the overhang, making sure that my gaze never strayed downward.

All my muscles were fired up but not yet burning. Sweat dripped from my chin onto my bare chest, and it felt as if time had drifted into slow motion. I had woken up this morning feeling like crap, from the alcohol, but also from not knowing what my next move would be with Daiyu. Our short exchange had been so strange.

I shook my head, not wanting to dwell on these thoughts. I couldn't afford to lose my concentration right now. Any mistake could be a disastrous one. I took another deep, long breath to clear my mind, neck extended to look for my next grip, when the intercom chimed. I knew my doorman Xiao Huang's face would be on the monitor by my door, even though I didn't bother to glance down.

"Yeah?" I managed through gritted teeth.

"Miss Jin is here to see you, Mr. Zhou?"

I cursed.

"Mr. Zhou?" Xiao Huang's disembodied voice drifted up to me.

"Just Jason."

"Yes, Jason," he replied.

"Please tell Miss Jin to give me a few minutes."

Xiao Huang cleared his throat. "She's actually on her way up now." He sounded apologetic. "Miss Jin insisted that you had an appointment." And everyone knew that Miss Jin was the only daughter of Mr. Jin of Jin Corp—who probably owned half of the 101 building.

I almost laughed but didn't have enough breath. My front door chimed at the same time. "Jason? It's Daiyu. We met last night?"

"Of course." I cleared my throat. "Come in."

My front door unbolted at my voice command, and Daiyu entered, shutting the door noiselessly behind her. I imagined seeing my apartment through her eyes for the first time. It was a study in glass, antique woods, and metals. My king-size bed was set to face the wall of glass and views of Taipei, its low platform and headboard crafted from titanium. Victor had purchased two antique curved-back chairs, beautifully carved, with a square titanium tea table nestled between them. A round glass table with two red brocade side chairs served as my dining table and desk.

"Jason?"

I watched from above as Daiyu walked slowly into the apartment. She was dressed in tight dark purple pants paired with an ivory sweater. The heels of her knee-high boots clicked against my concrete floor. She looked stylish and assured. She looked hot. I couldn't hang on any longer and swung for the horizontal bar closest to me, grabbing on with both arms, then swinging my legs through, so I could dangle upside down by my knees from the bar, letting my sore arms hang downward.

My movement caught Daiyu's eye and she glanced upward, then let out a small gasp. "What are you doing up there?"

"Climbing. Sorry, I wasn't expecting you."

"But you're not using the rope." She gestured to one of the belay-bots near the wall.

"Are you impressed?" I asked, my head feeling hot and full from the blood rushing into it.

"By your poor life choices?" she replied. "No."

"Not even a little?"

She crossed her arms across her chest. "Not even a little."

"Well, damn." I grinned. Her face looked pale in the early afternoon light.

"Come down, Jason. *Please*." Her dark brows were drawn together. She actually looked . . . angry with me.

*Great second impression*, I thought. *You've got her now. She'd love to take a foolish new guy into her confidence.*

I dropped down from the bar by my arms, then swung from one horizontal bar to the next across the ceiling, until I reached the other side of the rock wall. From there, I chose the easiest path downward, jumping when I was five feet from the ground. The belaybot whirled over and offered me a towel. I swore its digital face looked accusingly at me. I wiped my face with the soft cotton cloth before turning toward Daiyu.

"Hey," I said. The belaybot offered me a cold bottle of water before spinning off. I took it and offered the bottle to Daiyu, but she shook her head.

"Mocha, please," I ordered. "With whipped cream for Miss Jin."

The espresso machine hummed to life, and I gulped down half the bottle of water, then smiled sheepishly.

Her arms were still crossed, but one hand had risen to cover her mouth, hiding a frown or a smile, I couldn't tell by her expression. She wasn't shy about taking me in with those brown eyes either. Shirtless in front of her again like that first morning we "met" after her kidnapping, I scanned the few pieces of furniture I had for a discarded shirt. A towel. Anything.

She dropped her hand. "Do you do that often? Climb without a harness?"

"No. Never, actually. That was my first time. Not thinking straight after last night's party."

I started to cross the large chamber, where a black T-shirt (designer) was draped over one of the brocade chairs, when she held up a hand, then stepped closer and pointed at my bare chest. I felt my face flush—but she wasn't looking at my face.

"Is that real?"

It was the tattoo I had gotten in memory of my mom—a single calla lily—on the left side of my chest, above my heart. It had been her favorite flower. She'd take me to the calla lily festival every spring on Yangmingshan, to admire the sea of white flowers surrounded by dark green leaves. That tradition, and the farmlands harvesting the blooms, were lost after the earthquake and fires on the mountain.

Something else that could not stay.

I had gotten the tattoo a few months ago, in a rare drunken haze, after finding out that Daiyu would be my target to befriend. Arun had accompanied me to the best tattoo parlor in Taipei at two a.m. and was drunk enough himself that he never protested my subject of choice. He hadn't even asked why.

I touched the tattoo with my fingers, still tinged in white powder from the climb. "It's real." This tattoo, at least, would live as long as I did. However long that might be. "It's . . . my mom's favorite flower."

She nodded, then met my eyes. My blush had already faded, thank gods.

"I don't know anyone with a real tattoo," she said. "None of my friends would commit to an alteration that was permanent."

"Well, I was drunk." I crossed the room and grabbed the shirt, pulling it over my head before running a hand through my short hair. I had paid for the tattoo with my cut from the kidnapping. *Her* kidnapping. "It's my first and probably my last."

"It's beautiful," she murmured. "I think it's sweet how close you are to your mom. Is she in Taiwan?"

I went to the kitchen just as the espresso machine beeped three times. The mocha was waiting inside the glass vestibule, with shaved chocolate on top of the whipped cream. The rich aroma of espresso and chocolate filled my senses for a moment as I drew the large ceramic cup out. "No. She's still back in California. It's only me here in Taipei." The lie came easily enough. I hated lying.

And all of this was a lie.

"I don't see my mom often—she lives in Hong Kong," Daiyu said. "She hates my father."

"That's too bad," I said from the kitchen. "Do you miss her?"

"I miss the idea of her. We're not close."

But her mother had been the one to accept Daiyu's call during the kidnapping while her father was unreachable. How close was she to her dad, then?

I set the mocha down on the dining table, closing my MacFold; the thirty-two-inch laptop neatly folded itself into quarters. I still couldn't get enough of that trick. It made my old MacPlus look like something dredged up from an archaeological dig. I picked up the laptop, now just eight inches long and half an inch thick, and set it on the marble kitchen counter. "Sit."

She reached the table in a few purposeful strides, and I couldn't help staring at the long lines of her body, the litheness with which her hips swayed. Sitting down on the dining chair, she raised the large mug to me when I joined her. "Happy New Year," she said before taking a sip. "This is delicious."

Daiyu cradled the cup and took in her surroundings as unabashedly as she had stared at my bare chest. As if she owned all of it. An absolutely proprietary glance, one that I had never seen from a *mei* before—a confidence I had never felt but now must feign. It was too easy for me to forget that Daiyu was a *you* girl when not in her suit. She exuded a confidence coupled with a genuineness I was drawn to.

But if anyone was the epitome of all that the *you*s stood for, it would be the daughter of Jin.

I could never forget that.

"Nice place," she said, her gaze returning to the dramatic views of Taipei below.

Taipei was a city located within a basin, surrounded by mountains. This meant that the pollution was especially bad here, more easily trapped. The thick haze that hung over our city was a daily sight, unless storm clouds blew through to drench us in acid rain. I'd never seen the mountains that I knew were in the far distance in my three weeks of living in this apartment, a view that I knew existed from my research on the undernet of the 101 building.

"The view's the best part," I said.

She nodded, then took another sip of mocha, before turning her face toward me. "It is. Except for the brown haze that sits over us." She pointed into the distance, and then, as if she could read my mind, said, "There are mountains out there. But I've never seen a mountain before in my entire life."

"Ah." I swallowed, afraid of what I might say by accident. I remembered the conversations we had before, when I was her kidnapper. But she recalled none of it. The weight of this, beyond the fear of her possibly remembering, was disconcerting. Talking to her made me feel lopsided, askew. "But during your travels—"

Daiyu gave a humorless laugh. "My father travels a lot for business. But I have never been outside of Taipei." She nodded at my suit sitting in its glass pod set in the corner of my apartment. "He's grooming me to take over the company business. I spend a lot of my time at

Jin Corp, not on trips abroad. Secretly, I keep hoping that he'll have another child. And my new sibling could take over the job."

Surprised that she would reveal so much to me, we sat silent for a moment as I lightly tapped the glass table with my finger. "So you're an only child?" I made a pretense of asking; I knew that she was.

She nodded.

"You must be close?"

She smiled an enigmatic smile. It did not reach her eyes. "My father is a hard man to get close to. Most times he treats me like another product he's created—another investment."

Daiyu gazed out the wall of windows as I took in what she said. Finally, I asked, "Daiyu, why are you here?"

I didn't want to push her away. But it was a natural question to ask given the situation. And I needed to make this encounter as normal as I could. It's what I would ask any girl I barely knew who just appeared at my doorstep. "Do you do this a lot?" I went on. "Show up at a near stranger's door?"

"No," she interjected. "I never do this. It's just that meeting you last night . . . I thought you were interesting. Familiar almost." She turned and smiled at me, and I forced myself to keep my pose natural, feeling suddenly naked for sitting at a glass table. "I've always wanted to visit California," she said in English tinged with a posh British accent.

"There are many mountains there," I replied, also in English. "Maybe you can attend a university in California?"

"I wish." She reverted to her precise and educated Mandarin, giving me a wistful sidelong glance. "I'll be going to National Taiwan

University. I don't think Father will ever allow me to leave this city. And even here, I'm trailed by three bodyguards everywhere I go."

I raised my eyebrows, remembering the beefy *you* boy I had punched in the nose at the night market.

"They're downstairs now," she said, mistaking my expression for surprise. "I wouldn't let them come up. They can wait in the damned lobby forever as far as I'm concerned."

I laughed, because she sounded like every rebellious teen I knew, even given her vast wealth and privilege. "I'd love to visit Jin Corp," I said, trying to sound as casual as possible. I curled my fingers into a loose fist. If I were anywhere but here, I'd be spinning my butterfly knife to ease my nervous energy—but rich *you* boys didn't do that.

"You would?" She studied me over the rim of her cup, and I somehow held her gaze before my mouth twitched into a smile.

"What? Is it so strange? Your father manufactures the most expensive personal product being sold right now—worldwide. And the suits *are* an amazing feat of engineering."

She put the mocha down and wandered over to my suit's pod set in the corner of the large studio. "This is nice. Your first?"

"No," I lied. "I have one back in California. The air in the Bay Area is bad, but it's even worse in LA."

Daiyu turned to me and nodded. "Father has a lot of clients in the LA area. It's one of our largest markets in the United States, along with New York City." She began walking around the apartment, trailing a hand along the rock wall. "How about a trade? I take you on a personal tour of Jin Corp, and you"—she stopped by a belaybot

125

and tugged on the rope—"you teach me how to rock climb."

"What?" I replied without thinking, I was so caught off guard.

"It's more than a fair trade," she countered.

I laughed again. "That's not what I meant. You want to learn how to rock climb?"

"It looks fun." Daiyu tilted her face up to take in the twenty-foot wall and rubbed her hands together. "It looks like a challenge."

I shook my head. "You surprise me."

"How could I surprise you if you don't even know me?" She was pulling off her ivory sweater, and I wasn't sure which panicked me more, that or her question.

"Preconceived notions, I guess."

"Which are stupid," she said, voice muffled under the wool. Her sweater rode up to show her abdomen, and for a terrible moment, I thought everything would come off at once—and I'd have Jin's daughter standing in her lace bra in the middle of my apartment.

I was beside her within seconds, grasping at the bottom of her sweater.

"What are you doing?" she asked through the soft, opaque material.

Her stance had tensed, and too late, I saw the edge of a black top beneath the sweater. I reached for the fabric, my hand grazing against her bare stomach, and that was enough for me to imagine myself helping her *out* of her top, instead of pulling it down. "Just being a gentleman," I replied smoothly, surprised my voice didn't hitch, and tugged the shirt down to cover her exposed torso.

Her head emerged after taking the sweater off, revealing the black tank top beneath, and our eyes locked. She smiled at me, as if she had just read my mind. My hand still cupped her waist, and I casually let my arm drop. *Gods.* I barely noticed the dozens of *you* girls flaunting their prefect bodies, but the sight of Daiyu removing a sweater could make my mouth go dry. It wasn't because I was attracted to her that I was so thrown. That was a given. What terrified me was that I liked her.

Daiyu continued to undress, unzipping, then removing her brown boots. Her feet were clad in black stockings and she bounced on the balls of them, turning to scan the rock wall again. She threw a glance over her shoulder and winked. "I'm ready."

"Right now?"

"Why not?" she replied breezily.

"It's the best way to begin the new year," I joked. "Tell the belay-bot what size shoes you wear."

Daiyu spoke to the silver, egg-shaped bot and it retrieved climbing shoes from the depths of its belly. "They fit!" she exclaimed as she jumped up and tested the feel of the shoes. "Now what?"

"We'll strap you into the harness and you can climb. I'll reset the wall to beginner level. I can talk you through it." I took the harness and held it before her. "Your legs go through these holes here." She laid a hand lightly on my shoulder as she slipped into the harness. "Great. Now we just need to tighten the harness at your waist."

She was more slender than I was. I adjusted the straps, too aware of my own reluctance to touch her now, but I had to, to make certain the harness fit right. I ran my hands along the small of her back and around her waist, keeping my gaze down, tugging at the harness to make sure it was on correctly.

Resetting the wall configuration with a voice command, I then grabbed a pouch of powder and clipped it to one of the rings on her harness. "Dust your hands and you're ready to climb. The bot will be belaying your rope."

Daiyu eyed the bot with its impassive digital touch pad as a face. "Couldn't you hold my rope instead?"

"The belaybot is stronger and absolutely safe. I bought the best on the market," I said. "You can trust it."

"I trust you. . . ." She paused. "I'd trust a *person* holding the rope more."

Our eyes met for a brief moment, and I nodded. "Okay." I slipped on my own harness and pulled the length of thick rope from the belaybot, then made a figure-eight knot for Daiyu, looping it through her harness. I gave the rope another tug to make sure everything was secure. "Tell me when you're ready to climb and ready to come down. Make sure I give verbal confirmation each time."

I hadn't belayed for another person in a while and checked the locking carabiner on my belay loop before adjusting my grips on the thick rope. "Just select the handgrips easiest for you to climb up the wall," I said. "Use your legs as much as you can to push upward."

"Ready," she said to me.

I nodded. "Climb. I've got you."

She began scaling, quite quickly, up the rock wall. She was tall and lean but had muscle definition in her arms—something else that surprised me. I pulled the rope, taking up the slack as she climbed farther up, without hesitation.

128

"Do you work out?" I asked.

"I've got a personal trainer," she replied without glancing down.

"You're really good." In fact, she was doing great for her first climb. "When you're ready to come down, say 'take' and wait for my confirmation. Then put your feet in front of you so your legs are parallel to the ground and sit back. I'll bring you down."

"I did it! I reached the top!" she exclaimed.

The belaybot beside me played a single bell being rung, then cheering noises. I glanced at it in surprise, and Daiyu laughed before saying, "How do I keep going?" She was searching the grips on the overhang across the ceiling.

"Don't," I said. "That's too advanced for a first climb."

She ignored me. I felt her weight shift, tugging against my own harness as she reached overhead and found an overhang grip. I worked the rope, cursing in my head. She was safe enough, but if she fell off the wall, it'd still be a heart-stopping and nasty surprise. I was confident I could break her fall, but if something went wrong due to a fluke, I couldn't afford to have Jin's daughter hurt, much less seriously injured. If that happened, Jin would have me jailed, or simply send one of his thugs to beat me to a pulp. And if he somehow figured out our scheme, we'd *all* be dead.

"Daiyu," I gritted out, my voice full of warning.

I could hear her breathing, and I risked a glance up to see her clinging at an angle, hugging the overhang. "Just one more," she said.

Her arms strained as she took hold and pulled herself upward. At this angle, gravity was really working against her, and I marveled over how strong she was. I had expected *you* girls to be soft. And yes,

weak, being coddled and spoiled as they were. She had been coura-
geous in our interactions during the kidnapping; now I knew that
she was fearless.

I admired it, but that didn't make the task ahead of me any easier.

"All right," she said. "Take."

"Got it," I replied. "Sit back."

She thrust her feet out against the wall and sat back. I felt her
weight and began belaying the rope, lowering her slowly to the ground.
Daiyu kicked off the wall a little along the way, laughing the entire
time. When her feet touched the ground, her eyes were bright and her
cheeks flushed. Our eyes met and she gave me the most joyous smiles
I'd ever seen. My heart seized for a moment. Breaking our locked gazes,
I stepped forward and busied myself with her harness. The belaybot
rolled over and offered her a towel.

"You're what I imagine Meg Murry might be like a few years
older," I said, speaking the character's name in English.

"Meg Murry?" she asked.

"From *A Wrinkle in Time*." I straightened and smiled at her.
"Meg was stubborn and willful. You're more daring—but she comes
into her own. She's one of my favorite novel heroines."

"Ah. A literary allusion?" she asked.

I shrugged as I took off my own harness. "I was a world lit major.
I can't help but think in books." The first statement was a lie, but the
second was true enough. Books were my escapism, my retreat. They
were how I related to this senseless world we lived in.

"And who would you be, then?" she asked, crossing her arms, a
bemused expression on her face.

"It depends. Anyone from Liu Bei to Edmond Dantès to that poor bastard from 'The Tell-Tale Heart.' *Ba-dum-ba-dum-ba-dum*." I tapped against the bot's metal body for emphasis. "Awful business."

The belaybot rolled away, but not before spouting two indignant beeps.

"I see you tend toward the dramatic." She laughed. "I've read Poe in my lit class, but Dantès?"

"*The Count of Monte Cristo* by Dumas," I said. "The hero, Dantès, poses as a rich count and takes years to exact his plans of retribution and revenge." I realized too late how ironic that statement was, and how close to the truth to my own current situation. But our exchanges couldn't be built entirely on lies. And if I were to be sincere about anything, it would be in the books that I'd read and enjoyed.

"Between a paranoid murderer going mad and one disguised as someone else to seek vengeance—I'm not sure what to make of you, Jason." She brought her hand to her chin and narrowed her eyes, gauging me, and I returned her look, until she burst into laughter. "The climb was amazing," she said as she rested a hand on my shoulder and squeezed, as if it were the most natural thing in the world, and stepped out of the harness. And for a brief moment, I wondered who was playing whom here. "Thank you. You're a good teacher."

The bot rolled over, skirting around me, and took her harness.

"I've never tried teaching anyone before," I said. "But you're a natural."

Her face was glowing with a sheen of sweat as she used the towel, a smile playing on the corners of her lips. "I'm going to have to visit you more often."

My mouth dropped for a moment before I laughed too. "You're welcome to anytime."

"I'll take you up on that," she said and stretched her arms overhead, as if unable to contain her energy.

I hoped so.

It almost seemed too easy.

Daiyu gave me a casual hug when she left soon after, and her scent, citrusy and floral, lingered on my skin. I spent the next thirty minutes casting knives against the circular target set on the non-climbing wall, veering wide at first, like some half-assed amateur. My arm was unsteady, my concentration shot. I kept retrieving and throwing, lost in a focused rhythm, until I began hitting the bull's-eye over and over again.

The weight of the blade—the feel of the cool hilt in my hand—was reassuring and familiar.

It was what I needed.

This was the only thing that made sense to me right now, in this moment and within this world.

# CHAPTER SEVEN

Three days later, Xiao Huang personally delivered a long silver box to my door.

"What's this?" I asked.

He shrugged, then grinned so wide you would have thought I had tipped him a thousand yuan. "Have a nice day, sir," he said and touched the edge of his black cap, nodding once.

Perplexed, I pulled off the purple velvet ribbon and opened the box. Three white calla lilies were tucked inside, so perfect I touched a petal, wondering if it was real. It was—the flower cool and smooth. They weren't in season, but *you*s could grow most things in a greenhouse or have them flown in. A rectangular silver envelope rested at the bottom of the box with no name on it. I immediately thought of Daiyu. Was this some mistake? The card inside featured a traditional Chinese brush painting, a single pine tree perched on a rocky ledge, its needles laden with snow.

I opened the card. It was an invitation, the characters written in a hand well versed in Chinese calligraphy:

*You are cordially invited to a gala hosted by Jin Daiyu at the Jin residence. There will be a silent auction and all proceeds benefit the Children's Foundation. A 50,000 NT donation to attend is appreciated.*

The invitation gave the details of the party, noting that it was a black-tie affair. On the top corner, the characters written quickly but in an elegant hand, was a personal note from Daiyu:

*I had such a great time the other day. I hope you can make the party. Would love to see you.*
*xxo*

Turning the card over, it simply noted the title of the painting in the front as "Wintery Solace" by Jin Daiyu. She painted, too? Of course she did. I felt the heat rise to my cheeks as I stared at the delicate strokes for the pine needles. There had been no mention of the calla lilies, although Daiyu knew it had been my mother's favorite flower after discussing my tattoo. I'd never given flowers to anyone before, much less received them from a girl.

What was Daiyu's game?

I didn't know her well enough to gauge if this was simply a thoughtful gesture or polite *you* etiquette for teaching her to climb or—

What the hell was I doing?

I tossed the card onto the table and dictated a message to Victor. "I need a tuxedo. Make me look good."

It's a rough canvas I'm working with, Vic responded immediately, but I'm so brilliant at what I do, you'll be irresistible.

Laughing under my breath, I scrubbed a hand through my hair. It might be too soon to understand Daiyu's motivation, but what did it matter when I had received a personal invite to her exclusive party?

I sent a message to Lingyi: I'm going to Jin's residence. Daiyu invited me.

That didn't take long, she replied.

I think she likes me . . . , I nearly said, but instead dictated, "Why should it?"

I'm impressed, Lingyi responded. Give me 24 hours then I'll prep you.

Daiyu lived within walking distance of the 101, but Victor booked an airlimo for me for the gala night.

"You're not *walking* to this soiree," Vic said. "Absolutely not." He swept a hand over the black lapels of my Burberry tuxedo, then tilted his head and adjusted my bow tie. He had agonized over which brand and style tux I should wear and had finally settled on a sleek-fitting wool tux in a deep navy blue, tailored to fit perfectly. I had to admit I looked damned good.

"Stop fidgeting," Victor said. He tapped my chest. "The femto-cell is sewn into a hidden pocket here. Keep your jacket on at all times."

Lingyi had shown me the cell when we screen chatted; slim as a cashcard, it was able to divert all machinery online and within range through it, giving her access to everything. "The closer you are to the personal device or machine, the better," she had said to me.

Victor straightened. "You look immaculate—*almost* as good as me."

"Impossible," I said, laughing.

He stood back, eyeing me long enough I wanted to reach for a knife to spin in my hand.

"Really. I'm quite pleased with myself."

"I am nothing without you, Victor," I joked.

"I know," he replied, then turned away from me, retrieving something from a large bag. "Here." He passed me a huge bouquet of flowers. "These are for Daiyu."

I stared. It was a beautiful arrangement; I recognized chrysanthemums, lilies, and roses. "It's bigger than my head."

"You're there to make an impression, Zhou," Victor said. "Not to fade into the background."

I took the bouquet, ready to go. If I waited any longer, I'd start thinking too much, which was the last thing I wanted.

Vic glanced at his Palm. "Your limo has arrived downstairs."

The Jin mansion was set on bigger grounds than any other residence in Taipei, surrounded by massive gray stone walls in the Chinese style with carved beasts and flora decorating them. Although it was already dark, the entire estate was brightly lit. My black airlimo circled over the grounds, giving me a view of the Chinese courtyards and gardens below. The mansion itself was European inspired, reminding me of the Tuscan villas I'd studied on the undernet when I had been learning architecture on my own. It was built of cream-colored stone with majestic rectangular windows lining the first and second floors. We drifted over the tiled roof to land in a designated parking area behind the mansion.

I was fashionably late, per Victor's instruction. There were already dozens of expensive cars and limos parked in the large lot. A man dressed in a black suit opened the limo door and asked for my invitation. He wasn't overtly threatening, but it was obvious he was part of security, and my senses told me he was dangerous. I regretted being weaponless going in—but it was too much of a risk.

"Jason Zhou, huh?" the man asked.

I nodded, keeping my face smooth.

"You've never visited the Jin residence before?"

"No," I replied. "But I have a personal invitation from Miss Jin."

"We'll have to run a background check," he said, then scanned my face with his Palm, bathing my vision briefly in green light.

I stood still, relaxing my stance. There was no reason I should be nervous.

The man stared at his Palm for some time.

"Is there a problem?" I asked finally, mimicking the bored and impatient tone of all the rich *you* kids and their net diaries I'd watched. "I'd like to get in before the party's over."

He flicked a disinterested look at me and returned the invitation. "Enjoy the gala, Mr. Zhou."

My driver switched off his headlights, but the commercials continued to play across the opaque glass of the limo. He'd wait for me until the event was over.

I walked alone down the stone-paved pathway through the lush garden toward the front entrance, guided by red velvet ropes marking the way. The grounds were illuminated with hidden lights, as if by magic. I glimpsed a pond below rockery stacked poetically at its edge, more an art piece than a mountain. There was a moongate beyond the small pond, leading into another courtyard. Jin's estate was large enough that no traffic noise carried to where I strolled near the mansion. Turning a corner, I saw that the lush walkway opened into a large circular driveway with a stone fountain at its center, decorated with carvings of leaping koi fish.

Two doormen dressed in tuxedos stood at either side of the grand arch leading into the massive double doors of Jin's house. One bowed and proffered a hand, and I gave him my invitation. Their jackets were made of a deep silver brocade with the Jin character woven through it in pale gold. "It is a pleasure to welcome you, Mr. Zhou," the doorman said, and pulled one heavy wooden door open. I was bathed in blue light, and I realized the entryway scanned each person who entered for weapons. Walking through without incident, I stepped into a beautiful foyer with marble floors and a magnificent chandelier hanging from the domed ceiling.

Six security guards stood against the walls of the circular foyer, silent and observant. They were unobtrusive, but I felt their presence immediately. No music or voices carried to me from the gala; the mansion walls must be soundproof. Other than a large flower arrangement placed on the middle of a round stone table, the foyer was undecorated. I glanced down at the bouquet I clutched in my own hand, feeling tense and ridiculous. *I don't belong here.*

"Mr. Zhou." A young woman clad in a deep purple qipao decorated with the same pale gold Jin character glided toward me. "Welcome." She lifted a graceful hand. "Please follow me." I trailed behind her down one of the wide corridors leading from the foyer, then picked up my pace so we walked side by side. The corridor was composed of pillared archways, lit by intricate ironwork sconces along the walls. We passed one set of closed double doors and several floor-to-ceiling arched windows looking out to the lush gardens beyond.

We walked for some time in silence. I tried to take in my surroundings, in no mood for small talk. It astounded me how the corridor just went on, that an estate as large as this actually existed in the heart of Taipei. How many apartment buildings had Jin knocked down to build this opulent home? Finally, the woman stopped in front of tall arched double doors and opened them. Classical music and the low hum of many people speaking filled the sudden silence. "Enjoy, Mr. Zhou," she said and stepped aside. "Miss Jin has been waiting for you."

I covered my surprise by glancing down at the mixed bouquet I held. When I looked up, the woman had already slipped away. A small orchestra played on the far side of the wall, under a bank of tall arched glass doors framing them like a canvas. We were in a ballroom that opened out to the gardens and a pool beyond. About one hundred *you*s dressed in their finest mingled in the ballroom while servers weaved their way through the crowds carrying silver trays. One server stopped in front of me, offering small gilded dishes of scallops nestled over greens. I shook my head, and he drifted away. I had no appetite.

A chandelier as magnificent as the one in the foyer hung in the center of the rectangular room, with wall sconces casting a soft glow on the beautiful crowd. I saw Daiyu almost immediately, surrounded by a group of *you*s our age, each one of them holding a flute of bubbling champagne, laughing or smiling. The picture of wealth, happiness, and perfection.

I made my way to her, bumping a few elbows along the way—not the done thing, I assumed, by the sidelong glances I received. It wasn't until I neared Daiyu that I realized I had been holding the flowers thrust out like a weapon, my anger and discomfort rising with each jacket sleeve I brushed, with each diamond choker and large ruby or sapphire earring I glimpsed swaying above bare shoulders. Daiyu caught my eye and broke into a wide smile.

I stopped dead, loosening my grip on the bouquet. I hadn't noticed that my pulse had been racing, and sweat had gathered at the back of my neck, clammy against the stiff collar of my tuxedo shirt. I drew a slow, deliberate breath, and grinned back, shrugging sheepishly. *Hi*, I mouthed.

She broke away from the group and came toward me. Every one of her *you* friends tracked her movement like a hawk. It would have been ridiculous and funny if I wasn't already feeling so much out of my element. "Are those for me?" she asked.

I had forgotten the flowers and proffered them. "They are," I said, wishing I had asked Victor for a list of charming one-liners to use. "In exchange for the lilies you sent." I groaned inwardly. So *not* suave.

She breathed in the fragrance of the blooms, smiling into the bouquet. "Oh," she said, "these are lovely, Jason." Then she leaned forward and kissed me on the cheek, suffusing my senses with her subtle floral perfume. Several pairs of eyes narrowed among her group of friends, and I could actually feel their appraisal and suspicion from this short distance.

Daiyu was paying them no attention. She was clad in a sleek turquoise-blue dress, and the cut of it showed off her long, toned legs to full advantage. Her hair had been pulled back into a loose, elegant style, and her only accessory was a cascade of diamonds set in silver, plunging like raindrops between her breasts. I managed not to gape, but my eyes lingered on her longer than was polite before I remembered to say, "You look stunning."

"You look pretty stunning yourself." She smoothed a hand over my lapel.

Before I could respond, Angela charged up to us. "Jason Zhou from California," she exclaimed. "Where *have* you been hiding?" She grabbed me by one bicep and kissed me on the other cheek.

As much as I'd studied and followed the *you*s online, I could make no sense at all over the cheek kissing. Did I kiss them back? I thought Daiyu's kiss was a thank-you for the flowers. What was Angela's for, then?

"I haven't been hiding," I said, deciding not to return any cheek kisses today. Or ever.

Angela still clutched my arm, gazing up at me and fluttering her long lashes. She wore a strapless black dress today, and her lotus tattoos had been replaced by bats nestled among peach blossoms, one floating beneath each clavicle. "There's been a party every night since

New Year's Eve, and I haven't seen you at any of them!" She squeezed my arm in reprimand. I blinked when her unnaturally lit golden eyes turned a deep emerald, glowing subtly. Some new *you* fad she must have bought.

"Ah," I replied. "I'm not a party-every-night kind of guy."

She pouted impressively, her deep red lips reminding me of ripe fruit. "I think you two deserve each other." She pushed me toward Daiyu, then made a show of suppressing a bored yawn behind one hand. "Enjoy watching reruns together dressed in your onesies and sipping tea." Angela waggled her fingers at us, then flitted off.

I laughed and shook my head. "I'm not sure I can even picture that. A *onesie*?"

"They're pajama suits. Very soft. I have a purple one with cats all over it." Daiyu was pressed against my side, where I had bumped into her with Angela's playful shove.

I felt her warmth against my body. Neither of us moved or spoke.

Finally, she tilted her head, exposing the graceful column of her throat. "You look . . . uncomfortable."

"I am . . ." I paused. Should I play the part or speak the truth? "Very uncomfortable. I don't wear tuxes often, and I never attend extravagant galas."

She adjusted my black satin bow tie, which Victor had tied with care, and swept both hands over my shoulders. "But you look the part so perfectly." She smiled.

I hoped so.

Daiyu looped her arm in mine. "Let me introduce you to my friends."

"Is your father at the party?" I asked as casually as I could.

She gave me a sidelong glance. "No. He's on business abroad. California, in fact."

I let her lead me to her small group of friends. They were selecting various delicacies being offered by two servers on silver trays.

"Finally, you're back to introduce him." A plump girl with silver waved hair winked at me. She wore a long, pink dress that accentuated her every curve and a thick diamond choker that must have been worth millions. Extending an ivory gloved hand, she said, "I'm Meiwen."

I grasped her fingertips. "Hi, I'm Jason."

She smiled up at me, expectant. Her eyes had been carefully lined in black, ending in a thick sweep. Meiwen reminded me of a young, Asian Marilyn Monroe. The *you*s who had celebrated with wild abandon at the New Year's party with their angel wings and dragon-scaled skin were gone. Instead, everyone had opted for old-fashioned affluence and glamour tonight.

"It's nice to meet you," I said, and let go of her hand, but she held on for just a moment longer. Was I supposed to have given her a kiss on her hand, or leaned in to kiss her cheek? Too late. I could explain away any missteps by saying I was from abroad.

Daiyu introduced me to the other four *you*s, and I shook each of their hands.

One friend, Joseph Chen, clasped my palm tightly, as if in some contest of strength, and held it even longer than Meiwen had. "Whereabouts from California are you from?" he asked, staring me in the eyes.

"Los Angeles, but I studied in the Bay Area," I replied.

"Nice city," he said. "So you went to boarding school?"

I pulled my hand back; I was in no mood to play his alpha-male game.

"No, Cal," I said in English. "I went to Berkeley."

His eyes widened a touch behind his black Cartier frames, an accessory to match his tuxedo, I was certain, as all *you*s had perfect vision.

"Your family is friends with the Jins?"

Daiyu was standing beside me, talking to Angela, who had returned to the group after grabbing a tray with more champagne-filled glasses, which were quickly distributed. The other three *you*s sipped their drinks, pretending to follow Angela's chatter, when they were really eavesdropping on me and Joseph. The orchestra was playing loud enough that we had to speak in raised voices.

"I'm friends with Daiyu." I gave him a friendly smile. "What about you?" I could tell by the way he was acting that he and Daiyu had probably known each other since they were young, and he'd probably harbored a crush for her since he'd hit puberty.

Daiyu passed a glass to me. "Are you conducting a job interview, Joe?" She leaned into me, touching my sleeve casually with her fingertips. No one missed the gesture.

"Just trying to find out more about the new guy," Joseph replied, tilting his glass back and taking a long gulp of champagne.

"There's not much to find out," I said. "I've lived a pretty sheltered life."

Angela burst into laughter, and a few parents turned their heads to look in our direction. "The way you look?" She winked at me. "I don't believe it."

I resisted the urge to glance down—was my shirt untucked? Instead, I grinned and winked back.

"It's wonderful of you to attend and donate to such a great cause, Jason," Meiwen said. She swept back a silver wave with a gloved hand, her bejeweled finger catching the light.

"I'm here to support Daiyu." I took a sip from my own glass, wishing I had a cold beer instead.

"The Children's Foundation does so much for the kids in Taipei," Daiyu said. "The proceeds raised tonight will all be donated to go toward food, shelter, and medical care for children in need."

"You do wonderful work," a petite girl named Helen replied. She seemed to be a couple with Yongming, a muscular guy who looked like he was ready to bust out of his jacket. "And you know I love any chance to see Yong Yong in a tux!" The pet name she used for him confirmed my impression.

"What about you, Jason?" Helen asked. "Have you done any charity work?"

"I did help to rebuild homes in LA before," I lied. "But nothing like this."

"A man who goes out and gets his hands dirty," Angela cooed. "I like it."

I swallowed my champagne too fast, and coughed into the back of my hand.

Meiwen laughed. "You never quit, Ange." She stopped a waiter bearing a tray of cream puffs and selected one, nibbling on it delicately.

Angela took one too, but I passed. I could never get used to the idea of eating small bites of finger foods. Only those who had never gone hungry could really enjoy it. But despite the ostentatious lavishness of the gala, I was surprised that these *you*s cared enough to donate money for a *mei* cause.

"That sounds . . . charming," Joseph said, his tone indicating that he thought it was anything but. "Though I do believe it's better to put money behind something."

"Money is always nice . . . ," I said. "For those who have it."

Meiwen blinked, Yongming's dark eyebrows drew together, and Angela tilted her head, then took a long drink. The waiter drifted by again, and Angela picked up another cream puff. I almost laughed out loud, but the absurdity of it was quickly replaced by anger.

"What do you mean by that?" Joseph asked.

"I mean that the Children's Foundation seems like an organization that does a lot to help," I replied. "But maybe the best way to help is to prevent their parents from dying so young."

Daiyu's friends met each other's gazes in bewilderment.

"Dying from hunger and illness exacerbated by our polluted air and water, from the tainted foods," I went on, somehow keeping my voice even. "Maybe if more Taiwanese could actually *live* longer, there wouldn't be so many orphans in need?"

*Orphans like me.*

My neck felt hot, and I wanted more than anything to tear that stupid satin bow tie off and unbutton the tight collar of my perfectly starched shirt.

"You can stop now," Joseph said, his free hand fisted. "You're insulting Daiyu."

I lowered my head to calm myself, to try and curb my ire in the face of their ignorance. *What would Victor do?* He'd charm and compliment, not risk his cover by telling these oblivious *you*s the truth.

"I think he makes a valid point, though." Yongming's deep voice interrupted my thoughts.

I stared in surprise at the boy who reminded me of the Hulk in a tux, and he gave me a hesitant grin.

"I take walks through the city all the time," Yongming went on. "There are so many hungry kids without parents and sick adults on the streets lacking the necessary medical care. Raising money for the Children's Foundation helps; it's a great organization. But it's only applying pressure to stanch the wound, isn't it? We are not addressing the heart of the problem."

I had thought the guy had wrinkled his brow in confusion at my statement. But he had done it in thought. I had misjudged him—because he looked like a muscle head, because he was rich.

"You walk around the city, man?" Joseph asked, his tone dripping with distaste. "Those *mei*s can be dangerous. . . ." He shut up abruptly, flicking a glance toward Daiyu, who kept her gaze on the bubbles rising in her glass. I knew then that Joseph, at least, knew about her kidnapping. Maybe no one else.

Helen took a small step forward and took her boyfriend's hand, tilting her chin up. "Of course Yong Yong walks around Taipei. It's our city, after all. And it's why he wants to be a doctor."

Yongming smiled down at his girlfriend and raised her hand to

kiss it, the gesture of affection so natural, I could tell it was something he did often.

"I wanted to let you know I can see where you're coming from,
Jason." Yongming nodded at me.

Daiyu appeared pensive, then assessed me with an inquisitive
glint in her light brown eyes. Still clutching the colorful bouquet,
she looked like a goddess being wooed.

"I didn't mean to offend." I couldn't rely on grasping Diayu's
fingertips or kissing her hand in apology, and for an instant, I was
envious of Helen and Yongming and their obvious love and ease with
each other. "I agree that the foundation does good work," I said.
"There's just a bigger picture to consider. I think you"—I paused—
"*we* lead very insulated lives."

Joseph's mouth curled into a sneer for a moment, just long
enough for me to catch. It was obvious he didn't think of me as part
of "we" at all. I didn't know if it was out of jealousy or good instincts,
but I'd have to watch my back with this guy.

"No offense taken," Daiyu said. "I'm glad you said something,
because I think you're right: It's too easy for us to lead sheltered lives,
to fall into just one point of view."

I smiled, because she was speaking in literary terms now that I was
comfortable with and understood. The very opposite of what it felt like
for me to be at a fancy gala dressed in an expensive tux.

Yongming nodded, but I didn't miss Joseph's slight scowl as Daiyu
lifted her flute. "Still, I appreciate your donation tonight, Jason—all
your donations." She graced us with a warm smile, playing the role of
hostess perfectly. "I hope you're all having a good time."

Everyone nodded, and Helen raised her flute. "You always throw the best galas."

Daiyu clinked her glass with each of us as a server rushed in with another champagne-filled tray.

I took advantage of the distraction and drew closer, speaking into Daiyu's ear, "Any chance we can escape for a bit?"

A flush rose to her cheeks.

I needed to leave the crowded ballroom in order to isolate Daiyu's Palm for Lingyi to access, or, better yet, pick up on Jin's personal devices. I also really just wanted to get out of there.

"I'd like to put these in a vase," Daiyu said. "Let me give you a tour of the house, Jason."

I took pleasure in her friends' startled expressions but refrained from appearing too smug.

Following Daiyu across the ballroom, the long chamber was aglow with ambient lighting and the sparkle of jewels adorning the guests. She waved and smiled as we passed *you*s, but didn't stop to talk. The ones our age were enjoying the alcohol, chatting, and laughing, and their parents acted more reserved, but were also drinking. The small orchestra stopped playing and a single spotlight illuminated a woman sitting on a small dais with a guqin set on a carved stand in front of her. She began plucking on the seven-stringed instrument, and its notes filled the room, soulful and longing; a lament. Conversation tapered off as the guests turned their attention to the woman swathed in a pale green brocade tunic and skirt, her black hair pulled back in a long braid.

Several security personnel in their dark suits lingered along the wall, and one stood near the door Daiyu approached. "Can you step away?" I asked in a low voice. "It was selfish of me to ask."

"It's fine," she said. "I can leave for a while. There is enough food, drink, and entertainment to keep my guests happy."

She led me through the discreet door, which required a palm scan. "We have so many social and business events here," she explained without any prompting, "the security ensures unwanted guests don't wander through the rest of the house."

We slipped into an inner corridor, no less grand than the one I had been in before. The noise of the party disappeared the moment the heavy door closed behind us. "Do you host these galas often?" I asked, walking a step behind her, noting my surroundings. There were more closed double doors in this hallway. Glancing at my Vox, I saw that the femtocell was picking nothing up. I knew it was unlikely I could access Jin's devices given how secure the property was. Daiyu wasn't carrying her Palm tonight—I needed to get inside her bedroom.

"Once or twice a year," she said. "This charity especially is something close to my heart."

The corridor dead-ended with a thick wooden door in the Tuscan style, but with Chinese coins decorating the center of each square panel. The door required another palm scan from Daiyu and opened into a rotunda with a wide, curved marble staircase winding up the far wall. The wrought-iron railing of the staircase had an elaborate Chinese dragon motif.

We climbed the stairs side by side, our fingers brushing against each other. I had to force myself not to jerk back like it was an electrical shock.

150

"I've always hosted this gala alone," she said. "But some of my friends, like Meiwen, did help with the planning."

When we arrived at the top of the landing, I saw that this wide corridor was carpeted, providing a more intimate feel than the marbled floors downstairs. "Your house is impressive," I said.

A corner of her mouth lifted with wry humor. "My father does have a penchant for the grandiose."

The walls were lined with artwork, from classic Chinese brush art scrolls to Italian oil paintings. Built-in alcoves displayed vases, enameled boxes, or jade figurines. All originals, I had no doubt. Her house was like a museum.

"It's beautifully done—he has good taste."

"My father likes acquiring beautiful things," she said. "I think my mother was one of them."

She said it offhandedly in a casual tone, as if she were divulging some mundane fact. I lifted my eyebrows, wondering again what her relationship was like with her father.

Daiyu paused in front of another set of curved double doors, this one with a variety of birds etched into the pale wood. Surprisingly, it didn't require a palm scan, she simply turned an elaborate silver knob and pushed the door open. "Welcome to my bedroom," she said.

That was easy. I'd thought I'd have to persuade her.

It was more like a suite. Or the size of an apartment for a *mei* family of four. The far side consisted of three tall, arched windows opening onto views of the gardens below. A large canopied bed was set in the middle of the bedroom, draped in pale gold and green silks. The bed was strewn with cushions, and it wasn't made. She sat on the edge of it and slipped off her heels, flexing her feet. "These damned things hurt." She stretched her arms overhead like a languid cat, and I had a hard time not picturing the two of us helping each other out of our clothes.

A message popped up on my Vox, and I glanced at it discreetly, glad for the distraction. My femtocell had found a device near—Daiyu's Palm. Lingyi messaged two seconds after: *Give me fifteen minutes.* I slipped both my hands into my trouser pockets and took my time strolling around the large room. Bookshelves were built against one wall, filled with hundreds of titles. Curious, I glanced at the spines. It was obvious some were required reading from school, the usual classics, otherwise her tastes ran eclectic: mystery, fantasy, romance, and horror.

Random trinkets were placed on the shelves: a plastic unicorn with a rainbow tail woven into a braid, a fist-size pinecone, a jade figurine of a goat, and another one in gold.

"It figures the lit major is more interested in my books than he is in me," she said from the bed.

I laughed. "I thought I was getting a tour of your house." A long rosewood table carved with chrysanthemums was set near the shelves, serving as a desk. "But you're right: I can't resist looking at people's books."

She stood and reached for an antique vase that was on her fireplace mantel and disappeared into the bathroom with it and my bouquet. "I needed a break from the gala too," she said from the other room. "And nowhere feels . . . like my own space except for my bedroom. Everything else belongs to my father." She reemerged with the flowers in the porcelain vase. "There are no cameras in here."

I felt the hairs on the back of my neck rise. Of course Jin would have the best security tech on the market, and every corner would be under surveillance in his own house. Except for his daughter's bedroom. "Are you sure?" I almost said. Instead I went to her and reached for the vase, placing it on the rosewood table.

"They really are lovely," Daiyu said, giving my hand a squeeze. "It was very thoughtful of you."

I should tell Victor how he'd won me serious points with the flowers, but the guy hardly needed an ego boost.

She shifted closer, staring at me with those warm brown eyes, as if she could peer into my soul and read all my secrets. I forced myself to hold her gaze, steeled myself for that sudden moment of awful recognition. *I remember you—*you *kidnapped me.*

Instead, she broke into a slow smile. "You're shy."

*Gods.* Aloof, maybe. But not shy. I'd never been invited into a *you* girl's bedroom before, but I'd been invited by *mei* girls—and it always meant only one thing. It'd be so easy to slip my arms around her and kiss her, see where that kiss would lead. Wasn't my mission to "befriend" Daiyu? It didn't get much friendlier than that. But what if it ruined everything? Instinct told me she wasn't into flings; I felt like I was being tested somehow.

"Not really," I finally replied, grinning back at her. "I'm glad you like the flowers."

I walked over to the bank of arched windows, glancing at the expansive gardens below. There was a pavilion in the distance with a green-tiled roof, lit softly by golden lights. The view reminded me of *Dream of the Red Chamber* and the many scenes Baoyu and Daiyu spent in the lush gardens of their estate.

"So you live alone here with your father?" I asked, turning. She was leaning against a carved post of her bed, arms crossed, observing me.

"Just the two of us, yes," she said. "And whatever attendants he might have and our security team."

I searched the room for any photographs, the old-fashioned kind or a digital display. There was a single photograph in the room, Daiyu at perhaps ten or eleven, holding a fluffy white dog in her arms, laughing with delight at the camera. The image was tucked into a silver frame. No photographs of little Daiyu with her cousins, or extravagant birthday parties with friends, or even a studio portrait with her parents. The lack of these personal moments displayed in her bedroom seemed telling. "Is this your dog?" I asked.

"Her name was Mochi. My mom gave her to me for my eighth birthday." She picked up the silver frame and studied the photo. "My father forced me to give her away two years later because she knocked over a potted orchid plant and broke it."

I had to hold back on all the obscenities I wanted to call Jin. Instead, I said, "Your mom gave you Mochi to keep you company?"

Daiyu let out a small breath and nodded, setting the picture down.

I imagined her as a kid in this massive house, all alone except for her father's associates who likely never spoke to her. And Jin forced her to relinquish the one companion she had. I knew my childhood had been rough, and many times I had felt so alone. Daiyu must have experienced a different kind of loneliness. But in the end, maybe lonely was lonely.

"You don't ever stay with your mom?" I asked, my tone softer than I intended.

"My parents divorced when I was three," she said. "My father wanted full custody to spite my mother. As punishment for daring to leave him. She lives in Hong Kong, and I see her once every few years." She fingered the diamonds scattered across her throat. "What about your parents?"

"They've been married for twenty years," I replied without thought, having memorized my fabricated identity so it had become a second truth.

"Do you have siblings?"

I shook my head. "I'm an only child."

"I've always wished for siblings. . . . ," Daiyu murmured and was disrupted by a soft chime. She picked up her Palm at the side of her bed and moved her fingers across the screen, an amused smile quirking the corners of her mouth. "Angela wants to know if she was interrupting anything. She's on her way up."

I assumed she had security clearance as Daiyu's friend, since Angela obviously knew the way to her bedroom.

We chatted more, but the candid feel of the conversation had changed, and we moved on to less personal topics. It seemed barely two minutes later when Angela charged into the room without so much as a knock, her eyes bright with anticipation. I had just settled into a deep leather chair beside the bed, and Daiyu was perched on the bed's edge again. Angela took in the scene, and she seemed disappointed we weren't caught in a more compromising position.

"Hullo," Daiyu said in English.

"Oh," Angela replied.

"Were you hoping to join us for something other than conversation, Ange?" Daiyu asked with a wicked grin.

I laughed while Angela feigned innocence. Joseph appeared in the doorway, and I cleared my throat. Meiwen sidled past him, a vibrancy of color and swaying hips. "Don't just stand there like some oaf." She humphed.

I bit back a smile.

She patted the soft silver waves of her hair. "We lost Helen and Yongming on the way. They're making out in the garden."

"I see," Daiyu replied.

"I've never been in your bedroom before," Meiwen declared, heading straight into the bathroom. "Ooooh, look at this bathtub," her words echoed to us. "You can fit six people into this shower—don't get any ideas, Ange!"

Daiyu chuckled and Joseph shook his head.

"Only luxurious baths for me," Angela called back. She sat beside Daiyu on her bed and took her hand. "Since you're not doing anything," she said pointedly, "let's go back to the party."

I wondered whose idea it was to follow us: Joseph's or Angela's. A message appeared on my Vox from Lingyi: We're good.

Thank gods, she'd gotten access into Daiyu's Palm. Guilt prickled my conscience, momentary but cutting; I pushed it aside. This would never work if I second-guessed myself.

"I did put Jason's flowers in a vase," Daiyu said.

I stood, adjusting my tuxedo jacket. "I don't want to keep you from your gala, Daiyu."

"But I never gave you the tour." She slipped her heels back on.

"It's a big house," I replied. "Tonight probably wasn't the best time."

"Another day, then." She graced me with a small smile that only I could see.

My stomach suddenly felt hollow.

Angela pulled her friend to her feet. "I'm ready to bid everyone up on the charity auction!"

Meiwen rejoined us, the train of her pink dress sweeping behind her, and left the room with the girls. Only Joseph and I remained in Daiyu's bedroom. His stance tensed as I made for the door.

"Stay away from Daiyu," he said in a low voice.

I paused so we were near shoulder to shoulder. "She's the one who keeps showing up at my doorstep and inviting me to parties." There was no need to sound conceited or threatening, because the truth was enough.

He flinched, and I left the room.

# CHΔPTER EIGHT

I waited outside in Liberty Square in front of the Chiang Kai-shek Memorial Hall with throngs of other people. About one in ten in the crowd was suited. I'd never seen so many *you*s gathered in one place outdoors before, but Jin had made a nationwide broadcast via the news stations, com sys, and undernet that he was giving a big announcement here today—one that would change our lives forever. *You*s in their suits mingled with *mei*s in the crowds. Dozens of guards ringed the square, their tasers conspicuous at their hips. They were dressed in dark green uniforms, and their shirts all bore Jin Corp's insignia—the calligraphic character for "gold." News crews were stationed near the very front at the bottom of both flights of white steps, their cambots trained on the plaza above us that led into the hall's main entrance.

The memorial hall park was immaculately kept as a symbol of Taiwan's status. No grime or pollution covered the white garden walls that enveloped the park, nor the beautiful and brightly colored buildings within it. The park and hall used to be open to the general public, but too many bums were making their homes among the lush grass and colorful flower beds, so the government decided to open the park only on certain days of the year, or for special occasions such as this one. I'm sure Jin gave a large "donation" to make this happen.

It was a cold morning in January, and the pristine white walls of the hall with its double-tiered octagonal roof tiled in dark blue stood out dramatically in contrast against our smudged brown winter sky. My views and hearing were unobstructed by my glass helmet, as if I wore nothing over my head at all, but even though I could move in it and my sleek suit with ease, I still somehow felt separated from the rest of the crowd. Many *mei*s coughed on the outer edges of the square, a thick, hacking cough that made me shudder to hear it, and I was glad that I had my suit on, so I wouldn't catch their illness. The unbidden thought was followed by disgust and self-loathing that it came so easily—so automatically. It was so easy to be *you*. And to lack and want were the complete opposite: hard, cold, unrelenting, and hollow.

I couldn't feel the brisk air as I had the suit dialed up to a comfortable 72°F. I had turned off the com sys chat that had scrolled at the bottom of my helmet glass, where the *you*s in attendance speculated on what Jin's announcement would be, as well as where the party was after this. Never mind that it was not yet noon on a Monday. Daiyu was conspicuously missing in the conversation. She didn't participate often in their prattle, but my heart rate would always increase when I saw her icon appear, as my suit noted every time, much to my chagrin. We hadn't seen each other since her gala last week.

My friends had made me go over Daiyu's visit, the gala, and our conversations twice, although I found myself omitting minor details,

159

such as her secret wish that her father would have another child to take her place as Jin Corp's heir. How she had promised me another tour of her home with a smile. And in my own mind, I had gone over our interactions many times over—every inflection, every glance, every nuance—enough times that I would never admit it aloud to anyone else. She had said I seemed "familiar almost." She obviously didn't recognize me if she had seen my photo passed around, but I was certain that the kidnapping was ballooning within her mind, thrusting against the restraints of the memory-wipe. Would it hold? This concern I never mentioned to my friends either. They would only reassure me once more what the studies indicated, but they weren't the ones who had to interact with Daiyu, to befriend her only to work secretly against her. They weren't the ones who had to hold her clear and forthright gaze and not flinch away, knowing the truths that I did.

And all the lies.

More than twenty people dressed in red tunics and trousers accented in gold ran onto the plaza above us with drums and the crowd erupted in loud clapping. The drummers arranged themselves in a half circle with their drums placed in front of them. At the center stood a young man with a giant hanging drum, and he hit it with his powerful arms, a drumstick in each hand. I stood toward the middle of the crowded square, but my helmet was able to zoom in on any object within a half-mile distance. The other drummers picked up on his signal then began a powerful rhythm and beat against their own drums, hands flying so fast and in unison, they were almost a blur at times.

The strong cadence of the drumbeats filled the square, reverberating against the monument hall, against the glass and steel high-rises that towered around us, lit in neon lights and bright moving advertisements. Aircars and -peds zipped overhead, but the drummers with their agile fists and swirling sleeves made us forget all of this—took us back in time with their primal beats. Our reactions were completely visceral, as the people, *mei* or *you*, bobbed their heads and tapped their feet to the tempo that riveted us. In this moment, we were together and we felt as one.

The performance ended after a rousing solo from the young man at the center. A moment of silence followed after his large drum stopped reverberating on the last dramatic beat, and the quiet was palpable before the audience burst into cheers and applause. Many in the audience stamped their feet and whistled in enthusiasm. You could say whatever you liked about Jin, but the man knew how to put on a good show. As the drummers ran off the plaza carrying their instruments, two figures emerged from the hall's entrance, both clad in white suits. I zoomed in on them and saw that their sleeve edges were striped in red and a white sun design embroidered over a square blue background was set above their hearts—an exact replica of the Taiwanese flag.

How patriotic.

Although his helmet was tinted, I knew the taller individual was Jin himself. I glanced at the person standing beside him—a woman—and suddenly realized it was Daiyu. Not only did I recognize the long lines of her physique, but in the way she stood, legs slightly apart. If I could see beneath her tinted helmet, I knew her chin would be thrust forward in a challenge.

Suddenly, both Jin's and Daiyu's helmets lost their tint and we could see their faces. Jin began speaking, and he was directly projected in helmet to me. He was a good-looking man in his forties with a slight gray at his temples, and confident as only the richest person in Taiwan could be. Annoyed, I tried to turn the image off via thought, then voice command, but neither worked. All *you*s in suit would be seeing this broadcast—whether they liked it or not. The best I could do was minimize the broadcast in helmet.

"Fellow friends and citizens of Taiwan," Jin said. "Today is a momentous day." He raised both his arms up in a V, palms facing the sky for emphasis, before bringing them slowly down again to his sides. "Since the establishment of Jin Corp, our suits have reached a global market, becoming one of the most prized possessions worldwide for those who can afford it. Jin Corp officially put Taiwan on the map as a leader in innovation and technology, being seen as manufacturing the best and finely engineered products. My company has created jobs for thousands of Taiwanese and made the world take notice. No longer is the 'Made in Taiwan' label said with derision." Jin emphasized his last words with a fist thrust in the air, and the large crowd packed in Liberty Square hollered and clapped.

I looked more carefully at the masses around me—all the *you*s in suits were cheering, which was to be expected. But so were many of the *mei*s standing near me. Other than the pale man in his twenties with the hacking cough, all the other *mei*s beside me were dressed warmly and appeared healthy. The majority wore masks over their faces. It was true that Jin Corp created jobs for us, but at the same

162

time, their contracts were notorious for underpaying, because they received so many bids. Jin Corp was making itself rich from the sweat and blood of the people. It didn't have many fans among the *mei*s, so the enthusiasm I saw here seemed false.

"I promised you momentous news, and I won't hold off any longer." Jin beckoned with his hand, like someone who was used to being obeyed. Like royalty. Two figures emerged from the depths of the memorial hall to join Jin and Daiyu on the plaza, one man and one woman; both were suited. "Jin Corp has developed a much less expensive suit for the average citizen. These suits are basic and do not have the in helmet capabilities of our custom suits, but they do still give you regulated air, protecting you from the harsh pollutants you breathe every day."

The two figures turned a full circle to show off the suits. And as if to emphasize Jin's point, the plaza began to echo with the sounds of people with wracking coughs. I cast my gaze toward the outer edges of the square. No *you*s in suits stood there, and all the *mei*s looked more worn, with clothes that were threadbare, their hard lives lived etched as deep grooves in their faces. I saw Arun standing near one of the pine trees that lined the square. All my friends would be here today—but I was attending alone as Jason, with only a few *you* teens as new acquaintances I knew there.

"These more affordable suits start at two hundred thousand yuan," Jin said, "a starting price that is cheaper than most automobiles on the market."

The crowd began whispering excitedly among themselves, a soft din that became a palpable buzz.

"Affordable suits for yourself and your loved ones to prolong your lives." Jin flourished his arm at the two models wearing the basic suits. "Isn't that something worth investing in?"

The people around me all broke into raucous applause again, though I noted that few of the tired-looking *mei*s on the periphery clapped as enthusiastically, if at all. The guards stood with their arms folded behind them, as apart from the *mei*s as possible, like anything differentiated them other than their crisp clean Jin Corp uniforms. And the fact that Jin ensured that his guards were fed well so they were strong enough to protect him. That they received good medical attention. As you would keep your guard dogs.

"This is a new venture that was prompted by my daughter, Daiyu," Jin went on, and the cambots all panned to her.

Her face was clearly visible beneath her glass helmet. Her hair was pulled back and she wore more makeup than I had ever seen on her. She looked more grown-up as a result, beautiful yet severe. Daiyu nodded and graced the cameras with a small smile that barely showed her teeth—a shadow of what I had seen when she had gotten off the rock wall after her first climb.

"She felt it was unfair that so many Taiwanese are left to the harsh elements of our country, especially here in Taipei. Why couldn't we make a suit that would be more affordable—one that more people could buy? she asked me." Jin wrapped an arm around his daughter, but Daiyu stood stiff as ever, her face an impassive mask for the cameras. "It was due to her conviction that I began working on a patent for a less expensive and customized version of our suits. And I'm happy to say that we have partnered with Prosperity Bank of Taipei to finance these suits, so they can be made affordable for everyone."

Again, everyone cheered around me. "The suits will be available in early spring, but you can place your order now online or at any Jin Corp boutique," Jin said. "Jin Corp will also be giving away suits in promotion of our newest product. Raffles can be purchased for just one yuan at all 7-Elevens. One hundred suits will be given away to our lucky winners!"

I snorted. Jin's every generous gesture was a calculated move to increase business and profits.

More wild applause. But selling raffles was hardly giving anything away. I could see how Jin spun everything, from dressing in his patriotic suit to his carefully chosen wording. And Daiyu was a part of this? The cambots had already panned away from her, but I zoomed my view onto her face—her gaze was downcast as the crowd's excitement thundered around me. Then she raised her eyes, and it seemed as if she were looking directly at me. An impossibility if we weren't both in helmet. Her lips parted and she drew a breath—I could see it in the rise and fall of her chest—before she turned her face back toward her father.

Jin had both hands raised, triumphant, as he thanked everyone for coming. The park would be open to the public for the entire day to celebrate Jin Corp's announcement. Food and drink carts were set up around the park, and all items were discounted to one yuan, subsidized by Jin Corp. The four suited figures then disappeared back into the memorial hall amid fervent applause and shouting. People began to disperse after that. The *you*s climbed into aircars and some zipped off on their airpeds, while the *mei*s headed eagerly to the food

165

and drink carts stationed around the memorial park, excited to spend a nice and rare day there.

Suddenly, a shrill scream near me pierced the air, followed by shouts.

"He just collapsed!"

"He's dead!"

"It's contagious. Run!"

Two men thumped against my shoulder as they fled, panicked, and everyone else surged away in similar fashion. The air thundered with their cries and footsteps, and I tried to hold my ground until a man with wild eyes above his green face mask slammed into me, and someone slammed into him. I was on my hands and knees in an instant, as multiple feet kicked my legs and arms and strangers' knees bruised my ribs. Someone stomped hard on my left hand, and I shouted in pain, unable to pull it to my chest for fear I'd lose my balance and topple over entirely within the sea of people. Two *mei*s knocked into my helmet as they ran, and my head snapped back both times, ears ringing with the noise. I tried to push upward, but the press of people made it impossible. Then, as suddenly as it started, I seemed alone in the massive square. I rose unsteadily, tucking my bruised hand close, heartbeat thundering in my head.

Only two *mei*s remained with me and the sick man on the ground. I recognized him as the guy in his twenties with the hacking cough who I had seen earlier. He was lying on the cobblestone in fetal position, arms flung out in front of himself, his face deathly pale, except for two bright spots on his cheeks. He hadn't been trampled to death because everyone had steered a wide circle around him as they ran.

*Shit.*

I stooped down and touched the man's shoulder. His breathing was shallow, strained. Dark brown blood was crusted on his mouth, and I saw it on the cobblestone where he had stood and spat bloody sputum. I reached over to feel his forehead.

"I wouldn't touch him," said one of the *mei*s, a man in his twenties. He pressed a dirty handkerchief over his nose and mouth, and I saw that his fingernails were caked with grime. "You're in your fancy *you* suit, but your hands are bare. Don't want whatever he's got."

The sick man was burning up. *Command: what's his temperature?* I queried in my mind.

103.2°F flashed across my helmet.

*Gods.*

"We need an ambulance!" I shouted, raising my head to look around me. Jin's guards had retreated after the *you*s left—their only concern. A few *mei* gawkers remained near the edges of the square. All of them wore face masks. Their black eyes studied me: curious, desperate, frightened. Seeing the dark specks of blood reminded me of Yu Hua's novel: a hero struggling to support his own family by selling more and more of his own blood. Now, that wasn't even a possibility for most *mei*s—especially the poorest among us. Their blood was considered too dirty. Tainted.

The other *mei* who remained near, a girl wearing a mask covered with fluffy white cats and purple stars, snorted. "An ambulance? Let him die in peace. They'll bag him later and cremate him."

I stared at the *mei* girl. She didn't look more than fifteen years. Rolling her eyes at me, she said, "Rich, stupid *you* boy. Who's going

167

to pay for an ambulance? And his medical costs? Stop making a big show of it."

I glanced down at the man and saw the sheen of sweat collecting at his hairline and above his upper lip. He was burning up. Just like my mom had.

"*I'll* pay for all of it. We can't just leave him here. He's still alive."

The girl shrugged. "Probably not for much longer. We die on the streets all the time. You just don't know."

But I did know. Yet I had always turned my back, as most *mei*s did. What could *we* do? This was life. The truly poor and sick died in their hovels or in dark alleys. If they were lucky, a family member or friend reported their demise immediately. The unfortunate rotted until their rancid stench gave them away. Just one month in my $75 million apartment and I had already grown comfortable, removed from the grittiness of the streets. The hunger, illness, and deaths. I had grown soft. But here, now, there was something I could do. "Command," I said. "Get an ambulance to Liberty Square *now*."

CONTACTED. AMBULANCE IS ON WAY, flashed across my helmet.

The *mei* girl wandered off with the older man, neither glancing back even once.

I took long breaths to calm myself, wishing I could rub my temples. A pounding headache had emerged from nowhere right behind my eyes. Daiyu's icon suddenly flashed on the lower corner of my helmet. ACCEPT CALL?

I blinked and cleared my throat, before replying, *Yes.*

My glass helmet darkened, and Daiyu's face filled my vision. She had scrubbed the makeup from her face and let her hair down, tying it into a single braid.

"Hi, Jason." She smiled, and it was genuine. It lit her whole face. So different than the image of the blank-faced girl that had been broadcasted nationwide standing on the plaza of the memorial hall just twenty minutes ago.

"Hey," I said.

"I saw you in the square. I hadn't expected you to come."

So she *had* seen me in the crowd.

I gave a strained smile. "Of course. I wanted to hear your father's big announcement."

Her straight brows drew together. "What's wrong? You look strange."

I laughed. A tired but real laugh. "Too much partying last night?"

"That's a lie," Daiyu said. "Angela's been looking for you after my gala and keeps sending me sad messages. Jason, the absent and lost prince from California."

"Huh. I must keep missing her." A corner of my mouth tilted up. I could tell by the brief purse of her lips that she didn't believe a word of it. "So what's up, Miss Jin?"

"I wanted to fulfill my end of the bargain," she replied. "Are you free tomorrow for a personal tour of Jin Corp?"

Perfect. I was hoping she'd initiate the invitation rather than my having to ask. Less suspicious or desperate that way. This tour was crucial to our mission, and I needed to gather more intel for Lingyi.

An airambulance landed in the square, a stone's throw away from me and the sick man, its sirens and lights blasting. Daiyu's eyes

169

widened in alarm. She couldn't see what I saw, but she could hear everything.

"Yeah, I'm free," I said. "Come to my apartment and wear your suit." I paused. "Please."

*You* boys had good manners, didn't they?

She opened her mouth to reply, but I broke our connection before she could say another word.

# CHAPTER NINE

The paramedics hauled the sick man away after I gave them my cash-card number, saying that I would cover all medical costs. They knew I was good on my word simply because I was a *you*. The female paramedic said I could call the Three Hills Hospital for an update on his status the next morning, but I didn't even know the stranger's name. Lingyi sent me a message in the afternoon that I retrieved from my MacFold in helmet. Arun had seen what had happened in the square and left when the airambulance arrived. She wanted to know how I was and get an update on my situation. Her last sentences read: It was too much of a risk. You shouldn't have done it.

I deleted her message.

After a minute pause, she sent another message: I'm serious, Zhou. You drew unnecessary attention to yourself that could compromise the mission.

Heat flooded my face, and my vision went black for a moment. My hands were trembling with anger when I spat out my response: "So I should have just let him die? Like any other *you* would have?"

Like I was forced to watch my own mom die. Flashback to my

thirteen-year-old self grasping her fingers—too numb to cry—as she struggled for each rasping breath. I couldn't picture her face easily now, but I could still feel her hand in mine. She'd squeeze with the slightest pressure in response . . . until she couldn't anymore.

Lingyi took longer to reply this time as my heart raced in my chest: That's not what I meant. But the mission has to come first. You know that.

I wanted to scream. Punch the wall.

What if Jin was watching? she went on. You were already on his radar.

She was right. I did know. Our mission was paramount. And I had acted rashly for personal reasons. Compassion didn't figure into the equation for what we needed to do.

It won't happen again, I replied.

I know you have a good heart, Zhou. I've known from the start, she messaged. Then ended the convo with two pink hearts.

I unstrapped my Vox, threw it on my bed, and rock climbed the rest of the night. After almost three hours of scaling the walls and ceiling, my body finally gave out on me, and I hung upside down from a horizontal bar. I turned off all the lights with a voice command and gazed out the floor-to-ceiling windows at the shimmering lights of Taipei below. The 101 was ringed in red neon tonight, reflective of my own moods: Rushed. Impatient. Angry.

Trying to save the sick *mei* man might have been a huge risk. But I didn't regret my decision. Seeing him had brought back all the helplessness I had felt when my mom was sick, all the rage. I couldn't do nothing again. Like I'd done my whole life. I had to at least try this time.

I finally pulled myself upright when I began to feel dizzy, closing my eyes and shutting out the images of my city in hazy neon until I felt more steady. I climbed down the wall, the bot belaying my rope noiselessly as I descended at a breakneck speed, enjoying the exhilaration, like flying. I showered in my ridiculously grandiose bathroom, the only light provided by the glow of Italian glass tiles in sea greens and blues, then tumbled into my large bed, still damp and naked.

I slept a dreamless, heavy sleep, until the buzz of the door monitor woke me.

"Mr. . . ." Xiao Huang cleared his throat. "Good morning, Jason. Miss Jin is here to see you."

I groaned and stuffed my face into one of my large pillows. What time was it? I peered with one eye at the chrome clock set in the wall above my kitchen counter: 9:53.

"Tell Miss Jin—"

"Er, she's on her way up," he said.

"Ha!" I croaked. "Thank you, Xiao Huang."

I rolled gracelessly out of bed, then stood at the window, caught again by the city view. It was a particularly bad morning, and an impenetrable brown smog blanketed Taipei. These were the days when you felt the pollution most in your throat and nose, scratching and abrasive, when it felt as if you had a film of dust over your eyes. I rubbed my own eyes, as if just the memory irritated them, then ran a hand through my hair.

My door monitor buzzed again. "Jason? It's me."

"Daiyu," I said, my voice thick. "Give me a second. Please." Politeness was something I wasn't used to after living on the streets for so long. There was no need for "please" and "thank you" when you were starving, or getting mugged or beaten.

I went into my dressing room, paneled in rosewood, even more extravagant than my bathroom, filled with a wardrobe worth more than most *mei*s could ever earn in multiple lifetimes, and pulled on a black long-sleeved shirt and jeans without thinking. Victor would probably be pissed if he knew I was wearing the same few outfits all the time, considering how much he had spent. Hopefully, he'd never find out. I skidded into the bathroom, brushed my teeth, and washed my face before opening the front door with a voice command.

I heard the *click* of Daiyu's footsteps as she entered the apartment.

"I woke you," she said.

I came out of the dressing room and smiled at her, pulling a hand through my hair again, my idea of brushing it. Daiyu laughed. Seeing her always made my body buzz—a visceral response vacillating between anxiety and desire. She was dressed in a pale purple suit and casually held her helmet under one arm. Her black hair was swept back in a ponytail. I studied her expression and posture, trying to see if she remembered anything. But then, why would she be here?

"Good morning," I said. "I might have overslept. Mocha?"

"I'd love one." She settled herself at the dining table and placed her helmet upon it, comfortable and at ease, looking as confident as ever.

My own shoulders relaxed, and I felt the tightness that had been in my chest loosen. The memory-wipe was holding. "Did you want anything to eat?"

174

"I've already eaten," she replied. "But you can take me out to dinner after the tour."

I smirked. "Are you asking me out?"

"You'd know if I were asking you out," she replied.

I laughed and pounded a fist to my heart, as if I'd been wounded. "All right, then. Dinner together—but only out of convenience and necessity."

She arched an eyebrow at me and I dodged into the kitchen, too easily captured by that gaze. I ordered two mochas and toasted three slices of thick taro bread as I wolfed down a banana. Even after six months, I wasn't used to eating whenever and whatever I wanted. My body still remembered what it was like to be constantly hungry.

"Isn't it a school day for you?" I set her mocha on the table as she waved a hand in the air.

"It's my senior year. And I have an internship at my father's. The school's very flexible with my schedule." She took a sip of mocha, licking the cloud of whipped cream from the top.

I tried not to stare.

"Besides I'm at the top of my class," she said.

I sat down across from her and ate as her gaze wandered around the apartment. "No photos of family or friends?" She paused, then looked me dead in the eyes. "Why so Ro?"

Blood rushed to my head, pulse spiking. The same exact question she had asked me during her kidnapping. I reached for my mug, clasped it, and took a few long breaths, using the espresso's rich aroma as an excuse to slow my racing heart. "I haven't had the time. Guess I'm not sentimental," I finally said.

"Not sentimental?" Her full mouth lifted into a smile. "And you have your mother's favorite flower tattooed above your heart?"

I nearly choked on my drink, then wiped my mouth with a napkin. "Well. Exactly. Isn't that enough?" I gave her a grin. "No one knows about that tattoo except you." I didn't even think Arun remembered it, he had been so drunk.

She looked truly surprised then, but said nothing.

I shrugged. "It's new. So . . ." I crumpled the napkin with my hands. "I'll suit up if you're ready to go."

"Why did you want me to wear my suit? The limo's waiting for us downstairs."

"Because we're going to Jin Corp on my airped," I replied. I wanted us to be alone, away from the prying eyes of her bodyguards. It gave me better control of the situation.

Her eyes widened, and she shook her head, her ponytail swaying. "I couldn't. I came with three bodyguards, and they're waiting downstairs too."

"Come on. It'll be fun." I crossed the apartment and unhooked my suit, slipping it on, checking the places where I had hidden my knives. The light synthetic material conformed to my body, sleek beneath my palms as I zipped up the side, before grabbing my helmet. "I'm parked in the private garage on the nineteenth floor. We can go and they'll never know." I winked at her. "Let them wait."

"My father would kill me," she said.

"Don't tell him, then." I opened the door and cocked my head toward the elevators.

"What would the bodyguards think?" she added.

"Let them think what they want," I replied. "We're rock climbing for a few hours." I couldn't keep a corner of my mouth from lifting slyly. "Or whatever."

A wide grin spread across her face before she laughed, then grabbed her own helmet. She swept past me, and I caught her scent— fresh strawberries—and I was suddenly brought back to my lab on Yangmingshan, when she had removed her helmet for the first time during the kidnapping.

"Yes," she said. "Let them wait."

I shut the door behind me, hearing the *snick* of the autolock, before accessing the nineteenth floor with a palm scan at the elevator. We entered it together, and now I was hyperaware of her scent in this enclosed space, and how she didn't stand near enough to touch, but close enough that I imagined I could feel the warmth of her. I took a step away, pretending to be fixated on my suit's zipper. The elevator, one of the fastest in the world, dinged soon after, and we entered the private residential garage.

It was massive, a wide-open concrete space filled with the most expensive airlimos, sports cars, and luxury automobiles. Quite a few residents owned airpeds, and I led Daiyu to mine. Airpeds were named after the mopeds that so many still relied on for transporta-tion, but what Victor had purchased for me was really an airmotor-cycle: a Yamaha Blade in black, silver, and red.

Daiyu whistled and ran her hand along the black leather seat trimmed in red. "This is gorgeous."

"Your first time on an airped?" I asked.

She nodded, her eyes still studying the seductive curves of the motorcycle.

"I'm assuming your suit has the safety enhance?"

Her gaze flicked to me then. "And then some."

"How many suits do you have, anyway?"

"I haven't counted." She shrugged. "Over a dozen? My father often has me testing new enhancements Jin Corp is considering bringing onto the market."

"Like the Superman enhance?" I asked pointedly. Arun and I had gotten the details from Victor after our meeting; it was an enhance that gave the *you* X-ray vision, allowing them to see anyone they chose naked.

Daiyu's cheeks reddened. Then she gave me a slow once-over, her mouth twisted in a mischievous smile. I fought the urge to cross my arms, but instead tensed my body and stance. If she could see me naked, she was welcome to take her fill. I had a lot to hide—and my physique being ogled was the last of my concerns.

Her gaze finally met mine and she laughed. "No. I never tested the Superman. I didn't think much of that enhance, nor of the people who buy it."

I narrowed my eyes at her for tricking me, but my posture relaxed and I walked around the airped, checking the tires, rims, and propulsion system as Vic had taught me. Daiyu leaned casually against the leather seat, a smug expression on her face.

"Looks good," I said more to myself than to her, then lifted my helmet. "We'll connect in helmet?"

She nodded and we both slipped our helmets over our heads. I climbed onto the bike first and turned it on, checking that the lights and gauges were working, feeling the propulsion system hum to life beneath me. Regulated air filled my helmet, and I drew a deep breath of clean air.

"Get on," I said in helmet.

I felt the airped tilt with the weight of Daiyu climbing on behind me.

"There are pegs for you to place your feet. Just hold on tight and lean with me."

Her thighs pressed against me as she wrapped her arms around my waist. "Ready," she said. She sounded a little out of breath.

I revved the engine and we sped down the wide concrete path toward the steel wall as it slid open for us to reveal a glass outer wall, its edges lit in neon orange. "Hold on," I said, unable to keep the excitement from my voice.

I felt like a kid again right before his birthday party. Or how I'd always imagined a kid who got birthday parties would feel. The glass wall parted, and I sped through. We leaped into the air, the temperature dropping instantly around us even as our suits adjusted, and hung there for a heart-stopping moment before we lifted into the sky.

Daiyu gasped, and her limbs tightened around me. I could feel every inch of her against my body. My heartbeat raced as we surged upward, and I told myself it was from the speed of flying across the sky, not from the sensation of her clinging to me as close as a lover. I knew I liked Daiyu when I shouldn't. But I couldn't afford to like her more. Not for what I needed to do: lie to her and betray her.

Her laughter filled my ears as we soared over the lower buildings and wound between the taller ones, passing a few airpeds and aircars along the way, lit brightly even in the daytime. The curved lines of my own airped shone silver, to ensure that other drivers could see us. But beyond safety, it was obvious that the *you*s loved to be seen.

It was another cold winter day, and the sun was hidden behind clouds and pollution. The brightest light in Taipei didn't come from the smothered view of our sun, but from the colorful advertisements projected across the glass panes of skyscrapers. Many lower buildings also had giant projection billboards mounted on their roofs. We flew by a four-story-tall projection of a Taiwanese man and woman, dressed in business attire, enjoying Mr. Brown coffee together. Across the way, flashing on another building, a gorgeous flight attendant from Empress Air was advertising fast and inexpensive flights direct to Beijing.

"This is amazing," Daiyu breathed.

"Is it worth getting in trouble for?" I asked with a grin.

"Definitely."

We sped past the towering skyscrapers and soon left the taller buildings behind as we headed toward the district of Datong on the western edge of Taipei. We had maintained a height of about twenty stories, and the air was cold up here. Flying through the brown haze, I enjoyed what we could see of our city, instead of suffering a swollen throat and stinging eyes. The filth didn't seem as bad at all when you had a suit on.

Daiyu was warm against my back, so close I imagined that I could sense her heartbeat. As with rock climbing, she was fearless and a natural on the airped, leaning into the turns with me effortlessly. I took a few faster than necessary, just to feel her limbs tighten around me, hear the thrilled intake of her breath in helmet.

Jin Corp's octagonal structure was hard to miss as we entered the Datong District. Its exterior was painted a pale gold. There was no better representation of prosperity and wealth than its eight-sided shape and color. The company had helped to revive one of the oldest areas of Taipei, long in a slump since the commercial and economic centers had moved away over a century ago. After Jin Corp was built, new residences were constructed and the older buildings refurbished. New restaurants and cafes emerged to welcome Jin Corp's employees. Employees who would all be out of a job if our plan succeeded. I knew that in order to bring about a revolution, not only would *you*s be hurt in the process, but many *mei*s as well. It was something else I had to learn to live with.

*Means to an end.*

Wasn't that phrase usually used by villains in stories—or, at best, by misguided heroes?

But nothing big was ever gained without sacrifice. You grasped that fast enough as a reader, from Luo Guanzhong to Tolstoy to Woolf. My friends and I had debated for hours over our plan, back and forth, again and again. But in the end, the truth was a harsh and ugly one: in order to change the status quo, we had to be destructive. Seize control of the narrative. Redirect the plot.

I imagined blowing Jin Corp to smithereens, and it felt *right*. A clean slate. A new beginning.

"There's parking on the roof," Daiyu said, breaking into my thoughts. "But could you park on a side street instead?"

I nodded, and her arms hugged me tighter across my torso in thanks. Trusting. And in that moment, I hated myself for doing this to her. But I shoved the thought aside as quickly as it reared its head. Spying a narrow street near Jin Corp, I pressed the landing button and we skidded gently onto the concrete, riding a short distance until I parked and turned the airped off.

"You go first," I said, hoping my voice didn't sound strange.

She slid off of the airped with ease, leaving my back feeling suddenly exposed and cold. I got off and put down the kickstand.

"That was incredible!" Daiyu said. She reached over and took my hand, squeezing my fingers.

I almost snatched my arm back but controlled myself just in time, pressing my thumb into her palm before letting go. I was glad for my helmet, slightly tinted, as I was certain my expression must have appeared strained. *Gods.* My friends had given me the knowledge and all the material things to pass, but they'd never warned me of the emotional complications.

I guess they weren't expecting any.

"Still incredible for me, too." I grinned at Daiyu and forced away my thoughts. Forced away all the complications and focused on the girl before me, with eyes so bright that I could see them even behind her tinted helmet. "It's my first airped."

She admired the flying motorcycle, running her hand across the silver handlebars. "Will it be all right parked here?"

"It's got an obnoxious alarm. And is almost impossible to move when turned off."

Daiyu nodded and began walking down the residential street,

quiet except for the sound of a barking dog somewhere above us. The walls of the buildings were filthy with grime, and all the balconies and windows had iron bars over them. I cast a glance around the dim street before catching up to her. She was about four inches shorter than me but matched me stride for stride. Turning down another side street in the labyrinthine paths of the old district, she said, "I'll take us through a back entrance."

This was a narrow alley where Daiyu and I could barely walk shoulder to shoulder, with so little light penetrating it seemed near dusk instead of midday. I heard the faint trickle of water from a pipe and the scampering feet of rats. I was glad for my helmet, as I was too familiar with the moldy, stagnant stench of water that must have surrounded us.

"Why are we sneaking in the back?" I asked. "Are you embarrassed to be seen with me?"

I heard her soft laugh in the com sys. "I'm trying to keep you away from my father." She gave me a sidelong glance, mischievous. "He wouldn't approve of this private tour I'm giving to some new boy in my life."

"Is that what I am?" I asked with a grin. "Some new boy in your life?"

Before she could respond, a scraping noise made me half turn. Two shadowy figures were behind us in the long alleyway, and instinct told me they weren't just innocent pedestrians. "How much farther?" I touched her wrist. Had Jin's thugs finally caught up to me, so close to his own territory?

"Less than ten minutes. There's no direct path to the back

entrance." She led the way with assurance. Which made me think she'd done this before. Had she given more private tours, or had she visited her father's company secretly on occasion?

"Why?" She glanced at me, then turned as rushed footsteps echoed behind us.

"Stop!" one of them shouted in a gruff voice.

I spun to face the men but said under my breath to Daiyu, "Stay behind me."

She shifted so she stood behind me, a hand resting right between my shoulder blades.

The two *mei* thugs skidded to a halt a short distance from us, their worn and dirty faces twisted with greed. Not Jin's men. His were better fed. One held a short wooden staff, and the other a filthy dagger, thrust at us. They were thin, but desperation gave strength. I knew.

"Give us your cashcards," the one with the long, stringy hair shouted.

"That's useless," I said. "We'll just block access before you can cash out."

The one with shifty eyes waved his staff at me. "Take off your helmets," he screamed. "They can't do anything without their stupid fishbowls on."

I could hear Daiyu's rapid breathing in helmet, and her hand had moved from my back to my shoulder, gripping it tightly. I flicked out a knife from a hidden pocket in my sleeve and threw it. It thudded dead center in the narrow staff, an inch above the thug's fingers.

"Don't come closer," I said in a quiet voice. "I'll aim for between your eyes next time."

He jumped back in shock, shaking his staff, then tried to pull out the knife, which had embedded itself in the wood. "You useless arse," the other thug shouted and lunged at me, brandishing his rusty dagger.

Daiyu let out a startled cry, which sounded loud in helmet. Before I knew what was happening, she had lunged in front of me, neon red taser glowing in one hand. She pointed it at the man with the dagger, her finger on the trigger.

"Daiyu, don't!" There were two settings on a taser: instantaneous death or fried eggs for brains for the rest of your life. The reckless thug charged at us. Pushing Daiyu out of the way, I pulled another throwing knife and cast it—this one struck the center of the man's forearm and he let out an enraged howl as he buckled to his knees, his dagger clattering to the ground.

"Just go," I said, once his cries lowered into gasping curses. "Before you both die."

The other *mei* thug flung his staff aside and went to pull his partner up, shouting obscenities, before they stumbled away, disappearing down a narrow side alley. For a few moments, the injured man's cursing still reached us, echoing. Daiyu was leaning against the uneven wall, arm still extended rigidly, holding the taser. I touched her wrist and lowered her arm. "Give it to me," I said.

She shook her head. And I heard her panting breaths.

"Turn it off and put it away, then. Before you kill someone." The only "someone" left would be me.

Daiyu clicked the taser off, and it made a low whirring hum before the red lights dimmed. She slipped the weapon into a pocket in her suit leg.

"Hey." I put a hand on her shoulder, searching for her eyes. But she stared at the ground. "It's okay. They're gone."

She drew a long breath that shuddered through her, and without thinking, I pulled her into my arms. Our helmets made it so our embrace was awkward, yet she still leaned into me, and I felt her body tremble against mine.

I tightened my arms around her, as if that could steady her, make her fear dissipate. I told myself this was good. This was what I was supposed to do, to gain her trust, her confidence, to get closer to her. But a part of me knew that I wanted to comfort her, wanted to make her feel better. A part of me sympathized with Daiyu. And I'd use these feelings to my advantage, twist them to serve me.

After some time, she calmed, and I drew away from her. "I'll take you home. I'll call for an airlimo if you'd rather not ride my airped again."

She grasped both of my hands in hers. I suddenly envisioned when I had grabbed for her hand instead, when she had asked if she could go outside into Yangmingshan's thickets. Because she had never been in one her entire life. My hands had been callused then. They had softened since half a year ago, from my manicures, from leading my refined *you*-boy life, yet her hands were still softer than mine. "I *had* to do something," she said. "I couldn't just cower behind you and hide."

I wanted to take her chin, cupping her face in my hands, and was suddenly grateful for the clunky fishbowls we both had on. I wasn't thinking straight.

"Daiyu, I could never see you as a coward." That was the truth. "Do you always carry a taser?"

"I do." She did not let go of me but directed her words at our clasped hands. "Because of something that happened . . . last summer."

I felt the blood rush into my head, and I lowered my suit's temperature with a thought command, forcing my expression to remain concerned but neutral.

"I've been trained to use it. I've taken many lessons." She finally raised her face and met my eyes. "I could have killed them."

"I know."

"Why didn't you let me?"

I shook my head, my mouth tightening into a wry smile. "And have that on your conscience for the rest of your life? I'd feel responsible. It isn't noble and glamorous like they show in the films. It's never without consequence. Killing someone would change your life forever. It would change *you*. Look at Camus's *The Stranger*."

Daiyu gave a weak smile. "Camus, huh? Another French author I haven't read."

"Books aren't afraid to show you the truth," I said.

I tried to untangle our hands, but she only released one and led me back the way we came, toward my airped. Everything I said was true, but the most important reason I'd stopped her from killing the men was that I didn't want it to be all media news. "Daughter of Jin Kills Two Thugs in a Dark Alley" would be sensationalized and blasted for weeks across all news outlets: on buildings, in helmet, and all over the undernet. My false identity would come under heavy scrutiny. Our mission wouldn't be at risk—it'd be over. And if my and my friends' true identities were somehow leaked, my friends would be jailed for life.

But I'd be put to death. I had no doubt of that. I knew it when I agreed to kidnap Daiyu on my own.

"Jason," she said. Her tone, quiet and urgent, stopped me. "I don't ever want to hurt anyone. But after what happened to me . . . I have to protect myself. I've no choice."

I nodded, letting her know that I understood, though my helmet didn't move. The dark, damp walls seemed to loom inward. Oppressive.

"It's us versus them," she said.

I almost flinched.

"But it shouldn't be like that," she whispered.

I began walking again, heart thumping hard against my rib cage. "Are you sure you don't want me to call a limo?" I asked once more and pressed her hand to ground myself.

*Nobody's dead. Daiyu remembered nothing. And I'm still Jason Zhou. For now.*

"No," she replied. And already, her voice sounded stronger.

I remembered my first mugging on the streets, when I was fourteen. I had fought and survived, bloodied but alive, and hid in a hovel for two days. Too sick with fear and rage to do anything else.

"I don't want to see anyone. I don't want to . . . deal with people right now." She gave me a sidelong glance. A silent plea.

"I'll take you anywhere you want."

By the time we had reached another winding alleyway and turned down it, it felt natural that we were walking hand in hand. It was an easy role to play.

After a long silence, during which Daiyu looked over her shoulder twice into the deserted passageway, she said, "You saved my life. *Thank you* seems inadequate."

"I got us into this situation—"

"Do you always carry knives?" Her dark eyes were intense, quick and sharp in her pale face behind the glass helmet.

"Yes," I replied, thinking fast. "I won first place for the knife-throwing competition back at Berkeley. Twice."

"You did?" She sounded more dubious than amazed. "That's a thing?"

It was now. I sent a message to Lingyi via thought command to make sure she planted the necessary fake photos and undernet posts to back my lie. "Sure. I'm hurt you're not more impressed."

Daiyu let out a low laugh, even if it sounded shaky.

Less than a minute later, Lingyi messaged me in helmet: Got your request. Nice of you to get in touch. Done. But did you have to win first place twice?

I cleared my throat to hide my smile. Sarcasm noted.

We reached my airped where we had left it less than half an hour before. I climbed on and Daiyu swung on behind me, as if she'd been climbing onto sleek motorcycles her entire life. The airped roared to life, and I revved the engine as we sped down the street like we were being chased by demons before it lifted into the air.

My heart surged with it.

It got me every time.

Daiyu's arms were wound snugly around my waist, then she leaned closer. Her breasts pressed against my back, and one hand glided up to rest over my heart. Right above my tattoo.

"I *was* impressed, just so you know," she said in that rich voice. And it sounded like she was whispering directly into my ear. I felt the hairs at the back of my neck lift. "You have perfect aim."

I laughed.

Prideful.

Foolishly pleased like the Monkey King.

I took a sharp turn, and she gasped as she leaned with me, fingernails digging into my chest. A sense of protectiveness washed over me. Just as it had when I turned to face the thugs. I needed to keep Daiyu safe. *Wanted* to keep her safe. I didn't miss the irony, as we left the Datong District far below us, that the person she needed most protection from, the one who could inflict the most damage in the end, would be me.

# CHAPTER TEN

I woke but didn't know where I was. My whole body ached, as if some-one had run a moped over me, then backed up and done it again. My head hurt the worst, throbbing with each heartbeat. *Gods.* What was that beeping noise? I forced my eyes open. I was lying in bed. Yes, my king-size bed. In my expensive apartment. And my Vox was flashing urgently on the nightstand beside me. I reached for it, and even that took effort. I fumbled with its screen, trying to answer the call.

Finally, I saw Lingyi's face on the tiny screen, looking frantic.

"Zhou!"

I opened my mouth to reply, but no sound came out. My throat felt swollen and sore.

"Ai!" she exclaimed. "You're sick."

I blinked at her, then suddenly realized how hot I was. And how parched.

"I've been trying to get ahold of you all day. Zhou, *listen.*"

My eyes had drifted closed again, and I willed them open, staring at the blurred image of Lingyi's small face. I knew there was nothing wrong with the Vox—it was my vision.

"That man you checked into the hospital," she said, "the one you tried to save in Liberty Square, had pneumonia."

My hazy mind worked on that last word. Just like my mom had.

"Jason!" It was the first time she had used my English name, and it felt as if she had flung cold water in my face. "His death was exacerbated by the flu. An avian flu strain that the hospital had never seen before. Highly virulent. Arun was suspicious Patient Zero happened to be at Jin's announcement. I did some research and connected him to Jin." Her voice hitched, and I stared at her pinched face, rendered too pale against her dark purple hair. She took off her glasses and rubbed her eyes. "Zhou, Jin *released* this flu strain—you might have caught it."

*Shit.* A spasm of dry coughing seized me, wracked through my body until I felt limp and bruised.

"Zhou!" Lingyi sounded very far away. "We need to get help for you—"

I cut off our connection.

My mind was turning as slow as my ancient MacPlus on a bad day. But I knew one thing—no one could see me. I was highly contagious. If Jin's avian flu strain could easily pass from person to person, we would have a pandemic on our hands.

My Vox began buzzing and flashing again. Ignoring it, I tried to call my doorman, Xiao Huang, by voice command but only managed a croak. I rolled toward the other bedside and swiped at the half-empty glass of water sitting there, miraculously not knocking it over. I poured the water into my mouth with a shaky hand, and most of it splashed over my face. But it was enough.

192

"Xiao Huang," I said. The front door monitor buzzed, indicating he was on.

"I'm sick," I rasped.

"So sorry to hear that, Mr., I mean, Jason."

"Absolutely no visitors"—I drew a breath—"are allowed."

"Yes, Jason. But—"

I cut him off too.

My Vox had stopped buzzing. I lay like deadweight in the plush bed, feeling as if I were a candle burning up from the inside. My body throbbed with pain. I closed my eyes. Not wanting to move. Not wanting to breathe. Wishing the aches would go away. I would probably die like this.

And in the end, I couldn't even save that sick wretch in Liberty Square.

I became delirious after that.

I dreamed of Daiyu.

She came to nurse me, wiping a cold cloth across my brow, against my chest; murmuring softly as she coaxed me to drink water. She was in suit, and I tried to grab for her gloved hand. *I'm sorry*, I wanted to say. *Sorry.* I didn't know what I was apologizing for.

Everything.

She swept my hair back from my forehead, damp with sweat, then held my hand. Her glove was cool against my hot skin.

It was morning.

But I couldn't see her face.

▲▼▲

When I woke again, it was in darkness. How much time had passed since I had spoken with Lingyi? I stared with blurred eyes out my wall of windows, onto the city below. Beautiful as ever. I had never glimpsed a night sky thick with stars, but Taipei's neon lights were eternal.

My body felt battered, weak. But the constant ache was gone. I struggled to sit up, easing myself against the cold titanium headboard. I was thirsty. And starving.

"You're awake."

I almost jumped out of the bed in surprise. Daiyu was sitting at the dining table, a soft glow from the screen she had been reading reflected against her glass helmet. She wore a pale blue suit, its long sleeves illuminated with a silver starburst design.

"Daiyu. What are you doing here? I'm sick." I didn't even bother to ask how she got in. Xiao Huang was useless against her.

"That's why I came." She stood and crossed over to me, sitting on the edge of the bed. "I called and you answered your Vox, looking flushed and talking gibberish. I knew you had no family in Taipei. I wanted to make sure you were okay." She reached over to touch my brow with a gloved hand, and I flinched from her. "Your fever's passed."

"How did you know . . ." I stared at my loose fists, trying hard to gather my thoughts. Put up my defenses. Did I give anything away in my feverish ravings? "That I didn't have family here?" I would have sounded defensive if my voice weren't so weak.

"You said your mom was in California, and that you had no cousins left here," she said. "I guess I assumed."

"You need to leave. I think I caught something highly contagious—"

"It's all over the news," she said, her expression grim beneath her glass helmet. "At least a dozen people in the city have been infected with this new avian flu."

*The flu that your father released*, I wanted to say.

She leaned closer, probably scanning my temperature and pulse with her suit. "You kept saying, 'I couldn't save him,' over and over again."

Panic in my aching throat. *Gods.* Did I say more than that?

"You tried to save that man who collapsed in Liberty Square," she said. "After my father's big announcement."

Jin. He had planted that man in Liberty Square the day he announced the sale of more affordable suits. What better way to spur sales—through panic and illness from a virulent flu strain.

"He died," I replied in a hoarse whisper and shifted away, trying to put distance between us. "And if I somehow passed this on to you—"

"I was in suit the entire time I was here, Jason," she said. "You don't need to worry about me."

"I was in suit too, when I tried to help that man."

"My suits are better." She paused. I glanced at her, but she had drawn back, her features obscured. The effect, her rich voice—so familiar to me already—juxtaposed with her alien suit was disconcerting. "And I'm wearing gloves," she added.

195

I was angry with her. Angry that she'd come into my apartment, uninvited, as if she owned the place. Angry that she'd seen me so weak. But most of all, furious that she'd taken such a wild risk. For someone she barely even knew. "You shouldn't have come," I said, my words hard and clipped. "Even if you do own the best suits on the market."

"I'm fine. We have a decon pod at home anyway. It kills everything."

I let out a half-crazed laugh, despite myself. She was so secure in her wealth. I bet no one she cared about had ever died. Hell, even her grandparents were still alive.

"What?" she asked. Her tone was sharp.

"Like a specimen kept in a jar," I said. "Is this how we're supposed to live?"

She didn't reply. I suddenly realized I was naked beneath the thin sheet, so I couldn't even get up if I wanted to.

Finally, she said, "Why did you do it? Try to save that man?"

"What. And just do nothing instead?" I felt disgusted that she would even ask. It must have shown on my face, as she rose and walked away from me, standing before the floor-to-ceiling windows. I wanted her fishbowl off. I didn't want to talk to her like this, faceless. It put me at a disadvantage.

"But everyone does. Turn their eyes away. On a daily basis." She pivoted back to me. "It's why I urged my father to create a more affordable suit. So not only the rich can benefit from it." Daiyu paced the foot of my bed. "But my father . . ." She crossed her arms, shoulders tensing. "My father is always a businessman first. And before

I knew it, he had doubled the price of the suit, made a deal with Prosperity Bank . . . and the raffle. That ridiculous raffle!" Daiyu's frustration was palpable.

I should have placated her, said her intentions were good. Which was the opposite of what her father was doing to the *mei*s. He'd see us all in graves just to make a yuan. But I felt weak, vulnerable, and angry. And I wasn't certain in my still-hazy mind if Daiyu's intentions *had* been good.

"You can't tell me you didn't know—that your father would make a profit on the broken backs of *mei*s. Happily. You're his daughter, after all."

She spoke so low I barely caught her words. "You would think the worst of me?"

I closed my eyes, head swimming. "I don't know, Daiyu. I don't know you." I winced, my swollen throat aching. "I don't know how much you see."

Her silhouette against the windows reminded me of another day, when she stood gazing out on the lush green of Yangming-shan from my now-abandoned home. The 101's neon blue exterior told me it was Friday. I'd been out cold for three days.

"What have I done that makes you think I'm so horrible?" She whipped around, stalking back to the bed. Her movements were bold, but her voice betrayed her hurt. "You say you don't know me, but you seem to have made plenty of assumptions already."

I drew a ragged breath. She was right. I had judged her before I had ever met her, simply because she was *you*. But no matter how much she cared, did it matter when her perspective was from a place

197

of distance and comfort that her tremendous wealth afforded her?

"I understand you want to help the *mei*s, but—"

"I'm beginning to see more, Jason," Daiyu said. "And I'm here because I was worried about you. Is that so hard to believe?"

"It's foolish to risk getting sick." I swallowed. "We barely met."

"I know you better than you knew that stranger you tried to save in Liberty Square."

I blinked, caught off guard. "That's different."

"How so?"

In too many ways I didn't want to explain, all of which would expose my true self and past to her. My Vox beeped, and I answered it, relieved to be interrupted. Lingyi's small face peered at me from the screen. "Zhou! We've been—"

"I'm fine now," I cut Lingyi off, then moved so she could see Daiyu over my shoulder. "I've got a guest."

Lingyi clamped her mouth shut and stared at me. I could only imagine what I looked like and ran a hand through my hair. The ends stuck up. "Okay," she said. "Call me later." Lingyi broke our connection.

"New girlfriend?" Daiyu spoke in such a casual tone that I slanted my head, but her glass helmet only reflected the blue neon of the building.

Instead of answering her question, I said, "I really need to use the bathroom."

She leaned over the side of the bed, then tossed my boxers onto the sheets. I probably looked stricken, because she said, "I didn't undress you, if that's what you're thinking."

I rolled to the other edge of the bed and pulled my boxers on, not bothering to cover my backside, too frustrated for modesty. I had the vague notion of tugging off my clothes in fever dreams, so hot it felt like the material burned my skin. Not a dream, then. My first step was unsteady.

"I've made rice porridge," Daiyu said. "I thought you might be hungry."

I stopped halfway across the apartment. She was a dark shadow lined in blue and silver, intimate and remote. I was pissed at her on so many levels—over her privilege, over her casual certainty that anything she wanted, she would get—but it finally sunk in that she had come because she did care for me. Heat suffused my neck, rose to my face. I blamed it on a low fever and tried to ignore the guilt that settled in my stomach.

"Thank you, Daiyu," I said. "Really."

"You saved my life too," she replied in her rich voice.

"I didn't realize we were keeping score."

"No," she said as she walked into the kitchen. "Friends don't need to."

I holed up in my rich apartment for five days straight, seeing no one except for Daiyu, who visited and brought me food while she stayed in suit the entire time. Arun had warned that I would be contagious and to remain quarantined. We played Chinese chess, and she won every game. She had school assignments and spent many hours reading or working on research projects. After a few days, I got used to seeing her in the late afternoons at the dining table, as the Taipei skyline began to glimmer behind her at dusk. It was so that I almost began to believe that this was my life.

I was glad for her suit, which separated us. Because every time our eyes met, something intense ricocheted between us. I was still weak, but that didn't prevent me from climbing often in those five days we spent together. Anything to distract me from her tantalizing proximity and my own sexual frustrations. If she was named for the tragic heroine in *Dream of the Red Chamber*, then I would be the hero, Baoyu—and our relationship was doomed from the start.

"What do the bodyguards think of all the time you spend here?" I asked out of curiosity one afternoon. She was chauffeured to the 101 in a white airlimo, just as Iris had said from her surveillances.

"I gave them all a paid vacation." Daiyu's grin was clearly visible behind her glass helmet.

"But your father—"

"I got access to his account and sent the message that way."

I laughed, incredulous. "You mean you *hacked* into his account and pretended to be him."

She crossed her legs demurely and flipped through an ancient textbook on Chinese folklore, feigning innocence. I could smell the must of its pages even from where I sat across from her, a distinct scent that always transported me to a different time, a different place.

"I didn't actually sign off as him," she replied.

I shook my head, amused. I loved how she always surprised me. "And your driver?"

"My driver is well paid by me," Daiyu replied, still looking very pleased with herself. "And a brute. He's all the bodyguard I need."

I hoped he was better than the one I had taken out when I had kidnapped her last summer. Then an irrational fear gripped me, that I had somehow spoken this aloud, or that she could read the truth in my eyes. I took refuge on the rock wall again, not using a harness for the second time, needing to focus myself through sheer adrenalin. She didn't say anything.

When it came to Daiyu and me, so much was better left unsaid.

# CHAPTER ELEVEN

On the sixth day, I finally ventured out so Daiyu could take me on a personal tour of Jin Corp as she had promised. Lingyi had instructed me to gather info on the building's security setup and layout, to observe as much as I could. She had found Daiyu's eight-digit personal code for access throughout Jin Corp on her Palm, but the restricted areas required a brain wave scan. She sent a grab device that could capture the brain wave scan for our use if I could somehow convince Daiyu to take me into a high-security area.

I talked to Arun via Vox; he had his own instructions for me. Convinced that the virulent strain of avian flu was being manufactured in Jin Corp itself, he wanted me to keep an eye out for any laboratories hidden behind thick vaults.

"I'm close to getting my antidote to work, Zhou," he said to me. His face was tiny on my Vox, but I could still see the dark circles beneath his eyes. "I can help to curb this epidemic, but I need a sample of the actual flu strain to test and make certain my antidote can kill it."

I turned on the wall screen after speaking with Arun. It lowered from the ceiling, and I clicked to a news channel. Muted, the screen showed paramedics dressed in full hazmat suits loading the sick into ambulances. "At least three dozen already infected with dangerous flu virus in Taipei" flashed across the bottom of the screen. "Three deaths have been reported."

A reporter dressed in a black suit wearing a mask stood apart from two ambulances. It was clear from his rigid stance, leaning away from the scene, that he didn't want to be there. "We have no information on this new flu, although scientists believe it is a mutation of an avian flu strain with a high fatality rate. Doctors are recommending face masks be worn at all times and for people to stay inside."

I suited up. Even though I was feeling back to full health, my mood was grim. The last thing I wanted to do was tour Jin Corp with Daiyu and feign my rich-boy role. But time was slipping from us, people were dying, and my friends were relying on me.

Daiyu picked me up in her white limo. It was only my second time riding a luxury aircar, and I tried not to gawk at the projections across all the windows as I sank into the long white leather seat. Daiyu had chosen an underwater scene, submerging us in blue waters shimmering with faint sunlight. Iridescent jellyfish floated by, and strange puffer fish bobbed in and out of view. And although there was plenty of space, she slid down to sit right beside me, close enough that our thighs touched.

I dialed down my suit's temperature with a thought command. I had kept my distance from Daiyu during my recovery, and her proximity now brought a flush of warmth that had nothing to do with a fever. I was grateful for the suits that separated us. She spent the time talking about the strange sea creatures that drifted past: a majestic lionfish on full display, and a slithering bright blue–and-yellow ribbon eel. "The lionfish have venomous fin rays," she said as one swam past our window.

The rendered image was so real, I was half convinced we were gliding beneath the sea.

"The beautiful creatures are often the most dangerous," she murmured.

We had both taken off our helmets, and I raised an eyebrow at her comment, but she was studying the lionfish intently. We swept through clusters of seaweed, and Daiyu pressed a button on the panel. The images slowed on our windows, and we drifted among the seaweed.

"These are one of my favorites," she whispered and pointed at a stalk of pale green kelp. "A leafy sea dragon."

I didn't see it at first but then discerned a fantastic creature among the leaves, as if made from foliage itself. It nestled against the seaweed, almost completely camouflaged. "That's amazing," I said. The seahorse perched among the green, quiet and serene. "It's so peaceful."

I felt Daiyu's gaze turn to me, and our eyes met. I grinned, but her own smile barely touched the corners of her mouth. Unnerved, I reached over and clasped her hand for a moment, her skin cool against my own hot palm. "What?" I asked.

*I remember*, I waited for her to say.

*You were the one.*

She shook her head, then smiled again, but it was wistful,

tinged with sadness. "So many of these sea creatures are gone now. Extinct."

"Ah," I said. "That is sad."

She nodded solemnly and pressed something on the panel again, and the oceanic views disappeared, revealing a hazy Taipei skyline, shimmering just after dusk. A few airpeds zipped past us in the other direction, toward the heart of the city. She pressed close to me and rested her head against my shoulder, twining our fingers together, the gesture natural and familiar.

I hoped she couldn't detect how fast my pulse raced. I knew that I liked her more than I should, and she acted as if she liked me back. It was exactly what I wanted—what I had set out to do: win her trust, charm her. Yet I couldn't stop the guilt that expanded through my chest, couldn't separate the truth and deceptions caught between all the jumbled emotions I felt.

We began to descend, passing high-rises, their windows glowing like beacons. Bright advertisements played across glass buildings, illuminating our interior in neon greens, reds, and blues—very different from the underwater scenes.

The airlimo landed down in front of Jin Corp, and the door opened automatically for us to get out. She rose and slipped the helmet over her head, and I did the same. "Keep your glass tinted," Daiyu said to me in helmet as she walked to the wide golden doors. "And let me do the talking."

"As you wish," I said, more than happy to oblige.

The doors slid open noiselessly and we stepped inside the grand vestibule. Daiyu crossed the expanse of ivory stone floor to stop in front of the large circular rosewood counter and removed her helmet. "Ah Ming," she said. "I'm bringing in my classmate Edward. We're working on a school project together."

"Miss Jin," the young security guard said. "Of course. If I could just get a palm scan and collect his details . . ."

Daiyu gave an imperious wave of her hand. "My father knows. Edward is my guest." She graced Ah Ming with a stunning smile.

Ah Ming grinned back. The guy didn't have a chance. "I suppose . . ."

But she was already sweeping past him to the curved golden doors leading into Jin Corp proper. "You are a darling, Ah Ming."

She winked at him while punching her eight-digit code into the glowing blue touch pad set beside the doors. I had already memorized the sequence—the same one Lingyi had found hacking into Daiyu's Palm.

"We'll be done in a few hours," she said breezily and waved toward the young guard and nodded for me to follow.

I hid my smirk and stepped into a wide corridor behind Daiyu, as the doors slid closed behind us. "You can keep your helmet on and tinted," she said in a low voice. "There are cameras everywhere, and you look nothing like my classmate Edward."

"Is that a problem?" I asked.

"My father knows Edward's family. They are loyal clients and have bought at least a dozen custom suits." She led the way down the corridor. "He wouldn't object to my giving Edward a tour. Anyone else, and we'd be in trouble." The ivory stone floors continued here, and the walls were painted in a dark green bamboo design set against a pale golden background.

"Well, thank you, Edward," I said.

Wide redwood doors lined both sides of the hallway, each carved with Jin Corp's symbol. Lights set in the arched ceiling overhead cast the corridor in a warm, welcoming glow. The setting exuded professionalism, along with wealth and class. You were left with the impression that important tasks were being performed here, and performed well. I scanned the hallway, searching for emergency exits leading into stairwells. We passed one farther down, a nondescript ivory door with a discreet red EMERGENCY EXIT sign lit above it.

We would use those stairs when we were ready to bomb the building. A shiver ran down my spine. The thought of blowing up Jin Corp, creating destruction and mayhem, seemed surreal juxtaposed against this composed and swanky backdrop.

Soft classical music was piped in from the building's sound system. A small tour group of five people was clustered ahead, led by a woman dressed in a stylish red *you* suit with a gold sunburst design across the front. Her hair was swept back in a clean bun, and she spoke animatedly, but in soft tones. They had stopped in front of a long display case set into the wall, showcasing the prototypes and styles of Jin suits throughout the years. The tourists' heads swiveled around, taking it all in.

"The first floor of Jin Corp is open to the public for our investors, business partners, clients, and tourists," Daiyu said as we walked past the tour group. She smiled and nodded at two women dressed in expensive business attire. They cast curious glances my way, but neither stopped to speak with us. "Tours are conducted daily, but everyone is subjected to a palm scan and background check before entry is allowed."

*Except for me*, I thought.

"I'm fortunate to be your personal guest, then," I said.

Her eyes widened. "Why? Do you have something to hide?"

I laughed, even as my neck grew hot. "I mean, to be able to get a behind-the-scenes tour."

We walked past a global display of suits sold worldwide, from Los Angeles to London, Mexico City to Cairo. I paused, as a large image on the wall had caught my eye: a younger-looking Jin shaking hands with an Asian man who looked oddly familiar to me. As did the woman standing beside him, wearing a crisp, light blue dress. The caption read: *Jin Feiming strikes the largest US deal with Simon Lee to directly import suits into California with a large distribution center based in Los Angeles.*

Lee was my mother's maiden name, and I realized suddenly I was looking at my maternal grandfather. My mother resembled my grandmother in the photograph enough that there was no mistaking it. I had known my mother came from a well-off family, but I had no idea they were part of the truly wealthy buying into the *you* mentality Jin was selling.

"Jason?" Daiyu said, touching me lightly on the shoulder.

I flinched, then made an effort to unclench my jaw.

"What is it?"

I turned to her with a half smile. "Maybe I was having a moment of homesickness. Jin Corp's reach is impressive."

Daiyu glanced at the global map, illuminated dots marking

major manufacturing plants, distribution centers, and bestselling cities abroad. "It's why my father is always traveling. He wants the whole world to be suited."

She didn't return my smile, but instead walked on. We stopped at an elevator and she punched in her security code at another blue touch pad. I hadn't worn any recording devices because I couldn't risk getting caught, so I had to rely on memory for everything I observed. We entered the elevator and Daiyu selected the fifth floor, the highest in the building.

I couldn't stop thinking about the image of Jin with my maternal grandparents, each of them brimming with life. My anger and betrayal were underscored by sadness. They had tried to reach out to me after my mother had died, but I'd broken off all contact. At thirteen and orphaned, grappling with rage and grief, the gesture seemed false—too little, too late. Now the knowledge that they could have possibly saved my mother, had enough wealth to hire the best medical care for her—that hurt the most. But not once had my mother ever said to me, *Call your grandparents for help.*

Estranged and probably stubborn to a fault. I was my mother's son.

"There's a showroom on the ground floor for tourists to see how suits are made," Daiyu's voice broke into my thoughts, "but only investors ever get to see the actual factory floor."

The elevator doors slid open and we stepped into another wide corridor. Floor-to-ceiling glass panels gave a bird's-eye view of the factory below, taking up the entirety of the fourth floor. Dozens of employees wearing white lab coats worked at various stations, and I could see at least ten suits being made on the floor.

"These are all custom," she said, standing near the glass pane. "They're producing the cheaper suits on the second floor."

I watched as an employee placed a glass helmet over a suit that was fitted on a life-size dummy, and the sleeves lit up in intricate bright purple designs.

"As you know, the custom suits are made specifically for one person," she said. "When measurements are received, a mannequin is created to replicate the person's physique, so we can ensure fit and wearability." Daiyu began walking the circumference of the corridor, set in the octagonal shape of the building. Double red-wood doors flanked the other side. "This is the executive floor," she said. "My father's office is located here, but also those of the design teams. This is where the scientists and engineers brainstorm to create improved suits with even better technology and enhances. It also houses all the computers and servers that keep our suits worn by clients functioning."

While the ground floor had felt warm and welcoming, the feeling on this floor was exactly the opposite. The empty corridor was dimly lit, and the thick double doors appeared foreboding, guarding secrets within, and keeping strangers out. I noticed none of the doors had the blue touch pads that had allowed us access so far throughout the building. Instead, a curved glass dome was set overhead by the entrance of each door supported by a steel column. She followed my glance. "Brain wave scans are required to enter the highest-security areas within Jin Corp," she said. "This floor is highly restricted."

So Lingyi's intel was right. I needed to convince Daiyu to use the brain wave scan and somehow capture a copy of it.

Daiyu was gazing down at the expansive factory. The space was clean and well lit, but entirely clinical, without the clutter in Arun's lab, making it feel more intimate.

"Why a brain wave scan?" I asked.

"It's the best security option on the market currently." She turned to me, arching an eyebrow. It felt almost like a challenge.

"I'm not surprised," I replied. "Nothing but the best for Jin Corp." I walked over to the steel column, peering at the curved dome set overhead. "How does it work? I've never seen one before."

Without prompting, she brushed past me to stand beneath the dome.

She faced me, and too late, I realized I should have slipped the device Lingyi had given me onto the column before she came over. Now there was no way for me to do it discreetly.

The machine turned on with a low hum, then a crosshatch of laser beams flashed across the top of Daiyu's head, so her features were tinged a ghostly blue. "Our brain waves are unique, like our fingerprints," she said. "A recording of my brain wave was captured to help with authentication—"

She was interrupted by the door beside us beeping once, and the gold doorknob was illuminated in green. Stepping away from the glass dome, Daiyu opened the heavy wooden door, then shut it again. The green light dimmed. "We had to think of an image as our brain waves were being scanned and recorded, and then must focus on the same image when we use the scanners for entry."

"What's the image?" I asked, curious.

"The *Jin* character," she replied.

I detected a trace of sarcasm in her tone, but wasn't sure if I was imagining it. Palming the slim device back into a hidden pocket in my suit, I cursed myself for not having played this better. What could I do to make her use it again?

Going to the center of the landing, I gazed down at the employees working diligently at their various tasks and imagined this large wall of glass exploding outward, showering down on everyone on the factory floor below. Shrill screams and blood everywhere. We definitely needed a ruse to get everyone out of the building. As much as I loathed everything Jin Corp stood for, there would be no innocent lives lost if I could help it.

We slowly walked the entire circumference of the floor, and Daiyu stepped into the elevator again. This time, we stopped on the third floor. The corridor was paved with gray tiles, not as opulent as the ground floor. Laboratories behind glass windows flanked both sides of the narrow hallway, revealing more employees wearing white lab coats bearing Jin Corp's insignia placed above their hearts.

"Is this where they do the testing?" I asked, watching a technician gauge the durability of various materials at his workstation.

"Yes," she said. "For the suits, but it also houses the labs for scientific research."

This caught my attention. It was what Arun had told me to look for.

I observed as much as I could without drawing Daiyu's suspicion, noting the emergency-exit stairwells on this floor. But nothing I saw seemed out of the ordinary: technicians testing different materials used for the suits and helmets, engineers working on different 3D models of new designs, and artists sketching to render patterns on custom suits.

"What's that?" I asked, pointing at an oval structure shaped like a giant egg housed in a lab that looked exactly like the one Arun worked in.

"That's a decon pod," Daiyu replied. "The same one that we have at home. There are two located on this floor."

This only reaffirmed Arun's suspicions that the avian flu was being produced on-site.

We soon reached a portion of the floor that was housed behind steel doors, with brain wave scan stations set beside them.

"Another restricted area?" I asked. Here was my chance to have Daiyu use the scan machine again. But how?

We had passed several employees in lab coats along the corridor, but this part of the building looked deserted, silent and empty. It felt like a dungeon formed of steel, the massive doors revealing nothing of what went on behind them.

"Yes," she said.

"Do you know what they do in there?"

She crossed her arms, studying the thick steel doors. "I don't," Daiyu said. "But I know that my father has been working on a secret project for a few years now."

I untinted my helmet, and she held my gaze, assessing me. Was I being too obvious? Had I looked too long through one window, shown too much interest? Did she notice me memorizing the layout of everywhere we went, marking each corridor and emergency exit?

"I'm sure he'll make a big announcement soon about the

endeavor," she said. "But now you have me curious too."

I gave a devilish grin. "Let's go see."

Just then, one of the steel doors slid back, releasing a draft of cold air. Daiyu tensed, laying her hand lightly on my arm. "Keep your helmet on but untinted."

A tall man exited, wearing the same white lab coat as everyone else, clutching a stack of files. He was reading notes, murmuring to himself, before he noticed Daiyu and me standing on the edge of the restricted area. When he recognized Daiyu, his eyes widened. "Miss Jin," he said. "Good evening."

She nodded at the man, smiling. "Dr. Lu. You're here late."

"Yes, got caught up in what I was working on." His dark eyebrows drew together. "Can I help you?" He cast a glance my way. It was not a friendly look. "This is a high-security area."

"Really?" Daiyu said, lifting her chin. "Even to me?"

The tall scientist shifted on his feet, his uncertainty and discomfort obvious. "I . . . I think you'd have to ask your father, Miss Jin."

She flashed that disarming smile. "I was just giving my classmate a small tour," Daiyu said, her tone casual and light. "I'm taking him to Vivian to see my newest suit."

Dr. Lu brightened. "Vivian. She is so talented." He pressed the files he held protectively against his chest. "You're fortunate to have her as your designer."

"Definitely. We were just headed that way."

He nodded at us as we turned around, then pushed past us in his haste to where he was going.

She gripped my arm to stop me and cocked her head back

toward the restricted laboratory. I winked. We didn't say a word as she stepped beneath the brain wave scanner. This time, I slipped the capture device onto the column right as she got under the dome. I wondered if the scanner would grant her entry, and by Daiyu's uncertain expression, she didn't know either.

Three seconds later, we heard a loud *click*, and the steel vaulted door eased open with a soft *whoosh*. Daiyu pushed it a fraction and peered inside. I took the opportunity to remove the device and slip it back into my pocket, hoping it had copied her brain wave scan. She beckoned with her hand, and I followed. The door glided shut, but was at least a foot thick. The large lab was empty, with two rectangular lab benches strewn with machines and equipment. An array of test tubes set in a large tray was placed on a small rolling cart between them. Much bigger machinery lined the walls of the lab. It was freezing, and Daiyu shivered, being suited still but without her helmet on to regulate her temp. I dialed my own suit up to a comfortable seventy degrees.

"What happens if we get caught?" I asked.

She shrugged. "I have access to this lab, so security can't argue that this is off-limits to me."

"But it is to me," I said, cocking my eyebrow.

"True." Daiyu grinned. "I know the Jin security team doesn't review recordings unless they have a reason to."

"So don't give them a reason?"

"Exactly," she replied.

Daiyu wandered around the large room, hugging herself to keep warm.

"Was Dr. Lu acting strange to you?" Daiyu asked in a soft voice.

215

I had the same exact thought: The man was hiding something. "Maybe he's just awkward." Daiyu didn't need to know what we suspected.

She let out a soft laugh.

I meandered through the long laboratory, studying everything with unabashed curiosity. An enclosed refrigerated case against the wall caught my eye, and I went over as casually as I could. Three test tubes were nestled under the glass case. I leaned down closer to look at the vials. H7N9S had been labeled on all of them, and the test tube rims were banded in red.

"What do you think it is?" Daiyu asked.

I almost jumped, not hearing her approach behind me.

H7N9 was an avian flu strain. I was certain H7N9S was the mutated strain that Jin had released, and what Arun was looking for.

"I'm not sure," I lied. "We should probably go. Dr. Lu might return soon."

She agreed and pressed a large square release button by the steel door. It sighed open, and we slipped out, making sure the door was securely closed behind us.

"I'd still like to take you to see Vivian, my designer," Daiyu said.

We walked side by side, and her hand brushed against mine, long enough that it didn't feel accidental. It brought a flush of heat through my body, to my annoyance, that she could elicit such a visceral response with the slightest touch. Even with everything else going on during this tour.

The labs behind windows only required a personal code, which Daiyu didn't bother to hide from me when she used it for the third time.

Daiyu greeted a woman in her thirties, who was tall but stocky, her black hair pulled back in a tight bun. The overall effect would have been severe if not for her face lighting up with pleasure when she caught sight of Daiyu. "Miss Jin!" she exclaimed. "What an unexpected surprise." The woman stood beside a long white table with a light blue suit laid across it. It was unfinished, but one sleeve was lit in an intricate webwork of silver stars.

"I was working on a project with my friend"—Daiyu nodded toward me—"and had to stop by to see my favorite designer. How's the new suit coming, Vivian?"

Vivian nodded, barely giving me a glance, but waved Daiyu over to the table. "You came just in time. I was beginning to set the design."

They discussed what Vivian was working on for Daiyu's newest suit: a star theme. Daiyu talked enthusiastically about her favorite Chinese constellations and the stories behind them. I glanced around the large lab where everyone worked diligently at their stations. The entire room was filled with white furnishings, glaring almost in its lack of color other than what was displayed on work screens. One young man in his twenties gave me a curious look. He obviously knew who Daiyu was but went back to his work a moment later. I saw a life-size 3-D rendering of a suit design projected on the back wall of his station.

During their animated discussion, a message flashed across my Vox from Lingyi: Got it. We're good.

A copy of Daiyu's brain wave scan had transferred successfully from Lingyi's device.

By the time we left Jin Corp, over two hours had passed. Ah Ming was still seated in the grand vestibule, and Daiyu gave him a smile as we exited. "Have a good evening, Miss Jin," he shouted after us.

It was past nine, and her white limo pulled up to the curb a minute later. "Want to grab dinner?" Daiyu asked.

I was caught off guard and didn't hide my surprise. "I can't," I said. "I'm meeting someone."

I wanted to report to Lingyi immediately, but I also couldn't go because I *did* want to spend more time with Daiyu. I liked being with her too much. I liked her too much. And it needed to stop. When we parted ways, she drew closer for a hug, but I blocked her by putting a hand on her shoulder. "Thank you for the private tour, Miss Jin," I said.

She smiled a small smile, but not before I saw the disappointment in her eyes.

I had gotten what I needed from her.

My job with Daiyu was done.

Twelve days after Jin's big announcement at the memorial hall park about the cheaper suits and the collapse of Patient Zero, the death toll had risen to over two dozen in Taipei from Jin's flu strain. Although the disease was spreading rapidly, the government had yet to officially declare a state of emergency, as only poor *mei*s had been affected. Many who died were already suffering from illness and had compromised immune systems or were homeless and living on the streets, but Arun assured me that this avian flu was *bad*. "It can wipe out half of Taiwan if we don't do something to curb it," he said. "You *have* to return to Jin Corp and steal a sample for me."

So three days after Daiyu gave me the tour, on a Sunday in the dead of night, I went back.

Just after two a.m., I took my airped and flew to Jin Corp. I was fully suited but disconnected from the com sys so my whereabouts couldn't be tracked. Armed with Daiyu's security code and the capture device that had recorded and could "ghost" her brain waves for the scan (Lingyi had assured me that it *should* work), I let the euphoria overtake me. Racing faster than two hundred mph, I soared over Taipei, the trendier districts filled with young *you*s and *mei*s alike, looking for a good time. The flashing signs and lasers in these areas were a stark contrast to the dark, quiet buildings in places that were abandoned or occupied by the less adventurous, who were fast asleep.

It didn't seem the youth of Taipei were taking notice of the flu epidemic, too jaded to care about another outbreak, and too oblivious to know how lethal this one actually was. So many lives depended on whether I could smuggle one of the samples out for Arun. Failure was not an option.

I guided my airped back into the shadowed labyrinthine streets behind Jin Corp, parking on a narrow, deserted street. Without hesitation, I wound my way through the dank alleyways, my path illuminated by my helmet and suit. This time, I had half a dozen knives hidden on me, although they would be useless if I triggered security and Jin Corp went into lockdown.

Ignoring my increased heart rate displayed in helmet, I found the back entrance that Daiyu wanted to sneak me into the first time we tried to visit Jin Corp. The touch pad was dark but took on a faint glow when I punched in Daiyu's personal code with a gloved hand. I waited, heart pounding in my ears, and the door clicked open quietly after five seconds. I used the motion detection enhance Victor had gotten for me to search for any signs of movement beyond the thick walls. Seeing nothing, I slipped inside.

I was on the ground floor of the emergency stairwell, maybe one I had passed while touring with Daiyu. We had exchanged two brief messages the day after the tour, and nothing since. *Maybe she got the hint*, I thought with regret. Annoyed my mind had wandered to her, I forced myself to focus. Detecting no motion beyond the emergency exit leading into the main part of Jin Corp, I tinted my helmet and stepped into the wide, empty corridor. It was in a part of the ground floor I hadn't passed with Daiyu, but I recognized the general decor, and headed in the direction of the elevator.

Soon, I passed the main vestibule entrance, the Jin suit models and global displays, and stopped at the elevator. The building felt deserted, but my enhance had picked up the security guard sitting at the main entrance. I punched in Daiyu's code, and the elevator came to life and opened its doors to me twenty seconds later. I pressed the third-floor button, praying that Dr. Lu or anyone else would not be pulling an all-nighter this weekend.

Crouching low, I exited the elevator, remembering the glass windows which allowed views into the labs. My motion enhance detected nothing, so I rose. The labs on either side of the corridor had dimmed lights, the eerie silence prickling my skin, even while suited. I walked toward the restricted area, then used my enhance to try and scan for activity behind the vault. The enhance flashed red in helmet: FAILURE.

*Gods!* The vault was too thick for the enhance to work. I had to risk it. Removing my helmet, I stuck the capture device back on the column of the scanner, drew a long breath, and stepped beneath the glass dome. It hummed to life, and I imagined what I'd do if Lingyi's gadget failed. I wore a face mask, hiding the lower part of my face, but everything would be on camera. Our only hope was no one was watching or would have any reason to review tonight's footage. My vision was bathed in blue light, then the scanner fell silent. Pulse racing, I waited for my fate; the steel door eased open several seconds later.

I tucked the device from the column back into a pocket. Lingyi had not failed me. I put my helmet back on and listened at the door's opening. Hearing nothing but the soft whirring of machinery, I went inside and shut the vault behind me. The lights had been dimmed in the empty laboratory, but flickered on to full brightness when I entered. It felt even colder than when I had sneaked in with Daiyu. Going directly to where the flu virus was stored, I peered through the glass top, then carefully removed a duplicate vial from a pocket. Arun had made me a replica that looked exactly like the three stored inside this case from my description. I visually compared the vial to Jin's and was satisfied.

Unless they retested the sample, no one would know the difference.

Putting the decoy vial away, I ran my hands over the rectangular steel case. When I had visited with Daiyu, I didn't get the chance to study how to access the vials. There had been no noticeable touch pad on or near the case. The time ticked away relentlessly for me in helmet. Two thirty-six a.m. already. Gliding over the lower edge of the case, my gloved hand felt the outline of a square button. I pressed, and a touch pad extended outward. The only thing I could think of to do was to enter Daiyu's personal code, knowing it was unlikely she'd have access.

Surprisingly, the glass case lifted open, releasing an even colder burst of air. I took a vial out and slipped our placebo in its place. Securing the sample into a hidden pocket, I exited the lab, relieved to see an empty corridor. Halfway to the elevator, I heard someone whistling a soft tune and wheels being rolled across the tile floor. Cursing, I ducked into one of the doors on the right as a janitor turned the corner.

He hadn't seen me. But just as I was feeling smug over my fast reflexes, the lights in the lab turned on, triggered by my motion; the janitor stopped whistling. "Hello?" he said. "Who's there?"

*Shit!*

I rolled behind a workstation, out of view of the glass windows that lined the entire upper part of the labs. The wheels continued to roll, slower now, coming closer. Then silence, and the *click* of a door opening into the room I was in. "Hey," the janitor said in a gruff voice. "Anybody there?"

I didn't move, didn't breathe. I could take him down with a sleep spell injection if necessary, but that just left a doped-up janitor for someone to find the next morning, giving security reason to go through all their recordings. For the second time that night, I prayed for luck to be on my side.

"Useless technology," the janitor said after a long moment.

He rolled his cleaning cart into the room, and I took advantage of the noise to palm a syringe into my hand. It was a night of crap choices. But he wheeled past my workstation and kept going to the other end of the lab. I observed his retreating back and slipped out of the room, running toward the elevator at a crouch. My clock read 2:49 a.m. in helmet.

The elevator seemed to take much longer to arrive. By the time I exited out the same door I had entered, it was past three a.m. Leaning against it, I slowly let the tension in my muscles go. I'd been sweating without realizing and dialed my suit temp down with a thought command. The moon had all but disappeared behind Taipei's polluted haze, so I used my helmet's glow to light my way. I stopped for a moment and withdrew the vial when someone shoved me hard from behind.

I spun around and saw a *you* boy in a red suit, illuminated with deep purple designs.

"Why did you break into Jin Corp?"

I was so stunned, the boy got another shove in. This time, I glimpsed Daiyu's friend's face behind the helmet: Joseph Chen.

"I didn't break in," I replied in a calm voice.

"Why aren't you connected to the com sys, then?"

He tried to push me again, and I stepped out of the way. "I don't owe you an explanation," I said.

Joseph ripped his helmet off. "Let me *see* you."

I knew what Joseph was itching for—a fight. Ignoring him, I turned to leave. He slammed into me from behind and I spun around. Smacking a palm against my chest, he grabbed for the vial still clutched in my hand. Afraid the vial might shatter between our wrestling over it, Joseph swiped it from me. He held it up, triumphant. "What did you *steal*?"

Pissed, I removed my helmet too. "You followed me."

He grinned. "I live in the 101 too. Saw you in the garage taking off on your airped. I was curious."

"I didn't take anything," I lied. "That's mine. Give it back." My words echoed ominously in the dark alleyway.

"Bullshit," Joseph said. "I *knew* you couldn't be trusted. What is it . . ." He twisted the vial's stopper. "Some kind of drug?"

I clamped my hand over his wrist, gripping hard. He tried to jerk his arm back, but I was much stronger. For all of Joseph's bravado, I was certain the guy'd never been in an actual fight before.

"Whatever," he said and dropped the vial.

I caught it just in time, my heart in my throat. *Gods.* But before I could secure it back into my suit, the clueless *you* boy hit me in the cheek with a loose fist. Pain registered immediately on Joseph's face as he shook his hand. The guy really didn't know how to fight.

I had no choice. I couldn't risk him remembering or following me back to the 101, haranguing me the entire way. I punched him hard in the jaw, hard enough to leave a bruise. Hard enough to make it swell. It had to look like a mugging.

Joseph stumbled back, the whites of his eyes standing out in the dark.

Tucking the vial safely away, I reached for a syringe dosed with a memory-wipe. I stabbed Joseph in the back of his hand.

"What the hell was that?" He stared at me, mouth open, then crumpled to the ground.

I patted him down, searching the hidden pockets in his suit. Cashcard. Six thousand yuan in bills. Taking the notes, I tossed the cashcard on the ground beside him. I checked the Palm tucked in one of his pockets, making certain it was juiced and transmitting his location. I almost felt sorry for him.

He'd have a killer headache tomorrow morning.

Lingyi called for a group meeting the next day.

I went after dropping off the vial at Arun's lab. He thumped me on the shoulder before he took it in his gloved hands. "You kick ass, Zhou!"

I grinned at him. "I hope it's what you need."

He stayed behind and skipped our meeting, wanting to test the sample straightaway.

My friends' energized excitement shot through me the moment I stepped into headquarters. Iris was dangling from a thick rope notched into the twenty-foot ceiling, swinging deftly; she had managed to string red lanterns and paper firecrackers from the high ceiling for the lunar new year. I watched, mesmerized as she maneuvered from one rope to the next. Victor was sitting at the dining table, staring at his Palm. But Lingyi was watching Iris too, her head thrown back so her bob swept against her shoulders. She was grinning, obviously as in awe as I was over Iris's acrobatics. Iris felt Lingyi watching, glanced down and winked at her; there was an openness in her face that only ever emerged for Lingyi.

"All right, Iris," I said. "Stop showing off already."

Iris pinned the last red lantern and gold-trimmed firecrackers before shimmying off the rope as easy as anything. "Zhou. Wait till you see what Victor got for us!"

Vic, hearing his name, joined us in the sitting area. He adjusted his cuff links and straightened his vest.

Lingyi settled onto the red velvet armchair, tucking her feet beneath her and pulling down the hem of her long white skirt. She took all of us in with one sweeping gaze, dark eyes piercing behind her thick black frames, then said, "I've discovered that Jin Corp has a backup site for their security systems in a building located near Snake Alley. Let's call it the citadel. Victor and Iris have already scoped it out, and it isn't as heavily guarded as Jin Corp's main headquarters. Only eight to ten security guards manning it at any given time. Iris and Zhou, I need you two to break into the building so I can access their security system. It's self-contained and completely offline. I need physical proximity to those machines in order to hack in."

"How?" I asked.

"You climb," Victor said. "I got the latest high-tech climbing gear for you to do it too."

Lingyi then proceeded to carefully lay out our plan in detail.

"You're assuming Daiyu's security code for Jin Corp will work at the citadel," I said after we went through everything three times. "What if it doesn't?"

"Then we're screwed," Lingyi replied.

I laughed, and it sounded too loud. "That's reassuring."

"I can work on hacking the touch pad when you're on-site. But the truth is, you can only log in a few tries before alarms go off with

226

security." Lingyi tucked a strand of her thick purple hair behind her ear. "We'd have six tries, tops. And that's nothing when we're talking eight-number combos."

"So Daiyu's code *has* to work," Victor said.

"Zhou said that she has an internship at Jin Corp," Lingyi said. "It'd make sense she'd have high-security clearance, especially as Jin's daughter and successor."

"That's a bit of a leap, though, isn't it?" Victor steepled his fingertips and lifted his eyebrows. "If Iris and Zhou fail, they'll be thrown in jail. Jin won't show mercy in their punishment—he has the best lawyers. But maybe that'd be better than actually succeeding and following through on this suicide mission."

I snorted. "Tell us how you really feel, Vic."

"It *is* a risk," Lingyi agreed.

"We always knew that," I countered.

Lingyi bit her lower lip, then said, "If you or Iris want to abort the mission—"

"I don't," I replied, cutting her off. "I want to do this."

"I'm with Zhou," Iris chimed in. She was in the corner doing chin-ups on the metal bar. I'd never seen her sit for longer than a five-minute stretch.

Lingyi nodded once. "Victor, are you still in?"

"Do I have a choice?" He gave her a lazy smile, eyelids dropping slightly, as if he were ready for a nap. "You lot would be hopeless without me. It's terrible odds, though." He switched to English. "We're gambling with our lives, and the house always wins."

The odds had always been against us, but once committed, I was all in. There was no going back now. We wouldn't know unless we tried.

Lingyi rose. She was the brains behind our group, the hacker, the planner, the boss. But as her friend, I could tell how tense she was and realized how much we had riding on this break-in. If we failed, we were as good as dead.

"I can't stress how important it is to follow the plan exactly as I've laid out." She looked at each of us in turn again and held our gazes long enough so we felt the weight of it. "Am I clear?"

"Yes," we all replied, except for Iris, who had climbed onto the padded platform. Dressed all in black and standing perfectly straight at the edge, head dipped, she reminded me of a match ready to be struck.

"Iris?" Lingyi said, quiet but firm.

Iris executed a perfect backflip onto the floor before she responded, "Yes, boss. I heard you." She stretched her arms overhead like a panther.

Lingyi colored but didn't press the issue. It wasn't like her to get flustered. The stress of running the mission was definitely getting to her.

This break-in had to succeed or our objective would be at a standstill. And time wasn't on our side.

# CHΔPTER TWELVE

Three days after I broke into Jin Corp, I got an unexpected message from Daiyu while I was throwing knives at my target wall. Excitement spiked through me when I saw her icon on my Vox. I was acting like a hopeless, infatuated boy.

Hey, I've been busy with my senior project, but wanted to let you know they found my friend Joe behind Jin Corp, unconscious.

I had been searching for any bit of news on this, but had come across nothing.

What? I responded, unable to ignore the guilt threading through me. What happened?

Looks like a mugging. He woke finally with a fever and is delirious. The doctors think he's caught that flu going around. He can't remember anything.

I broke into a cold sweat. That was not part of the plan. The only way Joseph was exposed to the flu strain was because he had touched the vial I had stolen, or because I was still contagious. Either way, it was *my* fault.

I'm sorry, I replied. I hope he gets better.

But I knew from Arun that he thought the fatality rate of this mutated flu strain was as high as 80 percent.

They've sent him to a quarantined facility outside of Taipei, to try and give him the best treatment. I'm scared for him.

I swallowed hard. There was nothing I could say to comfort her, much less share the ugly truth. *I'm* the reason your friend might die, Daiyu. Please keep yourself safe, I simply said instead.

You too, Jason.

A soft chime; she had disconnected.

I scrubbed a hand through my hair, feeling like an utter ass and a horrible villain.

"Xiao Huang," I said aloud, paging the doorman through the building's com sys.

"Yes, Jason?" He peered at me through my front door's monitor.

"I'd like to send some flowers to Joseph Chen's family. What floor do they live on?" I didn't really want to send flowers; it would have been a disingenuous gesture given the truth, but more so because I wanted to monitor the family.

"I'm sorry, Jason," Xiao Huang mumbled. "That's, er, classified information."

"Why?"

"I've been instructed by the building supervisor not to divulge any information about the Chens." Xiao Huang appeared more pale in my monitor.

"Really," I said. "Because I will come down and get the information from you personally if I have to." I cast a knife at the wall target, and it hit with a satisfying *thunk*. Throwing two more in quick succession, I went on, "I don't think either of us wants that."

I saw the protrusion in Xiao Huang's throat working. "The young Mr. Chen got sick, you see, and now they think his mother, Mrs. Chen, might have caught it too."

"What floor, Huang?"

"The eightieth," he said in a resigned voice.

"Thanks."

"Yes, Jason. But I'd steer clear. They think it's that killer flu strain going around." He clicked off, the first time he'd ended an exchange between us first.

I collected the knives from the board and threw them again, then put on my suit and took the elevator to the eightieth floor. The Chen's grand double doors were blocked with bright yellow tape. One panel stood open, and I glanced inside. Four people wearing orange hazmat suits were in the lavish living room. The government, or Jin's people? Two walked toward the front door, and I quickly slipped back into the elevator, returning to my own apartment on the sixty-eighth floor.

I spent the next hour trawling the undernet for any news of Joseph Chen's illness. Nothing. Since Daiyu knew about her friend falling sick, it made sense that Jin knew as well, and had intervened, quickly covering up the fact that a rich *you* who used his suits had caught the airborne avian flu. It was fine for the *mei*s to get infected, but a *you* suffering the same fate would be poor business.

Even as I came to this conclusion, I saw an unmarked air-ambulance fly from the 101's garage, disappearing into the horizon. I couldn't tell Daiyu what I knew, and I decided not to tell my friends, either. What would it help? I'd just add it to my growing collection of misdeeds and personal sins.

Maybe by the end of all this, I wouldn't be able to look anyone in the eye. Or maybe I'd do just that, and simply not care any longer.

The citadel was situated in the midst of run-down abandoned apartments and shuttered businesses. Only homeless, downtrodden *mei*s came near the area—and even then, they remained hidden in the derelict hovels. It was a ten-story windowless five-sided structure made entirely of concrete, situated in a no-fly zone. That permit alone must have cost Jin a few million at least. The only way in on the ground floor, protected by thick steel doors, was manned by security guards 24/7. The rooftop was unguarded, except for a webwork of sensors protecting it.

Victor and I crouched under the shade of a gutted building. We had paid off the homeless *mei*s who squatted there, giving them money every morning we had arrived, scoping out the citadel's comings and goings. They took the money without a word. Some nodded wearily at us, not meeting our eyes. They were all filthy and disheveled, with that all-too-familiar hunger in their pinched faces. They left Victor and me alone after getting their daily payoff.

It was an unusually warm day in early February—humid, with thick brown smog blotting our anemic sun. Sweat gathered at the back of my neck, slid down between my shoulder blades. For once, I regretted wearing a black T-shirt and missed my temperature-controlled suit. Disgusted with myself, I drew a long breath of our polluted air, pungent with exhaust and the stench of urine. Then had to fight the urge to puke.

"What's wrong with you?" Victor asked. He was dressed as sharp as ever, in a button-down short-sleeved white shirt, tucked neatly into dark gray pants.

"Nothing," I said. "It's been a week already. Are you sure about this?"

Victor peered at me over his designer Italian sunglasses. "The generators are maintained monthly. The tech's due to return soon."

Before he finished speaking, a white van pulled up outside the citadel. The characters for LU'S SERVICE AND SUPPLIES were stenciled in blue across the side. A man in his thirties wearing a navy cap jumped out from the driver's side and slammed his car door shut. He hurried toward the double steel doors, then pulled out his wallet to flash an ID at the door monitor. A few moments later, a security guard from the citadel emerged, dressed in a nondescript gray uniform.

"See?" Victor grinned and cracked his knuckles.

The security guard tramped toward the square concrete building that housed the backup generators adjacent to the citadel. We watched as he unlocked the thick steel door to the building with two different keys, then both men disappeared inside. The two keys were kept on a lanyard, the kind you could put around your neck. About forty minutes later, both men emerged from the generator building.

Victor pulled out the front of his tucked shirt, mussed up his perfect hair, and lurched out from where we had been hiding. By the time the guard had locked the generator building's door again with both keys, Victor had already stumbled across the deserted street, weaving drunkenly and singing in a high-pitched voice. The guard was chatting to the technician in front of his van when Victor

233

waved, before careening head on into the guard. The guard shoved him off, cursing loudly, and Victor veered away from the men to bounce against a tree, almost slipping to the ground. He cowered there, balled up.

I knew Victor had lifted the keys from the guard's pocket and was now taking a 3-D scan of both keys. Sweat collected at my hairline, and I wiped my damp palms against my dark jeans. Vic was a pro, but I was still nervous as hell watching this go down. The man drove off in his van, and the guard disappeared back into the citadel. Victor teetered his way in the same direction, then doubled over, making loud retching noises. He put on such a good show, I was almost convinced he *had* been drinking. When he straightened, I saw that he had discreetly dropped the keys to the ground and proceeded to disappear down another dilapidated side alley. He had said he'd take a circuitous route back to me.

"Make sure the guard comes back out and finds those keys," Victor had instructed. "If he doesn't, go out and find them for him if you have to. Otherwise, they might change the locks and we're screwed."

Not three minutes later, the same guard came out, head swinging from side to side. Victor had made sure he dropped the keys in the direct path the guard had taken back from the generator building, and sure enough, the guard bent down and picked up the keys from the ground, circling his fingers through the lanyard this time, before heading back into the citadel.

Five minutes after that, Victor returned to my side, his shirt tucked back in, his hair smoothed into place, dapper as ever. "We're in, kid."

At least into the generator building. Iris and I still had to climb and break into the actual citadel. But I took Victor's success as a good omen. I wasn't the superstitious type, but we needed all the luck that we could get.

I loped through Snake Alley's covered market. The crowds were thinner on a Thursday night, but there were still enough people out that I blended in with ease. Brightly lit shops and restaurants flanked both sides of this popular Taipei destination. The air was thick with deep-fried foods, cigarette smoke, and more exotic smells. Large snakes nestled in glass cages for customers to gawk at, their thick bodies coiled, appearing ready to strike. Turtles clambered over one another in red and blue plastic tubs, smelling of brine and rotten eggs, so pungent my flimsy face mask was of no help. Made into soups, both the snakes and the turtles were believed to have strong healing and medicinal properties. Although these days, you were as likely to get seriously sick from eating the reptiles due to filth and disease.

More pedestrians had worn heavy-duty face masks since news of the "super" avian flu broke. The government had ordered the slaughter and disposal of thousands of chickens, but the outbreak had already killed dozens of *mei*s and had moved beyond just the homeless or weak. The fatality rate hovered at 80 percent, just as Arun had predicted. It wasn't considered an epidemic, though, because no *you*s had died yet, their lives somehow worth more because they owned more. I realized after my illness that I had survived by sheer luck; having succumbed to a similar strain when I was ten years old, I had built some immunity.

News of Joseph Chen's illness never broke, and four days after I had seen the men with hazmat suits in the Chen's home, the property was put up for sale. Perplexed, I took my airped up to the eightieth floor. The entire home had been emptied of furniture, as if the Chens had never existed. It filled me with a sense of foreboding, as if Jin had murdered the family and I had been an accomplice.

I never messaged Daiyu to follow up on her friend. The longer we didn't speak, the more convinced I was it was better to make a clean break of it.

Unsurprisingly, raffles for Jin's more affordable suits were selling like mooncakes before the midautumn festival. Chinese pop-song beats mingled with the voice of a man talking over a loudspeaker as he demonstrated skinning a thick yellow boa before draining it of its blood. I felt Iris's presence like a twinge at the back of my head. If I turned, I knew I wouldn't be able to spot her, she was so stealthy in her tailing of targets. But she was behind me somewhere. We had agreed to meet at the citadel just a half mile from Snake Alley ten minutes apart. The building was easy enough for Iris to scale, being a stronger and more agile climber than I was. Victor had gotten us climbing shoes and handholds that could stick to concrete as easily as a gecko to a flat wall using van der Waals forces, he'd explained. They were so new on the tech market, they weren't even being sold yet. But Victor had managed to get them, like he got everything else.

The hard part was deactivating the sensors that formed a dome above the top of the citadel, which would trigger Jin's alarms if Iris and I tried to climb onto the building's rooftop. Replicas had been made of both keys to the generator building, and Victor had gotten in without a hitch earlier and turned off the autotransfer switch so backup power wouldn't kick in. Lingyi, hacked into the Taiwan Power Company, was ready to shut down the electricity within a mile radius of the citadel. Now Iris and I just needed to get into the building undetected.

I emerged from Snake Alley and turned down a small side street with a few pedestrians. Dirty walls, iron bars, and endless lines of laundry drying pressed in on both sides. At eleven p.m., the residences were mostly dark and quiet. The farther I walked from Snake Alley, the more deserted it became. Broken windows of empty, abandoned apartments and doorless frames gaped as I passed them. I wondered how many homeless *mei*s were sleeping inside these buildings, which looked ready to collapse at any moment.

I reached the citadel's towering column of concrete, and it reminded me of a giant stone monster. Looking up at the flat, blank wall, I felt the adrenaline course through me. I stretched my arms overhead and rotated my shoulders, loosening up. We had chosen a moonless night to break in, and with the thick smog settled over the city, the area was dark except for two floodlights at the citadel's entrance. Reaching into the pouch slung at my waist, I powdered my hands. I'd never climbed anything so high before, much less without a harness.

I took out the handholds, testing them against the concrete wall. They had short handles as the grips were attached to six-inch circular discs able to adhere to any flat surface. Other than the shoes made of the same material, these were the only things that would be keep-ing us on the wall. As long as we held on. Iris and I had practiced climbing at headquarters with the gear. She took to it straightaway, but it didn't come intuitively for me. I flicked my wrists in the way Victor had shown me to deactivate the handhold's grip on the concrete, practicing several times.

A faint stir of air was the only indication that Iris had arrived. She pulled a black knit cap over her shock of short platinum hair and winked at me. "Hey," she said and tilted her chin up. "Not so bad."

Yeah. Not so bad if I didn't plunge to my death to be flattened like a scallion pancake. "Sure," I said out loud. "Easy."

She grinned, but I could only see the humor in her dark eyes above her face mask. Iris wore the same black cargo pants as I did, and a short-sleeved black tee. Only she had half a dozen syringes sheathed on each side of her pants, within perfect reach to stab someone with a sleep and memory-wipe spell.

"Is the area clear?" Lingyi spoke into our earpieces. She was monitoring all of us on her MacFold from our headquarters. I could picture her in my mind, in a bright tank top, pushing the black frames of her glasses up as she typed. Arun, who wasn't needed for this operation, had some lab crisis to deal with and was the only one in the group not linked in to our com sys.

"Yes, boss," Iris replied. "Will let you know when we're at the top."

She nodded at me and we both pulled on our climbing shoes and strapped on our handholds before gripping their handles. "Go parallel to me," she said and thrust her handhold against the concrete. Iris was eight feet up the side of the wall before I even scrambled on. The pads of my climbing shoes stuck like glue to the concrete and I maneuvered my way upward, getting used to the flicking motion

238

of my wrists and roll of my ankles to deactivate the grips each time.

It was a lot harder than Iris made it look. All my muscles strained as I clung against the wall, heart thumping hard against my ribs. My eyes watered from the polluted air, especially sensitive now that I spent the majority of my time breathing clean, regulated air. I used my legs to push myself upward, driving the handholds against the concrete as I did so. Risking a glance upward, I saw that Iris was already a third of the way up the citadel, climbing like a damned spider. Focusing on building rhythm and momentum, I ascended. There was no room for panic or error.

By the time I reached the top, I was so pumped, I felt I could scale another ten stories. This close, we could see the webwork of pale blue lights that crisscrossed its way over the citadel's rooftop.

"All right, boss," Iris said. "Cut the lights."

"The autotransfer switch is on maintenance bypass mode," Victor interjected from the generator building. "We're good."

Iris and I waited, and I could hear my own breathing as we hugged the cold concrete. "Working on it," Lingyi said. "Hold on."

I blinked the sweat from my eyes. "Any day now, boss."

Iris wasn't even sweating and perched on the wall with such ease, she might have been lounging on a sofa.

"You're a robot, you know that?" I said through gritted teeth.

The corners of her eyes crinkled.

Just then, a buzzing sound arced above our heads, and the city blocks went black around us. Distant honking of cars and mopeds from afar drifted to where we were. People shouted and cursed in panicked voices.

"Now," Iris said, and we both heaved ourselves over the side of the building, clear now of the sensors.

The rooftop was empty. We crouched low to the ground, scanning our surroundings. My scalp and arms tingled, as if the webwork of sensors had left a lingering hum in the air around us.

"We're good, boss," Iris said.

"Great," Lingyi replied.

Just then, the night sky fizzled above our heads and the blue sensors flickered back into place. The blocks surrounding us were once again lit with dim streetlights; the neon signs of Snake Alley flashed in the distance.

"That was twelve seconds," Lingyi said into our earpieces. "The generator never kicked in. If we're lucky, security won't be bothered to check and will assume the power lag was a hiccup. Victor, I need you to hide and clear out if they come around sniffing."

"Got it, boss," Vic said.

Outages were not uncommon in Taipei, and we used that to our advantage.

Iris nodded to me and we stripped off our gear, pulling on our regular shoes and black gloves before running over to the only exit, a single steel door that jutted out from the middle of the empty rooftop. A blue touch pad glowed beside it. Victor had sent a small cambot flying over the building to scout it before our mission. But the winds had been strong, and although we were certain of the webwork sensors, the images of the door and touch pad had been blurry.

"It looks exactly the same as the ones at Jin Corp," I confirmed. "I'll try Daiyu's access code."

Whether Daiyu's code would work in the off-site building was a crapshoot. I punched in her eight-digit code, heart pounding. For five long seconds, nothing. Then a loud whir emitted from the steel door and it *thunk*ed, swinging open inwardly.

"Yes," I said and exchanged high fives with Iris. "We're in, boss."

"Good," Lingyi replied. "You want the ninth floor."

Inside, there was no touch pad, which indicated that the door was designed only to keep people out. I shut it behind us, hoping security hadn't noticed that the rooftop door had been accessed. It was our way in, but also our only way back out. Iris led the way down the narrow stairway, lit by dim blue lights.

I followed her along the concrete steps, which descended at a steep angle. She slunk as silent as a panther, and every scrape of my foot sounded too loud in my own ears. The stairs terminated on the ninth floor; our only exit was the steel door that opened with a push bar. Iris pulled her motion-sensing goggles on, and their green rays sliced through the thick concrete walls. "Clear as far as I can see," she said.

She pushed the bar without hesitation and stepped through, looking both ways, then beckoned with one hand. I was still high on adrenaline, hyperaware of my surroundings, feeling like I could smash through a door or jump between buildings if I had to. The hallway was long and disappeared on both sides in sharp turns due to the five-sided shape of the building. A double steel door stood before us, with the same blue touch pad for security. Iris and I exchanged glances.

I waited while Iris walked the circumference of the floor, scanning for movement beyond the thick data-center walls. Her goggles were able to detect even the slightest twitch—the rise and fall of the chest as a person breathed, when a throat worked as someone swallowed. After a few minutes, which seemed too long, she jogged back into sight and nodded to me. Holding my breath, I punched in Daiyu's access code again. This time, the machine flashed in red: WELCOME JIN DAIYU.

*Crap.*

The double steel doors slid open, expelling a gust of cold air and the smell of machinery. We stepped inside and the doors closed behind us.

"We're in," Iris said to Lingyi. "But the touch pad recognized Daiyu's security code and identified her."

"Will security be notified she's in the building?" I asked, feeling light-headed.

"Unlikely, because they expect to greet every person at the front entrance, so an alert would be unnecessary," Lingyi said into our earpieces. "But it just takes one glance at the logs for whatever reason for this to be over. We need to move." Lingyi sounded in control as always, but I could still detect the edge in her voice. "Once I have access to Jin's security system, I can wipe your use of Daiyu's personal code from their logs."

"Right, boss," I said, flexing my fingers. "I'm ready."

"Are there machines?" Lingyi asked through the earpiece.

"Hundreds," I replied.

Rows and rows of steel racks housed blinking servers. A low hum vibrated through the expansive concrete space. The data center was also five-sided with a ten-foot ceiling, dimly lit with blue lights at each corner where the five walls met. I clicked my Vox on to bright to use as a flashlight, walking down a random row of machines. "What am I looking for?" I asked.

"The security servers are housed on this floor," Lingyi said. "Any one of them will do."

I walked down a dark row, surrounded by blinking green and blue lights, with an occasional red or flash of yellow, and chose a server farther away from the entrance. "Got it."

Iris had disappeared down another row of machines, prowling as she always did.

"Are the lights all blinking in one color?" Lingyi said in my earpiece.

"Yes. Blue."

"Perfect," Lingyi said. "Just turn on the Palm I gave you and direct it in front of those blinking lights. Press the green door icon."

I did as she said. The door icon vibrated when I pushed it and emitted a green ray of light onto the rectangular server in front of me. "Done."

"Now, just hold still," Lingyi said. "And hope that this works."

The vents expelling the cold air hummed around me as I stood motionless, praying to the Goddess of Mercy. I wasn't religious, but it couldn't hurt. Lingyi had explained that Jin's security system was entirely contained and offline. It was why breaking in and gaining access was crucial; otherwise, there was no possible way to infiltrate their systems. Lingyi needed physical proximity.

"Doppelganger's doing its thing," Lingyi said, her pitch slightly raised in excitement. "It's almost in."

Lingyi had written Doppelganger, a program that, instead of breaking into Jin Corp's security system, would mimic itself as part of the system. *We don't try and trample through the impossible doors they've built*, she had explained in easy terms for us nonhackers. *We wedge into the frame and then slither our way in.*

Nine minutes later, according to my Vox, the blinking lights on the server suddenly all began to flash yellow.

"Uh. Boss . . . ," I said.

"I see it. I know," she replied. I could hear rapid and soft clicking as she worked on her keyboard. "Hold on."

Sweat dampened my forehead and the back of my neck, despite the chill air whirling around me. Iris appeared from nowhere like a phantom by my side. Neither of us spoke. The yellow lights blinked five times in rapid succession, then all turned a solid glowing blue again. The green door icon on the Palm swung open, and a small female cartoon with Lingyi's purple hair pranced out, then proceeded to do a jerky, triumphant jig.

"We're in!" Lingyi said.

*And when we get in, we make ourselves look exactly like the rest. We make the system think we've been there all along.* Then Lingyi waved both her hands with a flourish, as if she were doing a magic trick.

"You did it!" I exclaimed. Iris and I bumped fists in celebration.

Lingyi's laughter carried through so clearly, it was as if she were in the data center with us. "Not without your help." Her elation was palpable. "Now get the hell out of there!"

"Right, boss," I said. Tucking my Palm away, I waited as Iris checked the vicinity with her goggles, then nodded, and we quickly left the data center and were back in the stairwell within minutes. Again, Iris led the way. When we pushed through the exit door, the air felt damp and warm compared to the dry, cold air within the citadel.

"Can you cut the lights for us again, boss?" Iris asked.

"I'm good to go," Victor said from the generator building.

We waited near the wall, careful not to trigger the blue sensors. Aircars wreathed in neon zipped in the far horizon, headed toward the high-rise districts, where the parties were just beginning at this hour for the *yous*.

Lingyi cursed again. "The power company's shut me out. They must have rebooted the system after the initial blackout I forced." She was typing faster than she was speaking. "It'd take a few hours for me to hack in again. I've got access to the citadel's security system through our Doppelganger program, but activating a shutdown of the sensors will give me away. You're just going to have to risk triggering their alarms. If we're lucky, it'll still work out."

"Crap," I said.

Iris was already pulling on her climbing gear, cool as ever. "We'll deal with trouble as it comes, boss." She tilted her chin up at me. "You're a good fighter, right? And a fast runner."

I laughed despite myself as I pulled on my gear too. "I'm a survivor."

"I can back up on the ground," Victor added through the earpiece.

"Stay hidden unless needed," Lingyi ordered. "The fewer people involved, the better."

"Got it, boss," Victor replied.

"Go when I go," Iris instructed. "Side by side, like on the way up." We both went to the wall's edge, facing the fifteen-story drop below. "Ready?" Iris asked.

I nodded, rolling my wrists.

She hoisted herself onto the shoulder-level wall with ease, and I followed. The entire rooftop flooded in red lights the minute we triggered the sensors. I slammed my handholds into the concrete wall, trying to find purchase with my shoes. Going down was much more difficult and awkward than the climb up. An alarm blared even as pulsing red light filled our vision.

"They've put the building on lockdown," Lingyi said. "I'm monitoring everything from within."

I wrenched my arm in my rush, not deactivating the handhold with the necessary wrist flick, and swung out from the building, clinging on by one grip and one foot. My heart leaped into my throat; I was certain I'd fall to my death.

"Steady," Iris said, and her calm voice brought everything back into focus, even as the blood roared in my ears.

I flexed my arm still connected to the wall and pulled myself back, muscles straining, then thrust my shoe against the concrete, making sure I had a firm hold with all limbs before descending again, falling into a quick rhythm.

"They're sending five men out," Lingyi said. "They've scanned the cam recordings, but I'd wiped everything, so they think you failed on your attempt to break *in*. Exactly as I'd hoped. They're waiting to intercept you on the bottom for questioning."

Iris jumped down onto the ground just as two men rushed toward her with red tasers drawn. Before I even reached the ground, she had kicked the tasers from the hands of the two men and twisted one's arm behind his back, before stabbing him in the neck with an injection. The big guy immediately slumped to the ground. I landed as she pulled two more syringes from the side of her pants in one swift motion, and jammed one into the throat of the guard scrambling on the ground for his weapon. He dropped like a sack of rice. The other three guards arrived, shouting in alarm as I flung my handholds down and reached for my throwing knives. One. Two. I knocked the tasers out of their hands, drawing blood from only one of the guards as Iris dispatched her third.

The unwounded guard charged at me, swinging wildly, eyes bulging. I ducked easily and punched him in the face, my knuckles exploding from the contact. He never knew what hit him when Iris slipped behind and stuck the injection at the back of his neck. He folded like raw, boneless chicken.

"Done," Iris said. Her breathing had picked up, and there was a sheen of sweat on her face, but her expression gave nothing away.

I got my handholds and had to dig around for my knives, rolling a guard over to retrieve one of them. My pulse was racing, and my hand tremored when I tucked the knives away.

"Security inside doesn't suspect a thing. They've never had a break-in before," Lingyi said into our earpieces. "They're waiting for the guards to bring you two back trussed like pigs. Time to disappear."

"I'm already out," Victor replied in our earpieces. "You guys were pros."

I imagined him making his way down a dark, narrow street. I

would bet money he had a nice dress shirt and cuff links on. Even for a break-in.

Iris nodded once at me, as if she were sealing a deal with a business partner, then turned and dashed into the night. I took a twisting alleyway on the opposite side. We'd see each other again at headquarters.

"You did good," Iris said into my earpiece. "I think those guards were out of practice." I could hear her smug confidence.

"You're a machine," I replied to Iris, breathless, because I was sprinting at full speed.

Lingyi's familiar chuckle came from across the ether. "That's why I love her."

# CHAPTER THIRTEEN

We met at headquarters two days later to debrief. On my way there, I grabbed five orders of scallion pancakes and fried dough wrapped in sesame flatbread for my friends from one of the stands on the street, smiling when the *mei* girl gave me a free hot soy milk for the large order.

Lingyi met me at the door, ecstatic and glowing, and assured us that Doppelganger had insinuated itself completely into Jin Corp's security system. She had spent much of the last forty-eight hours glued to her MacFold, studying Jin Corp's layout and inner workings—devising the best way to infiltrate and blow up the building.

"The easiest way is to trigger the fire alarm," Lingyi said. We were eating in the sitting area as she brainstormed aloud. "Jin Corp has a tight protocol set in place. All employees must evacuate the building within ten minutes, then are allowed to return ten minutes after. That gives us twenty minutes."

"I would suggest detonating the bombs within three minutes after the building has cleared," Victor said, which led to a long discussion on the logistics of where the bombs should be placed and how many were needed.

"During the fire alarm, Jin Corp's main security system will give access to the backup—in case of emergency. This means I'll have full control of the system." Lingyi projected images and video of Jin Corp's interior and floor plans as we continued to talk through possibilities. After two hours, Lingyi called for a break. But as I rose from the sofa, she said to me, "You should cool things off with Daiyu. You got what you needed from her."

I blanched, and Victor raised one dark eyebrow. It sounded so cruel when spoken aloud, even though that had been my same exact thought after Daiyu had given me a tour of Jin Corp.

"I haven't talked to her in a while," I lied. In truth, guilt had gotten the best of me, and I had messaged her to ask if she had news about Joseph. Daiyu responded that he was still quarantined in the facility outside of Taipei and recuperating.

Iris grabbed an apple from the bowl on the kitchen counter, every movement spare and smooth. "You're losing interest, that's all. You can play that, right?"

I could feel Lingyi scrutinizing me over her MacFold.

"I don't think it hurts to have Zhou continue to woo her," Victor said. "It's always good to keep the enemy close."

"There's sense in that," I replied before I could control my traitorous mouth. "It could be to our advantage if we remained friends."

I'd made the mistake of agreeing with Vic, something I rarely did.

"Wait," Lingyi said, tapping her hot pink fingernails against the glass table. "You don't actually *like* her, do you?"

I felt all eyes turn to me. Arun folded his arms across his chest.

He had tipped his orange spiked hair with indigo dye and looked like an aggressive rooster.

"And so what if he does?" Victor leaned back in the armchair. "As long as it doesn't interfere with him gathering intel. Not everyone can turn their feelings off so easily, Lingyi," he drawled.

The chamber went silent, like we had all sucked in a breath and held it. Lingyi colored, and Iris gave half an eye roll, then continued her push-up sets in the corner. Arun stared at his boots, seemingly fascinated by the laces. Lingyi, Iris, and Vic worked together well enough, but he had never hinted at his feelings for Lingyi so pointedly before. He had always acted like he didn't care, pretended to be unaffected. But we all knew the truth.

They had only dated a few months before Lingyi ended things, soon after Iris joined our group. Neither discussed the breakup with me, but it was clear enough that Lingyi thought it was more casual than Victor had. He tried to appear blasé, but he had fallen hard for her. Although he'd had plenty of hookups, Vic hadn't seen anyone seriously since.

After a long moment, Lingyi said, "Feelings can complicate things. . . ."

Victor's dark gaze slid to Lingyi, and she opened her mouth as if to say more, then clamped it shut again. "Victor, if you want to talk—"

He gave a nonchalant flip of his hand. "No. I don't want to talk. You're the boss." Vic flashed Lingyi a charming smile and winked. "But you should respect Zhou's choice. He knows what he's doing."

*Do I?*

I shrugged and kept my face smooth. "Whatever. It's over."

I proceeded to ignore Daiyu's calls and messages to me in the next few days, chucking my Vox onto the bed each time and shoving a pillow over it—annoyed with myself over how much I *did* want to talk to her.

How much I missed her.

The next day, Arun messaged me via Vox: Bad situation. Headquarters now.

I left the 101 by the back exit, the one used by celebrities to dodge paparazzi. But I used it to avoid having people wonder why I was leaving without my suit on. I couldn't go to headquarters suited as a *you* boy—it'd draw too much attention.

The crowds were thin this morning. Another dozen *mei*s had died in the past three days from the new super avian flu strain that had yet to be officially identified by our media. Experts reassured the public that although the fatality rate was higher than normal, most deaths happened to those who were already suffering from secondary illnesses or had seriously compromised immune systems. Instead of just normally compromised immune systems, downplaying the fact that it was airborne among the *mei*s living in hovels and on the streets. They failed to notify the public that this flu had already spread among young and healthy *mei*s, and they were dying too.

But the undernet was humming with the news and speculating on government conspiracies, keeping tally of their own death count.

I thrust my hands into my leather jacket, not meeting anyone's eyes in the gray haze that blanketed our city. Despite the face mask

I had strapped on, the reek of petrol and automobile fumes still suffused my every drawn breath. I was relieved to turn onto our headquarters' empty street, to get away from the pedestrians drifting through the sidewalks with hacking coughs, the honking of taxis, and the loud noise of mopeds.

I knocked on our headquarters' worn wooden door and it unbolted without Lingyi answering, filling me with unease. I stepped inside, and the heavy door whirred shut. My stomach clenched at the scene before me. Iris and Lingyi were laid side by side on makeshift beds in the sitting area, reminding me of corpses. Both girls were pale, with bright spots on their cheeks—the only reason I knew that they weren't actually dead.

They'd caught the super avian flu strain.

The sofa and chairs had been pushed against the walls. Arun was crouched over Iris, feeling for the pulse at her wrist, then resting his gloved hand against her brow. He wore his yellow hazmat suit that I knew he kept at his lab for experiments. It was as if we were in a biological warfare zone.

The window was shuttered, and he had the lights dimmed, so the room felt dark and somber, reminding me of a crypt. Arun lifted his eyes. I could see they were red-rimmed, even behind his full face mask.

"Zhou." His voice was rough, muffled. "I was coming over to give Lingyi an update."

It hadn't taken more than a few days for Arun to confirm that the H7N9S sample I had taken from Jin Corp was the mutated airborne strain that had been released in Liberty Square.

"I've been working nonstop to try and get my antidote to work," Arun said. "I'm so close, I can almost feel my mother's presence in the lab with me." He drew a long breath that shook.

My friend shifted his gaze to the girls. He appeared insect-like with the gear obscuring his face. "When I arrived, they were both already fevered and delirious."

I knew for certain they hadn't gotten ill from me. I had stayed away from all my friends while I was still contagious. But the flu was too widespread now, with a panicked government that had done nothing to intervene.

Arun struggled to his feet, as if he were an old man instead of eighteen. "Don't worry. You can't catch the same flu twice. That's why I didn't bring a respirator for you."

"They're not protected," I said, panic rising. My throat worked. "They've never had the avian flu."

In that moment, we both jumped from the loud *thud*ding at the front door. "Let me in!" Victor shouted.

Arun sighed and clicked on his Palm to speak through the hidden intercom over the door. "We can't risk you getting sick too, Victor."

"Zhou's there," Victor said accusingly.

"He's already had this flu."

"I don't give a shit," he shouted, sounding completely unlike himself. I'd never heard Victor raise his voice before. The front door *thud*ded again, even louder this time. Victor was kicking at it—with his expensively made shoes. He *must* be pissed. Frantic. "Let me in!" he roared.

Arun and I exchanged glances and he shrugged, pulling a full face respirator from his backpack along with a pair of gloves. "He'll lose it if we don't let him in," he said, and released the door a breadth, so Victor couldn't push his way in. "Put these on first. No guarantee you won't catch it, though. Your risk to take."

I heard Victor grunt in anger, then Arun released the door all the way and Victor trampled through, like an elephant ready to charge. He was dressed in a gray pin-striped suit; the clear respirator looked incongruous over his tanned face. His eyes widened when he saw the girls. "We need to get them to the hospital," Victor said, rounding on us both. "What are you two doing standing there like fools?"

Arun tried to clasp Victor's shoulder, but he jerked away, crouching down by Lingyi. He swept a damp lock of purple hair from her brow. "Sweetheart," he murmured in English.

"A doctor won't be able to do anything for them," Arun replied in a quiet voice. "The hospitals are overwhelmed. It's better to keep them quarantined here. And it's safer to keep our anonymity—"

Victor leaped to his feet, fists clenched. "You're putting the mission before their lives?"

"We all put the mission before our own lives when we agreed to this," I said.

Victor pivoted and cocked his elbow, as if he were ready to hit me, but instead shoved me hard by the shoulders. I reeled backward but caught myself. "Besides, it's what Lingyi wanted. No way she would have us compromise the mission," I said. "Not now. Not after all we've gone through to get this far." I returned Victor's glare with my own, my face feeling hot and tight.

"I went along with your haphazard schemes, and look where it got us." He threw a hand toward the girls, dark eyes bright with tears. "Lingyi would never have agreed to any of this if you hadn't pushed for it, Zhou!"

I lunged at him, and Arun intercepted; our bodies slammed, knocking the breath from me. "Lingyi does what she wants. She believes in this mission. I know you love her—"

Victor made an involuntary choking noise, and my anger dissipated. He was lashing out in fear and pain, I recognized that. I'd done it plenty of times myself. I swallowed and forced my voice steady. "But Jin did this. He released the flu strain so he could make more money at the cost of *mei* lives. It's why we have to follow through."

Arun grabbed Victor by the arm. "I'm keeping them hydrated and checking their temps. The doctors can't do any more than that." Arun loosened his grip on Victor, then flexed the fingers of both hands, as if he wanted to throttle something. Arun looked like he was about to throw up.

I refused to give in to the panic or fear, because underlying that was a familiar helplessness and despair. Something I had never wanted to feel again after watching my mother die. An eerie calm settled over me. I would do anything to make certain my friends survived.

"Arun, sit down," I said, moving toward him. "Maybe you caught it too."

Arun slumped down on the sofa pushed up against the wall, head bowed as if it were too heavy to lift up. "It's not that." He let out a sigh that misted his respirator for a moment. "I've got an antidote."

Victor fell to his knees in front of Arun, not giving a thought to his tailored pants. He took Arun by a shoulder, so tightly Victor's knuckles went white. Arun didn't even seem to register Victor's iron grip. "You have an antidote for this?" Victor spoke slow and deliberate. "And you haven't given it to them?"

"I can't!" Arun cried. "It's my newest batch. And the last time . . ." He punched a fist into his thigh. "Zhou, you saw what can happen. The lab monkeys hemorrhaged to death. I can't risk that on Lingyi and Iris!"

"But you've developed a newer antidote, right?" I asked.

Arun nodded, eyes wide and solemn. "This latest batch hasn't been tested yet."

"So test it!" I said.

"The monkeys won't arrive for two more days," Arun replied. "And even then, I'd have to infect them with the flu virus first. From everything I've gathered on the undernet, this super avian flu hits heavy and fast. We don't have time."

One glance at the deathly pale faces of the girls, and I knew he was right.

"They have an eighty percent chance of dying from this, Arun," Victor said. "Don't you think it's worth the risk?"

"If they died from my antidote—," Arun said.

"They'll probably die anyway if you aren't willing to help," Victor cut him off, sounding furious. "I'll inject them myself if I have to. I know you brought the antidote; I can see it in your face." He jumped to his feet and stalked over to Arun's open backpack.

"All right!" Arun rose, following. "I'll do it."

Victor stepped out of the way, and Arun retrieved a long case, pulling two syringes from it. "I'll do it," he said again, barely audible this time.

"I agree with Victor," I said. "You said yourself you were so close."

Arun shook his head. "'So close' is not good enough in science. 'So close' is not what you inject into your friends. But you're right: It's worth the risk if you look at it from a statistical vantage point."

I almost smiled, because this was so Arun. I was certain he didn't agree to use the antidote because of our emotional pleas. Arun had agreed because he had done the mathematical probability in his head.

He crouched by Iris and uncapped the syringe, but his hand shook too much as he held it near the crook of her elbow. He straightened and drew deep breaths until he leaned down again, this time, injecting the antidote into Iris's arm. Arun then moved to Lingyi's bedside and did the same.

Victor and I stood at the feet of their beds, silent, like witnesses in some ancient ritual. Arun joined us after he was done, fists clenched at his sides. "Now we wait," he said.

"How long before we know?" I asked, my eyes never leaving the girls' pallid faces.

"If the nanobots do what they're supposed to, it'll take a few hours for them to stunt the existing H7N9S viruses in their systems. Then it's a matter of waiting for their immune systems to take over." Victor folded his arms across his chest. "We'll know within eight hours how this will go."

Victor threw an arm around Arun, and Arun let him. "They'll be all right," Victor said, trying to sound confident. "They're strong. They'll pull through."

Arun slung his arm around my shoulder too, so we stood together, like oath brothers. My heart felt heavy. I wanted to believe him.

We stayed with the girls. Their complexions remained pale, with a bright flush in their cheeks. Both began to shift more in their beds, sometimes mumbling incoherently, or moaning as if in pain. They succumbed to ragged coughs, even in their sleep. Half-conscious, Iris's eyelids fluttered once, and I took the opportunity to prop her up gently, giving her water to drink. She opened her eyes fully after she finished the cup, but they didn't focus on me. Instead, she turned her head toward Lingyi, and a small whimper escaped from between her lips, a weak noise that I would never have expected from her. Iris, who was unfazed in any situation, who seemed indestructible. Quick to wink and smile, quick to rebel, but always emotionally distant somehow. Closed.

I laid her head gently down, and her lashes flickered again, as if she was struggling to remain conscious. Then, with obvious effort, her arm snaked out from beneath the thin sheet, damp from her sweat, and she reached over to clasp Lingyi's forearm. Lingyi didn't stir. Iris's fingers worked slowly, like a lumbering spider, toward Lingyi's wrist, before gripping Lingyi's hand in her own.

Iris let out a soft sigh, and her eyes closed. But she never let go of Lingyi's hand.

Arun had pulled up a chair and sat five feet away from us, palms clasped. His leg jittered. I didn't think he was even aware of it. If the nanobots' programming went haywire, Arun had explained, if they began to self-replicate by themselves or infiltrated an organ—

the brain, the heart, the lungs—if the nanobots went rogue, the girls could be dead within hours. The damage to their internal systems would be quick, painful, and irreversible.

I remembered the monkeys' convulsing bodies in those clear cages, blood dribbling from their noses and mouths, and had to force myself not to shudder.

Behind me, I could hear Victor pacing, back and forth, back and forth, with restrained grief and fury. I had been designated the main caretaker, since I had already had this flu. I wiped the girls' faces and upper chests with a cold, damp cloth, trying to cool their fevers. Three hours in, Arun gave me a large iced sugarcane juice to drink, along with two hot steamed pork buns. "You need to give yourself some fuel too," he said. And although I had no appetite, I washed my hands and ate and drank everything.

Arun's brown complexion had an underlying pallor I'd seen after his mom died. He hovered over me, then walked circles around the sitting area, flicking his eyes toward the girls nonstop.

"Is it my imagination or are they looking more flushed?" Victor asked.

I touched Lingyi's forehead. "She's burning up." I scrambled to Iris and touched her cheek—she felt just as hot. I took their temperatures, and both had fevers over 103°F. My heart raced, feeling helpless.

"This can't be good," I said, barely choking the words out. "They're getting worse."

Arun gave me another bucket of iced water. He wrung out a cloth and passed it to me. "All we can do is to try and keep them cool for now. Their bodies are fighting the virus. They might get worse before they get better."

But Arun looked like I felt—like we were ready to cry at any moment.

I ran the cold cloth under Lingyi's chin, across her shoulder blades and her upper chest. She was dressed in a light blue tank top—her favorite article of clothing, in a rainbow of bright colors, no matter what the weather. I then did the same for Iris. Her arms were slack, weighted. It was hard to believe it was these same arms that had taken down three guards with lightning speed just a few nights ago, the same arms that could climb and strike with such strength.

Another three hours passed, and we said nothing to each other. Time seemed to stretch on endlessly, as I tried my best not to follow the girls' every breath, deathly afraid that this one might be their last. The only sounds within our headquarters were the ragged coughing fits from Iris and Lingyi that rattled their entire bodies. I gave them water when I could and continued to try to cool them down with a damp cloth.

In the early evening, Arun stopped midpace and said, "I think they're looking less feverish."

I had been watching the girls so closely, my vision felt blurred. I touched Lingyi's cheek, then Iris's, then took their temperatures. "They're both just below 100°F!"

"Yes!" Arun exclaimed. "The antidote must be working."

"Thank the gods," Victor muttered, cracking his knuckles with nervous tension, his gaze focused on Lingyi's face. He looked ready to collapse to his knees.

Lingyi's straight, black eyebrows were drawn slightly together, as if she were anxious or vexed. If I had any doubt of Victor's feelings for her before, I didn't anymore. I felt for him. Why was it that we so often desired someone we could never have?

Arun rubbed his temples. "We aren't in the clear yet. These next few hours are critical. But I can't stand to just watch anymore." He looked like he'd tug out his own hair if he could. "I'm going to make some rice porridge," he said. "I have to do something."

Victor, who considered himself the better chef, followed Arun into the kitchen. I was glad. He needed something to keep himself occupied too. Vic, who was always so blasé about everything, was beside himself with worry.

I listened to the two bang around in the kitchen as they cooked together, and I sat down at the end of Lingyi's bed, resting a hand on her knee. Some time later, she opened her eyes and stared at me. "Zhou," she croaked.

"Hey," I said, smiling, trying to sound normal. My fingertips tingled from overwhelming relief. It felt as if my heart had been in my throat the entire day. "How do you feel?"

"Like shit," she rasped, then broke into a dry cough.

I went to ease her up and helped her drink some water. She gulped thirstily, then collapsed back on the pillow. Suddenly aware that she was clutching Iris's hand, she bolted upright again. "Is she okay?" Lingyi asked, frantic. I squeezed her arm, trying to calm her.

"She'll be fine, boss," Arun said. "You're both recovering nicely." He and Victor had come over the minute they saw Lingyi had woken.

Lingyi eased herself onto her side, so she was facing Iris. "Dar-

262

ling?" she whispered in English, then trailed her fingertips down Iris's arm, before cupping her face, gentle as a lover. "Iris, my heart, come back to me." This time in Mandarin.

And it was as if I had been kicked in the chest. I could feel Arun and Victor stiffen in shock behind me. They were as surprised as I was. Lingyi and Iris had been together for two years. We all knew it. But neither had ever been overt with displays of affection, not physically or in words. They had always been very private in their relationship. So much so that I'd often forget they were an item—other than the fact that wherever Lingyi was, Iris was almost always near, like a lethal shadow.

Iris gave a soft groan, and her eyes fluttered open. I'd never seen her so exposed, so unguarded; she appeared younger than her seventeen years. Her face was soft, not composed, masked as it usually was behind a smirk or wink. "Lingyi, I'm so sorry," she said. "I think I caught it first—"

"I could never regret our kisses." Lingyi's mouth twisted into a weak grin. "You didn't know." She rose onto her elbow and stroked Iris's face again, gazing down at her with tenderness.

Iris returned Lingyi's look. We all had our defenses, our hard surfaces, but Iris had built a wall higher than anyone I knew. Now I saw the love that filled her eyes, something that she had always tamped down when she was around us. To appear tougher, untouched, and unaffected? I didn't know.

But I understood her hesitation, the instinct for self-sufficiency for the sake of survival. Loving someone was risky. Loving someone left all your weaknesses exposed.

The other two guys finally stirred behind me. We exchanged

glances, our surprised expressions mirroring each other's. Victor went to kneel by Lingyi's bedside and spoke her name in a choked whisper.

"If you say something inane, man," Arun interjected, "I'll punch you in the mouth."

I laughed, surprising myself. My arms felt limp from relief that the worst of it seemed over, and I was emotionally wrung out. I'd risked my own life before—kidnapping Daiyu, breaking into Jin Corp—and had faced illness and death. But seeing it happen to my friends, that was different.

Victor ignored Arun. "I couldn't bear the thought of losing you, Lingyi," he said. "*We* can't lose you. You're the heart of our mission—the core of our group."

"No one's losing me. I'll be here to boss you forever," Lingyi murmured, then turned to him and smiled. A hesitant smile, almost shy if I didn't know Lingyi better.

Vic cleared his throat, but he smiled back, just a fraction. "I'm holding you to that." Still masked, Victor "kissed" his gloved hand, then pressed it against Lingyi's cheek.

As he half turned his face away from the girls, I saw his eyes were shadowed, the raw pain flashing across his features before he composed himself in a heartbeat. To Victor, being put together meant never letting others know how you truly felt. He wanted us to believe that nothing mattered to him except his next deal, and the profit he'd make. He didn't realize how much he gave himself away to those he was close to. Vic always had our backs and cared deeply, for his friends and for a better Taiwan. If I ever told Victor that I knew it was all a front, he'd be pissed.

We clustered there, with Arun clasping my shoulder, and my hand resting on Lingyi's knee. Victor cupped her face a moment longer as she and Iris laced their fingers together. Connected. Unified. And of one mind on the task that lay before us.

It should have made us strong, but instead I was suddenly struck by our fragility. How we were playing with danger and poised on the brink with a deadly plunge downward.

Victor was right. I loved each of them like family, and I had led them to this precipice.

Later that evening, Lingyi and Iris were well enough to eat the rice porridge, smoked chicken, and pickled cucumbers Victor had prepared for them. Arun had also stir-fried some long beans for us slathered in garlic and scallions, filling the dining room with their mouthwatering aroma. The girls were weak, but their temperatures were almost normal. Even their coughs had subsided. I ate with them while Victor and Arun left to get something from a cafe. The girls could be contagious for up to a week, Arun had said.

Daiyu messaged me after dinner. I hated how my chest tightened just from seeing her name on my Vox. Are you avoiding me? she asked. I stared at the message, irritated by the conflicting emotions she stirred in me. I turned off my Vox, ignoring it, while Iris and Lingyi chatted with each other about a new film they wanted to see once they recovered. Their heads leaned in, forming a space that included only each other, openly intimate. Almost dying from this flu had changed them.

Drumming the glass table with my fingers, I tapped my Vox back on after a few moments. Sorry, I replied. Friends have been sick. Ten seconds later, she responded: Sorry to hear. See you soon?

I rubbed my eyes, knee bouncing beneath the glass dining table.

Lingyi touched my arm. "You okay?"

I nodded without looking at her.

Then I unstrapped the Vox from my wrist, put it on silent, and shoved it into my jacket pocket.

Arun and Victor returned two hours later. They both hauled groceries; fruits, vegetables, and bottles of fresh juices and iced teas peeked from the tops of their overstuffed bags. Victor brewed chrysanthemum tea before joining us at the dining table. Iris and Lingyi sat with blankets wrapped around their shoulders and their knees pulled up, snuggled against each other.

"You're both looking much better," Arun said. "How do you feel?" He'd put his hazmat suit back on before entering headquarters, and Victor still wore his respirator.

"Human again," Iris replied. "This flu strain is no joke."

Lingyi nodded. "Arun, your antidote saved us."

Arun tucked his chin, a flush coloring his cheeks. "Yeah. I'd tested it with mixed results before. This new batch hadn't been tested. Didn't think I'd be using my friends as test subjects." He exhaled a long breath.

"We didn't give Arun much of a choice," I said.

Lingyi blew Arun a kiss. "You're amazing. *This* is amazing. Do you have more antidote stocked?"

"A dozen," Arun replied. "But my lab can replicate more in a few hours."

"We can release the antidote to the public and help curb the spread of this flu," Iris said. "Prevent more *mei*s from dying."

Arun shook his head. "It hasn't been approved yet by our FDA. There's no way the hospitals will distribute this."

Lingyi made a frustrated noise.

"Then let's take this to the streets ourselves," I replied.

My friends all stared at me, and I grinned. "Seriously. Victor, you've got networks everywhere. Arun and you can head the operation."

"It probably can't save those who are too far gone—but it can help many of the others." Arun's dark brown eyes were bright with excitement. "It can help to contain the spread of this flu if we get to enough of those afflicted in time."

Victor was already on his Palm, typing swiftly. "They're burning the bodies," he said in a grim voice.

"What?" I said.

"My contacts confirmed that the government has been burning the bodies of those who have died from this flu and rounding up other *mei*s who appear to be sick and quarantining them in warehouses."

"Locking them in, you mean," Lingyi replied.

"But I've not heard any of this on the news broadcasts!" I exclaimed.

"They're downplaying it to avoid panic spreading," Arun said. "And endangering the public at the same time."

"Still, Jin's plan is working." Victor actually sneered, evident even beneath his respirator, the openness of it so discordant with his usual smooth facade. "The sales of raffles and orders for his new, cheaper suits have skyrocketed with each passing day—no matter how much the government and media have tried to spin it."

"And knowing what I know about viruses," Arun added, "Jin's suits can't guarantee the wearer from getting sick. Look what happened to Zhou. Viruses *will* find a way."

"We're getting shafted from all sides." I felt rage swell along with all the emotions I had tried to suppress when the girls' lives were in danger.

"Not if we can help it," Victor replied. "The warehouses aren't even guarded, according to my source. It'll be easy enough for us to break into those sites and administer the antidotes."

"We can take to the streets, too, set up discreet 'vaccination' stations," Arun said.

Lingyi nodded. "Iris and I are out, but I can monitor news of the flu on the undernet. Track where it spreads on top of Victor's contacts."

"I can help on-site," I offered, but Lingyi shook her head.

"We can't risk you blowing your cover, Zhou. Better to keep away in case someone recognizes 'Jason.'" Lingyi yawned, looking wan and exhausted, and Iris put her arm around Lingyi's shoulders, hugging her close. Iris's platinum hair contrasted like a lick of white flame against Lingyi's deep purple. "Victor and Arun can handle this," Lingyi said.

"I could use Zhou's help," Arun replied. "I've asked for two more hazmat suits at my lab, so you won't be able to see his face clearly anyway. With a third person, we'd be able to move faster and save more lives."

"I want to," I added. "I promise to be careful."

Lingyi studied both of us in turn, then agreed with reluctance. "Because it'll save more lives," she repeated. Although she's the one who knew the most about my past, I had never gone into detail regarding my mother's death. But Lingyi nodded to me once, and I suspected she knew how much this meant to me personally.

I bumped fists with Arun, glad I could actively help the sick *mei*s and contribute. I thought of the memoir *Grass Soup*. Zhang endured decades of prison and labor camps during the Cultural Revolution and did everything he could to survive—including eating grass soup.

I knew that the Taiwanese people's will was strong—that we endured. But we needed at least a fighting chance.

# CHΔPTER FOURTEEN

We decided to meet Arun on campus at his lab the next evening, giving ourselves some time to rest, and also time to manufacture more antidote.

I was exhausted and headed back home to sleep. Long moments passed before I realized I thought of my apartment in the 101 as "home" now.

Getting off a few stops early, I walked the rest of the way. No matter how tired I was, I could never tire of the vibrancy of this city. The crowds were thinner tonight, and those who braved it wore thick masks covering their faces. But vendors were still doing business on the streets, doling out fried dumplings, meats grilled on skewers, fried leek cakes, and cups of rice noodles in broth. I grabbed a bag of candied sweet potatoes cooked in sticky syrup, finishing it before I entered the 101 through the private entrance, then immediately crawled into bed.

I slept until noon, rising to take a long shower, pulling on designer blue jeans and a gray, long-sleeved shirt. I brewed a triple espresso for myself and was just firing up my MacFold when my door buzzer rang. Daiyu was framed on my door monitor. *Aiyo.* She buzzed again. "I know you're home, Jason," she said. "Xiao Huang told me."

I obviously hadn't been tipping Xiao Huang enough. At least, not as much as Daiyu tipped him. The doorman knew which resident was home even when the private entrance was used, as each of us had to give a palm scan to gain entry. I kept silent for a long moment, then voice-commanded the front door open.

Daiyu strolled in, a vision in tight black pants and a red sweater that hugged her form. She wore black heeled boots that resonated sharply against the concrete floor. Her long hair wasn't swept back in a ponytail for once, making her look older to me. My heartbeat picked up, as it always did when I saw her—a combination of my fight-or-flight instinct kicking in mingled with my simple *want* for her. My pulse spiked every time. I hadn't seen Daiyu in over two weeks.

I leaned back in the chair, crossing my legs in front of me. "Hey," I said. "Shouldn't you be in school?"

One look in her light brown eyes—lit by some inner fire—told me I was in trouble.

She sat down at the dining table across from me. "I have my internship at Jin Corp today."

"So shouldn't you be there, then?" I took a sip of my espresso, but it tasted too bitter now, and lukewarm. "Isn't your father waiting for you?"

"He's been gone. Busy promoting the cheaper suits abroad."

I could feel her gaze on me, never leaving my face. I pretended to fiddle with my Vox. "You don't want me to meet him, do you?"

I couldn't meet Jin. There was always the risk that he'd recognize me from the image he had been sending around with those thugs. Unlikely, though still a possibility. But Daiyu had made that easy for me.

*Why?*

Daiyu shrugged. "My father gets weird about boys I . . ." She broke off and swept a hand through her hair, flustered.

Boys she secretly rode airpeds with?

Boys she ditched school to see?

Boys she barely knew whom she nursed when they got a killer flu?

Boys who kidnapped her and held her for large ransoms?

I forced myself to meet her eyes.

"Why do you seem so familiar to me, Jason?"

I almost jerked back, but tensed just in time. Damn these trendy glass tables that didn't allow for me to clench my hands or fidget. I got up, shoving my fists into my jean pockets, wishing I were feeling the heft of a knife handle in them instead. "I don't know," I said. "You seem familiar to me too."

I paced, trying to calm myself. Wondering if the memory-wipe was finally losing its hold on Daiyu.

Was she *remembering*?

She rose from the table too—smooth and elegant compared to my agitated movements. Standing before me in a few strides, she grabbed for my arm, and her subtle strawberry scent followed a second later.

"Maybe we knew each other in a past life?" I asked, trying to make my tone light.

She gazed up at me but didn't reply.

I could only think of one way to distract her and took a step forward. Close. Closer than I should ever be. "Does this feel familiar, then?" My voice had gone rough, and I swallowed. Fought the impulse to clear my throat.

She nodded imperceptibly.

I raised my other hand and trailed my fingers through her soft hair, before cupping my palm against the back of her neck, leaning in, and kissing her. She stiffened at first, then swayed into me, and I could feel her melding against my body in parts: her breasts, her hips, her thighs. She wrapped both arms around my neck and opened her mouth to me.

*Gods.*

My body felt electrified, every nerve standing on end. Crackling.

But I held back. *Tried* to hold back. I shouldn't have done this. Though she was urging me to kiss her deeper, seeking me with her tongue, so I gave in to the sensations. Gave in to the kiss. My hand gripped her waist, the other still clasping the back of her neck. Daiyu let her palms wander, across my shoulders then my chest, trailing her fingertips down my stomach. All the while exploring, tasting me with her lips and her tongue, as though if she kissed me long enough, she'd find the answer she sought so desperately. The reality was so much better than anything I'd fantasized. My body couldn't help but react. And she felt it too, because she ground her pelvis into me. I made an involuntary sound at the back of my throat, jumping out of my own skin, fighting the urge to tug her toward the bed.

I grasped her wrists and stumbled back, breaking our kiss. We were both out of breath, and she stared at me, face flushed. Dazed.

"Daiyu . . ." I took another unsteady step backward.

"We've never done that before," she said in a husky voice. "I would remember."

I laughed—low and raw—amazed I could draw enough air.

"So why does it feel like I've met you before?" she whispered and gripped my chin, forcing me to see her.

"I don't know why," I replied, twisting my head. It took everything I had not to kiss her again, to finish what we had started. "I don't know what you want me to say."

She caressed my cheek for a moment, then let her hand drop. "I don't know what I want you to say either."

A sudden downpour, and a gust of wind slammed against the floor-to-ceiling windows as heavy rain pelted from the heavens, obscuring the weighted silence that hung between us.

Victor and I were back on the National Taiwan University campus to meet Arun by six p.m.. He was unshaven, with dark circles under his eyes, but ecstatic, because he and his team were able to manufacture over two hundred antidotes. And they were making more. Victor had hired a nondescript blue van for us to drive to Wanhua, a district in the southwest of Taipei, where sightings of the large warehouses with sick *mei*s trapped within had been confirmed. It had been decided that an aircar would have drawn too much attention. I helped Arun load the syringes carefully placed in sealed holding trays into the back of the van. Arun showed us how to wear the hazmat suits, and we put them on before starting off.

As Victor drove through the streets of Taipei, I couldn't stop thinking of Daiyu, and that staggering kiss we had shared. She had left right after, and we said nothing more to each other than good-bye. She wanted the truth, and I couldn't give it to her.

Rooftop billboards beamed down on us—beautiful men and women trying to sell us beautiful things. The chill wind swept through my rolled-down window, rough against my face. We had discussed our plans and strategies while on campus, but had fallen silent during the drive. I was nervous but excited. If my friends and I could help *mei*s infected with Jin's virus, it would seriously curb the flu's spread. A sense of anticipation seemed to fill the van, and I knew Arun and Vic were eager to get to our first site too.

Victor parked on a deserted main road in Wanhua, empty of cars and people. A few gaping storefronts lined one side of the street, and the other side was dominated by the remains of an abandoned park, overgrown with brush and weeds. A large concrete warehouse stood adjacent to the park—what used to be a biscuit factory. The street lamps were few, and the ones that were working provided scant light. We got out of the van and slipped on our full face respirators.

The old factory was a square building with no windows except at the very top, the panes cracked and broken. Very dim lighting came from within, so weak I wondered if it was a trick on the eyes. The tall wooden door was secured with a large but cheap padlock. Didn't take me more than a minute to pick it; the lock gave with a loud *click*. Victor, Arun, and I looked at each other, and I eased the door open.

The scene that greeted us infuriated me and made me want to retch at the same time. At least fifty people were crammed into the warehouse, lying on the concrete ground with nothing more than

275

thin blankets. The government couldn't even be bothered to provide cots, because I suppose they were expecting all of them to die. Moans, coughs, and weeping echoed through the empty warehouse. I couldn't smell anything with my respirator on, but I saw enough vomit and urine on the floor, and dirty bodies glistening with fever sweat to imagine what it must be like.

Arun turned on a powerful lamp and was greeted by cries of alarm and hoarse voices begging for help. The sick ranged in all ages, although I saw more lined faces and heads covered in gray among them. At least eight were children, many curled up on their sides, faces flushed with fever. I gagged, fighting down nausea.

It was obvious that everyone who had been left here was poor and homeless, without family or friends to speak up for them, to demand they be treated as human beings, not like rabid dogs thrown into a cage to die.

Victor cursed.

"Let's get to work," Arun said, his voice cracking.

He demonstrated the best way to inject the antidote into the forearm. We made quick work of it through the ranks. A few tried to protest, asking in fear what we were doing, unable to believe that we were trying to help—not giving a lethal injection to kill them. After what they'd gone through, I didn't blame them. I gave as many reassurances as I could, but in the end, they were too weak to fight us off. We were done in an hour and left for the next stop.

Within fifteen minutes, we pulled up to a second warehouse. This was an abandoned clothing manufacturing company, and we had to navigate between dusty sewing machine stations to reach another forty *mei*s locked inside. While Victor and Arun were unloading water jugs to leave behind for those who might recover, I removed my gloves and checked my Vox for any messages or news.

The undernet was on fire tonight with sightings of three men outside one of the holding pens. *They are not dressed like the others who push the people in and bring out the bodies to burn*, one informant reported. *Saw one pick lock to break in*, another poster added. *Me*, I thought. This was followed by a flurry of speculation as to who the people were and what they were up to. Someone was curious enough to investigate. An hour later, another post: *they were in there for a while. taller guy came out and i got a glimpse inside when he held the door open. looks like they are injecting people with something.*

The discussion erupted into more frenzied hypothesizing and conspiracy theories. Most agreed that we were there to kill the sick, to try and curtail the virus. I didn't know what this meant for our operation, but the answer came soon enough. Victor shouted one word of warning from outside. I peered from behind the old wooden door just as three men stepped from a black sedan that had pulled up behind our van. They were dressed in black suits, hiding multiple weapons, I was certain.

*Crap.*

I was only carrying one knife on me tonight.

"We're not looking for any help," Arun said. Even behind his respirator, I could tell his chin was jutted out.

Without listening for more, I sprinted to the small emergency exit door on the opposite end of the floor, praying it wasn't jammed or would somehow set off the alarm in the derelict building. It resisted, but finally creaked open with a low whine. The men were facing Arun and Victor, stances tense, their necks thrust forward. A red taser glowed brightly in the hand of one of the thugs, and he waved it aggressively, ready to fire.

I crept out, easing the emergency door shut noiselessly behind me. The street was dark, lending cover as I circled around to the back of the men and ran toward the group, their loud arguing drowning my quick footsteps. I palmed my knife into my right hand, but it was too risky to cast it—the man with the taser might fire anyway; I'd also lose my sole weapon.

So I did the only thing I could and hurled myself into him at full speed, slamming him to the ground, away from my friends. He grunted, arm flung outward, and the taser crackled. He could kill me in an instant.

Cursing, he thrust the taser upward. Instinctively, I stabbed his arm, the sharp blade hitting bone. Crying out, he buckled under me and dropped the taser. I pinned his arm to the ground with one hand and wrapped my other around his throat. "Who do you work for?"

He sputtered, his features twisted with hatred and tried to throw me off, but I had my knees planted on either side of him and shoved harder on his windpipe, squeezing. His eyes bulged.

"Answer me," I said.

"Zhou!" Arun called from behind.

I looked toward Arun, and four more men had emerged from another black sedan. Seven in all now. We were outnumbered.

Victor had pulled Arun back, a hand clasped on his shoulder. But everyone's attention seemed to be on me.

"I'll kill him," I said, voice muffled behind my respirator.

There was no sound except for the ragged breathing of the man pinned beneath me.

"Kill him, then," one of the thugs said. "But you're coming with us."

I recognized him even in the dim streetlight: Da Ge, Jin's right-hand man.

I lunged for the dropped taser, still crackling a lethal red, and fired. All the men fell to the ground, avoiding the laser that arced over them. "Run," I shouted at my friends. They ran, Vic pulling Arun by the arm.

Da Ge and another man were scrambling to their feet, and I fired the taser again. Da Ge dodged, lightning quick in his reflexes. The other guy wasn't so lucky. I shot and tagged him square in the chest. He dropped instantly, convulsing on the ground. Victor and Arun disappeared into a dark alley. It had given my friends enough time—

I didn't finish the thought as I felt a sharp prick on my exposed wrist. The man under me had jabbed me with a syringe. "Sweet dreams, asshole," he said as the world went black around me.

I struggled to consciousness, my head heavy as stone, temples pounding. My mouth had been stuffed with a rag, and my throat worked, parched. Slowly, I opened my eyes. They felt swollen; my vision blurred. I had been thrown into some storage room. Boxes and old machinery were crammed against the walls. The thugs had tied me to a metal chair, bound my hands behind my back and my ankles together with rope. My limbs were numb, and I tried to rotate my shoulders. Pinpricks, then sharp pain flared in my joints and arms.

I had no idea how long I'd been out. Could be hours. Even a day. A wave of nausea swept over me, and I fought it. If I threw up, I'd choke to death on my own vomit. Slowing my breathing, I willed my pulse to stop racing, my mind to stop screaming in panic.

The only exit was a metal door with a round knob. I strained my ears, trying to gather any clue as to where I might be. Nothing but the buzzing of the dim fluorescent light above me, casting the dusty room in its lurid glow. I scanned the empty walls, raised my pounding head to look up at the ceiling. A square ventilation grille was set right above me, but I had no delusions of escaping through the vent. My bleary eyes caught a red light in a dark corner. I blinked rapidly, trying to focus. A camera, and it was recording. Which meant that someone could be watching.

I heard the sharp sound of footsteps before I heard the lowered voices. Dropping my chin, I shut my eyes just as a key jangled in the doorknob. The metal door banged open a moment later.

"He's still out," said a gruff voice.

"Well, wake him," another man said in a bored tone.

Someone stalked up to me, wrenched my head back by a fistful of hair, and ripped the rag from my mouth. I didn't want to react but gulped one breath. Then a slap hit me so hard across the cheek my head snapped to one side, the sound loud and resounding in the chamber. My ears rang with it. The spike of adrenaline that shot through me made my head swell with heat, my fingertips tingling. The thug tried to hit me again, open-palmed, but I twisted, wrenching my shoulders in their sockets, and he smacked my jaw and neck instead. The sting of it brought my mind into sharp focus.

"He's awake, Da Ge." The oaf smirked, revealing teeth stained yellow from smoking. I could smell it on him.

Da Ge approached, his thin frame towering over me. "What were you doing outside the temporary hospital ward?"

"You mean the holding pen?" I spoke to the concrete floor. "Where they were letting sick *mei*s die?"

"Who the fuck cares?" Da Ge drawled. "What were *you* doing there?"

"Just meeting my friends."

"You're dispensing meds. Undernet says that whatever you're doing is working." He cracked his knuckles. "That some of those wretches are actually recovering."

I raised my head and stared into Da Ge's face, saying nothing. He had mean, ruthless eyes and cutting cheekbones, reminding me of a shark.

"What were you giving them?"

I didn't reply, and in a blur, he punched me in the face, and my head slammed back against the metal edge of the chair. Blood spurted from my nose; I could feel my cheek swell beneath my eye.

I coughed, then spat at their feet; blood ran into my mouth and dribbled onto my shirt. Rage filled me, and it tasted of blood and bile. I couldn't feel any pain, only a tightness in my face.

Lowering my head, I gave a loud, wracking cough. I spat again and continued coughing, so hard that the metal legs of the chair bounced against the floor.

I could feel the two men watching me. Waiting.

Finally, I stopped and wiped my nose as best I could against my shoulder. "I think I got what they got," I said in a choked whisper. "You know what it is. The media's been downplaying it, but it's a highly contagious form of avian flu." I jerked my chin up and met their gazes. "The one that has an eighty percent fatality rate."

Both men took a long step back without even realizing.

"Lying bastard," said the stockier man, but his eyes darted uncertainly from me to the closed door.

"Better to return in suit next time," Da Ge said.

"Oh, it's too late for that, gentlemen. And a fancy *you* suit won't protect you. Viruses always find a way." I gave them a bloodstained smile, feeling every bit as monstrous as I knew I looked. "It's airborne, and you've got my blood and spit splattered all over you."

"Let's go," Da Ge said, striding for the door.

The muscular thug whipped out his taser as his boss was slipping into the corridor.

"Jin wants him alive," Da Ge said from outside. "Let's go up to the lab and use the decon pod."

I could barely hear Da Ge as the oaf stalked out after him, thudding the door shut with a loud *clang*.

I remembered the egg-shaped contraptions on the third-floor lab during our tour. I was sure I was somewhere in Jin Corp.

And Jin was on his way.

# CHAPTER FIFTEEN

I dozed off, despite my pounding head and aching arms. The sleep spell took the edge off my pain. I jerked awake when I heard the metal door screech open but quickly pretended to be out.

"What did you do to him?" A man's voice, assured and educated.

I recognized it and looked through one slitted eye. Expensive leather shoes and tailored suit. Jin.

Only Da Ge had returned. "Just a few smacks."

Jin shifted closer so I could see the edge of his gray suit jacket. His nails were manicured, and he wore a thick gold band on one hand and a carved jade ring on the other.

"Fools," Jin said. "I told you I needed to question him. How well do you think that goes when he's got his brains dribbling from his nose?"

Da Ge shuffled back, and I saw him bow down in subservience. "We didn't hit him so hard."

"Yes, you did," I rasped and raised my head, looking Jin square in the face, surprising both men. My cheekbone was swollen, and my limbs now screamed for circulation. But my vision was not as bleary, and I knew my gaze was clear when it met Jin's.

He was a good-looking man in his forties. I had studied his profile and photos extensively. But he looked even younger in person, with a content healthy glow that I'd only ever seen in *you*s. And though Daiyu got her looks more from her former model mother, there were mannerisms—a certain way Jin tilted his chin, how he took in and assessed a situation immediately with just one glance— that reminded me of her. There was no question that Daiyu was her father's daughter.

"Have you given him food?" Jin asked in a cold, detached tone, although he didn't glance away. "Some water at least?"

I swallowed then; my mouth was so dry, my throat swollen with pain.

Da Ge's narrow eyes flicked over toward Jin, his expression unreadable. "Didn't think to."

"Well, go!" Jin roared.

Da Ge left the cramped chamber, closing the door with a loud *thunk*.

"I apologize." Jin sighed and pulled up a chair from a back corner, shifting machinery parts and servers out of the way so he could sit across from me at a short distance.

I stared at him.

"Do you really have the super flu like you claimed?" Jin asked, a small smile playing at the corners of his mouth. I wanted more than anything to punch the smug look from his face. Instinctively, I knew that Jin had never known fear or rage, had never, ever felt helpless.

I shrugged noncommittally.

"I was only half following you and your friends' endeavors while abroad. Didn't know what you were about." Jin laced his fingers, pressing his thumbs together. "But my interest was piqued when reports came back that whatever you were doing seemed to be helping those infected. Something that could work against a virulent flu strain never seen before? How is that?"

I didn't reply, then licked my teeth and tasted blood.

"I see," Jin replied. "It's a good thing my men can follow some direction, as they picked up a few samples of what you dropped on-site. It's being analyzed in my lab upstairs as we speak."

"We've already sent the antidote to the FDA for approval," I said. "In case you were thinking of stealing it."

Jin laughed. "What would I need antidotes for? My business is not in curing the world of illness. I'll make sure your antidote isn't approved by the FDA. In fact, I'll see to it that your entire lab is shut down." He rose and dusted off his trousers, the movement efficient but somehow elegant. "I'm impressed, however, if you actually did succeed in producing an antidote for a virus that I personally know didn't exist outside a test tube until recently." He paused, then smiled graciously, as if I should be grateful for the compliment.

I jumped to my feet, dragging the chair with me, and rammed my head into Jin's torso. He shoved me by the shoulders so the legs of my chair jounced back to the ground, jarring my entire frame. My shoulders screamed from the impact.

"You have nerve," Jin said. "I'll give you that." He pulled on his sleeve cuffs, ran his hands over his expensive suit jacket. "I kill people who get in my way."

"Kill me, then." I sneered at him, not caring if I died as long as I could protect my friends.

285

He raised his eyebrows. "Not before you answer some questions first." Jin slanted his head, scrutinizing me with those sharp eyes. I'd seen Daiyu do the same to me, and I couldn't suppress a shudder from the intimacy of it. "I want to know," Jin said, "why you seem so familiar to me. Why you *sound* so familiar to me."

I shook my head to bring myself back into focus, but said nothing.

He hauled me up by my shirt collar, grasping hard enough that I choked. "You're that punk kid that stole three hundred million from me," he said. It wasn't a question. "The features are a little off from the image, but . . ." Jin narrowed his eyes.

I should have been afraid. Instead, I felt the fury rise in me, being face-to-face with the man who had ordered Dr. Nataraj murdered, who might as well have helped kill my own mother the way he kept *mei*s down like roaches beneath the heel of his expensive shoe. A man who cared more that he had money stolen than a daughter kidnapped. Jin didn't loosen his chokehold on my shirt, and my vision began to swim. Mustering the last of my strength, I reared back and head-butted him again right between the eyes. Pain exploded in my forehead; Jin reeled back, cursing.

I stumbled and fell into the chair hard, laughing. But no sound came. My limbs had turned boneless, and my ears rang.

Jin was rubbing his forehead, and I regretted I hadn't hit his nose or mouth to draw blood. Still, I felt a smug satisfaction to see him in pain.

"I will root out each and every one of your friends," Jin said in a cold, calm voice. "They won't die as pathetically as you will, but they'll spend the rest of their lives in a jail cell."

It didn't matter what he threatened me with. But sick fear cramped my empty stomach when he mentioned my friends. What could I do? How could I warn them? I was good as dead.

The door pushed open, brushing Jin's shoulder, and Da Ge entered with a bottle of water. His eyes darted around the room, taking in how my position had changed.

"I'm going home for the night," Jin said.

Da Ge shoved my chair back, pressing the bottle against my mouth, not caring that much of the water splattered down my chin and onto my clothes. "Want me to kill him?" he asked.

I gulped at the water, trying to drink enough and not choke. But my eyes never left Jin. Jin half turned, and his gaze swept over me once more. "I'll have lab results tomorrow from the syringes we picked up on-site." He glanced at his Vox, strapped to his wrist by diamond-studded gold links. "Kill him after I question him in the morning."

He gave a nod, as if wrapping up a business meeting, and left the room, closing the door quietly behind him.

Da Ge threw the empty water bottle into a corner, and it rattled noisily. Checking to make certain my feet and hands were bound securely, he then stuffed the dirty rag back in my mouth without saying a word. He clicked the buzzing lights off when he exited, so I was left in complete darkness.

I let my head drop, exhausted, praying that sleep would knock me out of my misery.

Again, I dozed off, but I didn't know for how long when a pulsing

287

alarm, like a polite car horn, began to blare. "Attention," a soothing female voice said in precise Mandarin. "Please leave the building via your nearest exit. You have ten minutes." The fire alarm had sounded. I immediately thought of my friends and the discussions we had just a few days back.

If I had recognized Da Ge, I had no doubt that Victor did as well. Which meant they would have been smart enough to tap into the security cameras to search for me within Jin Corp, and bullheaded enough to attempt to break in and rescue me if they had seen me on-screen.

My chest shook with laughter, smothered by the rag stuffed in my mouth.

Then I suddenly realized what the break-in meant. My friends couldn't use the fire alarm ruse twice. Not without arousing suspicion from Jin security. We were planning on bombing Jin Corp within the week. Would they be doing it tonight instead—trying to save me and plant the bombs? I would. Especially knowing Jin kept more of his avian flu virus on-site. No opportunity wasted. We all risked our lives when we had agreed to this, I had said to Victor. The mission came first. If they couldn't find me, I'd blow with the building.

The sleep spell had worn off, leaving my head and bruised face thrumming with pain. I struggled against the ropes that bound my hands, my arms uncooperative, my hands tingling, as if being stung by a thousand ants. Wiggling my fingers, I wrenched against the restraint, but it was useless. The fire alarm blared on, unrelenting and insistent.

I had faith that Lingyi would have sent one of our friends to find me, but whether I would be found in time was a different matter. Switching tactics, I tried smaller movements, testing the ropes, attempting to ease any kind of give along my wrists. I still had a knife tucked against my upper thigh, but it might as well have been on the moon.

A sudden loud popping noise, and the metal doorknob clattered onto the concrete. Yellow light filtered in from the fist-size hole. Hope surged in my chest. Was it Arun? Victor and Iris would be detonating the bombs. The door pushed open, flooding the chamber with dingy light, and the figure that stood against its glow was immediately recognizable to me, even though she was in suit.

Daiyu.

I blinked hard, shaking my head, almost believing it was a hallucination. But she flicked on the lights and her confident stride dispelled any doubt. Tucking her gun away in the holster strapped at her waist, she crouched down. Her touch was light against my shoulder. Gently, she removed the rag from my mouth. I drew a long, shuddering breath.

Her hand hovered above my swollen cheek. "I can't believe they did this to you," she said. Her helmet was half-tinted, but I could still catch the hard glint of her eyes.

"Daiyu." My throat was raw, and the word came as a croak. "What are you doing here?"

She slipped behind me, working on the rope that bound my hands first. "My father returned from abroad today, sooner than expected. I track his whereabouts through his Vox, which he always wears. He arrived at Jin Corp when I was about to leave my internship for the day," she said in a low voice.

The rope loosened slightly, and sensation flooded back into my arms, tingling my hands—painful but wonderful. I flexed my fingers and for a moment, I felt Daiyu grasping them before the rope slid off. Shaking my arms out, I rubbed my shoulder joint, wincing.

She crouched back down at my feet in front of me, unknotting the rope binding my ankles. "I avoided running into him but was curious when he headed away from the elevators that led to his office. I became even more curious when I saw Da Ge join him."

I imagined Daiyu sneaking around, tailing her father, but making it look as though she had every right to be where she was—because she was Jin's daughter.

"I followed them down here and heard enough. I knew my father was capable of questionable choices in his business practices, but"—she gave a rough shake of her head that I could see even with her helmet on—"I had to come back and free you." She tugged hard at the rope. "There are no blurred lines when it comes to murder. Even my father should know that." The bitter note of her tone didn't disguise the hurt and disappointment I heard there.

*But he doesn't care*, I thought. Anything to further his own agenda. Did Daiyu just find out tonight that her father was capable of murder?

"He's ordered people killed before." It was cruel to say it so bluntly, but she needed to know the truth. Especially now, when Jin Corp was about to blow.

"I had no actual proof before, but now . . . ," she replied. I barely heard her above the steady drone of the fire alarm. The rope slid off my ankles, and she pulled me gently to my feet.

I swayed, then felt Daiyu beside me, wrapping an arm around

my torso, steadying me. Her closeness comforted and disconcerted me all at once.

"Three minutes," the polite female voice reminded us. "Please exit the building. You have three minutes."

"Imagine my surprise when my Palm told me my security code had been accessed at the front entrance," Daiyu said. "I knew it had to be your friends—the ones Da Ge didn't capture."

My vision darkened for a moment, barely perceptible in the dim room, and I felt light-headed. She had *let* me see her code during that personal tour, hadn't she? Even though Lingyi had already hacked the info. How long had she been tracking our use of it? And why? How much did she know?

I shoved away from her. "You remembered it was me," I said in a hoarse whisper. Me who had kidnapped her and held her for ransom.

"I knew," she replied.

Those two words punched like bullets into my chest. And I felt my breath sucked from my lungs, as if I were being bulldozed flat. I would have doubled over if these last months of training, of pretending to be someone I wasn't—someone smoother, harder, more confident—hadn't become inextricably tied to me. I had turned into Jason Zhou, was more comfortable as him, than I had ever wanted to be. While I was angsting over lying to Daiyu, she had been playing me all along.

"We have to go." My tone was firm, not giving away the tumult of emotions that were overwhelming me. "They're bombing the place."

"You used the fire alarm to clear the employees out," she murmured. "Nice."

"Two minutes," the polite female voice reminded us.

Once the building was cleared, the bomb would likely go off within a few minutes. I knew that was how Victor had planned it.

"Come on!" I grabbed her hand, because no matter what happened between us, I wouldn't be able to forgive myself if she didn't make it out safely.

"I know the nearest exit," she said and took the lead. "In the upper-level basement."

We ran together, my heart going double time from desperation, from holding Daiyu's hand in mine, and the corridor stretched longer in front of my eyes, expanded, as if in some fun-house nightmare.

"Thank you for exiting in a timely manner," the female voice said above the alarm.

Time was up.

We dashed up one flight of stairs, side by side.

Pummeling against the emergency door on the landing, I pressed the exit bar and slammed against it like a brick wall. Locked. *Gods.* Flinging her arm out to push me back, Daiyu unholstered her gun. The barrel lit in red and she pulled the trigger. Her arm jerked upward from the explosion of the shot. A neat round hole the size of a fist appeared where the jamb would be. The air was tinged with smoke. I pushed against the bar again just as a deafening boom erupted above us, shaking the building to its core. The exit door wouldn't give. Another long boom followed immediately after, and Daiyu and I fell into each other. She tucked her head into my shoulder and I wrapped my arms around her, holding her tight against me, the glass of her helmet cold against my cheek.

The ground rumbled beneath our feet as the entire building shifted and groaned, like a monster awakening. My ears rang, even after the building quieted. With one arm still wrapped around Daiyu's shoulder, I shoved at the door again.

"It's useless," Daiyu said. She sounded as if she were speaking to me from the other end of a long tunnel. "Jin Corp's in lockdown, and these doors are impenetrable. I just got the company-wide message in helmet."

"We're trapped, then?"

"No," she replied. "I know a way out."

She slipped away from me, and I followed. I watched her straight back as she pushed a door, which opened into the main corridor on the ground floor. The golden ambient lighting I had seen during my tour had dimmed, replaced by red lights that pulsed, casting the wide hallway in a macabre bloody glow, like some horrific scene from *The Shining*. The fire alarm had ceased, and there was no sound except for our echoing footsteps and the monstrous moaning of the building. A distant ringing still filled my ears.

Daiyu half turned to glance back, and a rush of conflicted feelings surged through me when our eyes locked: chagrin that she had fooled me so completely, relief that she at last knew the truth, but most of all, fear. Fear that neither of us would make it out of this building alive. I had signed up for this from the start. She hadn't.

A moment later, a thunderous roar shook Jin Corp, a different sound than the explosives that had gone off. The ground rocked, and I closed the short distance between us. She grabbed my arm and we both dropped to our knees as the building heaved and shuddered. "The floors are collapsing above us," Daiyu shouted.

I stood when the building stilled and pulled Daiyu to her feet.

"This way," she said.

She stayed by my side now, as if afraid we'd lose each other somehow in the empty corridor. The dimmed golden lights flickered overhead, then cut out entirely, leaving only emergency lighting. Dust particles blasted out from the vents, carrying the scent of fire and electrical smoke. Tears streamed from my eyes, the smoke was so strong, and I coughed uncontrollably.

Daiyu pressed her fingers against my palm, and I let her guide me as gray tendrils began to fill the hall too fast, turning the air darker around us. We ran through the wide corridor, past the sleek gold sliding doors leading into the foyer. Another loud *boom* knocked us off our feet, and the entire building shook, as violent as an earthquake, followed by the sound of concrete collapsing. Another powerful *thud*, and we fell again; this time, Daiyu pulled me to my feet.

"We're almost there," she shouted, but in a moment of sudden silence, it sounded like a gunshot through the empty hallway.

Our world shuddered around us as we ran, and the smoke grew so thick, the air became almost opaque. I had taken off my shirt and pressed the fabric against my mouth and nose but knew it wouldn't be too long before I gave in to smoke inhalation. The visibility was so poor, I nearly careened into someone. Both Daiyu and I shouted in surprise, but the other person uttered nothing. Catching a glimpse of platinum-blond hair, I choked out, "Iris?"

"Zhou!" she exclaimed when she realized it was me. "Thank gods, Arun couldn't find you—"

"Daiyu got me," I shouted over the noise. "She knows the way out."

Iris gave a curt nod, her distrust of Daiyu clear in her dark eyes. "Zhou's here. We're headed out." She was reporting to Lingyi.

We stumbled forward together. I was grasping Daiyu's hand, and Iris gripped me by the shoulder so we wouldn't lose each other. "Vic's already out?" I asked.

Iris didn't reply, and I stopped, thinking I hadn't heard her in the commotion, but one look at her stricken face, and I knew. I jerked away from both girls. "We have to go back!"

I turned and lunged toward where we had come. The corridor was black with smoke and dust. A strong hand clenched my arm, stopping me. I charged forward; Iris might be strong, but I outweighed her.

"Zhou," she screamed. "Stop. Zhou!" She broke into a fit of coughing.

Victor. *No.*

"It's too late!" Iris screamed. "We lost connection with him after his second bomb detonated. He was having trouble setting the timer. . . ." Her voice broke. "Lingyi told him to go, but he didn't listen."

Someone else grasped my other hand. "Please, Jason." *Daiyu.* "We'll all die. Please come with us." I could see the tears streaking down her face, despite her filth-smudged helmet.

Somehow, I knew Daiyu wouldn't let me go without following. And although I was content to run toward my own death, I couldn't let hers be on my conscience, too. I nodded and let Daiyu lead us again to the exit. Iris brought up the rear, as if she didn't trust me not to break away again.

Maybe she understood me better than I realized.

We swayed on our feet as the building rocked, crashing to our knees over and over again. *This must be what hell is like*, I thought, unable to breathe, unable to see, surrounded by the rumbling of earth and stone and gulping death with each inhalation. I ran after Daiyu in a haze, only aware of our fingers twined together, my other hand clutching Iris's.

My mind kept riffling through memories of my friend, offering stark images, snapshots in time.

Victor tying the bow tie for my tuxedo with care. *I'm nothing without you, Victor*, I joked. *I know*, he replied with that devilish grin.

Victor leaning over me, his dark eyes filled with concern. After he basically shoved me out of a high-rise window. *You all right, kid?*

Victor, the pain-in-the-ass older brother I'd never had. No, I wasn't all right. Nothing will be right again.

*I* was supposed to be the dispensable one. *I* was supposed to take the majority of the risks. Not Victor, who had doubts about all of this from the start. Not Victor, who could charm his way out of anything.

But not this time.

Daiyu finally stopped at a steel door that required a brain wave scan. Her face was flushed and pallid in alternating beats as the red lights flickered around us. She began tugging at her helmet, then pulling at her collar, but her fishbowl wouldn't budge. "Could you get the helmet off me?" she asked. "My suit is dead."

The purple neon lights of her suit had dimmed. I pulled out my knife and wiped my eyes, still coughing. But I held my breath and lay a hand on Daiyu's shoulder. "Don't move," I said.

I was the unsteady one, but I forced myself to focus, then carefully slipped the tip of the blade under her suit collar and cut the material. Her chest rose up and down too fast, making me nervous I'd nick her by accident. She was hyperventilating. "All the suits are useless now," she said between rushed breaths. "My father wanted to be sure that if Jin Corp didn't exist, the suits wouldn't function."

Finally, I had carefully slashed through the circumference of her collar and lifted the helmet off her head. She drew a long breath then coughed uncontrollably. Wisps of black hair stuck to her forehead and cheeks.

She stood underneath the curved glass dome by the door, as blue lasers enveloped the top of her head, sliced across her temples and forehead. The door slid open, and we fell out, gasping for air.

Iris shoved the door closed; it sealed with a *snick*. We were in an alleyway behind Jin Corp, safe . . . for now. As if reading my thoughts, Daiyu said, "My father built the exterior of the building to withstand bombings, so it cannot collapse."

Even as she spoke, the octagonal structure shook violently. "I don't think we should test that theory," I said. We ran away from Jin Corp, winding our way through dark alleyways, Daiyu's Palm the only light illuminating our path. Finally, after we had put distance between us and the building, I stopped, lungs aching.

"Let's disappear, Zhou," Iris said. It was the first time I had ever seen her look so winded, ready to collapse like I was. "The cops will be here soon."

I paused for a long moment, my mind unable to focus, still reeling from losing Victor.

Daiyu's fingertips grazed my hand.

I glanced toward her, surprised.

Iris lifted an eyebrow. "We've gotta get out of here."

"Go on without me," I replied. The thought of returning to headquarters without seeing Victor flashing a cocky grin was unbearable. I didn't want to share my grief. I needed to hold it alone first.

Iris flexed her gloved hands. "He's not coming," she said. It took me a second to realize she was speaking to Lingyi.

She stalked toward me then, and I took a step back, not wanting to fight. At this point, I knew I'd lose. Instead, she stuck her earpiece into my ear.

"Come home, Zhou," Lingyi said, her voice thick. I could tell she had been crying.

"Is Arun all right?"

"I'm here, bro. Where *were* you?" Arun asked. "I searched all through the basement."

"There are two levels," Lingyi said in a low voice, having overheard Arun's frantic query.

Arun had been on the wrong floor.

"I need some time," I finally replied, hoarse. "Victor's dead." I knew they must have known, but I needed to say it aloud.

"Oh, Zhou." Lingyi broke into a long sob. "I know. Go with Iris. Please."

My vision blurred. "I can't." I felt Daiyu's hand again, her fingers pressing gently against my palm. "I'm going with Daiyu."

"She's Jin's daughter, Zhou," Iris said, not bothering to keep the contempt from her voice.

I met her gaze. Her dark eyes gleamed faintly from a faraway streetlight. "And she saved my life. She saved yours."

"You're angry," Lingyi replied. "Because we failed to find you. We left you there—"

"No," I cut her off. "I'm not angry. It was always the mission first. We all knew that." We had abided by it, and lost Victor because of it. At this moment, when we should have been feeling triumphant, I only felt numb. Grief swelled in the shadows, waiting, and all too familiar.

"It was the hardest call I ever had to make," Lingyi said, sounding broken. "I had to force Arun out of the building."

"You did right." I wiped the ash and tears from my eyes. "It's why you're our boss."

She hiccupped a tiny laugh. "Then come home. I command it."

"I'll see you, boss." I removed the earpiece and handed it back to Iris.

She had been crying too, but looked so furious, I feared she would try and drag me with her by the ear. Instead, she turned without a word and ran into the night, disappearing like smoke down a dark alleyway.

Distant sirens wailed, drawing closer.

"Jason," Daiyu said. "Your secret—what your friends did tonight—I'll never tell."

I nodded, wanting more than anything to fall into her arms, to hold her. Because it felt like I'd lost everything again, with Jin Corp's collapse.

"Thank you for . . ." What? Saving my life? Promising to keep our secret? "Everything." I kissed Daiyu's hand before letting go.

She caught my wrist again firmly. "You told your friends you're coming with me . . . tonight."

"I was being presumptuous," I said with a faint smile. Even that hurt my bruised face. But I did choose her. I didn't explain that this choice would wedge a divide between me and my friends longer than just one night. I knew that Lingyi and Iris would see it as a betrayal, as embracing the *you*s. I didn't know where Arun would stand. Victor would probably tease me relentlessly for choosing a girl over my "ideals"—but it was more than that. I had gone into this seeing the world in stark contrast: black and white, us versus them. Now I knew it wasn't as simple as that.

Then my mind stuttered. Vic was gone. Dead.

"No, you weren't," she said.

"But first tell me why," I said, voice rasping. She tilted her face up toward me, and the single light farther down the alley cast her face in shadows. "Why did you let us use your security code? When you *knew*?"

"I didn't know anything for certain," she whispered, her voice faltering too. "But I had begun to track my father's activities and started to suspect . . . things. He had given me high clearance at Jin Corp, but I was able to send a message to security as him, requesting the highest clearance for me. Full access. I saw what he had been doing—bribing the politicians against environmental reform, threatening them if they didn't cooperate . . ."

That's why we had been able to use Daiyu's security code at the citadel, why she had access to the restricted lab so we could steal the flu virus. Jin had underestimated his own daughter.

"I didn't know if I could trust you, but I followed my instincts and took a chance." She slid her hand into mine, and the corners of her mouth lifted ever so slightly. "There's something I want to show you."

I hesitated a moment, then nodded. I had been the one who had judged her, made presumptions because she was *you*. She had surprised me again and again, but tonight, after all she told me, I wasn't surprised. It made sense. Daiyu loved Taiwan as much as I did. I remembered the girl silhouetted against the glass wall in my old home on Yangmingshan, the wild jungle foliage as her backdrop. She had looked outside with such wistful yearning. I hadn't understood then that it wasn't only the *mei*s who had suffered in our pollution-ravaged city. We walked together in silence, then she turned onto another empty street. The air was humid with rain, smelling almost of spring, and a toad croaked somewhere in the distance—a deep and satisfied noise.

She could be leading me straight to her father. Or toward a group of criminals waiting to take care of me once and for all. But I didn't truly believe it. My friends and I had completed our mission. It was done. And tonight I chose to follow my heart.

# CHΔPTER SIXTEEN

Daiyu led me farther into the twisting alleyways. This was the same area where we had been approached by two desperate muggers last month. And although I kept my ears tuned to the noises around us, I was filled with a sense of brashness after what had happened tonight. Exhaustion mixed with excitement tinged with grief. I didn't really care where Daiyu was taking me, as long as I was with her. Somehow, after all the lies, and beneath both of our agendas, I suddenly understood that I trusted her.

Despite everything.

"Are you going to tell me how you remembered?" I finally risked asking, breaking our silence.

She pressed her lips together and shook her head. "Later."

She finally stopped in one of the narrow streets, a short ways from a Yamaha Blade, exactly like mine, but the most expensive model, tricked out with a personalized paint job and actual gems embedded into its body and frame. The bike was painted a deep, seductive red, with golden flames decorating its front panel and sides. Inexplicably, two silver horns jutted from the handlebars. Daiyu saw where I was gazing and said, "Because I was born in the year of the goat."

A year younger than me. No wonder she was so stubborn.

"This is *your* airped?" I said.

She approached the gorgeous motorcycle and the instrument panel lit up in neon blue. Golden lights hidden in its body illuminated the entire airped on the darkened street, creating a halo around it. "Yes, mine."

She climbed on, and I simply stared, admiring the way her body moved, how she settled herself comfortably on the gold leather seat, straddling it with her long legs.

*Damn.*

Daiyu gave me a measured look, then smiled a slow smile. She knew exactly what I was thinking. "Come on. Climb on."

"Won't your father be looking for you?" I asked.

Her shoulders tensed, and her straight eyebrows drew together. "I messaged him good night hours ago. The door to my bedroom is locked. He'll be too preoccupied tonight to think of me."

I got on behind her, winding my arms around her waist, holding her close. I could feel the tension in her body, her muscles taut. "I thought you'd never ridden on an airped before?" I said against her ear.

She let out a sigh and relaxed against me. "I lied," she replied.

Daiyu revved the engine, and the Blade purred as it sped down the empty street. "You seemed to enjoy showing off," she said above the noise.

I rested my forehead against her shoulder and laughed as we lifted into the air, and my heart surged with it. She was absolutely right. I had enjoyed it.

▲▼▲

Daiyu flew through the empty skies cautiously, as I was unsuited and hers was defunct. An accident would mean certain death. We weren't near the center of Taipei, and at not yet three a.m., there was little air traffic in this area unfrequented by *you*s looking for a good time. To my surprise, Daiyu seemed to be headed toward Shilin and the Yangming mountains, back to where this all started—where I had kidnapped her last summer. I watched Taipei unfurl beneath me, a maze of narrow streets, dark alleyways and brightly lit boulevards. I loved this city, my city, and wondered if what my friends and I did tonight would help it in the way that we had hoped. Galvanize the nation.

*Please don't let Victor's death be for nothing.*

If I had learned anything growing up, it was that there were no guarantees in life. But that didn't mean you simply sat back and never tried. I shivered. My expensive leather jacket did little to ward off the chill wind flying so high, but my chest was warm. I could feel my heartbeat against Daiyu's back. We were near the base of Yangming-shan when Daiyu steered the airped onto a wide road, shutting the system and kicking down the stand.

After the rush of air against my ears and the hum of the airped's propulsion system and engine, the sudden silence seemed loud.

"We're here," Daiyu said and waited for me to get off the airped before she slid off.

I glanced around. We were on an empty road that wound upward toward the mountain, untraveled because no one visited the haunted peaks anymore, after the earthquake and fires. I saw nothing but then glimpsed the curve of a dome hidden behind a thicket of trees set farther back.

"Come on," she said. Daiyu walked toward the trees, and I followed.

We soon reached a large clearing, cut back to accommodate the structure I had glimpsed from afar. The building was made of ivory stone, smooth and circular, with a domed roof. A square vestibule was set at the front, with wide silver doors. It reminded me of the old-school observatories I had seen on the undernet, back when astronomers could actually study the stars and solar systems from within our cities. Now the skies were too polluted from Seoul to London to Mexico City.

"What is it?" I asked.

"It's my senior project," she said and gestured toward the entrance. "You'll see."

"You *built* this for your senior project?" It must have cost millions.

She nodded, unperturbed, and opened the elegant silver doors with a palm scan. The doors were etched with delicate plum blossoms—Taiwan's national flower. Gold lights set into the arched ceiling came on, illuminating the empty chamber. I walked with Daiyu inside, admiring the jade tile work on the floor. "The vestibule isn't finished yet"—she waved a hand—"but soon."

The expansive chamber smelled of stone and wood, construction. Regulated air pumped from vents above.

"There's a restroom." Daiyu pointed to a cherrywood door on the right-hand side.

I slipped inside. After using the facilities, I stared at myself in the wide expanse of mirrors above the marble sinks. My short hair stuck up every which way from the airped ride, but also from my time spent as a prisoner. The lower half of my face and neck were smeared in dried blood, and my left cheekbone was swollen, making the eye appear squinted. I only had on my black leather jacket over dirty jeans, as I had used my shirt to cover my face while escaping Jin Corp, and lost it somewhere along the way. I looked every bit like a street urchin trying to be something I wasn't.

*I tried, Vic*, I thought, looking at my reflection until it blurred. *But you were always the suave one.*

I washed my face and neck, then rinsed my mouth out. My head and cheek throbbed, but nothing I couldn't deal with. I'd been beat up worse.

There was a light knocking on the door, startling me despite its muted tone. My heart raced, and the ground tilted beneath my feet; for a moment, it felt as if I were in Jin Corp again, with the building collapsing over me, my vision obscured by smoke. Daiyu entered carrying a silver cup. I let out a breathless laugh, gripping the marble restroom counter. "You have no sense of privacy at all, do you?" My voice cracked.

"You've been in here for a while." She offered the cup. "I thought you might be thirsty."

I was, now that she mentioned it. Suddenly, it felt as if I could fall to my knees from thirst. I drank, and ice-cold sugarcane juice slid down my throat like some miracle elixir. I didn't set the cup down until I was done, already feeling more alert. "Thank you," I said.

She was leaning against the counter, facing me, close enough I felt her body's warmth.

"Jason—"

"I'm sorry," I cut in. "I'm sorry that I lied to you and used you. You were a necessary means to an end." *Shit.* I sounded like a robotic jerk. Gripping the counter edge again, I went on, "But it doesn't mean that . . ." I faltered.

*. . . it was all a lie.*

*. . . I only pretended to like you.*

*. . . the kiss we shared doesn't still blow my mind.*

". . . I ever wanted to hurt you," I finally said. Staring at my knuckles, I knew how foolish I sounded.

"You used me," Daiyu replied. "But I used you too."

That was true. She played me better than I could ever have guessed. Who was actually running the show this entire time? Lingyi and our group, or had Daiyu simply *let* us?

"That night you woke up from the flu, and you were so angry with me," Daiyu murmured. "I told you I was starting to *see*. Starting to learn more and more about what my father was doing. How truly horrible it was for *mei*s in our country. But I also saw that you couldn't trust me."

I looked at her then, and she graced me with a sad smile.

"You couldn't truly trust me," she repeated. "And I didn't blame you."

"I was the one who kidnapped you, Daiyu, who stole from you. Why did you trust *me*?"

She took my hand then. "I took a leap of faith."

We exited the restroom, and Daiyu led me to another set of silver curved doors, following the shape of the circular building. A palm scan and they slid open without a sound, disappearing into the walls. The lights within the inner chamber came on and Daiyu stepped inside. It was a hall, probably seating no more than one hundred, cozy and intimate. A raised circular dais stood at the center of the room, with plush chairs surrounding it, all reclined. I glanced upward at the high, domed ceiling, an expanse of white.

"A theatre," I said with sudden understanding. "You've built a dome theatre?"

These were popular a few decades ago, and there had been one in Taipei. But it soon went out of fashion, being too expensive for most *mei*s and not high-tech enough for the *you*s, who preferred putting on sim suits for a fully immersive experience. Daiyu's eyes flicked toward me, and she gave an enigmatic smile. She went to the dais and pulled a blanket and pillows from beneath it, making a nest for us on the small stage. Climbing on, she lay down and patted the space beside her. Although her pose was natural, she was exuding nervous energy, some unspoken tension that made me jittery in turn. What was she going to show me? What had been *her* story all this time? I got onto the platform and stretched out beside her, our shoulders touching.

She was avoiding eye contact, focused on her Palm, typing one-handed. The lights in the theatre began to fade, and I felt my pulse pick up, not knowing what to expect, yet filled with wary anticipation.

The theatre dimmed gradually, until we were in full dark. But then the domed screen above us took on a glow, so subtle at first I

308

didn't know if it was my imagination, until I recognized the Taipei skyline, precise as a paper cutout, with the skies brightening behind it. Thin wisps of white clouds were scattered across pale blue, a color I had never seen with my own eyes. Beyond, I glimpsed the sloping lines of distant mountains, the mountains that surrounded our city, that Daiyu had pointed out from my apartment in the 101, somewhere in the unseeable distance. Mountains that might have been as real as ancient dragons, for we had no proof they existed in our skyline except from old images of Taipei. And the sun crept up between them, bright and fierce. Blazing. I squinted, turning my head to the side as it rose between the peaks and climbed, godlike, and the skies deepened to an indigo blue around it.

Taipei was lit beneath, with fewer high-rises and no aircars, awash in colors from what the sun and skies gave. Instead of being smothered in a blanket of brown or gray. My heart hurt to see it—to see how it was supposed to be.

"Blue skies," I whispered.

Daiyu squeezed my hand. "I kept returning to that conversation we had in your vegetable garden."

I ran my thumb across her knuckles, not knowing how to respond.

"After I saw the footage played for the first time here," she continued, "I wondered why we ever let it go."

From lack of foresight. Greed. Hubris.

"I think I can even feel the warmth of the sun."

"It's because you do." She turned to me and smiled. "I've designed the theatre to be experiential."

"It's incredible."

She was using her Palm again, and the scene changed gradually before our eyes. At first, early morning mist obscured the landscape, but as the day brightened, the fog dissipated, revealing trees on the mountains, denser and greener than I'd ever seen. I recognized the thickets of Yangmingshan, opening up to a sea of calla lilies with their white blooms turned upward. It was an aerial view, from decades-old footage. A cool breeze swept over my face as the camera panned, and farmers walked between the endless flowers, all wearing hats to protect them from the sun. What I had seen, visiting with my mom, had been a muted version of this, the colors dulled, the expanse narrowed and clipped. But it had still been beautiful, walking among those blooms, holding my mom's hand.

These hues from so many years past hurt my eyes, as if my vision wasn't used to such pristine color. Such brightness. So different from the glimmer and flash of neon lights I had become accustomed to. A small figure waved in the distance, surrounded by calla lilies, and the camera zoomed in. A little girl with an upturned face, beaming, clutching a bouquet in one small fist and holding the brim of her sun hat with her other hand. She thrust the flowers in the sky, pointing at the camera overhead, and her mother approached from behind, laughing, putting a hand on her daughter's shoulder. They waved together, smiling up at the camera, and it panned out until they became dots, swept across the field of flowers below, before lifting to show the horizon, the lush mountains punctuating the skyline.

A knot rose in my throat and I swallowed it, even as a light breeze brushed against my cheeks. I could almost smell the earth again, the mountains and pine. Something that I'd missed since being forced to leave my makeshift home in Yangmingshan. The image froze and slowly faded from the screen, until it was only white once more and Daiyu and I were lying in a dimly lit theatre. It felt still. Encapsulated.

"I created this for you," Daiyu said in a soft voice after a long silence.

"But how did you—"

"I've spent so much time trying to understand you. Your motivations," she said. "Trying to figure you out." She let out a small breath. "You didn't say a word when you kidnapped me."

I involuntarily snatched my hand back—we had watched the short films with our fingers entwined. Blood surged into my head, filling my ears with white noise for a moment.

"It took a long time to walk back to your home," she continued. "Two hours and twenty-seven minutes to be exact, according to my suit."

"Your suit?" I repeated, uncomprehending.

"I never remembered anything, Jason. I still don't remember." She turned on her side, shifting closer to me, so I could smell her clean scent, the strawberry shampoo she used. It took every inch of my will not to shrink from her. I didn't know if I was ready for what she was about to tell me. I had no clue as to what she would say. How would she end this?

"Your memory-wipe held," she continued, "but my father was using me to test a new enhance, without my knowledge. My suit recorded the kidnapping. We had imagery from whenever I wore my helmet, and voice recording for the entire time. The camera didn't work properly, so everything was dim, fuzzy. But the voice recording was crystal clear."

I breathed in and out, in and out, letting that sink in. This was how Jin had created a bad rendering of me.

"I would never have known, if one of his thugs didn't come around one day showing me that poorly made image of you. When you still had the longer hair, dyed blond." She was speaking to a point behind me, beyond my shoulder, not looking in my eyes. "He wanted to know if I recognized the boy in the photo. If I could tell him anything at all. To think hard." She made a derisive noise. "He gave himself away like a bad chess player staring too long at the piece he wants to move next. My father had told me I had fainted that evening at the night market, even though I'd never fainted before in my life. When I tried to ask more questions, I couldn't. All three of my bodyguards had been replaced. My friend Marie, who was with me that night, kept telling me it was exactly how my father said." She paused. "But she distanced herself from me, and I saw the fear in her eyes."

I lay on my back, gazing up at the domed ceiling, saying nothing.

"I was suspicious," she said. "My father left his MacFold open one morning while taking a business call and I went in and made myself admin, giving myself remote access. He never suspected a thing." Daiyu gave a bitter laugh. "So I went through his files, and found the recording of the kidnapping, all of it. And his messages sent directing his men to search for you, to find you, and to kill you. The money was secondary. It was a matter of principle and pride. How could some worthless kid make a fool of him like this? My getting kidnapped was also secondary. It was about him. In the end, it's *always* about him.

"I watched and listened to the recording hundreds of times," Daiyu continued. "So many times that I have our entire conversations memorized. I would never have been able to recognize your face from it, but your voice . . ." She pulled out her hair band, letting her ponytail loose, then proceeded to twist the band between her fingertips. "I thought you sounded familiar at the New Year's party—but it was noisy. So I showed up at your apartment the next day to be sure. And I *knew* after that visit, it was the same voice from the boy who kidnapped me in the recording." She glanced at me for a second, before her eyes flicked away.

"Daiyu," I said, my voice hoarse.

"No. Don't interrupt," she replied. "Let me tell this."

I let myself look at her then, and she went on, avoiding my gaze.

"You didn't say a thing after you kidnapped me, but you talked on the whole way back," she said.

*Did I?* I tried to think back to last summer, after I had jabbed the memory-wipe into her hand, when she had begged me not to. I remember catching her, lifting her into my arms, feeling both guilty and relieved. It was a long walk back, and I was exhausted and hot. I remembered stopping twice to rest, while the evening darkened around us. I couldn't recall what I might have said to her.

"A running monologue the entire time. You kept apologizing. You explained you had to do this, for me to please understand. And that it was nothing personal and that you hoped I wouldn't remember—that it wouldn't affect me in any profound way." She let out a wry laugh. "If I hadn't found my father's recording of the kidnapping, I probably would have moved on soon enough. After all, I remembered none of it. But instead, the exact opposite happened. I became obsessed. You told me all about your mom, about losing her to that terrible illness, how you'd been living on the streets for these last five years. You were at the center of this mystery." She touched my shoulder then, startling me. "You never made it sound like you were stealing to keep the money for yourself. You talked as if you had a plan—a goal."

"And you wanted to know what I was about," I said.

She nodded. "It made absolutely no sense when you showed up at the party, so willing to befriend me. Pretending to be a *you* boy. But then you asked for a tour of Jin Corp—"

Daiyu had turned the tables, when I had thought I was being so cool, so sly.

"After the kidnapping, I had convinced my father to do the cheaper suits for the *mei*s and stopped spying on him." Daiyu's mouth tightened. "But your showing up, and your interest in my father's company, made me curious again. I began going through his files and saw that he wanted to add the image- and voice-recording enhance in *all* the cheaper suits. Without telling the consumer."

"*Gods.* I'm sorry, Daiyu," I said. *Sorry that your father was a selfish, immoral asshole.*

She gave me a half smile. "When I pointed out how wrong this was to my father, lying that I had overheard him talking about it in a business deal, he ignored me. It was a free addition! he declared. Something that could be used by the police in case of emergency or by the government to track any criminal activities. It was a free *benefit* with the suit. And in exchange, my father would be able to cull data on the consumer habits of the Taiwanese and all his clients worldwide."

"Of course," I said. "Data he could sell at a premium." *Not to mention have access to all the private moments and conversations between people.*

She nodded. "My father made his own fortune. He's always seen himself as the hero of his own story, and the rest of us, secondary characters existing only to serve him. The idea of privacy is ludicrous to him. How did this enhance *hurt* anyone? Privacy is a privilege that you could buy if you were rich enough."

I snorted. "Like clean air, food, and water? Like good health care?"

"I don't agree with him," she said. "I never bothered to think through the implications of my father's actions, of his business practices, until after my kidnapping." Her cheeks colored. She was embarrassed, even though I was the criminal in this scenario. "I had always pretended I didn't see, but it was only when I read the plans for this enhance, and confronted him, that I understood . . . how warped his thinking truly was. He believed it was in his right to lie to the people, bribe and intimidate politicians—do whatever was necessary to get the results he desired." She was clutching the thin blanket between her fingers, staring at the pattern with unseeing eyes. "I could partially justify in my mind his wanting to . . . seek retribution for what you did. I made sure that your paths never crossed. But when I heard him casually say he'd kill you after questioning you . . . I couldn't make any more excuses for him."

I caressed her cheek with the back of my hand.

"There's more, isn't there?" she whispered. "More that I don't know."

I nodded.

"Tell me everything," she said. "Later."

"All right," I replied. From the beginning, I had thought we were on opposite sides, fighting against each other, when all along Daiyu had wanted what my friends and I had wanted. My heart had trusted her long before my mind would allow it.

She reached for my jacket again and began to pull it from my shoulders. Her mood had changed, and she was looking directly into my eyes.

My thoughts stuttered midstream. Every nerve ending went into hyperdrive, my body instantly remembering, as if I had never broken our kiss.

She slipped the jacket off. "Can it just be us now? For tonight?" Her pupils were dark, infinite pools. "No more lies?"

Daiyu leaned down and captured my lower lip with her supple mouth, and then we were kissing, her fingers running across my bare back, my hand reaching for her suit zipper, brushing past her arm, her breast, before finding the pull and tugging. The sound of her suit unzipping while she pressed herself against me, undressing me as we kissed, made my mind reel.

She pushed back a long while later, her palm warm against my chest, and gazed down, drinking me in with her eyes. Unabashed, she took her time. I stroked her shoulder blade, the curve of her waist, letting my hand run over the swell of her hip. Her long hair fell like a curtain, sweeping across my shoulder, and I eased off her suit top, revealing a simple black T-shirt beneath. My fingers grazed her stomach, lifting the edge of her shirt; she helped me, pulling it off, and my breath caught. She had nothing on underneath. "I've wanted this for so long," she whispered.

It was such a bold declaration, so like Daiyu—the girl who was used to getting everything she wanted, who always managed to surprise me. The girl who persisted all alone in finding the ugly truths about her own father. Yet there was a vulnerability in the arch of her neck, in the way her eyes softened in the dim light as she searched my face.

*I took a leap of faith*, she had said to me.

It was my turn to jump.

"Me too," I said, kissing her fingertips. "I'm yours."

Her full lips curved into a smile.

For the remainder of tonight at least, our worlds would hold only each other.

# EPILOGUE

## THREE MONTHS LATER

The news reporter stood in front of the abandoned Jin Corp building, as the cambot panned from the double gold doors upward. The
exterior of the building had held, just as Daiyu had said it would, but
the interior was almost completely destroyed.

"After three months of investigations, there have been no new
leads on the bombing of Jin Corp. The main challenge has been that
the hundreds of security cameras revealed no unusual activity the
night of the attack, and most cameras stopped functioning after the
four explosions destroyed much of the building." The news reporter
was dressed in a gray skirt and light blue shirt, not a hair out of place,
despite the humid weather.

*Victor's in there.*

*Lost in the rubble.*

I sat in my large bed, propped against the cold headboard. Spring
rain came in sheets, so thick it obscured the city views below. Fingering

318

my Vox restlessly, I forced myself to watch the news update, ignoring the burning behind my eyes.

"Crews have been trying to clear the inside of the building, but the environment is highly volatile, and progress has been slow," the news reporter continued. "In the meantime, another indictment has been brought against Jin Feiming for bribery and coercion as three more e-mail exchanges surfaced between politicians and a man who went by Mr. Wu, a criminal directly linked to Jin with evidence provided by the same anonymous source. The e-mails detail Wu preventing the introduction of environmental laws to improve Taiwan's polluted air and waters through threats and bribes under Jin's direction. Jin Feiming left for Beijing just a few days after the bombing and has not returned since. He has never addressed the accusations lodged against him but has the most prominent attorney in Taiwan, Chao Haiping, working in his defense."

Lingyi and I had exchanged only a few messages since the bombing. So it was Arun who had told me she was the anonymous source behind all the leaks on Jin. I had already suspected it, but the knowledge made me miss Lingyi and the way she always followed through with conviction.

The screen cut to footage of Jin in Beijing; he stood in Tiananmen Square with the Forbidden City behind him.

"It's with great excitement that I announce the building of a new Jin Corp just outside of Beijing," Jin said, smiling with charm into the camera, his dark eyes bright with enthusiasm. "The loss of our original Taipei headquarters was unexpected, but only a minor setback. I can't think of a better place to rebuild and manufacture even better suits than before, with more features and cutting-edge enhancements—"

A reporter shoved a small silver microphone forward as others followed suit. "Mr. Jin, could you please address the allegations from politicians back in Taiwan who have stepped forward and accused you—"

Jin didn't even blink but continued as if he'd heard nothing. "I absolutely expect the new Jin Corp to be up and running within the next year. With the impressive resources we have here in China and the unrivaled workforce, I fully anticipate bringing new suits onto the market at price points that every person can enjoy—from the working man to those who can afford more luxury." He nodded graciously, happy and at ease. "I promise they will be available again globally within two years' time."

"Mr. Jin, with your suits defunct now, shouldn't our main focus be on cutting back pollution and improving our environment?" the reporter asked.

Jin lifted his dark eyebrows in amusement. "That's a fantasy," he replied. "Childish, naive dreams. We humans are consumers; we use resources and we buy things. And why shouldn't we? There will still be a demand for Jin suits when we come back onto the market." He swept a hand behind him, and the Forbidden City was barely visible, the palace's curved rooflines melting into Beijing's heavy smog. "And none too soon."

The camera cut back to the original news reporter standing in front of the abandoned Jin Corp building in Taipei. "Meanwhile, the

Old Taipei Theatre that was opened and funded by Jin's own daughter, Jin Daiyu, has had long lines since its grand opening in May. Let's go to Peng Jielan for the story."

My heart lurched at the sound of Daiyu's name.

The wall screen showed her in a sleeveless pale blue dress, cut short enough to reveal most of her stunningly toned legs, as a crowd of rich *you*s swarmed around her in fancy dress. She had attended alone, as head of the theatre and the hostess of the gala. Jin might be in disgrace with some in Taiwan, but his name and his wealth still carried weight.

The evening was a raging success, the *you*s were whisked home in their aircars and limos, trapped once again in regulated spaces, wondering why the government didn't actually do something about the polluted air. Especially since they didn't have their suits to venture out now, like before.

The images from the glittering opening gala had been replaced by the facade of the actual theatre, with the lush trees of Yangmingshan as a backdrop framing the domed roof.

"Since the opening of the Old Taipei Theatre," the new reporter standing by the theatre's silver entrance said, "there have been rumblings on the undernet as well as among the wealthy about the state of Taiwan's air and environment. Many of the wealthiest Taiwanese have stepped forward to advocate the introduction of environmental legislation to improve Taiwan's pollution. The new bill will be brought up to vote in the fall."

The reporter smiled winningly into the camera before they cut to previously recorded footage. Angela's face filled the wall screen.

She showed much less skin since the last time I saw her, wearing a black sweater and turquoise skirt that emphasized her curves. "Why shouldn't we have better air? Clean, breathable air?" she demanded, speaking right into the camera. Her hair was longer and swept past her shoulders, but it was as red as ever. "Why should we be forced to cower and hide in regulated spaces, trapped inside like dogs?"

The corner of my mouth twitched upward. Hadn't I used almost those same exact words when we were making our plans?

"But the *mei*s"—the unseen male reporter stopped himself—"those who couldn't afford suits have been living under these conditions for years. Why do you care *now*?"

Angela blinked her wide, kohl-lined eyes. "Because it affects me now," she said in a tone that told the reporter in no uncertain terms he was asking a ridiculous question.

I laughed under my breath.

More images from the gala played across the screen, Daiyu posing with politicians and celebrities alike, looking stunning and regal. I knew from my research before going in as Jason Zhou that she was fiercely protective of her privacy. Now she was on a personal campaign to help push environmental legislation through, and she was using her image and status to full advantage.

I had kept limited contact with my friends and hadn't seen them again as a group since Victor's death. I wasn't ready to face them together, to accept their sympathy or shared grief, and be reminded so starkly in numbers that we had lost one of our own. I couldn't deal with their suspicions and scrutiny, or be questioned again on where my loyalties lay.

Arun's antidote had helped to curb the spread of the virulent flu Jin had released. When it was clear what the antidote could do, the FDA quickly approved it, and it was manufactured and distributed throughout all hospitals. Arun had become a local hero, and I'd always smile when I saw him on-screen, his orange hair usually spiked, wearing a white lab coat for interviews. Dr. Nataraj would be so proud of him.

My apartment door clicked open, followed by the familiar sound of boot heels resounding against the concrete floor. I didn't need to look to know who it was—I'd given Daiyu official access to my apartment a month ago. Not that she hadn't been coming and going as she pleased for as long as I knew her. A corner of my mouth twitched upward at the thought.

"I've brought fresh-baked buns," she said, and set a rectangular box on the glass table. Her gray jeans were darkened by splotches of rain, the flower blouse she wore turned sheer, clinging to her wet skin. She wrung the water from her ponytail, completely at ease and unaware of how I was staring.

Then she met my gaze and her lips curved in a knowing grin.

Ah. She did know. Fooled again.

I smiled back, then laughed and extended my hand.

She came to me, droplets falling from her like stars, and clasped it.

We had wanted to change the world.

This was only the beginning.

# ACKNOWLEDGMENTS

*Want* began as a short story I wrote in 2011 titled "Blue Skies." It was the first non-fantasy story I had written since I was a young adult myself and also my first told as a first-person narrative. Zhou intrigued me from the start and so did Daiyu. Beyond the two characters, I wanted to feature Taipei, my birth city, and bring it to life for my readers. I love Taiwan so much and am so thrilled that *Want* is one of the first YA books to be set there. I was both excited and terrified when I decided to expand the short story into a novel and got to know Zhou and Daiyu even better, while creating supporting characters who were just as interesting to me.

My eternal gratitude to Michael Strother, who acquired *Want*. He saw Jason Zhou exactly as I wanted to portray him and pushed me to take the story to an even higher level. Michael is the main reason this gorgeous cover features my Asian hero's face so prominently, something we very rarely see on young-adult bookshelves. Thank you for believing in me and this story! I am beyond lucky to have Jen Ung as my editor for the latter revisions on *Want*. Thank you for asking those questions about my characters and relationships so I could delve deeper. Your support and enthusiasm have been invaluable to me!

This book benefited very much from my beta readers' feedback. Hugs to these fabulous friends and amazing women writers who took the time: Leah Cypess, Deva Fagen, Malinda Lo, and Sarah Rees Brennan. Special thanks to Malinda, whose feedback was especially helpful to me, and to Sarah, who has provided excellent comments and suggestions for my last three published titles!

My critique group, as ever, did the heavy lifting for this manuscript: John Atcheson, Kirsten Kinney, Amy Mair, and Mark McDonough. Thank you especially for John's expertise and input on the manuscript and Amy for lending new eyes to the story.

Thank you to my dear friends Joseph C. Chen (so dear I named a character after him in the book and then infected him with the virus I kept asking questions about, ha!) and Dr. Marcus Doane, who were both troupers in fielding this layperson's questions on viruses and more. Love to my own m for answering computer- and security-related questions.

I used my fabulous librarian friend Lalitha Nataraj's surname to give to Arun and his mother. Thank you for all the support and adventures in these past years. I'm so glad you mistook me as a fellow librarian so many years ago and introduced yourself.

Jason Chan is an incredible artist and seriously nailed it with his cover art. I feel so lucky! And thank you to both Karina Granda and Regina Flath who helped with the jacket design. I could not have asked for a more stunning cover!

Thank you to everyone at Simon Pulse who has welcomed me so warmly, and to the publicity and education and library teams working so hard behind the scenes to help promote this title.

Much gratitude to my agent Bill Contardi, who has been there with me from the start. I'm looking forward to more anon, always.

And last but never least, love to my sweet pea and my munchkin, who are growing up too fast.

November 18, 2016
San Diego, CA

# THE BOMBING

## LINGYI

Lingyi was their leader. And she was sending them headlong into danger—possibly even to their deaths.

She forced herself not to dwell on this, on every possible awful outcome. She needed to keep the surge of panic at bay. If Lingyi lost focus, her friends would pay for it.

It was a huge risk to blow up Jin Corp the same night they needed to save Zhou, but they couldn't use the fire alarm ploy twice. It was tonight or never. Still, it hadn't felt quite real before—a challenging game, a far-fetched fantasy. But there was a sense of finality tonight, when she had kissed Iris once before the group departed. They had all agreed to do this, had worked for months toward this end, but planning and doing were two very different things.

She feared for their lives.

Lingyi studied the nine video feeds pulled up on her wall screen. Three were from the body cams attached to Iris, Victor, and Arun, following their every movement. The other six were from Jin Corp, with one trained on the main entrance and lobby, one directed at the back door her friends would use, and another showing Zhou, who was slumped in a chair, unmoving. She toggled between various corridors and areas in Jin Corp with the other three feeds.

Lingyi paced the small area of her sitting room. Iris had always insisted they needed a bigger apartment, but Lingyi thought this was perfect. Cozy. She had chosen to orchestrate everything from her apartment tonight instead of their headquarters. Headquarters was too filled with the presence of her friends—echoes of them at every turn. She hadn't expected to feel the same hollow emptiness in her apartment.

Iris wasn't sprawled on their sofa, napping, with a hand tucked beneath her ear—her favorite pose. She was nearing the back entrance of Jin Corp, and from her body cam, Victor and Arun were right beside her. Lingyi tapped the screen that showed Zhou in that basement room littered with old machines. Flickering fluorescent light illuminated the space. She stared at Zhou, trying to detect any movement at all; the rise and fall of his chest, the jerk of a knee or shoulder, but saw nothing. There was no sound from Jin Corp's feeds, and she was terrified for him.

"You there, boss?" Victor's voice came in close and clear, as if he were standing beside her in the room.

Lingyi jumped. "Here. Everything looks good." She made her tone light, not letting the anxiety slip in. They needed her confidence and guidance so they could do their tasks quickly and right. "The building's quiet. Move fast. I won't have access to the security system until the fire alarm is triggered." If a security person happened to see them slip into the building, it'd only make things harder.

Iris used Daiyu's access code to try and enter the building. Lingyi held her breath, her heart in her throat. After a few seconds, the door clicked open and they each filed in, letting it close securely behind them.

"Arun," Lingyi said into her earpiece. "Zhou is in one of the rooms in the basement. Go down one level."

"Got it, boss," Arun replied.

They had gone over everything at headquarters earlier that day. But Lingyi couldn't help but call out the commands, directing each of them to their tasks. It gave her a false sense of control. "You have twenty minutes once the alarm goes off," Lingyi reiterated.

They knew, but Lingyi's palms dampened with sweat from saying it out loud. Arun headed down a dark stairwell, emerging onto a long corridor filled with blank doors. It was dimly lit; he began trying the knobs. He didn't expect to run into anyone down there.

The majority of the doors swung open, revealing empty rooms filled with machinery and other junk stored below the building. He used the motion detector for the rooms that were locked to try and locate Zhou. Lingyi's heart speeded up every time, but the detector never found him behind the locked doors.

Arun was cursing under his breath, and everyone could hear it. "I've already checked all the rooms on the right side. I need more time."

He picked up his pace, running from one door to the next, his cam bobbing with the motion.

"I'm coming up on the fire alarm," Iris replied. "The longer we hold off, the more likely we'll be discovered."

"Just five minutes." Arun was panting.

Five minutes to give security a chance to glance at any of the cameras that showed Arun, Vic, or Iris skulking around. Five minutes could give them all away. They'd already discussed and argued over this earlier in the afternoon. Iris was right.

"We don't have time," Vic said in a grim voice. "Stick with the plan." Lingyi knew Victor loved Zhou like a brother—it couldn't have been an easy thing to say.

"He's somewhere down there, Arun," Lingyi said, her chest constricting. Was she issuing Zhou's death sentence? "Iris, sound the alarm."

Iris's gloved hand pulled down on the red handle. A pulsing alarm immediately filled Lingyi's earpiece. A soothing female voice broadcasted over the building's sound system, "Attention. Please leave the building via your nearest exit. You have ten minutes."

Lingyi swung into her seat at her glass-top desk, accessing Jin Corp's main security system now that the alarm had been sounded. The building was in emergency mode. Even the security crew had left their areas. Lingyi watched as a few employees trickled out of the main entrance. At this time of night, they were mostly security and custodial staff.

Vic and Iris stayed out of sight as Arun continued to run down the basement corridor, trying doors. Lingyi checked on Zhou's feed. To her immense relief, he had woken, probably from the blaring noise of the alarm. He looked around, slowly rolling his shoulders, possibly trying to get out of his bindings. "Hang on, Zhou, Arun's on his way," she said, even though she knew he had no way of hearing her.

"I can't find him!" Arun shouted in frustration.

"Keep looking," Lingyi replied. "He's down there and awake!"

Arun began screaming Zhou's name over the sound of the insistent alarm. But Zhou's mouth was bound, and even as Arun shouted, Zhou gave no indication he could hear him.

Lingyi forced herself to turn her attention to the ground floor.

Vic and Iris were running down a wide corridor and stopped at an elevator. Seven minutes in, and the building already looked empty. There were a few stragglers hurrying toward their nearest exit. "The elevator is clear," she said, toggling between the security cameras.

"Thanks, boss," Iris and Vic replied at the same time.

They entered the empty car, and Victor punched the third- and fifth-floor buttons. He then adjusted the silver cuff link at his wrist. Vic had put on a sleek gray suit with a silver vest and blue tie knotted perfectly at his throat. Lingyi almost smiled, would have teased him under any other circumstances. Iris slipped out on the third floor, and Victor got off on the fifth and highest floor. There wasn't enough time to set a bomb on each floor with only two people, but they could strategically set two each on the third and fifth. The bombs would be powerful enough to destroy the inside of the building.

When Iris had argued that she should take the fifth floor, because she was faster than Victor, and the location was riskier, Vic had countered that he had a better handle on the tech, should anything go wrong. In the end, Lingyi made the final call, like she always did. Victor would take the higher floor. Lingyi suddenly realized she could feel her heart thumping hard against her chest, as she followed both Iris and Vic on their feeds.

Arun's panicked voice burst into their earpieces. "I still can't find Zhou. I've checked every room down here twice. We have to abort!"

Lingyi lifted her head to the wall screen, then jumped from her seat, fighting the sick feeling in her stomach. She touched the feed that had displayed the dingy basement room Zhou had been trapped in. It showed only an empty chair. "He's gone!" she shouted.

"What?" Arun stood stock-still in the middle of the basement corridor. "Where did he go? Is he still in the building?"

Lingyi pushed up her glasses with a shaking hand. "I don't know. But we can't abort now."

"First bomb is set," Iris said.

"First bomb is set," Victor replied not ten seconds later.

There were eight minutes left before people would be let back into the building.

They were halfway there with two bombs set. No turning back now.

Lingyi skidded back to her desk, toggling through all the cameras located within the basement of Jin Corp on her computer—more than two dozen. Most of them only showed empty, dark rooms. "Arun, you have to get out. I don't know where Zhou is."

He let out a long string of curses. "I won't just leave him!"

Lingyi ignored the sudden stinging pressure behind her eyes. *Zhou.* She flicked between the feeds again, seeing nothing. She loved him like a brother too. Now she was sealing his fate, abandoning him. "Arun. There's less than six minutes and the bombs are going to blow." Her voice cracked. "Go. Leave the building now!"

"Second bomb set," Iris said into their earpieces.

Arun was staring down on the floor, both hands clenched into fists. "Fuck!" he shouted, then began running toward the stairwell. She watched until his feed showed he was out in the alleyway again, behind Jin Corp.

Lingyi let out a long breath, even as she swiped at the corner of her eye, knocking her glasses askew. Readjusting them, she checked on

Iris's and Victor's progress. Iris was in another stairwell, headed down to the ground floor. Vic's feed showed him fiddling with his second bomb. The timer was counting down already, but one of the three lights that controlled it glowed red, while the other two were green.

Something was wrong.

"Victor," she said into her earpiece, trying to keep her voice even. "Leave it. Now."

He didn't budge. She watched in horror as he worked the wires with his long fingers. Victor wore a rectangular titanium ring on his right hand. Lingyi felt like she was floating out of herself for a moment, adrift. The clock showed less than three minutes before detonation.

Then she slammed back into her body and was screaming again, "Victor!"

"I heard you, boss," Victor replied in a calm tone; cool and collected. "But we're down two bombs without Zhou's help. They all have to blow for the maximum damage we need. I've almost got this." A hand reached up, out of view, and Lingyi saw the word MUTE light up in green on his feed.

"No!" Lingyi screamed.

"Boss," Iris's voice came in through the earpiece. "What's going on? Where's Vic?" She had stopped in a stairwell.

"Keep running, Iris," Lingyi ordered. "Clear the building!" She was trying to draw enough breath. "Now!"

The clock began counting down from one minute. Vic continued to work the wires patiently. Iris stood frozen in the stairwell, and then the first of her bombs went off, so loud Lingyi ripped out her earpiece. Iris's feed shook from the impact, and she was running again, bursting through the emergency exit door onto the ground floor.

Lingyi felt light-headed. Terror smothered her, like a monstrous beast sitting on her chest.

The ground shuddered beneath Victor. He flicked a switch on the bomb, and the light that had been red suddenly turned green. The digital clock started counting down from ten in red. Vic had been crouched over the bomb, but straightened now. He brushed off the sleeves of his suit jacket, then flashed her an *okay* sign with his hand. There was a burst of blinding white light from his feed two seconds later.

"Vic!" she screamed again.

His feed displayed only gray static.

Frantic, she toggled between all the screens, searching for him, knowing what she was doing made no sense. The cameras within Jin Corp showed only chaos, shaking walls and crumbling floors, machinery collapsing onto each other. Iris's feed was obscured with dust and smoke. Tears blurred Lingyi's vision. She grabbed the earpiece and put it back in her ear. Lingyi had to get Iris out.

"Head to the main entrance," Lingyi directed, her voice wavering and thick. She cleared her throat.

"Should I wait for Vic?" Iris asked, pausing at the sliding doors that led into the main entrance area.

"No," Lingyi managed to croak. "I lost his connection." She couldn't bring herself to say anything else.

Iris didn't speak, then pressed the button to open the curved golden doors, revealing the grand foyer. She ran to the front entrance, but the doors wouldn't open for her. She slammed her hand onto the square button, then pounded on the steel doors, but nothing worked.

Lingyi searched through Jin Corp's security system. "The building's in lockdown." She tried to override the command, then worked on manually opening the front entrance. Nothing worked. Lingyi checked who had initiated the lockdown. Jin. Not two minutes after the first bomb went off. "Nothing will open now, not without special access."

"How do I get special access?" Iris shouted above the rumbling noise.

"There are some emergency exits on the ground floor. Turn right. We might be able to use Daiyu's access code to open them." But Lingyi was only guessing. She couldn't face the notion that she might lose Iris, too.

Iris was trying to navigate through the smoke-filled haze in the corridor, when she exclaimed, "Zhou! Thank gods, Arun couldn't find you—"

"Daiyu got me." Lingyi heard Zhou's familiar voice crackle through her earpiece. "She knows the way out."

Lingyi held herself taut, because otherwise, she would collapse onto her desk from relief. Zhou was alive, and Daiyu would take them to safety. Iris was speaking to her, but none of the words were registering. Instead, Lingyi found herself searching through every camera still working in Jin Corp, looking for Victor's familiar shape. He was always slick, always a step ahead. If anyone could actually cheat death, it'd be Vic. She squinted at the corridors filled with smoke, searched the rooms sparking with live wire, writhing like electric serpents.

She checked Iris's feed but couldn't see anything except thick smoke, and the vague sense of someone moving in front of her. Suddenly, she heard Zhou screaming that they needed to go back. To find Vic. Lingyi wanted to say something but couldn't form the words. She heard Iris instead, her love, her heart, convincing him to keep heading toward the exit—telling Zhou that Victor was gone.

*No.*

Lingyi couldn't see. She wiped her nose with one sleeve, then blinked hard, flicking through the security cameras. There were fewer and fewer that still worked, and all of them showed chaos and ruin; gaping maws, fire, and smoke. She could hear voices speaking on Iris's feed, but Iris didn't say anything again. Then they were outside, clear of the crumbling building.

Lingyi drew a long breath that erupted into shaking sobs.

They were out.

Iris and Zhou were safe.

Iris's feed jostled as they ran away from Jin Corp. Lingyi felt as if she were floating outside her own body again, untethered. Then Iris spoke directly into her ear, summoning Lingyi back to herself. "He's not coming."

Lingyi tried to grasp what Iris meant. No, Vic wasn't coming. *Vic was dead.* Then she saw Zhou standing there beside a girl who looked vaguely familiar. "Let me speak with him," Lingyi said, her voice cracking.

Iris stalked toward Zhou and shoved her earpiece into Zhou's ear.

"Come home, Zhou," Lingyi managed to say.

"Is Arun all right?" he asked.

"I'm here, bro. Where *were* you?" Arun interjected from his earpiece. "I searched all through the basement."

"There are two levels," Lingyi heard the girl standing beside Zhou say in a quiet voice. Daiyu.

Arun had been on the wrong floor, because Lingyi hadn't studied the building plans thoroughly enough.

"I need some time," Zhou finally replied in a hoarse voice. "Victor's dead."

"Oh, Zhou." Lingyi broke into a sob. "I know. Go with Iris. Please."

A long pause. "I can't," he finally said.

Iris and Zhou argued, but Lingyi barely heard them.

Lingyi couldn't blame him. She had ordered Arun to abandon him—good as dead. "You're angry," she said. "Because we failed to find you. We left you there—"

"No," he cut her off. "I'm not angry. It was always the mission first. We all knew that."

She did know that. But Lingyi had been the one who had been forced to make all the tough decisions, had forced her friends to abide by the hard choices. And now Vic was dead; and his blood was on her hands. She'd failed them. She said more to Zhou, but it was as if someone else had taken over—someone blathering meaningless words.

Finally, the voices stopped in her earpiece.

Lingyi folded her arms onto the cold glass and rested her head down on them. Most of Jin Corp's cameras had winked out by now, displaying static. She closed her eyes and felt hot tears slide down her face.

The image of Victor giving her an *okay* sign flashed before her eyes, before he, too, had been consumed by gray static.

Lingyi lost track of time.